THESE VALLEY DAYS, 2

BETHANY-KRIS

Published by Bethany-Kris

www.bethanykris.com

ISBN 13: 978-1-989658-60-4

Editor: Elizabeth Peters

Cover Design © Mignon Mykel from Oh, So Novel

For my nan who once told me that she dreamed of writing a book about a sexy man who would whisk her away to a cabin in the woods where they'd fall madly in love and fuck like bunnies. Delaney might not be you, nan, but I wrote the book all the same.

CONTENTS

1. 1
2. 11
3. 20
4. 27
5. 38
6. 51
7. 57
8. 64
9. 71
10. 80
11. 88
12. 96
13. 107
14. 114
15. 126
16. 134
17. 145
18. 152
19. 163
20. 173
21. 182
22. 194
23. 201
24. 213
25. 221
26. 233
27. 242
28. 252
29. 262
30. 276
31. 283
32. 291
33. 304
34. 313
35. 324
36. 333
37. 346
38. 358

39. 371
Epilogue...376

1.

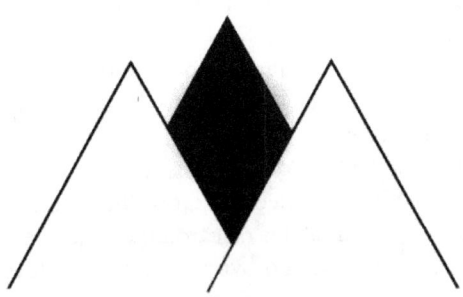

"You're absolutely sure you want to do this?"

Was that a real question?

"Give me something else to look at in the mirror, Margot. I *need* it. It's this or a tattoo of my last name. I've considered making the appointment."

Maybe that would get Delaney out of her own damn head. A late birthday gift since she'd gone on like her twenty-fifth was just another Sunday.

Margot's nose crinkled in disgust. "Really, you'd want *Reed* ... just somewhere? You've got more creativity than that, Delaney."

"I was going to make it cute," Delaney tried not to whine.

And failed.

"On three?" Margot asked.

Delaney nodded but kept her gaze on the apartment ceiling overhead instead of the redhead looming over the side of the couch.

"Okay—one, two, *breathe.*"

She gulped in a lungful of air as Margot plunged the needle straight through Delaney's left nostril.

"And let it out now," Margot urged.

Delaney did. The pain came and left faster than she remembered it from the first time she'd had the nose piercing done, but that was years ago. Somebody who didn't know what they were doing had an earring gun and it took weeks for the swelling to go down. Margot had skill and practice on her side, so the second of pain was over before Delaney had even blinked.

Tears raced down her cheek when she did.

"Jesus Christ," Delaney muttered under her breath.

Margot's wild curls bounced with her laughter as she reached over Delaney's prone form on the couch with gloved hands for something she'd sat on the tray. "It wasn't that bad, come on."

"I'm *crying*!"

"Your eye is watering. It always does." Her friend laughed. Blue latex came back into Delaney's view, and Margot said, "Sit tight, and I'll get this hoop in for you."

She remained still while Margot finished her work, sliding in a hoop at the end of the long needle that nestled nicely around the shell of Delaney's nostril. After discarding the needle to the clean tray on the coffee table, Margot wiped the river of tears that had trailed down the side of Delaney's face.

Margot beamed and lifted her eyebrows high. "Wanna see?"

Laughing, Delaney pushed up into a sitting position on the couch. "Yeah, where's the mirror?"

Margot pointed next to the tray as she rounded the couch and began cleaning up her supplies. Only a little ache remained around the piercing, but more interesting was how Delaney could feel the thin strip of gold looped along the side of her nose. Every flicker of her facial muscles made her more and more aware of the small piece of jewelry.

She hadn't even reached for the mirror yet.

Margot noticed. "Yeah, that'll get better. Give it a couple of hours."

Delaney wrinkled her nose again. "I don't remember this from the first time."

"Yeah, probably because you were lucky they didn't crush your cartilage and your brain could only focus on one thing—like the *pain*."

Fair point.

Delaney gave it to Margot.

"Give me a break, I was seventeen and *free*," she mumbled under her breath, picking up the mirror.

Margot shrugged. "True enough, but stupid is still dumb, Delaney."

Yeah, it was.

She admired the gold hoop framing the left side of her nose and how it added to the delicate swoop of her bridge and button tip. It confirmed what she'd believed all those years ago when she dared to get the piercing despite knowing how her mother would scream at her for it the first time she saw it—the look suited her face.

As for her mother all those years ago? Amanda didn't stop shrieking until Delaney had backed out of the driveway.

Delaney glanced away from the black-haired, hazel-eyed reflection in the mirror that looked so much like her mother's, thinking, *well, she won't see it to yell about it now.*

"You got quiet over there," Margot noted.

Of course, her friend would notice. Despite being well-liked and having a lot of friends when she was younger, Delaney always kept her circle small. Those people she truly let see her mask slip to find the human waiting underneath. One didn't need to wait long in adulthood to figure out that being human in public sucked.

People like Margot knew those quiet moments for Delaney were introspective seconds lost in the maze of her mind and hidden thoughts. Not necessarily a pleasant place to be, for what it was worth. Delaney rarely had a choice, though.

"Yeah, I did get quiet," Delaney admitted, handing the mirror across the coffee table for Margot to take. Not having something in her hands made her edgier. She'd forced herself to stop picking at the beds of her nails by keeping a manageable length set of gel nails on but as soon as those bitches started to grow out, her urge to pick began. It had become a vicious cycle. A sad by-product of the fact she hadn't smoked a cigarette in two years.

Once upon a time, all her nervous energy went into flicking ash from the tip of a cigarette and burning lungsful of secret smoke. Until the smell of smoke made her want to puke. She still needed somewhere to put the rest of her anxiety, though.

Her fingers were it.

Nobody said Delaney was perfect.

"I've considered taking up smoking again," Delaney said.

Margot gasped, her attention swinging from packing away her tools to Delaney. *"No."*

"Not seriously, Margot. I'm just …"

"Struggling?" her friend asked, as she took the recliner across from the matching blue couch.

"I don't like that word."

It implied weakness and Delaney took issue with that. Instead of saying so, because nobody liked to pick at a raw wound, she toyed with one of the many cushions on the couch. The fringe edge gave her fingers something else to do except be there for her to pick.

Like the sofa, the recliner got the same treatment with too many sham pillows with images of various boating objects.

Bexley took decorating *way* too seriously.

Mostly, because her cousin just didn't know when to stop. A color started a theme and then it would spread until it took over everything. She even managed to find lamps with large conch shell bases for the space. It was starting to bleed over into the two-bedroom apartment's tiny kitchen in little ways.

Delaney tried not to notice.

Most of the time.

"Okay, I'm starting to think you don't like the nose ring," Margot blurted out worriedly.

Delaney barked out a laugh. *"Really?"*

Across the way, with studs in both sides of her nose, and one gold hoop next to her right diamond nose ring, Margot shrugged. "I'm used to people telling me by now, and *yeah*—so you're a little lost in your head. You do that sometimes. I want to know what you think of your *face.*"

Margot pointed at her own for effect. It did the job.

Delaney grinned big.

Margot smiled back, and her eyes twinkled. "You okay, hon?"

Delaney sighed.

She got asked that question a lot more than she wanted to admit. Usually by the same few people who took notice of her lack of laughter and smiles—or really, how quickly it died or fell. Delaney had been stuck in this loop of lingering unhappiness for a while, and it was getting harder and harder to climb back out every time she made another trip around Sad-ville.

Population one.

A terrible place for a vacation, anyway.

"Delaney?" Margot pressed the longer she remained silent on the couch.

"Yeah, I'm fine," she lied lamely. Standing up, Delaney rubbed at her forehead and eyed the muted news playing on the television mounted between the living room's two tall windows. She could pretend like the busy Fredericton street, dusted with blustering snow, gave her something interesting to stare at. Really, she just didn't want to meet Margot's gaze. "Some days are better than others, but I'm making it work. Do you want something to drink?"

"No, I'm gonna grab tea from Timmies with Leya on the way out," Margot said.

Delaney saw her shrug out of the corner of her eye.

"Sorry, I did say I couldn't stay too long," she added. "The flight's at seven."

"No worries."

I need something to drink, though, Delaney thought. Preferably liquor because something in her gut said it was going to be a long night once Margot headed out to catch her evening flight to Toronto.

Margot said nothing as Delaney cut through the living room to make a beeline for the fridge at the far side of the apartment. She nestled what remained of her red wine from the night before and a clean glass in her arms to make her way back to the couch.

"I have missed you a lot," Delaney said, focusing on pouring the wine and not spilling it over blue fabric that had never washed well.

"I missed you, too."

Delaney glanced up over the glass on the coffee table. "But the expo, right?"

Margot laughed at that. "Yeah, the expo was what I really wanted to do."

A year traveling Canada with a team that put on a beauty expo displaying the talents of artists from all over the country kept Margot moving constantly. From one city to the next. New faces and personalities greeted her at every show. She met amazing people, learned from the best in her field along the way, and made connections that would not have been possible, otherwise. It sucked that she didn't make it home as often as her friends would like so they could catch up, but a life on the road seemed to suit Margot better.

Not even Delaney could ignore it, and nobody—not even her sorry ass—blamed Margot for running through the door that opened for her. The girlfriend Margot met along the way probably helped, too.

But Leya?

That girl was raised in a cement zoo—she wasn't cut out for small town, or even rural life. The handful of times Margot did bring her girlfriend home, it was abundantly obvious that the high-energy blonde with her manic energy couldn't stand remaining in one place for too long. Especially not a small place. Not to mention, Leya didn't pretend to *want* to spend real, quality time with Margot's family and friends.

Margot crossed her legs, always polite even in sweats and an oversized hoodie. "I really thought we'd get a few days together, but ..."

She trailed off, leaving Delaney with the option to speak for them both.

How could she explain?

Or apologize?

She hadn't even been able to do that to herself lately.

"I know, I flaked coming home," Delaney muttered.

Or rather, she was willing to let her friends make plans to gather for a week in their valley town to catch up after the Christmas season, but Delaney didn't follow through on any of it. Even her cousin went home to spend time with her sister—one of the only family members left who still spoke to the pair—but she remained three hours away in the city.

Safe in a crowd of faces that didn't know hers.

Away from familiar streets.

Alone.

Part of her liked that—it made spiraling into a darkness of her own making easier when there weren't other people around to see her do it. She didn't have to explain the hollow spot in her chest where her heart used to be that had been eaten away by her ever-constant guilt. A monster she just couldn't shake.

"Gracen says you haven't been home in over a year," Margot noted quietly.

"I'd rather not think about the time I did go home, actually," Delaney muttered unhappily.

Margot offered her a sympathetic smile that wasn't returned. Some shit she couldn't even fake. "You know, they've finally got the wood shop up and running on the Flats, now?"

She did know that.

Gracen sent a lot of pictures. It seemed like her best friend had found a creative knack to focus every moment of her spare time when she wasn't working in the salon Malachi had built onto the house for her.

"She was really hoping you were gonna get to the valley last week, Delaney, but I don't think she was surprised when you didn't show up, either. It still hurts, though. It's disappointing."

What isn't when it comes to me?

Nothing came as a shock, now.

Not when it came to Delaney.

"Sometimes, Gracen talks too much," Delaney replied.

She hoped it did the job to make her lack of interest in the direction of the conversation clear. It wasn't Margot's fault, really. Some things just couldn't be helped.

Instead, Margot challenged her with, "Or is it that she worries about you just enough, Delaney? I mean, come on."

The sharp comment hit Delaney right in the heart. "What's that supposed to mean?"

"Well, somebody's got to care about you. It sure as hell seems like you don't anymore."

Yeah.

Friends *always* knew.

*

"I'm sorry, I'm sorry," Delaney rushed to apologize the second she picked up the ringing cell phone. Almost too late—on the fourth ring, just before her voicemail picked up the call. "I'm sorry, Gracen, I swear I'm not ignoring you, okay?"

"You sure? Kind of seems like it."

Delaney rolled her eyes as she turned the Jeep off in the parking stall of the large lot in front of the strip mall where she'd worked at a walk-in salon for almost two years. "Come on, I know I didn't call you back, and you left a message last night, but—"

"I wanted to tell you that I wasn't mad you didn't come home to visit," Gracen interjected before Delaney could get another word out. Not that her friend could hear the woosh of relief that rushed from Delaney's chest at the news, but the weight was gone. *Mostly.* "Margot called from the airport last night and said you guys talked. She thought maybe she crossed a line, and I just want you to know it's okay, Delaney. I get that you're dealing with stuff you have to work through and that you're not ready, yet. That's *okay.*"

The very last thing Delaney needed to currently do was wipe away tears in the blustery parking lot of her place of employment, but so was her life lately. Mid-January was as harsh of a Canadian climate as one could get in New Brunswick, and with the freezing temps and shitty weather came Delaney's equally terrible mood.

Seasonal depression could be a real bitch. Especially piled on top of an already struggling mental state. She needed to get herself figured out, and *soon*.

"Thanks," Delaney mumbled against the heel of her wet palm.

"Yeah, of course," Gracen returned on the other end of the call. "Whatever you need, you know that. Margot didn't mention it because I asked her not to, but—"

"You guys need to stop talking about me when I'm not around to join the conversation," Delaney interjected.

Gracen scoffed. "Stop it—nobody's talking about you."

"Well—"

"Malachi and I got engaged over Christmas. I wanted to share the news with you when you came home so it could be something special ... not over the phone, or whatever."

Like this.

Delaney cursed herself for being selfish. "I'm sorry. Is the ring beautiful?"

"Like I picked it myself. I'll send you a picture?"

"Please," Delaney mumbled, trying not to sound totally fucking pitiful. As if she needed more reminders that she had been a trash friend.

"I'll send a couple," Gracen assured, still not seeming bothered. "We want to get married in the late spring—here on the Flats."

Delaney dragged in a shaky breath that she held inside her chest until the air burned in her lungs. Yet, she couldn't stop herself from letting it all out to say, "I'm definitely going to have to come home for that, huh?"

"I do need a maid of honor."

Yes, she did. It *should* be Delaney. Like they'd always planned from the time they were teenagers.

"I'm gonna be home for that," Delaney said.

"Just ... don't make promises, okay? I understand that coming back here isn't easy for you, but it's harder to make sense of it when you say one thing and willingly do another."

"I get it, Gracen."

A sigh crackled over the phone before Gracen asked, "You're just heading into work, right?"

Even from three hours away with only phone calls and texts throughout the week to keep their line of communication open,

Gracen fit Delaney into her life in small ways. Like remembering her odd work schedule that wasn't like the typical salon's nine-to-five.

"Yeah, and almost late," Delaney added, not hiding her annoyance. "It's half my fault, but partly Bexley's, too. I polished off what I had left of wine, fell asleep, and didn't wake up until my last alarm."

Gracen's light laugh filtered through the speakers. "Let me guess, Bexley didn't wake up, either?"

"I didn't even see her before my head hit the pillow last night. She was out somewhere. I dragged her out of bed as I was heading out the door. Who even knows if she made her first class?"

Gracen laughed again.

Delaney didn't excuse Bexley's weekend behavior, but she didn't step in to stop it. Friends. Drinking. Being *young*. Even if the girl wasn't of legal age yet to get in the bars, she managed it. Alongside her friends, too.

She let her cousin live if only because now was the perfect time for Bexley to do so. It often meant she didn't see her younger cousin on the weekends because throughout the week, her nose was stuck in books. She had one year left on her nursing degree before the real world would come and knock Bexley on her ass.

Like it did for everyone.

"She's lucky you're around to keep her on track," Gracen said. "So, who's doing that for you?"

Great.

Someone else had to jump on that train again. Nobody had time for that.

Delaney liked it better when no one had a clue about her problems, or the sad state of her life. As lonely as it currently happened to be. "Listen," she said to Gracen, "I've got two minutes to get inside the salon before Linda calls someone to fill my chair."

A lie.

She was on time, in the lot, and visible to her boss through the salon's windows below the glowing sign showcasing the business. *Styled Cuts - Unisex.*

Classy, really.

The job was a step down from the salon she had once owned alongside Gracen, but the three-hundred dollar a month chair rental couldn't be beat, she had four twelve-hour slots a week with her name on it and then a four day stretch of off time to do with what she wanted. The owner switched out stylists on the four day rotation to get double her bang out of the chairs, but Delaney didn't mind because it worked for her.

She made good money, could pay her monthly rental in a day's work with the right clients, and didn't have to think too hard to do it. She didn't have to invest emotional energy into something someone might take from her one day, and she didn't have the mental capacity to deal with a salon like it was a business anymore.

Not after everything …

Thankfully, Gracen didn't call Delaney on her bullshit. Apparently, all she really wanted to do was check in on her friend. Like she did on many other mornings.

"Call me for anything, okay?" Gracen asked before Delaney ended the call.

"Yeah, you know I will."

"Yeah," her friend echoed, "I guess."

What she didn't say that was still clear between them both?

But you don't.

Not anymore.

Luckily—if only for the moment because Delaney didn't want to deal with her feelings—she didn't have the time to think about her inability to be the best friend Gracen needed and deserved. As soon as she ended the call with Gracen, she found a text waiting from her boss.

Whenever you're done in the parking lot, there's a client in your chair. You're welcome. He's cute.

Fucking perfect.

Just what she needed.

2.

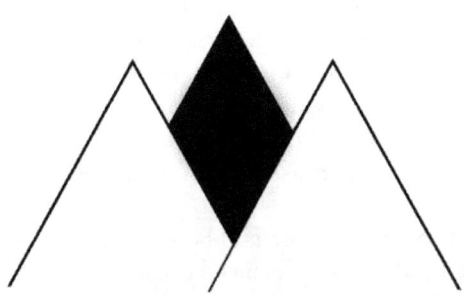

The man she found waiting in her chair *was* cute. At least, Linda could pick a good-looking face out of the crowd. The guy, with shoulders broader than the barber chair he sat in, preoccupied himself with whatever was in his hands—his phone, maybe?— and his dark-haired head remained down while he waited. He didn't notice Delaney enter the salon, despite the bell chiming overhead at her entrance or the woman at the back manning the cash register behind the reception counter pointing his way.

As if Delaney *didn't* know what chair hers was.

She gave Linda a half-hearted thumbs up on her way past the desk to hang her coat and bag up in the rear hallway with the rest of the employee belongings.

"That's new, huh?" her boss asked, pointing at her own nose but looking at Delaney's.

"Yeah, I thought I'd try something."

Linda grinned big. "It's cute."

"Thanks."

"Jean wanted to take him," the woman explained on Delaney's way by again, "but she's already got somebody in her chair for the next forty-five minutes, so today is your day, Delaney. Mr. Dalton said he didn't have that kind of time this morning, and you didn't have anyone booked in your first hour, right?"

"It's fine. I've got him."

"I'd get him, too, if I didn't have arthritis in my damn back," the woman muttered at Delaney's back.

Or it sure sounded like that's what she said. Really, Linda just didn't like to cut hair.

It never failed to amaze Delaney the way women could go

11

completely stupid in the face of a handsome man. It didn't make much sense to her—maybe because she wasn't one to let her physical attraction do the thinking and talking for her. The way a person's body felt shouldn't determine what their head or heart had to say about someone. Good-looking people—men included— were everywhere. She wouldn't look like a bumbling fool just because she had to talk to somebody who looked good, either.

"Mr. Dalton?" Delaney asked, coming up behind the man in her chair.

He had a good view of her, and how she barely stood taller than the top of his head, when he glanced up into the reflection of the mirror. His wide, friendly smile showed off straight, white teeth and welcomed her closer so she could distinguish the dark browns of his eyes from the pupils that zeroed in on her.

"How does Lucas sound?" he returned.

Delaney grinned. "I can call you Lucas."

He made the calls.

"Great. So, you're the lucky one, then?" he asked.

Delaney arched one eyebrow. "The lucky one?"

"Cutting this mop."

He gestured to the top of his head where his short crew-cut had grown out just enough to be noticeable. Of course, a bit of pomade could style his hair nicely even at the slightly longer length, but the cut of his blazer and the tightness of the red tie's knot hanging down from his throat told Delaney he probably didn't have the personality type to let his hair grow out much at all.

"It doesn't look anything like a mop, honestly." She smiled, stepping closer with a hand raised toward his hair. "May I?"

The man waved again. "Go to it."

She quickly realized he hadn't been playing with his phone when he sat the small item that had taken up his attention during her arrival to the top of the workstation's glossy black counter. Her hand flew up to toy with the bottom end of a plain gold cross that hung from a chain around her neck, but as she had become aware that the cross charm became a thing she used to self-soothe, she forced her suddenly trembling hand back down to her sides.

Now wasn't the time.

Certainly not for the shakes.

The pocket-sized Bible with gold foil lettering on the leatherbound cover almost seemed to mock Delaney from the corner of her eye. She hadn't seen one like that in years, but she hadn't opened her own in *many* more. Not that her lack of study meant she couldn't recite the damn thing from almost start to finish when hours every night of her childhood had been dedicated to Bible study. Her siblings and cousins had even liked to quiz one another, so they kept a competitive edge in quizzing during Sunday school.

Delaney forced herself to put the Bible out of her mind, so she could do her damn job. Teasing the longer bit of length on the top of Lucas' head, between her fingers she met his dark gaze in the mirror once again. "Are you just looking to trim it back up?"

"Nothing too scary," he agreed, winking.

The wink made Delaney glance away to fret with the chair as if she might pump it up higher. Not a chance with the height of him sitting there. She *had* to do something else, though. She could deal with a man who was attractive, but charm was a different kind of beast, altogether. Men with charm they knew how to use, on the other hand, could make a better woman's morals waiver at the best of times.

Just not hers.

Usually.

"And no fade," he added as she placed the leather satchel filled with her sterilized tools onto the workstation. "I don't need another reason to feel like my head is going to explode. I have enough as it is."

Okay.

No clippers, then.

"Somebody doesn't like fades?" she asked, digging through the bag to pull out the items she wanted to use. A comb. Scissors. Thinning shears. She found they helped for people who didn't immediately like the way the hair laid on their head after a cut. Sometimes, a quick run through with the shears turned someone's outlook around. "Your wife, maybe?"

Lucas made no apologies about lifting his bare hand for her to see. No ring glinted under the salon lights, but a fancy watch with a recognizable name stamped into the face did.

"No wife." He smiled tightly while she reached for the clean cape and rolled towel on the shelving unit beside her station. "I just don't think the fades are for me. Also, I've already washed it this morning. Trying to save some time here, you know?"

She didn't believe that for a second. His excuse about the fade—not so much the wife. She took him at face value in that regard; he'd not cared one bit or barely gave a thought about flashing a bare finger.

He had strong shoulders and a thick neck corded with muscles. Good for high fades. It might give him a more military appearance, however, and some people didn't prefer that.

Delaney opted not to push it. "Can we take the blazer off? The cape will be more comfortable."

"Sure."

He didn't hesitate to stand and shrug off the navy-blue blazer that hadn't been buttoned. She had the opportunity to properly admire the way his back and trunk-like arms filled out the dress shirt as he shifted the waistline of his pants at the belt before sitting back down in the chair, blazer folded in his lap.

Delaney wasn't the only person who noticed, apparently.

Dual, feminine *ohs* echoed from across the salon. Both she and Lucas turned at the sudden noise to find Linda had left her perch behind the desk to lean against the workstation of another stylist behind Delaney. How she hadn't noticed the change happening in the reflection of the mirror was another matter she didn't give much thought to.

She wasn't distracted.

Just doing her job.

The stylist at her back quickly turned the client in her chair back around to face her own station and mirror while Linda barely suppressed a smile at being noticed.

Delaney tried to play it all off. "Sorry about that. You'd think they never met a man with a nice smile before."

Lucas chuckled, and scratched at the underside of his clean-shaven, prominent jaw. The cleft in his squared chin became more pronounced when he laughed, but it was the shift in his gaze that said he was more uncomfortable than he let any of them know. It took a hell of a lot of control to keep his discomfort hidden.

"No worries, it's fine," he assured.

It wasn't. Professionalism counted for a lot in her business. As much as someone didn't come into a hair salon or barber shop looking to get judged, they also didn't expect to be gawked at and fawned over. All people wanted, for the most part, was a fucking hair cut. She could, however, focus them back where they needed to be.

"Let's get you trimmed up," she said, whipping out the cape to open it up.

Lucas smiled at her reflection; his gaze seemingly unseeing the background of the salon around them in the mirror. "Sounds good to me ... It's Delaney, right?"

"That's me."

He nodded once and settled into the chair with his eyes turned forward. "I'll remember it. Let's go." Then, without any warning, his smile melted into a smirk as he asked, "So, you think I have a nice smile, huh?"

She hadn't been ready for that comment, or the way his voice dropped with richness when he asked it.

It even made her blush.

Delaney used the cape she swept around his front, and hooked at the nape of his neck, as a buffer of sorts until the heat in her cheeks subsided. Even as she tucked in the folded towel between his tanned skin and the black cape, she did her very best to ignore the way he watched her in the mirror with a knowing grin.

Yep.

He'd definitely caught the blush.

"Are we cutting this hair of yours?" she asked, settling her nerves with a light laugh. "Or not?"

*

Lucas Dalton was a talker.

Real smooth, too.

Over the course of a twenty-minute trim, the man never quieted for more than a handful of seconds. He had a way with words, and conversation, too. It almost felt like sitting down for tea with an old friend as he pulled information from Delaney like ribbons while snips of hair fell in wisps around his shoulders.

Before she'd even dampened his hair with water from a squeeze bottle he had her admitting that she wasn't from the city, despite living here. His uncanny ability didn't stop there. The man learned her favorite colors—black and white until she died—her age and birthday, her latest read, and even her feelings about the recent weather. While he also kept the conversation entertaining.

A feat.

He could make her laugh, didn't prod into personal waters, and knew when to turn a question or comment around on himself if he noticed that it landed the wrong way with Delaney. All in all, he made her comfortable.

She was the one cutting *his* hair.

The irony wasn't lost on her.

If not for the Rolex on his wrist that she'd noticed earlier, she might have thought he was in management. A suit people would listen to. Didn't those sorts of people need a litany of communication skills? No manager she knew had the kind of money for a five-to-ten-thousand-dollar watch, though.

The disappointment slipping through Delaney after she'd pulled away the cape, and Lucas stood from the chair to get a better look in the mirror confused her—those twenty minutes flew by before she realized she could have taken a few extra minutes.

At least, he smiled about the cut.

Lucas brushed his palm back and forth over the short crop of his hair, messing it up in much the same way she had done to style it. "It's perfect, thank you."

"You sure you don't want maybe an inch of fade up your neck? It'll look great, trust me."

The man only shook his head. "I'll never hear the end of it until it grows back in, trust me."

So, it *was* someone else who didn't like the look on him. What a damn shame.

"Well, you're welcome. I'm glad you like it."

Lucas turned with his lips stretching wide. "I'm glad I landed in your chair this morning. I should have got this trimmed up before I left, but I definitely couldn't go back with it looking the way it did."

Delaney frowned openly. "You looked fine when you came in. You look great now, too."

She only said it because it was the truth, and his insistence that even a small bit of growth to his short style meant he must look unkempt was plain bullshit.

He shrugged, already slipping on his blazer. "I suppose the two of us will have to agree to disagree. How much do I owe you?"

At the front of the salon, the bell chimed. Delaney waved at the young woman, bundled in a parka with a faux fur trimmed hood, who glanced her way immediately.

Her next client. The one she'd booked a little after the start of her shift so she had enough time to shake off the morning jitters.

Before a walk-in named Lucas filled her chair.

Oh, well.

"Linda can get you paid up," Delaney told Lucas. "I gotta get the chair ready for my next client."

"Will do," he agreed, nodding. "Thanks again, eh?"

Delaney stepped to the side, allowing the man out around the chair. "I'm glad you like it." Then, she noticed an item he left behind. "Oh, don't forget your Bible?"

Lucas' next step hesitated, and he glanced over his shoulder. HIs gaze narrowed at the item dangling from her throat. "Are you a Christian?"

She had to think about it.

The answer was too complicated and would take a conversation they simply didn't have time for, nor would she share those intimate details of her life with a stranger that wore a nice smile. She could, and did, opt to whittle the truth down.

"I used to be," she admitted.

"Keep it? Or toss it," Lucas said just as fast. "I was trying to hold onto something—it's not working for me."

Sometimes, that was the harder reality to accept.

Delaney understood.

Preaching had never been her thing despite growing up in an ultra religious, fundamentalist family. She hadn't been the person who liked getting up in front of the congregation to pass along the Lord's word. Over time, she figured out that nobody really needed any of the things the person who stood at the pulpit said they did to be a follower of Christ.

"If you're trying to find a way to talk to God, just talk to Him," Delaney said. "Nothing in that Bible really gets around to explaining that part, but if it's what you're looking for, He listens. Just talk."

Lucas chewed on his inner, lower lip before muttering, "Yeah, thanks. I'll keep it in mind."

She didn't toss the Bible—even if she had no plans to read it, surely she could find someone who would. It remained on the edge of the workstation as she cleaned up the chair, and her next client took the seat. Lucas was shrugging on his wool jacket near the front, seemingly oblivious to the rest of the women in the salon who couldn't help themselves but watch the man ready to leave.

"I want to do something … *shaggy*," said the girl in Delaney's chair.

"You know, it's not really a style you can just do nothing for, right?" she asked. "It takes a bit of work to get it to look like a shag is purposeful."

The client didn't get the chance to respond.

The stylist who worked in the chair next to Delaney's moved to the power bar plugged in between their two stations. Whether she meant to change a cord out or remove one, whatever she yanked on sent sparks and a plume of black smoke rising.

It was the smell that did it for Delaney.

Charred plastic.

Something *burning*.

She didn't even notice the way the lights on their side of the salon flickered from the short because she was desperately trying to blink away the memories flooding her mind's eye. It could take mere minutes for a building to practically burn to the ground. One good lungful of smoke to choke out her tears.

She couldn't blink those away, either.

It was like Delaney wasn't even standing there in Linda's salon. Her surroundings morphed into a familiar sight, but flames licked at the floorboards around her feet and nothing about it was *right*.

It wasn't real.

It still felt like it.

Her night- and daymares of fire didn't happen as often as they used to, but the random intrusive images still took her by surprise every single time.

"Delaney—*Delaney!*"

"Are you okay?" she heard someone else ask.

Good God.

Why couldn't she *breathe*?

"Delaney!" Linda shouted close to her face.

The woman shook her shoulders hard.

That helped a bit.

Delaney blinked to find her boss standing in front of her, and Linda must have saw the flash of awareness. "There you are, huh?"

"I … I just need a second," Delaney managed to say.

Alone, she wanted to add, but didn't. *Couldn't*.

"Sure," Linda replied. "Take all the time you need. The bathroom, maybe? Clean up your face a bit."

A new, but familiar, voice joined the conversation. "Is everything okay?"

Oh, *God*.

Delaney swung away from Linda and the rest of the salon, including Lucas Dalton, who had yet to leave. Apparently. She made a beeline for one of two bathrooms at the back of the salon only to hear Linda filling in the blanks for the rest of the room.

"She has a thing about fire, I think?" Linda said. "Someone burned down her place a while back. She testified at the trial last year. The one upriver—didn't you hear?"

It looked like Delaney's day could get worse.

3.

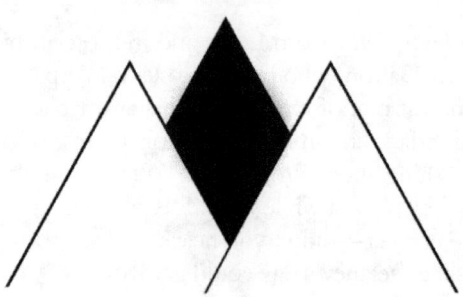

"I'm sorry, I'm sorry," Delaney mumbled, embarrassed, into her hands.

A sigh echoed from across the quiet apartment. The only true sign of her cousin's irritation even though Delaney's apologies had not stopped from the moment the two left the strip mall salon.

"Why on earth are you apologizing to me?" Bexley asked.

"You had classes, Bex. You didn't need me having a meltdown at work."

Putting the episode *mildly*, Delaney knew. The humiliation of hearing her boss recognize Delaney's plight and explain to the entire salon, including clients, why she'd freaked out kept her locked in the back bathroom and refusing to come out. Mostly because she couldn't get her hands to stop shaking.

Linda was understanding.

At least.

Delaney, when she felt up to it, would need to sit the woman down in private and make sure it was clear that she should never share her employee's personal business again. Certainly not in such a public manner. The last thing Delaney wanted to do was even think about her next three shifts at the salon for the week because she couldn't envision a path forward where the people at work wouldn't question her about things, now.

That was triggering, too.

"I didn't mind leaving classes to come help," Bexley said, joining Delaney on the couch.

She couldn't even manage to lift her head from her hands as the cushions shifted next to her, and a hand rubbed soothingly up and down her arm.

"It was all a refresher today, anyway," her cousin added, doing her best to minimize Delaney's guilt. Not that it would work. "You know, for coming back from break, and all. It's not a big deal, don't worry about it."

No, it *was* a big deal.

Despite having a license, Bexley didn't own her own car. She preferred public transport to go to and from school, or cabs if she was bar hopping on the weekend with friends. She hadn't hesitated to call a cab and come to collect Delaney and her Jeep at the salon twenty minutes away from her nursing college.

Fucking the rest of her day, too, surely.

"You shouldn't miss classes for me," Delaney muttered. "I'm twenty-five. My baby cousin doesn't need to be running after me because I can't get my emotions and thoughts under control, okay?"

Bexley sighed loudly again.

She let Delaney rant, though.

"I mean, it's been two goddamn—"

"Language, hey. Let's not bring God into it," Bexley interjected, sounding entirely too much like her mother—Delaney's aunt.

"It's been two years," Delaney snapped. Not at her cousin, really. Just the situation overall. "The Haus burnt two freaking years ago, okay? I should be able to see a few sparks and smell something burnt without having panic attacks, right?"

Bexley remained quiet next to her on the couch.

Delaney glanced her way, finally. "*Right?*"

"Maybe it's not that simple?" her cousin offered with a little shrug.

"What does that mean?"

Bexley tipped her head back and forth like she was trying to ease Delaney into believing what was about to come out of her mouth before she'd even said it. "You remember how Callie Smith counseled you and Gracen after the fire?"

"Yeah, those first couple of weeks were ..."

Bad.

Confusing.

Hell, honestly.

Neither of the women were in a good place—mentally, mostly—to deal with an arson that had been believed to be connected to Delaney's family. Callie, a social worker that Delaney and Gracen were familiar with, had offered to counsel the women should they need it.

Really, all Delaney wanted to do was forget it. All of it. Like it didn't even happen at all. She stuffed the memories of that morning down deep until she was numb and didn't even allow herself to think about the fire.

Unless she wasn't given a choice.

Like today.

A second fire in the valley town in less than a couple of months practically right across the river from one another, with a *plausible* connection, put the Haus and its owners in the spotlight.

To the town.

Police.

Delaney eventually changed her number because as the story grew, and arrests happened within the ranks of her own estranged family for the fire, she started getting random calls from reporters. That stopped after she changed her number and moved out of town on the advice of law enforcement until the trial of her older male cousin, Bexley's brother, and Levi—Delaney's brother—had finished.

She'd gone home to testify.

And not been back.

"Did you listen at all when Callie talked about what to expect *later*?" Bexley asked. "The salon burning, and then you feeling like you weren't safe to stay in town … that's all really traumatic stuff, Delaney."

"I handled it—"

"Yeah, pretty well," her cousin interrupted, bobbing her dirty blonde bob. "You did, and nobody can take that from you, but if dealing with it just means you ran or hid from it and didn't actually *feel* any of it, then—"

"Don't tell me I didn't feel anything when it felt like my whole world burned down that day," Delaney said, snappish and sharp.

Meaner than she meant to be.

"I'm sorry," she added. "I know you didn't mean it like that."

Bexley crossed her arms over her chest, crinkling the cartoon figures on her colorful scrubs. "Yeah, I didn't."

"I know, I'm just …"

Delaney struggled to find words. One of many struggles in her life lately. It sucked worse that she couldn't even explain the war she constantly fought inside her head. Was this ever going to end?

"You're just having a bad day," Bexley said, so Delaney didn't have to.

"A bad year, maybe."

Bexley laughed lightly. "*Well*, it's all the same. Feels like it sometimes, right?"

Delaney didn't confirm the obvious when neither of them needed her to. The sad state of her situation spoke loud enough for itself.

"The panic attacks and whatnot," Bexley edged carefully.

Delaney wished she could squeeze her eyes shut forever because of the building pressure starting to reach its peak inside her head. Migraines *always* followed her panic attacks. It never failed. "What about them?"

"It gets worse the closer you are to home, doesn't it?"

Despite the pain, Delaney's eyes flew wide to stare at the blank blue screen mounted on the wall. She'd turned the TV on when she got home just to get some other sound in the apartment other than her breathing and Bexley's quiet movements, but she never even made it far enough to turn on the satellite.

That took too much energy, too.

"I don't—"

"My bedroom is right next to yours," Bexley said before Delaney could think up another lie. "I hear when you're having bad nights. I listened as it got worse as the holidays came closer and you were supposed to go home to visit Gracen. I know these things, so why won't you admit there's a problem you're not dealing with?"

Jesus.

Delaney's nerves finally exploded. "Maybe that's what I'm trying to do!"

Bexley didn't flinch. "By gritting your teeth through it?"

"I'll wait while you figure out something better for me to do, okay?"

She meant for it to sound sarcastic.

Bexley was unbothered. "I think you should call Callie Smith again. I bet there's a reason this is happening and a way to help, if you'd be willing to try it."

"Help *what*?"

Meds didn't help. She tried the anti-anxiety prescription filled by her family doctor. The sleeping aids worked for a while, but she refused to gain a dependency, so that went out the window after a short period of time. The lack of sleep put her on edge even more, if that were possible, and certainly didn't help with the random spells of waking nightmares at the worst possible times.

Once, over burnt toast.

What was left?

Delaney's brain—her memories—were just broken.

That's how it felt, anyway.

Bexley pushed up from the couch, but stood close to clasp onto Delaney's jean-clad knee with a gentle, supportive squeeze. "Listen, don't feel guilty about calling me today. I don't care—I will always be there to help you. Like you helped me. I mean, this wouldn't even have happened to you if you hadn't stepped up for me, so you don't get to feel bad about reaching out to me once in a while. Isn't that what real family is supposed to do—wasn't that what you told me?"

Delaney blinked away a few stray tears, mumbling a shaky, "Yeah, I know."

"But you need to call Callie and try to get some of that stuff in your head and heart sorted, Delaney. Call her."

*

Delaney had to work up the courage over the course of the day to call her boss. A pathetic feeling, to be sure.

The woman was gracious when she did finally get Delaney's call.

"Don't worry that it's after seven," Linda assured as Delaney tried to get an apology out for the late time. "I'm just getting around to closing here, anyway. I had to wait most of the day for the electrician to get in and see what we're going to have to do about the half of the salon with no power at the moment. Looks like it'll take a few days to get everything fixed and back to normal."

"Still, I should've called—"

"When you were ready," her boss interjected. "And now you are. I hope you called to tell me that you planned to take tomorrow off—the rest of the week, maybe? After today, I think you need a break. Nothing wrong with taking it, girlie."

The woman didn't pose the question like there were options to the answers.

Delaney laughed weakly. "Believe it or not, but a part of me would just like to get up tomorrow and restart this whole day over like it didn't even happen."

On another day, she would done exactly that, too.

"But?"

"But I don't think I should, either," Delaney admitted. "Avoiding it isn't helping anything."

Not her proudest moment. Courage and pride were not always the same thing, and she was trying to figure out what fit where in her life at the moment. Including those two things.

"I am going to take the week to get some stuff sorted," Delaney went on to explain. "If it might bleed into another week, is that okay?"

"Perfectly fine, you do what you need. We are here and ready for you to come back whenever, Delaney. The other ladies were really worried about you today."

She bet.

Regardless of her feelings about her private information being shared with coworkers, Linda wasn't all bad. She probably hadn't given her slip of the tongue much thought considering the upsetting situation. Everybody had to give a little grace sometimes.

Delaney would try for this.

"Thanks, Linda. I'm *really* sorry."

"Don't apologize. Things happen sometimes. *And*, while we're on the topic, don't worry about your chair rental this month," Linda said. "It's covered. I know you can't apply for sickness benefits being I hired you girls into the salon as independent contractors, but if you need any help coming up with money to pay something, you let me know. Do you hear?"

It was sweet that Linda cared enough to provide Delaney with that kind of help, but it wasn't needed. She wouldn't explain that her savings and checking accounts were well-funded because the insurance had paid out for the Haus fire shortly after arrests were made, and her current living situation with Bexley in the modest Fredericton apartment cost far less than she made. Delaney was debt-free, could do *anything* if she wanted to, but here she was.

Stuck.

"I hear you," Delaney eventually said.

"Good," replied the older woman.

"I sincerely hope the girls didn't pool a fund to pay for my chair rental or something," she added after a moment. "I can cover it myself, if that's the case. They don't need to do that for me."

"Mr. Dalton wrote a cheque to me for that, actually, and then he had to head off. A plane to catch, or something. He really was in a rush this morning."

Delaney's brain took a second to catch up, and even then, she couldn't wrap her mind around what Linda had said. "Lucas—the first guy in my chair this morning?"

"He let *you* call him Lucas. The rest of us just got Mr. Dalton."

Huh.

How about that?

4.

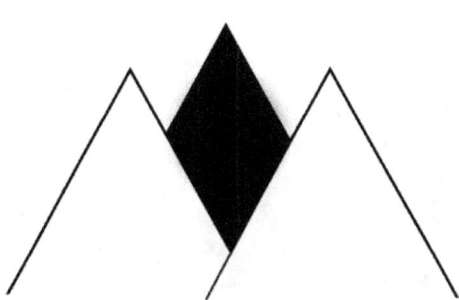

Three things about Dalton men carried across continents and generations never failing: their imposing size, laughter that boomed, and a family brewery with recipes older than the country they now called home.

Down the corridor of upstairs offices in the bottling factory on the east side of Saint John waited the largest of all at the far end with windows that overlooked the line below. Lucas didn't like to spend days stuffed away in the big office after returning from being away from the brewery.

Like he should still be down on the factory floor making rounds and walking the long blocks back and forth from the docks to barrels.

Despite taking over the day-to-day business and management of the brewery and plant in Saint John for his father a handful of years back so that Ronald could move his private office toward the center of the city, it was only supposed to be temporary. Before his father got up and changed location to work out of their warehouse and distribution arm across the country entirely. Without a lick of warning, too.

That left Lucas off the floor downstairs more often than he liked, and it was out of his control. There was something to be said for being seen by one's employees after a stint out of the city that tended to draw out the problem areas.

Be it a spat between coworkers, or a concern about a machine; even personal problems that someone might otherwise hide for the sake of professional appearances came to light when a boss gave his employee ten minutes of undivided attention. It probably helped that Lucas had been the willing shoulder to cry on—God knew they were big enough to hold others' weight—for a while, and his father didn't have the time or patience for things he called nonsense.

Like caring.

The brewery ran as it should, a well-oiled machine, when everyone was happy. From the loading docks at the far end of the plant to the high school student running the cash register in the gift shop at the front where the public was welcome to sign up for tours and tastings. They all made a difference to output, quality, and production, not to mention, experience, when they spent their shift working with a genuine smile.

It all mattered.

Lucas had to remind himself of those things more often lately. More than he should, honestly. He'd worked in the brewery from the time he was a teenager. Doing the same shit out front that everybody else who couldn't work in the back had to do. After high school, he maintained employment under his grandfather— who owned the majority shares of *Dalton Brewery* back then—while he worked toward a degree in business and management. The diploma guaranteed him a position managing the small army of employees until his late thirtieth birthday when he moved off the floor and upstairs where suits and ties made a daily appearance. Up here, he spent more time on the phone than he didn't.

Five years later, and Lucas still put more time in talking on the phone than he did getting his hands dirty downstairs.

But it was never enough.

"Is it *piss off Lucas* day?" came a holler from outside Lucas' office.

Followed by *that* booming laugh.

"Fuck my life," Lucas muttered under his breath.

Forgetting his place for the moment.

The phone conference was still live.

"My apologies, Mr. Dalton. Could you repeat that? It was a bit low."

"No need, something came up," he told the head of human resources who had him on a three-way call with the team of managers at the call center. "Can you finish this without me this week, Oliver?"

Never missing a beat, the man on the other end said, "Sure, absolutely. I'll debrief you in an email."

"Great, goodbye."

He didn't have time to consider if his reply had sounded as short to the others on the call as it did to his own ears before he cut it off entirely. Lucas barely had the chance to posture his body toward the opened doorway to brace for the oncoming visitor before the barrel of a man with energy that instantly filled the room darkened the space.

His little brother—by a whole decade—grinned wide and slapped the frosted glass door with his palm. "Did you miss me, fuckhead?"

Lucas tried, but the pulse of pain between his eyebrows had him pinching the spot to relieve the sudden tension. "Jacob, just *try* to give a shit when you're inside this place, okay? Try, that's all I'm asking."

"I give a shit."

Glaring at the twenty-five-year-old in the doorway who clearly didn't notice the giggles and jokes filtering down the hallway from the other offices, Lucas offered to Jacob, "Then get better at showing it, maybe?"

Defensive in a blink, Jacob straightened a bit with hunched in shoulders as he folded his once-beefy arms over his broad chest. Despite all the time his brother proclaimed to put into the gym, he'd yet to gain back a lot of the muscle mass that he'd lost in his earlier twenties.

"Jesus, man—why do you gotta sound so much like Dad, huh? I haven't seen you in like a week and a half, so I come all the way across the city when all I've got are trash morning classes, and you're being a prick. Whose talking about getting better at showing shit between us again?"

Goddammit.

Like a dagger to his heart, Jacob knew right where to hit Lucas when it really counted. A weakness in the older Dalton brother that only his younger sibling could latch onto because while a lot of differences separated the two, the things that mattered were exactly the damn same.

"I'm not like *Dad*," Lucas spat back.

Then, he did a double-take of the door, and his brain decided to remember the people just beyond his office.

"Close the fucking door," he snapped.

Jacob did, but he put in no effort to look happy about it. In fact, his arms remained crossed, and he refused to look at his older brother sitting behind the desk, opting to inspect the wall of shelves showing off the company's many awards.

"Not like Dad, right?" Jacob asked, oozing sarcasm. "Fuck, you've barely even changed this office. It all looks the same to me."

Then, he glanced Lucas' way. Sometimes, when Jacob got that mean gleam twist to his mouth, Lucas found himself thrown back to harder times with his younger brother. When Jacob had been all too willing—and quick, without even a thought—to hurt the one person who cared the most about him just to hide the demons in his own life.

Those moments scared Lucas.

That meanness in Jacob's expression worried him even more.

"What?" he asked Jacob.

"Not much about you looks different, either," he brother muttered, moving in for the kill.

"*Shut up.*" Lucas knew good and well he sounded like a child, but sometimes, things couldn't be helped. He forced his tone to be playful because despite the tense situation with his brother, Lucas didn't want to set Jacob off by saying something that might cross the lines. His brother learned early on from their parents' behavior that the quickest way out of anything was to run—and *fast*. "It's been a long few days, okay?"

Jacob scoffed, shoving his fisted hands into the pockets of his white hoodie with the maple leaf logo of his favorite hockey team. The two of them couldn't be more different with Jacob in distressed, acid-wash denim and laced up Doc Martens while Lucas wished he could breathe a little easier in his three-piece suit. One of them had the chance to live a little and take time to grow up while the other one never gave himself the opportunity to do the same— Lucas tried to keep that in mind when his baby brother was concerned.

After their pappy died, they only really had each other. The boys learned young not to expect comfort or help from their father who thought showing even conditional love for his child was the same as a handout to a beggar on the street. He'd been lucky enough to be the first grandchild of his grandfather, a man he'd been named after, and he'd doted on Lucas accordingly, and earned him shares in the brewery that had been held in trust. Something his father couldn't stand, and didn't share with Lucas until after his grandfather was dead and the will came to light.

Jealousy was a terrible monster.

Lucas did exactly what he had to so that Jacob didn't have to when it came to the family business. Including the *family* bit. Neither of the Dalton sons were particularly liked or needed by their father, and once they reached adult age, got cut off financially. Lucas chose to step up and help Jacob, so he didn't have to lower his morals to lose dignity crawling back to their father.

Besides, Lucas had to do that bullshit once a month—at least— whenever Dalton Brewery's CEO decided to leave his office downtown and came over to the east side to play boss now that he had returned to the city a few weeks earlier to spend the winter. A tyrant on the warpath, Ronald could leave real devastation in his wake.

Thankfully, that happened less and less with his father handling the company's business on the other side of Canada. Well, *when* the bastard stayed there.

"It's January," Lucas said, trying to keep the parental tone to a minimum because that never went off well with Jacob, "don't you have anything warm to wear other than that hoodie?"

Jacob rolled his eyes behind the rectangle-rimless prescription sunglasses his brother liked to wear in the winter months when the overwhelming white made everything seem brighter. Despite not being totally opaque indoors, Lucas couldn't get a good look at Jacob's eyes beyond their movement. Specifically, his pupils and their size. It bothered Lucas. Both that he couldn't see them, and that he wanted to at all. Not to mention, that he's already noticed the hoodie seemed looser on Jacob's tall frame. Lucas didn't want his mind to go to that bad place with his brother at all, but given the lack of quality time he had to spend with Jacob lately, he had to trust that everything was fine.

Especially when Jacob said so.

"Now, you sound like Mom," his brother muttered.

Not fucking likely.

"Get real. Mom was too drunk to care if you had something warm to wear."

That was their nanny's job.

The drinking got worse for their mother after Jacob came along although, at the time, Lucas was too young to understand why. Back before he knew what sex was and how babies got made, he couldn't put together why his mother's stomach grew and grew into a balloon. Overnight, he became the caretaker for a little brother he didn't even know existed until the day his parents brought the baby home. At least then, he finally had something to love him back.

"The sweater's fine," Jacob said after a minute of stillness between the two. "But seriously, bro, what crawled up your ass? It was like walking in on Dad for a sec—"

"Would you stop saying that?"

Jacob's jaw snapped audibly shut.

A part of Lucas hated that Jacob might be right—it got under his skin to have people constantly compare him to his father. More than anyone else in the world, Jacob knew it, too. Lucas considered bringing the conversation back to what currently concerned him about his brother, but he stopped himself. His defence against Jacob's comments didn't have to be to look for something equally bad or worse in his brother to point out.

That was the type of shit their dad would do.

Really, Lucas didn't mean to be so harsh. "Sorry," he muttered fast, "but you can't holler and swear down the hall when people are trying to work here, Jacob. People are *working*—they're making calls and doing meetings."

He gestured at the triangle base for his phone in the middle of the desk. "*I* was on a damn call!"

His brother had the nerve to look sheepish. "My bad?"

The problem with having a brother who didn't have a lot of responsibilities or expectations was that he also had yet to grow up. In a lot of ways. Lucas had a bad habit of excusing Jacob's shortcomings because of his biases. He knew the reasons why Jacob was the way he was—flighty and indifferent, and so he tried to give Jacob grace.

Sometimes, to his detriment.

Giving his brother grace didn't change the fact that they had already had quite a few hard years together. By *Jacob's* own actions, too.

Jacob had yet to find something he cared about except for his dog, a Mastiff rescue named Purdy that had passed from age-related illness a few months ago, his truck, and the quad on the back. Even the three-year degree in business had been stretched out for another two because his brother found too many other things to do *except* go to school. Before changing his direction in the last year to something else entirely. A bachelor's in exercise science.

Truly, that was a better fit for Jacob.

"It was just the head office for the call center in Freddy, but still," Lucas tacked on a little sharper at the end, "just think when you walk in here, all right? It's not a place to party."

Jacob grinned in the direction of the windows overlooking the factory line below. "*Actually*, there's enough liquor in this building for the whole city to have a party."

"That'll never happen, and aren't you the one who says sober means *sober*?"

"Fun sucker," Jacob bitched under his breath.

Lucas wished that was his problem. "Tired, is more like it, man."

He flattened his palms over his face, scrubbing hard to get a bit of blood flowing. Trips to Freddy every other week for a day here and there to be on hand for the recent management changes implemented at the head office for the call center left Lucas exhausted. He took the company helicopter back and forth because he wasn't built for long car drives on dark highways that seemed to stretch on endlessly.

He also wasn't sleeping in his bed as much as he would like. The bigger issue in his life. The *real* one.

"You need to relax a bit," Jacob said, his brows rising high like they did whenever he had a bright idea. "Oh, like go out with me this weekend—and by go out, I mean meet me at the gym where we can put on helmets and gloves and beat the hell out of each other."

Lucas chuckled, former memories of doing just that with Jacob over the past few years filling his mind. Those moments between the two almost always led into deep conversations about their lives and circumstances; or to confessions they might not have shared with anyone else.

"We never do that anymore, you know?" Jacob asked quieter.

"This weekend isn't great for me." Lucas blinked through his fingers. "I have the mayor's dinner and ball this weekend. You wanna go to that?"

A charity event thrown every winter.

A cringe pulled at Jacob's face. "Nobody wants to go to that, bro."

"Dad does. He's making me go, too."

And would likely ignore his oldest son all night, as well.

Lucas couldn't wait.

He got two and a half weeks of silence from him father, and had been stupidly hoping for longer. He should have known better.

Ronald continued to find interesting ways to punish his adult sons despite the men making every effort to give him distance and silence. Work and handling his father's responsibilities—without the actual title on his desk that he deserved—for the brewery made that harder for Lucas, obviously. Things had gotten more tense over the last twelve or so months.

He honestly believed that was because his father had started to face his harsh, stark reality. The loneliness awaiting him in his coming years. All the effort he put into making everyone else around him miserable had finally started catching up to the bastard.

Lucas wished he cared less than he did.

Ronald wasn't even worthy of that.

"I hear Mom's back in the area," Jacob noted.

"Living somewhere in Rothesay with her new husband," Lucas confirmed.

A realtor with whom she'd been having an affair for the last decade or more. Not even Dalton money and all the bubbly in the world had been enough to make Penelope stay when Ronald finally stopped pretending like he wanted her.

It was a messy thing … their family.

"Are you gonna meet up with her? They've been down in Florida since last winter, right?" Jacob questioned.

Lucas did his best to act busy with the papers on his desk, before shuffling them into a drawer where they didn't belong. Anything to drag out how long it took him to answer that question. "She did stop drinking."

Jacob sighed loudly. "Yeah, so *she* says."

"There was a time when she was a decent mom," Lucas added.

A hard scoff echoed. "*When?*"

Lucas would never be the bastard to tell his brother the truth: *before you.*

"I don't really want to see her," Lucas said, needing to get the two away from dangerous waters. "But I might if she reaches out and asks. What would it hurt?"

"A lot," Jacob answered immediately, "she's like an emotional leech, Lucas. She sucks the good right out of you."

All of them, really.

With parents like theirs, the two didn't have a chance at making emotional connections outside of their close circles. It contributed a lot to their close bond and guarded nature.

"If you do see her," Jacob said, taking one of the two leather bucket chairs across from Lucas' desk as a seat, "don't even hint that I want to speak to her."

"I won't."

An easy task, really.

Their mother rarely asked about her youngest son. As if they needed more proof about her missing maternal instinct.

Jacob huffed a hard breath, shoved his sunglasses high on his head, and then glared at a spot on the one that had once held a portrait of their parents. One of the few things Ronald did take.

"Just talkin' about them drains the good out of ya," Jacob said sadly.

"That's the truth."

Sometimes, they just needed to hear someone else say this shit they experienced *was* fucked up. Children didn't need a lot to grow up into decent human beings, and money counted for practically nothing when a home had no love.

Jacob cleared his throat, and his familiar dark gaze swung back to Lucas with less emotion than before after he dropped the aviators back down on his face. "How was Freddy this week?"

"Busy. It's settled now, though. I'll go back in six weeks for a check and to do a run through with the new people, but …" Lucas trailed off with a shrug. "I'm back home for a while."

While their main home office for the brewery remained in Saint John, the seaport city of New Brunswick situated on the Bay of Fundy, the call center for everything from their distribution lines to truckers had been relocated two hours away just outside of Fredericton. The relocation was new because the growth of the company demanded it in the last decade. What had started as a small enterprise for his great-great grandfather turned into an empire for his family.

An empire Lucas had started to hate.

Resentment could do that to a person.

Lucas didn't want Jacob to ever feel the way he did, and

perhaps if the young man found a place to focus his energy and passions, he wouldn't. On the other hand, Lucas would always be stuck right here.

"So ... that's a hard no for this weekend?" Jacob asked, his shaggy brunette hair a far cry from the short cut that his older brother kept trimmed neat.

Jacob never had to listen to Ronald bitch about it.

"Yeah, that's a hard no," Lucas replied. "Sorry, man."

Jacob shrugged and lumbered out of the chair to stand at his towering six-and-a-half-foot height. The age difference meant nothing when the two brothers stood toe to toe and looked one another in the eye. Not once had they come to blows despite sometimes coming close.

"We can figure out another time," his brother said, but he didn't sound particularly happy about it. "Do you have a date for the weekend thing, at least?"

Instantly, a black-haired, hazel-eyed pretty face flooded Lucas' mind before he could stuff the memory of Delaney's sweet smile away. Her reflection seemed to haunt him every time he looked in a mirror as if she was going to suddenly turn up behind him to say hello. It was a joke how fast she came to his mind first considering he didn't even have the woman's number to call her at all let alone ask for a date to a formal event that was sure to be stuffy *and* boring. He blamed his incessant thoughts of her on the fact that she'd been on his mind from the moment he left that walk-in salon in Freddy without knowing if she was okay.

"Well?" Jacob demanded, still waiting for an answer. The hopeful note to his question was about to get deflated faster than the birthday balloons the two brothers never had year after year.

"No on a date, too," Lucas admitted. "Frankly, I wouldn't punish a woman with a night alongside Dad and his friends, so ..."

"Fair enough, but aren't you tired of this yet?"

Lucas didn't understand. "I'm tired of a lot of things, man."

"Clearly not, you're still here. Doing what he can't be bothered to, Luke. I mean, it's up to you if you want to work yourself dead in this stuffy fucking office that smells like Dad," Jacob said, cutting across the floor for the door.

"It doesn't smell like him."

Over his shoulder, Jacob's eyes shifted suspiciously around the room. "Maybe it's just me, but—"

"It *doesn't* smell like him," Lucas insisted again.
Stronger the second time.
Jacob nodded once. "Who are you trying to convince?"

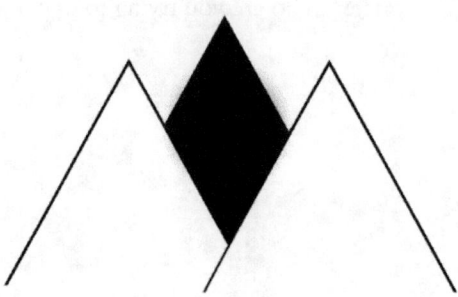

The mayor's twelve thousand square foot residence sat on an acreage just outside of the city's limits with private access from the road to both the house and a lake that wasn't big enough for a good boat run. Despite calling the yearly bash—with ten thousand dollar a plate expectation per guest—a ball, there wasn't ever any dancing. Just catered food by a chef whose name Lucas could never remember and rich people who wanted an excuse to dress up and get drunk.

Rarely could Lucas remember a time when wealthy people came together for a private party and didn't have a reason for doing so outside of talking about something they did to elevate their image, or to show off one thing or another. It could have just been the circles he had been made familiar with, but Lucas never cared too much for the performative activism and silent condemnation of people who had privilege and money.

The charity bit tacked on at the end of this particular evening was purely for brownie points, in his opinion. It gave the attendees the ability to say they were doing something, as if their CPAs weren't already allocating donations at the end of the year, anyway. Apparently, it was different when one went to a dinner alongside the wealthiest and most powerful in their part of the land and had their name added to a little plaque the mayor added to his growing wall year after year.

It gave someone *status*. While all they did was gossip and drink to get it.

He'd never cared for that.

His lack of concern for the lifestyles of the wealthy was never more apparent than when Lucas parked his Bronco SUV between a

Bentley and a Mercedes that didn't look as if the winter months had bothered the cars at all. The way their rims shined said they'd been washed and the paint had a wax, likely in a heated garage shortly before arrival at the mayor's family mansion. Everyone had to look their best; be at their greatest. It didn't leave much time or space for a man like him who couldn't quite fit in despite his proximity to the inner circle. He could not say the same, visually, of his two-year-old Bronco with its dirt-spattered sides that spoke of the factory's open-air parking lot compared to the rest of the vehicles lining the drive.

The white twinkle lights from Christmas remained lit around the eaves of the roof's high peaks all along the front, but there wasn't a Christmas tree or garland in sight. That season had long passed for the Alcott home, it seemed. The white lights overhead matched the ones wrapped around the trunk of the birch trees lining the drive and helped to illuminate the front of the property.

The wide, winding drive, cleared of ice and snow, so one could see the hand laid brickwork leading around the circular entry rounding a large water feature that was only lit, currently, but not running with water.

"You know," said a redhead wrapped in white mink a few cars down to the car dealership heir helping her along the drive, "I really could have done without these boots tonight, Benny. It ruins the look."

The thirty-seven-year-old, whom Lucas had brushed shoulders with on the ice in his private high school during hockey season, uttered frustratedly, "It's *Brennan*. Cut the Benny shit, Sheela."

"Only mommy gets to use that, right?"

"Your mouth is *not* worth a thirteen-thousand-dollar night, but you know, if you think open-toed stilettos are better for this, next year you're welcome to wear them and walk yourself, sweetheart."

Ouch.

The escort—Brennan already had two nasty divorces under his belt over his penchant for paid pussy—only heard one thing in the man's remark. "Who's bringing me next year?"

Brennan laughed at the expense of a woman more interested in her money than her dignity. Nothing about the situation felt right.

"Exactly," Brennan said, closing in on the front entrance of the lit up house.

Lucas, still cringing a couple of dozen paces behind the couple, slowed even more so the man up ahead had less of a chance of noticing him. If he could avoid conversations with a handful of people tonight—*perfect*.

Brennan was high on that list.

The mayor's personal assistant, a young, eager man, welcomed guests at the double doors before directing people inside by way of the bottom entry or the top of the house at the end of a zigzagging wooden ramp.

Lucas took the ramp option because regardless of the chilly temperature, he'd rather be outside watching the guests' children take on the snow-covered rolling hills on sleds and three-skis than inside making rounds with people he barely spoke to on any other given day of the year. He wasn't one for pretenses, but he also couldn't be a no-show when the mayor had personally made a call to him the week before confirming his father had passed along the invitation when Lucas didn't immediately RSVP.

He shot himself in the foot here.

Badly.

Few adults milled about on the upper deck that continued all the way around the house, monitoring the children. Lucas, polite to the one or two he did recognize, only nodded at the ones he didn't. Not even the sight of his own breaths making plumes of gray in front of his face could convince him to hide from the cold air outside.

Instead, he walked the deck and listened to the children squeal down below.

"Excuse us, sir," a young boy said as he and a girl of about the same age pushed beyond where Lucas blocked the stairs at the side of the house leading down. The two couldn't be more than ten or so.

Under his arm, the kid held a red rolled up silly carpet that would really let the two fly down the rolling hills. Typically, Lucas loomed over kids and some didn't take that well, so despite his quiet mood, he forced on a friendly smile to the cheeky two more interested in sliding than him.

"Sorry, mister!" called the girl on her way down the stairs.

"No worries," Lucas replied in a chuckle.

The girl, with ski pants pulled up high under the skirt of a pink dress that peeked out from under her parka jacket, beamed over her shoulder as she raced after the dark-haired boy. "You should slide, too!"

On another night with different people, maybe Lucas would. In fact, as a younger man he had. Having a younger brother ten years his junior kept Lucas' heart young ... in the ways that counted, he supposed. When he had been twenty and should have been enjoying the college life of a bachelor, he had a ten-year-old brother with a penchant for getting into trouble because he had *zero* parental guidance and needed a male figure to look up to. Someone to give him a reason to toe the line.

Lucas took the role seriously when he was old enough to grasp how growing up like he had with careless parents affected him. He'd wanted to make the outlook better for his brother somehow. Jacob, on the other hand, never let his older brother forget how to have fun when it mattered. Things worked out.

Tonight wasn't that night, unfortunately. His tweed coat and thermal-lined leather gloves might keep him partially warm, but the same couldn't be said for his Oxford loafers. Those weren't made to wade snow. The idea of freezing his nuts off and exhausting himself climbing back up the hill with the kids looked like a far better option than what waited behind him even if there wasn't a single adult out there enjoying the snowy hills with the kiddos. He didn't even turn to face the wide, tall windows overlooking the dining room inside, but he didn't have to, either.

Lucas could hear the party perfectly well.

He already regretted doing yet another thing to somehow please his father when in the end, the effort would be pointless.

Fruitless.

For absolutely nothing.

The fact Lucas showed up to something he couldn't and wouldn't enjoy for nothing more than to fulfill his father's request would continue to add to Ronald's constant *how high* mentality. How high could he make his oldest son jump before the man's knees finally gave out? Lucas didn't have many options when it came to Ronald. He could bend over backwards to avoid the man altogether, or make magic happen to give Ronald everything he wanted to keep the peace otherwise.

Regardless, only *Lucas* really suffered.

Luke, dude, he told himself to get out of his damn head, *you're being a bit dramatic here.*

Or wallowing.

It didn't matter. Neither of the two things would help and really only served to avoid the real problem facing Lucas at that moment. That he'd rather stand outside with his face freezing in the minus fifteen Celsius breeze than chance going inside where he might have to have a conversation with his father.

His gaze swung to beyond the corner of the house where he'd previously come up from the front. In the backdrop, he could see where Ronald had parked his Escalade. Only the front of the white vehicle was visible to him but the fact that it was there at all proved someone else had arrived, too.

The night, already fallen high in the sky, darkened around Lucas for an entirely different reason. Strange how that bullshit worked.

"*Dalton*! Lucas! I thought that was you, friend!"

Leaning over the railing to find the voice down below, Lucas genuinely grinned at who waved back. Standing next to the table where the children could get hot chocolate in foam cups, a familiar man laughed. The youngest of the three Alcott brothers, and a friend of Jacob's as they were the same age, Griffin wagged a finger in Lucas' direction.

"I'll be right up—don't move, man."

Lucas laughed. "Yeah, sure."

He'd always thought Jacob and Griffin got along well because the two had a lot in common besides just their age. Both being the babies of their families—with generational gaps between them and their brothers—made for an experience only they would truly understand.

He had personal reasons beyond just his father's expectations for not refusing this evening. Their families had brushed shoulders over the years, mostly aided by Jacob and Griffin's friendship. Of course, the boys' fathers ran in the same circles of prominent men in the city, too.

A smiling Griffin welcomed Lucas with a hard smack to his back after a tight hug. "I suppose I don't need to ask where Jacob is, huh?"

Lucas nodded off that comment. "Anywhere but here, you know?"

Griffin waved the news away, unfazed, as he stepped back from Lucas. "Yeah, *well* ..."

What could a person say?

Some family secrets were actually raw, open wounds that people just refused to treat. The obvious estrangement between the remaining Dalton relatives, his father had been an only child and most of Ronald's extended family were dead, was clear to the people who knew the family. At least beyond their family's name stamped on popular beer bottles and emblazoned on the trailers of eighteen-wheelers all across the country.

A company of *values*, they toted on job listings. Family values, in fact. It worked because their fifteen-hundred employees across the province and country held strong. The core values of the Dalton Brewery's work culture tried to reflect that by ensuring every employee felt appreciated and respected, like one might do for a family member, but the experience didn't carry on at the top of the tier.

There, they were just broken.

A living, breathing *lie*.

Lucas had gotten a little tired of it.

"How've you been?" Griffin asked, leaning sideways against the deck rail.

"Do you want an honest answer?"

Griffin's shoulder bobbed enthusiastically. "If it helps, go for it."

Lucas chuckled. "Nothing does, that's the point. I've tried everything to make myself give a shit about anything and not a bit of it has worked."

Boxing on the weekend for his anger. Church on Sundays because he thought God might be able to teach him about patience and forgiveness. None of it made much of a difference, and he was worried that his detachment from it all meant he was turning into the spitting image of his father—and not just physically, like he already did. The face in the mirror every morning reminded him of Ronald's lingering genes, but Lucas had stopped letting that affect more than just an annoyance he had to deal with being the bastard's son.

Well ...

Lucas ran a hand through his new haircut.

Mostly.

No, inside in heart, he was turning into someone who didn't care. That hit different.

"Oh, it's *that* kind of mood, huh?" Griffin asked after a moment of awkward silence.

"It's been a rough couple of years," Lucas admitted, glancing out over the rolling hills that were perfectly manicured lawns in the warmer months. "Dad's left me with a lot, and Jacob's finishing his last bit of college, so—"

"He told me you pay for his tuition and give him an allowance," Griffin blurted out. "Last time we talked, I mean. I didn't think things had gotten that bad with him and your guys' dad. I didn't even bother to ask him if he was coming tonight, or not."

"Already knew," he muttered.

"Yeah, sorry."

"Listen ..." Lucas shoved his hands into the pockets of his tweed coat to hide the way he had to flex the tension out of his fists. "Don't take what he told you to anybody—we're handling the family stuff *in* the family, you know what I mean?"

How would that affect the employees of their company to know the family-owned business responsible for their weekly pay and future retirement funds was a shouting match away from crumbling in the worst way?

They didn't deserve that, either.

Griffin scoffed under his breath. "I know what you mean. I get how that kind of stuff starts in families like ours, though. Dad told Sloane if he didn't give up the painting shit and get a wife before he turned forty that he'd be out of the estate entirely."

The man's green eyes darted fast to Lucas before he added lower, "You're not going to see him tonight, either. He's moved to Halifax with his boyfriend. Another hard line for Mom and Dad."

Jesus.

Lucas was *so* tired.

"He told me to get a therapist before he left last month," Griffin added. "I'm starting to think everybody should have one. Like a mandatory thing we can pull up when needed and say, *hey, these things are fucked and they're fucking with me.*"

A laugh passed between the two.

"You started therapy?" Lucas asked after, honestly surprised.

"Yep—why, you thinking about it?"

"I hadn't," he admitted.

Therapy probably wasn't the miracle key to fix his life, but it made sense why Griffin would put the suggestion on the table. Some things needed help to get worked out. He wanted happiness, and that kept being sucked away from him by a toxic family dynamic he had yet to manage. Avoiding and people-pleasing didn't put Lucas in a place that served himself first. He just happened to be in a shitty position where he couldn't talk to just anyone about these things. He'd not been raised that way, for one.

"You should try it," Griffin said, slapping Lucas on the shoulder as he passed by his friend to take the stairs down again. "I gotta get back to watching out for these damn kids. Can't have somebody burning themselves and threatening to sue."

Lucas didn't reply, but Griffin did something important for him at that moment. A silent friend to friend understanding that it was okay not to be okay sometimes.

He might try therapy. Like boxing and church, even though he'd not found what he really wanted or needed in those things. Then, nobody could say Lucas didn't try.

He simply needed to make it through the winter with his father before the man headed back out west to their second brewery and bottling plant, and dispatch in the country. The spot where he'd moved his new office and worked, when he felt like it, Ronald only came back home for an extended stay in Saint John for Christmas and the winter since his divorce.

The distance between Alberta and New Brunswick—basically a whole country—made things easier in the strained family. In some ways.

"Oh, and mind the den downstairs," Griffin called up to Lucas. "Everybody's smoking cigars with Dad down there, and playing pool. Pretending to like drinking his shitty scotch."

"Scotch isn't shitty, you just have no decent tast—"

"Your father is also down there," Griffin interjected, dead staring Lucas from below.

"Avoid the shitty scotch, don't see my father. Got it," Lucas said.

That's what mattered to him.

Might as well make this night bearable—*for himself*—even it was just pushing back the inevitable to a later date. Some things couldn't be helped.

*

Avoid the den.
Famous last words.

45

Lucas didn't get to avoid the downstairs den, the shitty scotch, or his father, after all. The second he entered the Alcott home, Tanner—the middle son and closest to Lucas' age, though the two weren't particularly close *or* friends—spotted him from across the room.

So much for a quick warm up of his fingers with the hopes of slipping back outside unnoticed. Lucas couldn't be so lucky.

"Teams!" Tanner shouted at him from the other side of the dining room like Lucas should immediately know what he meant. "You're here—I told your father we were doing teams for billiards at least once tonight, man. Right now, let's go … I just got Dad up and playing again, so he's in the right mood."

By the time Tanner finished his explanation, he had crossed the room to throw an arm around Lucas' shoulder with a hug that pulled him toward the rear hallway connecting to the room that led to the private den downstairs. He didn't know how to shove off the man's arm, or intentions, without seeming like a total asshole, so he sucked it up and let Tanner pull him along.

"Work kept you busy this year?" Tanner asked, making polite small talk on the way.

Lucas wished he wouldn't bother. "Something like that—I heard you were running for city council coming up, eh?"

Turning the topic back to Tanner worked to Lucas' favor. The guy was more than happy to talk about himself—always at the ready to sell the image of a proper Alcott—like their father, Mattos, Matty, to his friends, undoubtedly expected.

Tanner Alcott was a younger, more obnoxious version of his father. A man, personable enough with salesman's tongue, and a booming laugh that Lucas could already hear when he and Tanner rounded the top of the wood paneled staircase leading to the basement den. The cigar smoke hadn't quite carried all the way up the stairwell yet, but he found it halfway down like a wall the two had to walk through to get to the bottom.

Before they did, Lucas heard something else he didn't want to. *Someone* else, really.

"I'll play the winner this round," came the familiar voice, roughened with an exhale of smoke he *almost* coughed on.

As if Tanner could read Lucas' mind, his hand clamped to his companion's shoulder at the sound of Ronald Dalton's voice. He pulled Lucas slightly closer with a friendly shake as they entered the den downstairs side by side, announcing his arrival to the room with an overly loud, "Look who I found!"

A dozen or more familiar faces turned Lucas' way at Tanner's introduction—something that wasn't at all needed. A few hellos echoed from the men he would say hello to out in public but couldn't care less if their phone numbers were in his contact list. Making nice with friends of his father never settled well with Lucas.

"Lucas, hey," came the greeting of a man sitting on the stool under the neon light proclaiming the den a *Man Cave.*

"Hey, Ridge," Lucas returned, offering his hand for a fist bump from one Alcott cousin he didn't mind seeing around every once in a while.

Chatting with Ridge for a few minutes gave Lucas the chance to avoid jumping right into a conversation with his father—whom he hadn't spoken to in a good while—waiting just a few paces away at the far end of a red-clothed billiards table. Pool stick already in hand and with his eyes on the table watching the last few plays of the current game out, Ronald didn't seem interested or concerned with his son's arrival.

Appearances, however, were deceiving.

Lucas tried to focus on the question Ridge had asked about the brewery's shelf life on their barrels, but the smooth *plunk-plunk-plunk* of clean shots on the pool table one after the other kept him from answering.

Ronald looked his way, too, after the eight ball had dropped into a corner pocket after the final game call.

"Lucas and I will take Tanner and Matty," Ronald declared between the celebratory shout from the last winner.

Fuck his whole life.

Lucas wasn't even good at pool.

"Later," Ridge told Lucas with a nod toward the table. "We can catch up, yeah?"

"Sure, man."

Staying on his side of the den and pool table would have been preferred, but Lucas made his way over to his father's side along the far wall under another neon light showing off the Alcott patriarch's favorite beer.

Not theirs.

Lucas wasn't offended.

He had other things to worry about.

47

"How late were you—twenty minutes?" Ronald asked the second Lucas was close enough to hear his father's displeasure and complaints.

"Nothing's served, right?" Lucas returned, keeping his tone light.

Walking on eggshells to keep the peace with Ronald Dalton became a carefully balanced circus act that Lucas had gotten tired of playing over the years. Or maybe he just no longer wanted to look like a clown for doing something that never actually worked.

Sometimes, like around others, keeping the peace couldn't be avoided. No one wanted to get in between an infamous Dalton shouting match—God knew Lucas didn't want to have one, either.

Ronald, it seemed, had moved to other things to bitch about. "I heard your mother is back in town—let's hope I don't have to see her face."

Lucas remained expressionless at the comment Ronald made under his breath, so the two men at the other side of the pool table currently racking up the balls wouldn't hear.

"Have *you* seen her?" Ronald asked.

"No."

"Well, that's not shocking. You've only been around to see me since I came back from the west when you absolutely have to, I suppose," Ronald replied as if that said something about Lucas.

He refused to take the bait and ask *what*. The answer was obvious. Ronald expected Lucas to make his way downtown to Ronald's private offices to kiss his ass and personally deliver company reports—because they sure as hell didn't get together during personal time—but he refused to do even that for his father. In fact, Lucas found every excuse he could to avoid meeting up with Ronald since the man's return to the city.

"Are you going to spend any hours in the brewery this winter, or just work from your office downtown?" Lucas asked, trying to prod the conversation in a direction that served him.

Mostly, so he knew how to plan for his upcoming months.

Ronald sucked his tongue along his teeth before muttering, on a completely unrelated level, "I also hope your brother isn't going to show up tonight."

That hurtful comment made Lucas flinch.

"He's *not*, thanks," Lucas replied, "and he had other plans this weekend."

"What, playing with dogs or sitting in another meeting? Useless, all of it. And the only thing you do by paying his way and keeping him fed is enabling his nonsense on. Whatever," Ronald said, carelessly, with a wave of one hand as if he could wipe his youngest son away with a gesture and a word. "It's your mess. Otherwise, he's just a waste of my damn breath."

"*Dad*," Lucas muttered sharply under his breath, "have a little respect."

He always tried to draw the line with Ronald. That sweet spot where Lucas could stand every insult and mean comment about people he cared for coming out of his father's mouth. The story never changed with Ronald. The same person he could look in their face and smile became the next human he called an idiot in one of his rages.

Jacob wasn't perfect, nobody was, and his brother had demons, sure. Maybe he needed a bit more time to grow up than the rest of them, and made mistakes along the way, but Ronald could at least respect the fact that Jacob *tried*.

He tried to do better.

Be better.

That was more than Ronald could say for himself. He didn't need to take every possible chance he could to put Jacob down for nothing but doing better—but of course, Ronald did and would.

"Lucas," his father said in an annoyed sigh, "I won't pretend like I'm not happy to see that he didn't come tonight. I'm not interested in another scene where he has to go through the whole spiel about why he's sob—"

"I'm considering therapy," Lucas interjected quietly, knowing where his father's conversation would go, and the two across the table were waiting for Ronald to decide if they would flip to break, or not.

Giving his father something about *him* to latch onto and criticize to feed whatever misery lived inside Ronald seemed like a better route than listening to him insult and talk about Jacob when his brother couldn't even defend himself.

Sure enough, the therapy comment worked.

Ronald scoffed, *loud*. "The fuck you are—for what, to cry about how your mother didn't love you enough? Are you serious? You sound like an idiot."

That time, Ronald wasn't quiet at all.

No, the whole room heard it.

At least, Ronald had moved on from Jacob. That'd make this *one* game of pool Lucas would grit his teeth though mildly bearable. Very fucking little else.

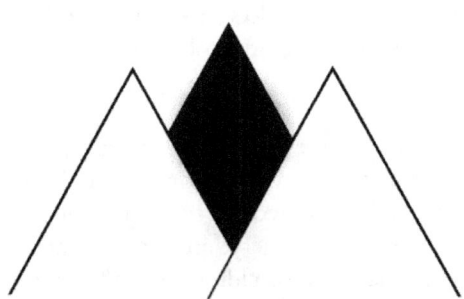

6

Callie Smith, a social worker, and part-time licensed counselor could make anyone smile by the sight of hers alone. Her short, black bob framed an animated face, and when she smiled at strangers in the same way she did to those she called friends, people couldn't help but smile back. A ray of freaking sunshine, Delaney bet the woman even woke up happy and full of joy.

If not, she hid it well.

In front of Delaney's Jeep, Callie did some version of a victory dance at having procured fast-food from the king of burgers—or so the restaurant proclaimed. She balanced drinks in a holder in one hand and a brown bag full of food in her other. It wasn't Delaney's favorite fast-food but considering she hadn't bothered with breakfast before hitting the road that morning, anything looked edible at the moment. Especially greasy or salty things.

She could pay for it later.

"Get in the Jeep," Delaney called, laughing, out the driver's side window.

Callie grinned her way into the passenger seat, plopping the drink and food to the middle console. "Are we eating here, or …?"

The potato chip factory next to the gas station and attached fast food joints wasn't a bad place to park in Waterville, but a person couldn't escape the distinct smell of grease in the air. Even inside a car. No matter the time of year, the factory made itself well known. She thought the smell did get worse in the winter months, though.

There wasn't much else to do or see in the small valley community further down river from Delaney's hometown. A big hospital where everyone within an hour's drive had to go to deliver babies or get treatment for something more than a Band-Aid couldn't fix. It was a momentary hub between the larger towns.

"I know a spot," Delaney said.

Callie shrugged as she buckled herself into the Jeep. "I'm up for whatever. I've got some extra time today. Things didn't go so great at the hospital."

"Oh?"

Silence answered Delaney's vague prompting.

She was never quite sure whether or not she should just outright ask Callie about her work with at-risk children and their turbulent families. Callie did everything from home checkups on open CPS cases to delivering children to and from medical or therapy appointments when their foster parents couldn't manage it. Her caseload continued to grow double and triple what she should handle, and the worst of humanity sometimes hid behind the walls and doors children called home.

It could be a lot.

Delaney didn't like to push.

"It'll work out eventually," Callie said, although it sounded more like something she meant for herself.

That was okay, too.

"Let's find a place to eat," Delaney said as she maneuvered the Jeep out of the parking spot next to Callie's unmoving car.

She hit the highway from the on ramp just offset from the gas station. Callie, who'd professed her desire for food the second the two met up in the parking lot, dug through the bag before Delaney had even merged completely.

The burger and fries weren't her favorite, but her mouth still watered as the hot greasiness of the food filled the Jeep's cab. Her stomach had to join the sad chorus with a loud rumble. Even her current passenger heard the noise.

"Sorry," she said with a mouthful of fries at Delaney's half-hearted side glare.

"I'm just a little jealous," Delaney admitted.

But honest with herself, too.

Delaney didn't have the skills to eat and drive—or rather, she wouldn't test herself in the winter on less-than-ideal road conditions, regardless of the studs in her tires.

The drive wasn't far. Delaney remembered the small road the government trucks kept cleared to store piles of sand for easy access during stormier weather. Sure enough, five minutes up the highway, there waited a snow-cleared path with a fresh layer of sand and a pile off to the side.

The road wove around a field and up along the edge of a rock face that overlooked the highway and the Saint John River further down below. At least, the two women had a decent view while they talked and ate. As long as Delaney kept the Jeep running, they wouldn't be bothered by the chilly winds outside.

"Here," Callie said the moment they'd parked.

She already had Delaney's wrapped Whopper and fries ready. Her drink sat in the cup holder with a straw shoved down the middle of the cover, too.

"Can we eat first?" Delaney asked.

She didn't tack on the rest of the important bits to the question; Callie would understand. After all, Delaney didn't get in her Jeep at eight in the morning and drive for two hours on a mid-weekday for nothing.

In a way, getting *this* far downriver had been a test. The fact she could even look down upon the Saint John River, capped in ice from one side to the other, and didn't have a clenching pit in her stomach making her want to get away said she'd passed.

So far.

"Yeah, let's eat," Callie agreed.

Delaney went for her burger first. By the time she got around to her fries after sucking half of her soda dry, they had gone lukewarm. It didn't matter. She ate those too. The saltiness made up for the lack of heat, and helped her to finish off what remained of her drink.

At some point, Callie reached over and turned on the radio. A station that focused on the top hit list in music, so every song was something recognizable or made someone want to dance along. All the noise and music did for Delaney was keep her from getting too far into the anxiety spinning a web of *what ifs* inside her head.

"So, you joined those trauma recovery webinars last weekend, right?" Callie asked suddenly.

Delaney, cleaning the tips of her fingers with a napkin, hadn't been ready for the question. "Uh … yeah?"

Callie smiled gently. "Yeah like maybe, or yeah like—"

"I did both. Saturday and Sunday night."

"And?"

"And what?" Delaney returned.

"Come on, Delaney. What did you think?"

"Honestly?"

Callie nodded, but no judgement waited on her face for Delaney. Her friendly, welcoming personality made it slightly easier for Delaney to say the hard things in front of Callie. She was one of the few people able to absorb it all without making Delaney feel ashamed or broken. Reaching out at Bexley's suggestion had been the right thing for her to do—a step in the right direction.

"At first, I figured it was a good way to waste a weekend," Delaney muttered.

"*Hey.*"

Delaney laughed, tossing the dirty napkin Callie's way to dunk it in the bag between them. "I only thought that because I thought I was going to be on camera with a bunch of other strangers talking about this awful thing that happened to me. I didn't realize it was meant to be more informative and—"

"*Recovery* based?" Callie suggested. "Like it said in the title?"

"I overthink a lot of things," Delaney said.

Only a little defensively.

Callie didn't prompt Delaney with another question about the webinars which gave her a second to think about them deeper than her initial feelings. In the end, it wasn't at all what she thought it would be—only one person happened to come on screen and talk, presenting his video slide of information on PTSD and recovery from trauma. He'd professed a dislike for labels, proclaiming what hurt one might not hurt another, and everyone should be free to recover at their own speeds. That was harder to do when people felt the need to compare their pain to someone else's in the crowd.

Mostly, Delaney got stuck on the labels. If only because they offered an answer, and she fixated on that part.

That probably hadn't been the intention of the webinar, but it solved a big problem for Delaney. Something that had been practically laughing in her face for over a year because she had been too scared to call it out by name.

She couldn't ignore how the ninety-minute webinars provided by the province's mental health services affected her. Delaney recognized herself in the list of symptoms, and in the paths of avoidance or deflecting, that kept her stuck in her trauma.

Outside perspective made a big difference for her when she could see her problems projected through the life or experience of someone else.

She wouldn't be the victim again.

She wasn't that weak.

Those things could both be true, but also harmful.

"I think I might have PTSD," Delaney admitted.

Putting it out into the world like that, even if it was only between her and Callie in the Jeep, was a huge step for Delaney.

"You can register every week for the webinars," Callie told Delaney, "just use the same link I already sent. If it helped, I mean, some people go back a couple of times to learn methods of retraining their thoughts or learning how to target triggers. It's—"

"I don't think I'll do it again," Delaney admitted.

Callie nodded supportively. "Once was enough?"

"I got the point." Delaney settled into her seat, folding her arms over her chest while she silently observed the movement on the highway below. With another week off before she had to return to work, a short car trip to have a face-to-face conversation with the only person she felt comfortable sharing these secrets with was more than worth it. Callie didn't have to make time in her busy days for Delaney when they could do a session over the phone or on video chat, but getting away from her current day to day life could also be self-care. Something she desperately needed. "I keep wondering if because I didn't really deal with the fire and how it messed with me, I gotta deal with this now, and in a way, that means they've won."

They meaning her family.

The cousin, and her only brother, that set fire to her whole world. Literally. The Haus burnt to the ground in less than a couple of hours. The fire started at the back inside the rear offices after the guys had broken windows. It took twenty minutes of water spraying from the trucks of the fire department before the men decided to call the building a loss and maintain the blaze until the building fell. The back had taken too much structural damage.

She stood there and watched it all, and it never really felt like she left that time or place.

"They didn't win," Callie said. "They're spending eight years in prison because your testimony about their movements and behaviors before and leading up to the fire helped to convict them. That alone makes you a survivor."

"And I should focus more on the triumphs of my hardships and not the event itself," Delaney parroted, remembering the advice about putting her past into a different perspective. One that didn't automatically place her as the victim. Reframing tragedy took mindfulness and patience. She still needed some practice.

"Exactly," Callie murmured. "You know, I think you're gonna do okay. It just takes a little bit of time for some people to really get to the root of what's keeping them stuck, but once you get it … *boom*. You're out of there, Delaney. Out of your head and all the rest. Just give it time."

She sighed. "How much is it going to take?"

Callie laughed lightly. "Why—do you have a deadline?"

Actually, yes.

"Gracen is getting married in the spring," Delaney said.

"Oh, really? I didn't hear that."

"It's a new thing. I don't know if she's started to spread the word, or …"

"No worries, I'll keep it secret."

Delaney wasn't concerned about that, really. Her anxiety focused somewhere else entirely. "I would like to be able to go back home and maybe stay there for a bit. I want to enjoy that time with my best friend. She deserves a special day, and I don't want to ruin it."

Callie's easy smile never faltered. "*You* won't ruin anything, and for what it's worth, you've already gotten past the hardest part of all of this."

"How so?"

"You recognized something wasn't okay. You asked for help, Delaney. Those are your first steps into healing." Callie put the fast-food bag full of trash on the car's floor before asking, "Do you think you're ready to get back to work next week?"

Well …

"As ready as I'll ever be," Delaney answered honestly.

7.

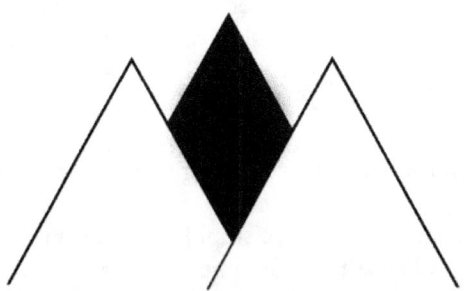

Linda turned the salon into a shrine to whatever holiday or theme took focus that month. Delaney couldn't say she liked the giant hearts hanging from the ceiling between rows of pink and white confetti strings, but it did give the place some charm. The small cupids pasted to the walls shot arrows into hearts stuck on every mirror.

A painted *Happy Valentine's Day* welcomed everyone at the front windows on their way through the doors. The small salon tucked away into the strip mall showed up and out. Nothing was too much, apparently.

She did find it slightly humorous that her boss spent a good week putting up all the decorations between her appointments—only esthetician clients as Linda proclaimed her back couldn't take the hours upon hours on her feet anymore—but would have to take them down in another day or so. Linda couldn't stand to leave a theme up more than a couple of days past a holiday.

Tacky, she said.

Right.

The decorations being old was the tacky bit. Linda was far too soft-hearted for anyone to explain it was practically the same thing. At least, to the extent *she* took the decorating. That made a lot of difference.

It kept the woman happy, though, so nobody had a complaint. Including Delaney.

She did, however, peel the heart and arrow off her station's mirror when Linda wasn't looking because it kept flopping down. Not in the way, really. The damn thing just wouldn't stay up and that bothered Delaney in a way she couldn't explain.

Her boss hadn't noticed.

Or didn't care.

Valentine's Day would be over by the end of the weekend, and when Delaney started her next shift of four straight days, the decorations would all be gone.

What was next?

Easter?

She couldn't wait for the pastel egg and bunny decorations.

Not.

Delaney laughed at her own stupid joke, drawing in the gaze of the girl who worked at the station next to hers. She pretended not to notice the curious stare while she finished a second sweep around her chair. Keeping her conversations with coworkers at surface level never gave them the chance to feel like they could prob too deep with Delaney.

That place wasn't safe.

Thankfully, the blown plug and lights had been fixed—whatever surge shorted the wires didn't cause a problem now.

She stepped into the backroom to put the broom and dustpan away with the others, and returned to her workstation to find she had missed a call from Gracen after not responding to an earlier text because she'd been busy with a client. Nobody looked at her twice for sitting in the chair and making a personal call, not that their boss particularly cared. She didn't have another client scheduled until after lunch, and since her most recent had finished fifteen minutes early, Delaney had lots of time to work with.

Or so she thought …

"It's almost my lunchtime," Delaney told Gracen when her best friend picked up on the second ring. "We've got to make a rule where you have to wait at least an hour before calling me when I don't answer a text during work."

Gracen didn't miss a beat, not even bothering to say hello or deny that she often pulled the trigger on calling Delaney before she had a chance to answer anything back. "Your schedule is so weird, though."

"Not untrue," Delaney agreed.

"I wasn't sure if you were working today or not. Sometimes, I mess it up."

That was a lie.

She didn't even bother to call Gracen on it when a simple

question could clear it up for both of them.

"Didn't I tell you my schedule for the next two weeks when we talked on—"

"I want to send you something, okay?" Gracen interjected.

Delaney's brow flew high. "Like, in the mail?"

Gracen laughed. "No. A picture."

"You want to send me a picture."

Delaney didn't pose the statement as a question because it wasn't one. Pictures from Gracen weren't anything unusual or new. Gracen sent Delaney pictures regularly throughout the week. It would be strange if she went a day without getting an update on something via a texted photo. It could be anything.

Of someone's hair Gracen thought had turned out particularly well. Even her property and new woodworking and epoxy projects with her partner. Often, she sent pictures of her cat, Mister Kitty, doing absolutely nothing but looking cute. Personally, those were Delaney's favorite of the bunch.

So, yeah.

Gracen sent Delaney pictures all the time, but she didn't call to preface doing so. That was different.

"Yeah, in a few minutes," Gracen clarified, a nervous edge trailing her laugh before she added, "I'll text it to you, but I wanted to give you a warning first. Like a heads up so you weren't thinking, *what the fuck, Gracen*? Do you know what I mean?"

Not particularly.

Delaney had missed something.

Clearly.

"This is weird, right?" Delaney asked. "It's not just me—you're being *weird.*"

The echo of Gracen's loud laughter told Delaney something she hadn't realized until that moment. Her friend had her on speakerphone. A lower, masculine chuckle, not quite in the background, confirmed her belief.

"Hi, Malachi," Delaney said.

Gracen had yet to stop laughing.

"Hello to you, Delaney," he returned. "And yes, she's being—"

"I'm not being weird," Gracen said before anyone could get a word in edgewise. "I'm getting tired of waiting, and I've convinced myself to hold back long enough hoping we could do it face to face, but it's *eating away at me here.*"

"She does overthink it a lot," Malachi confirmed. "The amount of times I've had to listen to her rant at me about whether or not she should just tell you ... Just tell her, babe."

Delaney blinked, imagining her best friend and *fiancé*—now— in their kitchen with the phone between them on the counter. She could picture it perfectly and that left her with a hollow ache in her chest that she couldn't explain. Maybe because she wanted to be there with them; the laughter didn't quite feel as warm and real over the phone.

All made up nonsense in her own head, sure.

On the other hand, it had been a long time since Delaney could honestly say she missed home. Especially in a way that left her longing to *be* there. Usually, those thoughts, or the lack of them, left her sad and ashamed.

Or worse, numb.

"Should I just do it, or send the picture?" she heard Gracen ask in the background.

"Oh, my God. Woman, *make a choice*," Malachi returned.

"I'm trying!"

His laughter rumbled on the other end of the call. "Do you want me to do it for you?"

"*No!*"

Gracen's sharp response slammed Delaney back into reality and out of her spiraling thoughts.

"Tell me what?" Delaney asked.

All of the sudden, Gracen's voice was far clearer and closer to the phone. "You're off speaker."

"Great, so will you tell me what's going on?"

"Yes and no," her friend returned.

"Gracen—"

"I know you're almost on a lunch break, so my plan is to send you a picture shortly and then you can call me back. I've hyped myself up way too much to just tell you over the phone when I did this whole thing with a picture yesterday at the hospital—okay? It's cute. Let me have this."

Wait, *what?*

"Why were you at the hospital yester—"

"*Delaney.*" Gracen's impatient sigh crackled over the speakers in Delaney's ear. "I'm sorry—I should have just waited until noon and sent you the picture but you know how I am. I get ahead of

myself. I know you're still at work, but I let Malachi get in my head
when I started waffling about things because you didn't text me
back."

"None of this makes sense," Delaney laughed into the phone.

Finally gaining the attention of a couple of her coworkers. The
woman in the station next to hers grinned her way, but quickly
went back to fluffing the blowout of the blonde in her chair.
Across the salon, Linda peeked in Delaney's direction from behind
the desk where she was currently filing off the remnants of a lady's
gel nails.

"It will," Gracen promised. "*Shortly.*"

Delaney spun her chair around so that the back faced the rest of
the salon. "Nothing bad, right?" she asked, quieting her voice more
than before.

"Something *great*, Delaney."

"Something you've known for a while and wanted to tell me?"
she prodded.

Just to see how far she could get.

Gracen scoffed. "Nice try, but also yes."

Her friend might as well have put them both back at square one
of their current conversation with that comment. Which might
have been the point.

"Since just before the holidays, anyway," Gracen added. "I
really wanted to tell you then, but—"

"I didn't come home."

"But that's okay," her friend rushed to say. "That's a work in
progress, right?"

Delaney grinned even though Gracen couldn't see it. "Yeah,
that's my work in progress."

She had just got Gracen off the phone, with a promise to call
her back when she finally took her lunch, as the bell over the
salon's front door chimed with a jingle. Her intention had been to
pick Bexley up over noon and take her out to eat, which she still
planned to do, but she froze in the chair once she swung it around
and saw who had come in.

He wore the same black tweed jacket as last time, but the
matching cap he pulled from his head to slap the snow off against
his palm was a new accessory. Lucas caught her staring across the
floor, and winked her way before turning to shrug off his jacket
and hang it up with his cap on the coat rack near the door.

By the time he scuffed the soles of his ankle-high boots against the entrance mat, Linda had already excused herself from her client. Except the boss didn't make a beeline for Lucas Dalton—instead, she came for Delaney.

With a big smile on her face.

"Thank me for this later, okay?" the woman asked, her grin turning conspiratorial.

Delaney couldn't help but look between Linda and the man finishing his business at the door as to not dirty the salon's floor more than necessary. "What did you do?"

"You know, he was *very* concerned about you," her boss explained. "Unintentionally kind, I think. I thought it was sweet. He might have called a week or so ago to check in. *Maybe* I mentioned I could fit him in to see you whenever he was in town if he just gave me a call ahead. Looks like things worked out, huh?"

Things worked out?

Her boss had lost the fucking plot.

"*Linda!*"

Delaney's whisper-scold only made the older woman *teehee* under her breath.

"You're *so* welcome," Linda said over her shoulder, giving a little wave to Lucas on the other side of the salon as she headed back to her own workstation. She stopped halfway to turn back and tell Delaney, "Trust me, that one is every bit a catch."

What fresh hell was Linda trying to walk Delaney into here, and since when did she play matchmaker?

Delaney couldn't decide whether to laugh or cry. Neither seemed appropriate given the current circumstances, so she plastered on a smile to greet the man heading for her chair. His friendly, charming grin made her own far more genuine when it leveled on her, though. She wouldn't deny the shot of heat that raced up her arm the second he stretched out his hand for her to take, and his grip practically swallowed hers whole.

"Mr. Dalton," Delaney said, her smile stretching wider.

"*Lucas*," he corrected.

Of course.

"Lucas," she echoed softer.

He nodded and squeezed her hand, clearly pleased. The suit from last time had been replaced by a corded-knit cream cashmere sweater that he filled out nicely, but his black slacks were still pressed with clean lines. There was something about his smile that deepened the cleft in his chin and the dimple in one cheek—he turned into a gentle giant before her eyes.

"I hope you don't mind me coming back," he said, pretending to give his reflection appropriate attention in the mirror behind them like his hair was some sort of mess. Barely even grown out, in fact. His gaze kept floating back to her more than it did the mirror, anyway. "I liked what you did."

He had yet to let go of her hand.

Surprisingly, she didn't mind.

"I guess I could fit in a walk-in before I take lunch," Delaney replied, trying to be cheeky. With not one clue if she had succeeded except for the laugh that boomed out of him. An appropriate sound for a man that towered over her with an impressive size.

"Perfect," he murmured, making her gaze zone in on the way his mouth moved with the word.

When was the last time she flirted with a man?

Embarrassingly long.

His handsome face made her want to try.

Dammit, Linda.

8.

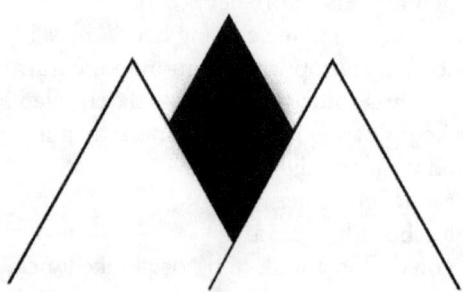

Standing, sweet Delaney reached Lucas' chest in height. Even so, he wouldn't call her waifish despite her five-foot stature. His hands could probably meet if he grabbed a hold of her waist, but she didn't lack in curves that stood out in painted-on black skinny jeans with plaid patches in the knees, and a loose-fitting black sweater with a dangerously low cut at the back, criss-crossing down her spine.

Leaving it open for him to notice.

And he did.

She'd pulled her hair up into a high ponytail so just the wispy ends brushed her shoulders. To be fair, once he had sat in her chair, making the two of them eye-level after she let out a bit of air, Delaney blocked Lucas' view of anything, but the teasing cut in the back of her sweater. While she fiddled at her workstation, wiping shears down and prepping a small trimmer to clean up his edges at the end of the cut, he had two options.

Stare at *her* in the mirror.

Or her back.

Her jeans *were* tight enough that it took effort to keep from admiring the shapely swell of her backside that he had an urge to fit in both his hands. A good grab would pull her right into his lap, and he had the strangest feeling she would fit particularly well there. Not that his thoughts were appropriate.

Or even wanted by Delaney, for that matter.

Lucas needed to get this shit under control.

Fast.

A handful of weeks away from the black-haired woman with the face of an angel had given him a chance to appreciate her a little more sitting in her chair this time around. Mostly because he knew the haircut wouldn't last very long, and honestly, he hadn't thoroughly thought out this side trip of his during his three-day trip to Fredericton.

All work, no play.

Hadn't that become his life in a nutshell?

At least, Jacob had been interested—probably because he couldn't remember a time Lucas mentioned a female after his twenties—when his older brother offhandedly remarked that he hoped to catch up with someone while he returned to the city to finish the transition of new management at the call center's headquarters. However, just saying *someone* wasn't enough information for Lucas' little brother. Jacob wouldn't leave it at that, so Lucas provided enough bare bones details to keep him from asking too many questions.

Mostly because Lucas didn't have answers.

Pitiful, huh?

"Mr. Dalton, I hope Delaney's keeping you entertained," came a new voice behind him.

Delaney turned away from the workstation at the same time he noticed who had joined their reflections in the mirror. The shop's owner, who demanded he call her Linda even though he hadn't offered her the same first name respect yet, beamed a couple of steps back from the chair in her bright red dress with polka dot hearts.

Adding the decorations in the place to her choice in clothing, and he had to wonder if the woman had a favorite holiday.

"I am—"

"Being wonderful," Lucas interjected, making Delaney's lips curve into the prettiest smile. Those dark eyes of hers skirted to his fast before darting back to the woman behind him, but nothing came out of that candy mouth of hers. She couldn't quite hide the slight pink coloring the apples of her cheeks. "I'm grateful she fit me in."

"Me, too," Linda replied, her reflection winking.

Delaney moved around the chair, a hand gesturing at her boss all the while. "Thank you, I've got this."

"Mmhmm. Mr. Dalton—"

"Lucas," he told Linda.

It only seemed fair that—after everything the woman had

helped him with here—he let her call him by his first name. Professionalism and privacy kept Lucas maintaining a wall between the person he allowed the public to see and the man who went home to a quiet, dark apartment every night. Almost always alone, now. It became something he could bank on. There was comfort in familiarity, after all.

Lucas wished he didn't lean so hard into it, though.

"*Lucas*," the woman echoed, nodding, "would you like a drink—coffee, tea, water?"

"I just came from brunch, actually. I'm good for the moment."

"Great. Call over if you need something," Linda said, spinning on her ankle-high wedge boots. She even waved her fingers over her shoulder as she went.

Delaney laughed under her breath as she pulled a clean cape and rolled towel from the shelves next to her workstation. She came to stand behind Lucas at the chair so they both faced each other's reflections in the mirror. "She's something else, that one."

"I like her," he noted.

"Oh?"

"She's helpful. Kind, too."

"She is definitely both of those things," Delaney said, and her grin softened a bit at the *kind* comment. She went ahead and fit the towel around his neck before also covering him with the cape and securing it on tight, too. "I would think someone who knows about being kind might recognize it in others, though."

Lucas, distracted with the way Delaney's one hand came to rest on the top of his shoulder while her other swept through the hair at the top of his head, didn't see where the conversation had headed. He enjoyed the way her fingertips squeezed tenderly, barely there at all, around tense muscles. Could she feel that—his stress? It weighed there and, in his neck, more than anywhere else. Not even a weekly massage helped to work it all out. He *tried*.

He couldn't pretend like the tension seemingly forever knotted into his body didn't melt away a little at her touch. Even seconds of relief were welcomed.

"What do you mean?" he asked.

"Kind people ..."

"What about them?"

"Well, *you*."

Lucas' gaze snapped up to meet hers in the mirror.

Delaney shrugged. "Thank you for what you did. Paying for my chair rental, I mean. You didn't have to—"

"I didn't really think of that as a kind thing to do. The right thing, maybe."

He'd not been able to stick around very long after his last appointment, but he had been able to see a vibrant young woman turn into a terrified, crying statue at the sight of a few sparks and a bit of plastic-smelling smoke.

Terribly, truly.

Even though he hadn't been able to forget about it, Lucas didn't think it was also his right to ask what brought on the reaction despite Linda's comment to the peanut gallery about a fire and whatever else. So, he didn't ask that day, but he had called the salon later in the day to check up on Delaney and offer to mail a check to cover her chair rental when Linda mentioned Delaney had taken a few days off.

"I try to be mindful about that sort of thing, but sometimes I just do it and never see it for what it is," Lucas muttered, more to himself than the woman standing behind the chair.

"Of—"

"Kindness," he filled in quickly. "Or of *being* kind. I forget sometimes, or I'll do something and remember there's a reason I try to wake up and choose kindness."

"I don't think you have to try, really," Delaney replied. "You smile, and it radiates."

Why couldn't he see that in himself, then? *Too busy seeing someone else*, his thoughts quickly filled in. The self-awareness served to do nothing but make Lucas quiet in the chair as Delaney began her work.

She didn't notice the somber change within Lucas, either.

He didn't mind.

"Same as before?" she asked, her dainty features lighting up.

"Same as before, please."

"No fade." Delaney patted his shoulders and smiled big. "Let's get to work."

Lucas found peace in watching someone else work. Especially if their job took a skill he had never mastered. Not that trips to a hairdresser had been a particularly fun day in his past—simply an appointment he tried to keep up, despite never finding a barber he cared to visit more than twice—but it was a different beast for him to sit still while Delaney circled his prone form in the chair again and again.

She used but a few spritzes of water to get his hair damp enough for her satisfaction before using a stainless-steel comb and a sharp pair of shears to trim his length between two fingers. Other than a bit of safe small talk, like learning his age and letting him complain about his tiring week, she put all of her focus into keeping his hair even. His style was a short, simple crop that was easy to maintain and didn't take more than fifteen minutes to upkeep in a stylist's chair.

So, as Delaney approached the end of the trim, cleaning up the strays around his ears before changing out the comb and shears for the small trimmer, to do the edges of the back of his neck, he prodded her into talking once more.

"Someone likes Valentine's," he noted.

Delaney laughed, turning the buzzer on and giving him a look in the mirror. "You think?"

Yeah, one could guess, eh?

"What about you—do you have one?"

Maybe asking a question like that as she was leaning in to keep the edge of his hairline straight while the clipper almost touched his skin wasn't good timing. He could have thought it through better, but Delaney just pulled back the clippers to give a bit of buffer room.

"A Valentine?" she asked.

"Mmhmm. Do you have one?"

He became hyper aware of the salon at that moment. All the time she worked and while they chatted, he paid no mind to the women with clients in their chairs, or the ladies packing up their stations to head out for lunch. They weren't exactly alone. This was her place of employment, as well. He'd not considered that there should be a proper time and place for everything, but the two of them weren't exactly afforded a different meeting.

Lucas would work with what he had.

"Delaney?" he asked quietly.

The buzz of the clippers continued, but he could tell when she squeezed them harder because of the muted noise. Her smile grew wide even though she tried to rub her lips together to melt it away. He took it as a good sign that she smiled, at least.

"Is there a reason you're asking me?" she returned.

As fast as she asked the question, like perhaps she was scared of what his answer would be, Delaney bent down to get back to work. He felt the clippers at his hairline on the back of his neck, but he also noticed her gaze darting to him in the mirror.

She arched an eyebrow at him.

Waiting.

"Would you be interested in dinner—if you don't have someone making you their Valentine, of course," he tacked on at the end.

"Of course," she echoed. "Hold still for a sec."

Her steady hands worked across the back of his neck. Lucas had never been more nervous waiting for someone's response. It made sitting still for her to get that straight edge right particularly difficult.

Then, Delaney straightened up, her attention zoned in on the back of his neck to determine whether or not she was satisfied. He couldn't figure out if her parroting of his words had been a confirmation to his request for a date, or not.

Nor could he make himself *ask*.

"A little on that side ..." Delaney muttered to herself.

At the same time his phone beeped where he'd sat it beside hers on the workstation before they sat down to begin. Well, he thought it was his phone until he reached forward to grab it, leaned back into the seat, and tapped the screen to light it up.

The image that popped up in the text banner on the locked home screen of the phone corrected his initial thought—it was *not*, in fact, his black phone. At a quick glance, it could be.

The clippers touched the back of his neck on the right side at the same time Lucas asked, "Is someone having a baby? That *is* a sonogram, yeah?"

He held the phone high enough that he thought Delaney could see, but at the same time, felt the slip.

The way the buzz of the machine revved slightly as it went higher on the back of his neck than it was supposed to. Apparently, he had not learned his lesson about keeping his mouth shut while she worked.

"Oh, my God," Delaney breathed out, yanking the clippers back before her palm cupped the back of his neck. Immediately, the clippers shut off. Her horrified stare found his blank face in the mirror before she closed her eyes shut and bit her lip, muttering, "I am *so, so, so* sorry."

He knew what she did.

He didn't need her to say it.

Lucas tried his hardest to even be *annoyed* that she'd let the clippers slip up the back of his neck, but it had been partially his fault, too. All he could do was shake with his rumbling laughter that he desperately tried to hold in to keep from alerting the rest of the people in the salon.

He felt Delaney's hand lift before it clamped right back down.

"Okay, it's not *that* bad," she told him. "Manageable."

"Bad enough for a—"

She cringed. "Just a little fade."

Her hand raised to show the inch or so she'd have to work with to blend in the mistake.

Lucas laughed harder.

"It's not funny," she insisted.

"It is, a little."

Delaney huffed, her hand still pressed to the back of his neck. "Is *not*. I've got more practice than I need to know how to keep from making these kinds of mistakes. You distracted me with all your talk of Valentine's and *babies*."

"More the baby, huh?" he tried to joke.

She rolled her eyes. "Yeah, more the baby."

"Here I was sitting here freaking out because you didn't say yes or no to dinner, but now I'm thinking that I should be asking something else."

"I said yes—*of course*, that's what I said."

"That's what you meant?" he returned.

Delaney didn't hesitate. "Next time, let's keep any and all surprises until *after* the haircut, huh?"

"That's what you meant."

It wasn't a question this time.

"I'll give you an address to pick me up, you give me the time," she said.

Fair enough. He could work with that.

"So, who's pregnant?" Lucas asked, grinning.

Delaney smiled back, shaking her head. "Apparently, my best friend."

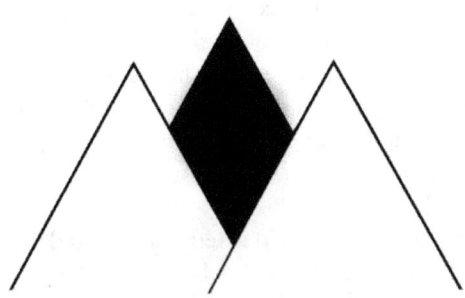

9

"Mira Belle," Delaney suggested.

"I'll put that one on the list."

It seemed to be an elusive list. One Gracen protected because she refused to go back down over the names she agreed were worthy enough to make the list, proclaiming the name she *did* pick would remain secret until the baby finally came along.

In the mirror of the portable, lighted beauty mirror sitting on the table, Delaney's reflection grinned. "Oh, that's my first one to get on *the list*."

"Stop saying it like that. Malachi does that, too."

Delaney giggled. "You're taking this name list *very* seriously, Gracen."

"It *is* serious! They're going to have this name for the rest of their life, Delaney. I want them to love it as much as I do, okay?"

Yeah, so it better be a good one, right?

"Eden Sophia," Delaney said, adding a new one for Gracen to consider.

"I definitely like the Eden bit."

"Eden ..." Delaney dug in her brain for a middle name that would sound good—a parent had to realize not only would they say the name a lot, but they could also be yelling it often, too; one would want the name to sound good being said in any particular way. "Oh, Eden *Reed* Anders."

Gracen's muffled laugh chirped over the phone before she muttered, "You know, that actually sounds good."

"I know, right?"

Delaney pulled that one entirely out of her ass, too. Not that she expected Gracen to use her last name even if she was the first official, not-blood related auntie of *Baby Anders*. Or, that's what she had taken to call Gracen's unborn baby in her head.

"Pizza sounds *perfect*," Gracen told her companion on the other end of the call. "Especially if you're the one making it."

Malachi's rumbly laughter echoed in the background of the call, but his words were a muffle that Delaney couldn't properly distinguish. The lull in conversation allowed Delaney the time to resituate her makeup on the table before putting the call on speakerphone.

Across the room, her cousin acted uninterested in the phone call. Or Delaney's makeshift beauty counter with every piece of makeup she had spread out like a buffet made of shimmers and rouge from one side of the table to the other. They didn't have a large enough bathroom to comfortably do much other than get in the bathtub or stand from the toilet to immediately be against the sink under a very small mirror.

She needed more room to work.

Not that she would use all of her makeup. Despite the mountain of makeup that took three bags to keep contained, Delaney rarely wore more than a natural look. A light foundation. Faint highlighter on the high points of her face. A nude shade of lipstick. Her most difficult choice was which eyeliner to use to make her favorite wing, but in the end, she almost always picked the same one for that, too. It was the blackest of black liner, and it went on smoother than anything else she had tried.

When shopping, her eyes were often needier than her hands and heart. If it looked pretty, she'd buy it. The fact she might already have the same shade of eyeshadow—that she didn't use— wasn't that important. Delaney was trying to get better about those bad habits. Money didn't grow on trees, but someday, the effects of her consumerism would end up in the ground when she tossed all of her expired products into the garbage. The trees wouldn't like that, either, right?

"You know," Gracen said, coming back to the conversation with Delaney while a familiar *mewing* filled the background, "I'm only ten weeks pregnant, and we're sitting here going through names like this baby is coming tomorrow. It's like when I went shopping and couldn't help but buy at least ten different things that were gender neutral because the baby needs *something*."

"Not even," Delaney shot back. "And you already started the

list, bitch. I was just helping you out."

Gracen cackled. "Yeah, that's true."

"Mmhmm, see. Everybody probably does this, anyway."

"You think?"

Gracen's quiet question shot Delaney through the heart with a spear of sadness she hadn't expected. That was probably a question a first-time pregnant woman should be able to call her mother and ask. Except Gracen no longer had a mother to call, and Delaney couldn't help in that department, either. Her mother wouldn't even pick up her fucking calls.

Not that she bothered to try anymore.

"Well, I don't really know for sure," Delaney hedged.

"Yeah, me either. I've got about as much experience with pregnant women and babies as Mister Kitty here."

At the sound of his name, the cat in the background meowed louder.

"I know, buddy," Gracen cooed to her vocal pet. "You're my best friend, too, huh?"

"Friggin cat, stealing all my love," Delaney joked.

"He does *not*. You sound just like Malachi."

To be fair, the cat *did* get a lot of attention and love. Delaney didn't have to be present in Gracen's life every single day to know she doted on Mister Kitty as if he were another human in her home in need of her time and affection. He had more toys than he could reasonably play with, a choice in various foods, and a bed in practically every room. All things Gracen was solely responsible for.

"He's not spoiled," Gracen said as if she could read Delaney's mind.

"Not at all, huh? Not even a little bit?"

"No, he's *loved*."

"Spoiled from love, sure."

Her best friend only sighed on the other end of the line when Delaney challenged her.

"Hey, are we making a long list of baby names or picking on me and my cat?" Gracen suddenly asked.

"Both are valid things to tease you about, thank you very much."

"Yeah, well … somebody here already does that everyday. You're gonna have to pick something new. Next name, please."

Delaney guffawed.

Gracen didn't budge, laughing as she demanded, "Come on, give me another name."

To be fair, Delaney didn't mean any harm by joking about Gracen's obsession over naming her unborn child. A baby, by the way, whose gender her friend did not yet even know. She thought it was sweet that Gracen wanted to put so much careful effort and thought into naming the child. Maybe someday, she could tell the story of how she picked the baby's name and the way those around her, even Delaney, helped.

"Amber ... Rose," came a suggestion from across the apartment.

Gracen still heard it. "I like it, but I also think I've heard it before."

"Probably a stripper name," Bexley muttered. "Sounds like one."

"It does not," Delaney argued.

Her cousin only flipped a hand indifferently over her shoulder where she sat with the back of her head facing Delaney. "I mean, it does, and I'm the one who came up with it."

More giggles rushed from the phone.

"That's terrible," Delaney said, more to herself than the other two women involved in the conversation. "How do you think a kid would feel if somebody told them their name sounded like a stripper's name?"

Gracen's amusement quieted.

On the couch, Bexley flipped through channels, unbothered. "If it's true ..."

"*Bex.*"

Her cousin didn't act as if Delaney had said a thing.

"What would *you* tell your kid if they came home one day and said to you," Gracen asked Delaney, "*Mom, so and so said I had a stripper's name*—what then?"

"Who would say that to a kid?" Delaney questioned.

Someone *horrible*.

"I might," Bexley chimed in.

Of course.

Delaney side-eyed her cousin who had still yet to turn around on the couch. "I'd tell them their name is as beautiful as the person—or people—who own it. And the only people who have something to say about their name are just jealous that theirs aren't as interesting or pretty."

She also wouldn't name her kid Amber—no offense to any Ambers, but it reminded her of names like Jessica or Tiffany. There were far better names to pick. Delaney didn't add that bit out loud. Just in case Gracen *did* like the name.

It was her baby, and she would name it whatever she wanted.

"I like my name," Bexley said, "it's not a jealous thing."

Right.

Delaney went back to her conversation, and what mattered there. Picking one's battles, especially when it came to family, was a real skill she had needed to master early in life. "For the record, we've been doing this for an hour, Gracen, and not once have we got into the boy names."

"I'm gonna let Malachi name the baby if it's a boy."

"Even if he names him something like Henry or—"

"Even then," Gracen interjected. "Also, I like Henry, so ..."

Delaney smiled at her reflection in the mirror. "Who knows? Maybe the baby will be a boy, and all this time we've spent going through names will be for nothing."

"Of course," Gracen added quieter, "I can't get him to tell me any of the names he might pick."

A hard laugh burst from Delaney. "Really?"

"Malachi says it's too early. He needs time to work on a short list."

"Like he has a long one to whittle down?"

At ten weeks along?

Delaney doubted that.

"What's the chance he already has a name picked out if it's a boy?" Delaney asked.

"Twin minds, you and I," Gracen murmured. "I've considered that might be the case only because he gets this stupid little smile on his face whenever I bring up a boy name I found and liked in this damn book."

"You have a *book* of baby names?"

Delaney thought Gracen was just trolling the internet or listing names off the top of her head like she had been, but apparently not.

"I might have picked one up a few days ago," Gracen offered as if it wasn't important.

"Have you considered ordering more?"

Her friend had little self-control when it came to shopping online and having things mailed directly to her door. Delaney remembered good and well what it was like to walk out of her apartment to find Gracen's latest order had been delivered in a giant pile on their stoop.

"*Maybe*," Gracen whispered, "but we don't have to get into all of that."

"Uh-huh," Delaney replied.

She had caught onto Gracen's tricks a long damn time ago.

"There could be a chance he thinks I might try to convince him to change the name if he tells me now. I mean, we do have another seven months to go, you know?"

"Would you?" she asked Gracen.

"Not on purpose."

Delaney snorted. "I bet he's just as invested in naming this kid as you."

She only knew about the baby for a day—Malachi had undoubtedly known since day *one*.

"Oh, he's invested," Gracen agreed with a low laugh, "in keeping me distracted with all sorts of girl names."

Huh. Did that mean ... "Someone believes you're having a boy."

Delaney meant for the comment to be a joke, but Gracen's answering silence confirmed that it might hold a bit of truth.

"Is that what you think, too?" she asked her friend.

Gracen let out a happy sigh. "I think ..."

"Keep going."

A chirp of a laugh answered back. "I think I'm gonna put Amber Rose on the list, too."

"*Yes!*" came the holler from the couch. Bexley even fist pumped the air. "Stripper names for the win."

Not too seriously, but throwing an old eyeliner stick at the back of Bexley's head all at the same time, Delaney told her cousin, "Stop calling it that."

She didn't miss.

*

"Any reason you didn't mention to Gracen that you had a date tonight?" Bexley asked as she leaned in the doorway of Delaney's bedroom.

"Uh, no?"

"Why was that a question?"

"Because I didn't really think to mention it," Delaney said, her tone posing it like a question even though it wasn't one.

It was the truth.

Delaney, standing slightly off kilter with one foot in suede ankle boots with a thick two-inch heel and another in a slightly shorter heeled boot that went up over her knees, eyed her reflection in the leaning mirror against the wall. Facing the foot of her bed, it cast rainbows in her room whenever the light filtered through the window and caught the reflective pane.

"You didn't think to mention that you were going on your first date in over a year?" Bexley's voice pitched higher at the end, like she couldn't mentally grasp the concept.

"I have more interesting things to talk about with Gracen," Delaney replied, turning on her taller heel to face her cousin. "Which is better—bootie or boot?"

"There's three feet of snow outside. The boots."

Delaney toyed with the hem of the short skirt where the dress fell to just below her mid-thigh. A sliver of skin showed when she moved and walked. Bending over would take careful mindfulness. "Yeah, but does the thigh-showing thing scream *try to find out what's under this skirt* or should I do a thick hose with the bootie instead?"

She wanted her look to set the tone for her date with Lucas. Something she would do for any man she agreed to go to dinner with—he wasn't a special case. The last impression Delaney intended to make was that she would be the *all-you-can-eat* buffet.

That was not the case.

There would be no menu including her.

"Who cares if he's thinking about what is—or isn't; are you wearing panties?—under your dress, Delaney? Weren't you the one who spent the last half hour ranting at me about saying a name could be a stripper name? What was that patriarchal, feminist crap you spewed at me again? I forgot, sorry."

Dammit.

"First of all, *yes*, I am wearing panties."

"Thank God," Bexley muttered.

"And I never said someone else couldn't look like they wanted a man's hands up their dress the first night he takes her out … just that I don't, thank you."

Not offering another detail more, Delaney spun back around to take in her dress and boot options once more. She waffled yet again. "Maybe the booties—"

"No, the boots, Delaney. The *boots*," her cousin stressed. "Because it looks sexy as hell with that loose sweater dress look, you know? Yeah, a peek of your thighs will show—good. That's the point. Skin doesn't mean *touch me*. Also, you rock those boots."

Bexley made good points.

"Good for you," Delaney muttered.

"What?"

She smiled, turning around to face Bexley before bending down to remove the suede ankle boot. "You actually said hell—I mean it's not *Jesus*, but …"

Bexley rolled her eyes. "Just because I'm taking a healthy break from my faith doesn't mean I think we should do things vainly."

"Mmhmm."

At least, one of them had given that part of their life some thought. Lucas' unwanted Bible remained untouched on the corner of her workstation, tucked behind the jar of Barbicide, at the salon. And of course, her cross necklace remained around her throat, but she didn't give God much more thought. For the moment, she couldn't emotionally or mentally afford to.

One thing at a time …

"So, what time is the date again?" Bexley asked.

Delaney fell to the end of her platform, queen size bed. The pale pink duvet fluffed up around her at the bottoms. As she worked her size seven foot into the leather boot, she told her cousin, "I've got half an hour before he's supposed to show up outside."

Which meant she managed to finish her makeup and get her hair curled into soft waves before having just enough time to pick an outfit. With that done, Delaney could breathe for a bit before her evening really got started. Just because she wouldn't put out for a man on a first date had no bearing on the fact that she *wanted* to—in fact, the man hadn't left her mind.

"A half an hour? That so?" Bexley asked.

"Yep, why?"

"And his name is …?"

Delaney gave her cousin a *knock it off* look. "Lucas. Lucas Dalton. Mind your business. Otherwise, if I don't call or text at least once an hour, call the po-po and pass the name along. You can even write down the plate number for good measure. Okay?"

She was joking. Mostly. It wasn't Delaney's first date.

Bexley rolled her eyes at the extremes, but she snickered as she exited the room as fast as she came, muttering, "The po-po ... Something is wrong with you."

Nope.

Delaney was just fine—most of the time. It was everybody else that didn't get things right.

10.

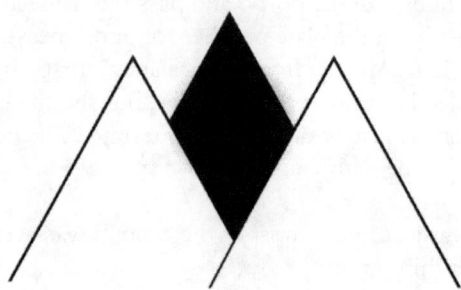

The noisy ringtone cut through the music on the radio, dragging Lucas' attention away from the road for a mere moment. Long enough to see who was calling, and to roll his eyes at the name on the dashboard.

J. Dalton, it read.

No surprise there.

His gaze went back to the road while he picked up the call from his younger brother using the button on his steering wheel. Without a proper hello. "Didn't I tell you that I was meeting up with—"

"Delaney, yeah. At six. That's why I'm calling," Jacob interrupted like it should have been obvious to his brother. "To make sure everything was good, you know?"

"Mmhmm." Lucas didn't believe that for a second. "Not to see if you could pry more details out of me?"

About the date.

Delaney.

Anything at all.

Jacob tried for every bit of it only to get Lucas's somber stonewalling in response. There wasn't much to tell—yet. Maybe he would when—or if—that changed. Lucas couldn't say. He had an entire evening to get through with Delaney yet.

His brother's chuckles echoed over the rental car's speakers. "My bad for being interested in your life when you finally have something *interesting* going on, bro."

He did have a point there.

Lucas still refused to concede. "Was it just your interest when you tried to get her last name out of me?"

"Nah, that was for research purposes. The online kind. The type you can't do because you won't get out of the stone ages and make a fucking social media profile. Even the brewery has its own pages, man."

Lucas didn't dignify the comment with a response because there wouldn't be one worth his breath. A waste of his time.

Nothing about mindlessly scrolling a glowing feed on the screen of his phone or laptop to watch the online lives of acquaintances and strangers play out appealed to him, and he wouldn't apologize for not pretending that it did to please his brother.

Besides, he doubted there was much about Delaney Reed— online or otherwise—for Jacob to find that Lucas hadn't already learned about the young woman. A social media profile felt like a resume in the way it laid out a person's age, interests, and surface history attached to a smiling photo or candid shot with friends.

He knew those things already.

Because she told him.

At least Jacob didn't hide his intentions. Lucas had to give his brother that, if nothing else.

"Plus, the crazy ones are good at hiding it sometimes," Jacob added. "Maybe I could have saved you a shitty evening, but now we'll have to wait and see how it plays out, huh? I will say, this way is better for me if we end up getting a good story out of it."

"Knock it off."

"I'm just saying—keep it mind." Jacob barked a laugh before saying, "Oh, yeah!"

His sudden declaration made Lucas sigh.

"What?"

"She'll have access to sharp blades tonight, too."

Jacob's cackles created static in the speakers, and he sounded far too pleased with himself and his teasing. Nothing stopped him from having a good laugh at his brother's expense. Lucas really shouldn't have told his brother about his plans for the date.

"Play your cards wrong," Jacob said, "and this night could go *way* left, bro."

"Go to hell, Jacob," Lucas returned, jokingly.

As much as he could manage, anyway. The minutes of levity gave him the chance to focus on something other than the nerves churning in his stomach, and the navigational screen focusing on his current address of destination.

She was a street away.

He tried not to think about it.

"All bullshit aside," Jacob said, pulling Lucas out of his nervous thoughts, "I hope you have a great night."

Lucas grinned, checking the rearview mirror as he pulled up to a red light. "Me, too."

In the background, a quiet robotic voice repeated that he should make a left turn and a right in thirty meters to reach the block of quaint apartments he could already see from his position.

"And you're staying out of trouble, too, right?" Lucas asked, choosing his words carefully so it didn't seem like he was prying too hard.

Jacob never responded well to that sort of thing, but Lucas felt like he had to keep checking in on his brother lately. Not for any particular reason—and every time he asked, Jacob assured that he was fine—but he couldn't escape the dread that had been following him whenever he let his mind focus on his brother. Like something bad was right around the corner.

"Of course, bro. Why wouldn't I be? Did you find flowers?" Jacob asked.

Apparently, Lucas should give his kid brother more credit. He remembered the one thing Lucas hadn't given much thought about regarding this evening—everything else was planned down to a T. Or so Lucas thought until Jacob pointed out something he lacked during their conversation earlier in the day. One might think a person could find a bushel of roses easily the day after Valentine's, but he had not been that lucky.

Lucas wasn't a flowers and dinner sort of man. Not that he couldn't—or didn't like to—wine and dine a woman, but his day-to-day schedule rarely allowed for a lot of personal time between his work and family obligations. His last date, a blind setup by a mutual friend, went nowhere fast. That had been more than a year ago. It wasn't a surprise that his brother had to remind him to bring something pretty and aromatic—flowers—for his date.

"I did find some," Lucas confirmed. "Well, I picked up a pot of Chrysanthemums. It works."

"Mums? She doesn't have cats, right?"

How would Lucas know?

"What does that matter?" he asked.

Jacob made a noise of indifference. "I think they're toxic to cats. And she's in an apartment. So it's not like she's going to have them outside."

"Great. Note to self—ask about a cat."

His brother laughed louder.

The prick.

On the other hand, his voice assistant, a program on his phone, heard the command, and replied robotically: *Note added to your task list, Mr. Dalton.*

Fuck his whole life.

Then, another thought poked Lucas.

"How did you know she lives in an apartment?" he demanded as the light turned green.

There was really only *one* way when Lucas put the information in a single spot.

Even if Jacob hesitated to answer. "*I mean …*"

"Did you log into my email to check my calendar?"

"You gave me nothing, bro," Jacob returned, his tone suggesting that his brother should have expected this end result. "Nothing—what did you think I would do? It doesn't matter. I also found *nothing.*"

"Jacob, stay out of my email," Lucas snapped. "For one. Two, mind your damn business."

"Yeah, yeah. Call me tomorrow?"

"Screw you."

Lucas hung up the call like he did when he picked it up.

No hello.

No goodbyes.

Jacob was lucky that Lucas loved the shit—for all his antics and the heartache his kid brother had caused him over the years, he was most grateful to be beyond those harder times. Sure, Jacob had his demons, and he struggled with boundaries sometimes, but Lucas gave him grace.

Or, he tried.

His brother's laughter was still ringing in his ear even after he'd pulled into the shared open lot for a square block of apartment buildings that all looked the same. Painted a quaint white with lace-like detailing at the apexes of the eaves, the buildings reached tall for the dark sky. He found the one building toward the back of the lot with the trio of letters over the entrance and parked in one of three visitor spots under a towering spruce tree. In the passenger seat, next to the black pot of maroon mums, sat his phone.

It blinked with a new text.

He picked it up to see the apology, well wishes, and a *call me tomorrow* from his brother, but he swiped it away with a shake of his head. He would call his brother in the morning, and they'd definitely revisit the hacking conversation, but there was no love lost there.

Jacob couldn't help himself.

Not when it came to Lucas.

He shot off a text to the number directly below his brother's in the recent contact list. Not that there was a lot to see in that conversation thread. His texts with Delaney had been mostly confirmatory of their date, times and so forth. His most recent message, just sent, said simply: *I'm outside whenever you're ready.*

Not wanting Delaney to come out of her place to search for the waiting car, he stepped out of the vehicle with the pot of mums and headed for the entrance door. His shoes crunched across the snow-crusted walkway until he came to a stop just beyond the double glass doors showcasing the lit entry and a back wall of mailboxes for the apartment. The call board outside the doors, labeled with every apartment number, took his attention for a minute.

Long enough to miss Delaney exiting from the second floor. Her descent caught the edge of his vision, and he greeted her with a smile on the other side of the doors. The blonde girl, leaning out of the second-floor metal door, said something that caused Delaney to pause and look over her shoulder.

Then, she pushed the door open. Stepping out into the cold air with him, she immediately shoved her hands into the pockets of her long, buttoned up tweed coat with a belt cinched at the middle.

"*Hey,*" she said, her breath full of air like she'd been in a rush. "Wow, it's cold."

"Hey, yourself," Lucas returned. He held out the mums. Their color matched the pom-topped hat, scarf, and finger mittens Delaney wore. All luck. "We won't be out in this weather for long. These are for you."

She took the flowers, saying, "Thank you."

The blonde inside had yet to leave the upper stairwell while still holding open the hallway door.

"Is that your friend?"

"Bexley. My roommate, and cousin," Delaney said, peeking behind herself once more. She waved at the young woman, but she still didn't move. In fact, Bexley openly stared between Delaney and Lucas, making sure both of them knew she was doing it. "She's too nosy for her own good."

Yeah, he had one of those in his life, too. He gave Miss Bexley a bit of grace for her narrowing stare lingering on him when he tried to ignore it.

"You don't have a cat, right?" Lucas asked.

Delaney swung back on him with a wide smile. "What?"

"The mums—I guess they're bad for cats."

"Ah, okay," she replied, surveying the tops of the flowers before lifting them for a sniff that curved her lips happily again. "No worries. No cats."

Without warning, Delaney stepped forward with an arm wide that she wrapped around his middle. Maybe it was the fact he had a good ninety or more pounds of muscle on the woman, but he didn't expect the force of her squeeze or how warm and soft she'd feel tucked against his chest. It took real effort to keep his next breaths steady as whatever candied-crisp perfume she wore wafted up with her next hug.

She kept the mums safe at the side and beamed up at him.

"You won't be offended if I leave these with Bex, right?" she asked.

God, no.

He was going to be more irritated by the fact that she had to let him go to do it.

"The flowers are yours. Do whatever you want."

She tossed him a wink as she pulled away and turned back for the door. Lucas tried to give the two women a bit of privacy by facing the parking lot when Bexley came down the stairs inside at her cousin's gesturing.

He still heard the quiet, "Nice to meet you, Mr. Dalton."

He grinned over his shoulder and waved. "You, too … Bexley, is it?"

The blonde nodded. "That's me. And you're Lucas, right?"

A chuckle escaped him at her pointed question to get his name right, and confirm her cousin had not lied. "That is me, yes."

"Get inside—your food is getting cold," Delaney pointed out.

"I can order something else," her cousin argued. "We've made introductions now, so we might as well talk a bit."

"Nope." Delaney shoved Bexley, now holding the maroon mums, back inside the doors. "*Goodnight.*"

The door finally shut.

Not that Bexley moved.

In fact, she smiled and waved at the two while Delaney rejoined Lucas on the walkway and hooked her elbow around his. As they headed for the idling car twenty paces away.

"That's yours?" Delaney asked.

"For the rest of the week." She shot him a curious glance, and he clarified, "A rental. I live in Saint John but travel back and forth to here for work at least every couple of weeks. I can't stand driving more than an hour if I'm behind the wheel, so I don't bring my vehicle very often."

"Oh, okay."

He didn't typically get rentals in Freddy, either. The half of a dozen cab companies and car services on his contact list made travel simple, and an easy write-off at the end of the year for his accountant. He'd made an exception with the two-door Lexus he rented to take Delaney out.

Not that he planned to tell her, of course.

It was just a car.

This was *only* the first date.

Lucas was still trying to feel this girl out beyond the four walls of the salon where he met her, but he wanted to. That was a damn good start.

He chanced a glance over his shoulder.

Delaney didn't miss it. "She's not moved, has she?"

"Not one inch," he confirmed.

She only laughed.

"It's good to have someone looking out for you," Lucas added as they rounded the car to the passenger side.

"Yeah, I guess."

"Sometimes, eh?"

Delaney shrugged, muttering, "Sometimes."

He opened the door for her, and waited until she was comfortably inside before closing the door. On his way back around the front of the vehicle, he waved to the woman standing beyond the entrance doors.

Bexley waved back.

Once inside the Lexus, his new passenger handed over the cell phone that had been in her seat, and then asked, "Any reason you asked for my shoe size this morning?"

Lucas shot Delaney a smirk while he put the car in reverse. "That, sweets, is a surprise."

One he had planned for later.

"*Sweets?*"

She didn't sound offended.

He took that as a win.

Lucas tried to keep his gaze on the rearview mirror while he backed out of the spot, but he couldn't stop it from cutting to her once or twice. The bit of pink color heating Delaney's cheeks and the way she watched him below the long sweep of her dark lashes stopped the sudden *should I or shouldn't I* game he found himself playing in his head.

Why not?

He wanted her to know he was interested.

In everything.

Anything.

"If you taste anything like you smell, it's appropriate," he offered.

Delaney guffawed in the seat next to his, but her grin melted into something sexy all the same. He reveled in the fact she didn't shrink away at the suggestive comment. "You're going to have to work for that."

So be it.

All he knew *was* work.

11.

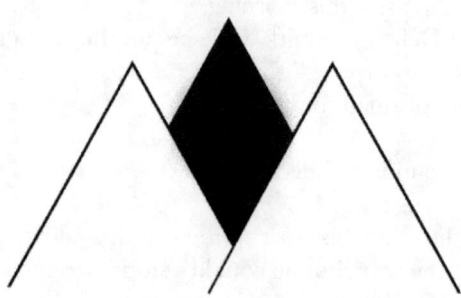

Manger—the name a nod to the French chef heading the kitchen—happened to be one of maybe three restaurants in the city that required a dress code of its patrons. Nothing crazy. Blazers and ties for men, and appropriate dress for their counterparts. It meant the usual diners tended to be professionals or someone looking for a step above the norm for their dining experience. Quiet people enjoying a good meal while discussing business or life.

The menu varied from extravagant dishes the chef learned while training in France to the steak and potato dishes that Lucas preferred when he dined. The curated list of desserts changed depending on the time of the year, but the infamous cherry cheesecake Manger was known for remained at the top regardless of the season.

Cozy tables surrounded by tan suede chairs with clam shaped backs faced windows overlooking a central part of town; or depending on the room, diners sat in front of digital fireplaces with water features dropping down from the ceiling that created partition walls for privacy. Dark colored stonework made hearths around the fireplaces and added to the calming ambiance of the place.

Lucas tried to get a table for lunch or dinner whenever he ended up in the city, but it always depended on his schedule. Especially when dining at Manger meant waiting a good while to actually eat, but that would give Lucas and his companion a chance to talk without food between them.

When he did get the opportunity to drop by the place, he typically ate alone, and had only met up with someone in passing that he recognized who was also dining at the same time. Perhaps that was why the host who greeted Lucas and Delaney at the front of the restaurant, one of three whom he recognized that rotated shifts, smiled a little wider at the sight of him stepping beyond the entry doors with someone at his side.

A woman, no less.

"Mr. Dalton," Curtis welcomed with hands stretching over the stone podium he would stand behind until directing them further beyond the entrance alcove. "And his *guest*—hello. I hope you're both having a warm night. It's cold out there."

"So far, not bad," he told the host. Lucas encouraged Delaney to head in front of him to shake the man's hand first with a press of his palm at her lower back, and she moved forward without hesitance. "Miss Reed, Curtis."

The host passed Lucas a knowing look and a smile as he shook Delaney's hand, still warm in mittens, with both of his. "Welcome to *Manger*, Miss Reed. Is tonight your first time at the restaurant?"

"It is," Delaney replied.

Yet, the woman stood there and gazed around as if the place had been made for her. Good. He didn't want her to feel out of place, but he also wanted her to enjoy the atmosphere and food. Manger was meant to be an experience.

One never got that first time back.

Curtis released his hold on Delaney's hand only to wag a finger in Lucas' direction, saying, "Now I know why you asked for the far side table, hmm?"

Delaney passed Lucas a curious look as he slipped in beside her and curled an arm around her waist. "A view and a fire," he explained.

Not well, he knew.

Her puckered brow said so.

"You'll see," Lucas added with a gentle squeeze to her waist.

Delaney shook her head with a smile, and gazed into the main dining room where there were fewer private seating spots and more patrons. They also had better access to watch the movement in the kitchen, and slightly more noise. Usually, he opted for the main seating because he could lose himself in the scrape of utensils against plates, the soft hum of conversation around him, and the laughter traveling out from the kitchen.

Lucas didn't care to get distracted by others tonight.

Only one person.

Delaney smiled up at him when Lucas pointed out the painting of the Saint John River in aerial view hanging over the mantle in the alcove in a rainbow of hues. In the bottom left corner, Sloane Alcott's familiar signature blackened the bright colors.

"A friend's brother made that," he told her.

"Really?"

"Yeah, I have a few of my own around the apartment." A collection of a half of a dozen acrylic paintings that Lucas held particularly close. He wasn't one for art, but there was something to be said for personally knowing an artist. "He said once there was something about the Maritimes ... they're stuck in his head in all those colors."

"I bet," she said, taking in the six-foot long piece of art again. "It's a hell of a way to see it, huh?"

"Nothing but the river is the color it should be, and yet—"

"If you know what it is, you can see it," Delaney interjected.

Lucas nodded. "Exactly."

The paintings he owned were focused more on the areas that were most familiar and sentimental to Lucas. He had the sudden urge to commission one of the river, now. Perhaps not one as big, though.

Another time ...

"Your table is ready whenever you both would like to head back," Curtis said after having clicked through the tablet on his podium. "Would you like to check in your coats and everything else?"

"Oh, yes, please," Delaney said before Lucas could get a word in edgewise.

He was close enough to help her with removing her jacket. The short sweater dress she wore underneath wasn't body conforming, but it clung to the swell of her hips and backside as she turned to pull her arms from the coat. The coat itself had been too long for him to appreciate just how high her boots went.

Right up to mid-thigh. Only a sliver of smooth, creamy skin peeked out between the top of her boots and the hem of her dress.

Complimenting Delaney seemed inappropriate given their current circumstances. Damn the weather for not giving him the chance to admire her earlier. Besides, they weren't alone, although they would be soon, and she was more interested in tugging off her mittens, hat, and scarf for Curtis to take than Lucas' staring.

Lucky for him.

His mouth had gone dry, anyway.

"And your coat, Mr. Dalton?" Curtis asked, the bundle of Delaney's items waiting where it hung over his arm.

The question brought Lucas back to reality, and the beautiful woman waiting for him with an equally gorgeous smile as she kept a tight grip on the short handle of her black leather purse. He did not think shedding his jacket had the same effect on the room, but who was he to say?

Delaney tucked close to his side once more the very second she could.

All the way to the far table.

*

They had barely sat down at one of the handful of fully private dining tables before Delaney excused herself to the restroom with a complaint about hats and her hair. It didn't matter how vehemently Lucas tried to assure her she looked perfect, and the hat hadn't done anything terrible to her waves of black locks, she wanted the proof for herself.

Left alone behind the wall of water falling between panes of fiberglass from the ceiling, he sat at the table situated between the window overlooking a snow-covered town and the fireplace crackling on the screen at his back.

"Are you thinking about the typical?" Curtis asked as he returned to the table with a water pitcher in one hand and a silver serving tray with glasses in another.

"I'll wait for her, and go from there," Lucas replied.

"Sounds perfect. Can I start you out with drinks—wine, or your usual ale?"

Lucas wouldn't be drinking much when he had to drive, but a glass of liquor that absorbed over the couple of hours it would take them to wait and eat couldn't hurt. "A bottle of sweet red and my usual, sure," he agreed.

Curtis agreed with a nod, and turned to leave. "I'll be back with menus when I see you're ready."

"Thank you. Oh, breadsticks, too."

A chuckle answered that. "Of course. Breadsticks, as well. I'll bring those right along."

Every table needed a basket.

It only seemed right.

The beep of his phone—a second, loud beep since parking the car—reminded Lucas that he needed to put the device on flight mode for the rest of the evening. Not that he wouldn't check it for emergencies, work-wise or Jacob-related, later, but he wouldn't be keeping a running commentary on the night with his brother.

At least, that's who he assumed had been texting him.

Lucas figured out that wasn't the case when he retrieved the phone from his inner blazer pocket. In fact, the separate texts hadn't even come from the same person.

His father had messaged first to ask for a meeting at the brewery when Lucas returned to Saint John the following week while the newest, a text from his mother, asked for lunch. Neither of the two had been in contact with him in recent weeks.

Not that he minded.

He *didn't*.

Lucas wished they hadn't messaged tonight, either. The last thing he wanted to worry, or even think about, was his fucking parents. They took up more room in his head rent-free than he cared to admit.

Instead of answering back, on both fronts, Lucas simply turned the phone on flight mode like he originally intended to do and slipped the phone back into his pocket without a second thought. Penelope had become accustomed to waiting for a response from her oldest son when she did reach out while his father, on the other hand ...

Well, fuck Ronald, too.

Lucas had to stop jumping through hoops to please an unpleasable man.

No excuses.

Despite putting the phone away, and his mind on pouring a glass of water to sip away the new taste of bitterness lingering on the back of his tongue, Lucas wasn't able to stuff the shitty turn of his mood when Delaney returned back to the table. Maybe his smile didn't reach his eyes.

"What's wrong?"

Lucas tried to laugh it off as he stood to help Delaney back into her chair before pushing it into the table a bit. She placed her purse next to the chair leg when he said, "Nothing—just a reminder that I forgot to turn my phone off tonight."

Her nose scrunched in the cutest way as she peered across the table at him as he retook his own seat. "Work?"

"In a way."

Did his parents—and all the baggage that came with his family's current estrangement—have to be on the table for discussion tonight?

He sure hoped not.

"I never asked you what you did for work," she noted.

The change in topic became an olive branch that Lucas grasped onto to save him for the moment. "It's a family business—you'd probably put it together if I gave you a couple of hints."

Her dark brows lifted high. "Oh?"

"We distill and distribute some of the most-consumed beer in this country, actually. The family's signature blend and a couple of licensed brews."

"*Dalton.*"

Lucas grinned at the understanding he heard dawning her voice. "*The* Daltons, yes."

"Oh, wow," Delaney said, a knot forming between her brow as she gazed between him and the table in front of them while she processed the news. "The company has a major hub here, right?"

He nodded. "A call center for the supply and employee chain. It's why I keep going back and forth every handful of weeks. Things have changed and grown over the last decade. We're still trying to catch up, I think."

"Is the brewery your favorite part? All that beer, I bet."

Lucas laughed. "Do I look like the type?"

"I think it would be part of the job, no?"

Maybe.

"I like the bottling plant more than anything," Lucas admitted, "but it was one of the first areas I remember exploring as a kid, so I might be biased."

Nostalgia could do that to a person.

Delaney leaned into the table, elbows propped up at the edge as she inched closer to him. "And what do you do, exactly?"

"Manage and oversee the eastern arm of the company. My father handles the west. The ten-year plan is getting something set up in the middle to break up the difference."

Or that was supposed to be the plan.

Who knew what the future held?

"At thirty-five?" Delaney asked, although she didn't say it like his age was a bad thing. "That must be—"

"A lot," he interjected, not wanting her to get confused about his job. It wasn't very glamorous behind the bottles formed with the family's company name on the necks, and their liquor being sold all across the country. The fissures and cracks behind the family's tight-knit facade when it came to the public and even their own company twisted what it should be into something far worse for Lucas. "I rarely get a break, and it always feels like there's something to do. I can't catch up sometimes."

Or there was someone to avoid ...

He didn't mention that bit.

Her pouty smile, shadowed by the dim lighting and flickering lights from the fake flames and glowing water feature, made Lucas aware that he had still yet to pay this woman the respect she was due. Her understated makeup made her natural beauty more apparent and highlighted the best features of her face from the small button nose above the plushness of her mouth to the sultry way her gaze swept over him.

She didn't have to try to look good sitting there.

She just *did*.

Confidence was the best accessory for a woman. He'd put good money on it.

"So, tonight must be a rare treat for you, then," she said softly.

"Delaney," he said, and her name on his lips drew her hazel stare to where he could hold it strong, "the rare treat for me tonight is you. Just so that's clear. You're the only reason I made an effort to do anything tonight in the first place."

She eyed the dark landscape beyond the window before her attention came back to him, and that sweet smile of hers had deepened.

"Oh?"

Lucas' head bobbed with his hummed confirmation. "Mmhmm."

He reached across the table to snag the open palm she offered for him to hold. The thrill of the rougher pads of his fingertips gliding along her silken skin to weave their fingers was as unexpected to him as the fact she wanted to hold his hand in the first place. The innocence and care in a simple touch couldn't be understated.

No matter.

He *liked* it.

Finally, he found the right—the *best*—time to tell her what he should have mentioned a while ago. "You look amazing."

"I might have waffled on the dress. And boots."

"Is that so?"

She laughed. "Believe it or not, but my cousin convinced me to wear it."

His grin split impossibly wider. "If I get the chance, remind me to thank her."

"And I still can't get you to tell me why you wanted my shoe size?" she prodded.

"Not a chance, no."

He would not ruin that surprise.

Delaney guffawed, but still, their hands stayed connected.

The return of Curtis to their section with leather bound menus, breadsticks, and drinks balanced on a serving tray broke the two apart.

Unfortunately.

"Richie will be around to get your order shortly," the host explained, handing over menus after placing the drinks and breadsticks.

A bottle of red wine sat taller than the beer Delaney reached for to spin so she could see the label and branding on the bottle.

Sure enough …

Her light laugh tinkled into the room, filling Lucas' chest with something warm and tight that he hadn't felt before. The sound of her amusement and joy did strange things to his insides.

"I should have guessed," she told him before spinning the bottle his way.

The Dalton Brewery logo stared back at him.

"I prefer rum at home, but anywhere else, I'm all about the loyalty," he said, shrugging.

The host between them chuckled, saying before he left, "Enjoy your evening."

Oh, they certainly would. Given the way Delaney grinned at him from across the table, things could only get better from here.

Lucas looked forward to it.

12.

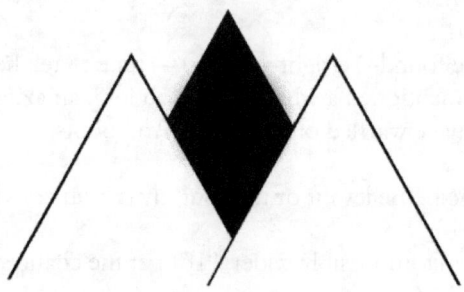

"Can I look *now?*" Delaney asked as her vision was still blocked by the scarf she had allowed Lucas to use as a makeshift blindfold.

For *her* eyes.

Unfortunately.

He chuckled out a quiet, "*Not yet.*"

Delaney sighed loudly.

Then, she did it again for good measure. Just to make sure Lucas had heard her loud and clear if not the first time. Her message must have made its way to him.

"Patience is a virtue, you know," he pointed out at her huffy silence.

Damn this man.

"Rich," Delaney returned, "coming from the man who can see our current location."

"Mmhmm, and soon, you will, too."

He had an answer for everything.

Secretly, she adored the fact that he had gone to so much trouble to make their evening fun for her. Including whatever surprise he had planned. He could have left their date at dinner and drinks; she would have been happy with that, too.

No, he went for more.

First dates weren't typically the best when people spent most of the time getting to know one another and moving past the awkward stages of figuring out if there was even an attraction.

She didn't have that issue with Lucas. His hand, snug and warm, resting just under the hemline of her dress on her bare thigh said he didn't have that problem with her, either. At least, the two of them worked that part out easily enough.

Under no other circumstances would she allow anyone to blindfold her for what they professed to be a surprise. She found it terribly hard to refuse Lucas when he had plastered on that charming smile of his and said he had a special use for her scarf if she was up to play a little game.

Maybe it was the three glasses of red wine she had drank alongside her medium-rare steak for dinner, but her mind had gone to a far dirtier place at first. Delaney hadn't been quite sure what to make of her thoughts, or that handsome grin Lucas leveled on her, but she didn't refuse him.

And look where it got her.

"You're lucky I like you," Delaney mused under her breath.

Next to her in the car, where he sat in the driver's seat manning the sporty Lexus, her date laughed a rumble of a sound that did wicked things to her insides. Maybe she simply heard every glorious note in his amusement and it stuck all of her chords in the right way.

Then again, it *could* be the liquor. That third glass had certainly been a risk, and while she left a couple of mouthfuls in the bottom of the glass, the wine had already hit her veins before she'd put her lips to the rim.

To be fair, Delaney didn't get drunk.

Wasn't drunk.

Just buzzed a bit. Enough to feel it and the heat the alcohol left swimming in her bloodstream. Nothing more and nothing less. She got enough of getting blackout drunk in her teenage years, and even had one emergency room visit to pump her stomach under her proverbial belt as the proof.

She learned her limit.

Long ago.

A couple of beers.

A half a bottle of wine …

She felt the car roll to a slow stop, and heard the gears shift as Lucas put the vehicle into park.

"Are we here?" Delaney asked immediately, already reaching up to remove the blindfold.

Lucas laughed again, and his hand left her thigh to catch hers before she could pull the scarf away from her face. "Yes, but wait."

"*For what?*"

She really should work on her patience. Thinner than a string of sewing thread, it could snap at any moment.

That strong hand of his found her thigh again.

And *squeezed.*

"Was that true?" he asked.

Delaney blinked behind the scarf, searching her flubbing brain for the answer to his question. She blamed the blank slate of her mind on the fact that his hand had yet to let go of her thigh, and if anything, she'd become hyper aware of each of his fingertips digging in.

Deliciously.

"Was what true?" she eventually asked.

"You *like* me."

She grinned despite biting her lower lip to try to suppress the reaction. Another fail on her part. "I think I said *you're lucky* that I like you, right?"

Totally different things.

Not really.

She honestly expected another quick quip from Lucas—he always seemed to have one at the ready for her smart comments, after all. Instead, his silence reigned louder.

Longer.

All she heard were his soft breaths.

The shift of him in the driver's seat, causing his hand to shift slightly on her thigh while his fingers skirted a millimeter higher under her dress. She didn't even know if he meant to do that, nor did she intend to ask, but she couldn't stop the subtle way her crossed legs tightened. The only proof that she would like for his hand to *keep* traveling.

Delaney needed to find her control.

Soon.

The longer Lucas remained silent, the more Delaney had to fight the urge to pull down the makeshift blindfold. She put all of that nervous energy into fidgeting with her fingers in her lap until he cleared his throat in the seat next to hers.

"Delaney."

"Hmm?"

"*Delaney,*" Lucas repeated, lower the second time.

Oh, she reveled in the huskiness she heard in his voice, and dared to daydream what it might sound like breathed in her ear while they tangled underneath bedsheets. A dangerous game for her to play.

"Yes?"

"I feel like you need to know I think it should be illegal how cute you look sitting there blindfolded and biting your lip."

"*Cute?*" she questioned with a chirpy laugh.

"I wasn't sure if you wanted me to use another word."

"I mean, other than the taste comment earlier, you have been a gentleman."

Opening doors. Pulling out her chair. Even helping her in and out of her coat at the beginning and end of their dinner. He never pushed her boundaries more than holding her hand at the restaurant, and *she* had been the one to place his hand where it currently sat while they drove. She appreciated his effort to be respectful and appropriate.

She also wanted him to cross a line.

Not far.

Just enough ...

"But?" Lucas questioned.

"Is there another word you might choose?"

Lucas' next breath came out hard, but *relieved.* "Sexy. Sexy is the other word. The only word, let's be honest here. And I've done this to myself by putting you in this position, but it's a tease to me. You sitting there like that is killing me. Like a gift waiting for me to unwrap. I'd really just like to kiss you, but I didn't ask, and I don't want to assume—"

Her mouth decided to work before her brain did.

"So kiss me," she whispered, smiling again.

Thank God her mouth heard her heart talking in her chest before it ever listened for her brain; those galloping beats of the organ screamed far louder than any rational thought coming out of her head, anyway. Even when it got her into trouble. This was not one of those times.

Lucas delivered exactly what she asked for, but the gentle press of his soft mouth against hers still shocked Delaney all the same. Enough that she jumped a bit in her seat, giggling and grinning wider until the first sweeps of his lips along hers coaxed her mouth open for him, and she gave into his silent demand. The first stroke of his tongue along her own dragged a shuddering exhale from her chest, but that could have been the way he grabbed her thigh harder while his other hand caressed the line of her jaw.

She shivered.

His kiss slowed to soft pecks until his chuckles rocked them both. He left her with the distinct taste of mint lingering on her tongue. Compliments of the wrapped candies he'd taken from the bowl on the podium on the way out of Manger.

Delaney had to fight the desire to reach out in the space of darkness around her to find him and pull him back for another kiss. One that bruised and left her breathless. One that wouldn't leave her aching for more.

Maybe this was better.

She'd come running back for a second.

"Okay," she heard him mutter, "you might as well take that off, now."

Really?

"Now?" she asked faintly.

Why did all the blood in her body suddenly decide to rush in her ears?

"I might like another kiss, you know."

"Yeah, definitely now or we're never leaving this car," Lucas said, the huskiness coming back thick in his voice.

His hand left her thigh, too.

A shame, that.

Delaney, left with no other option, decided to give into Lucas' request for her to remove the scarf blocking her vision. If only to tell him she wanted his hand back where it had been, *and* another kiss to make it worth her while.

Except the sight she found waiting beyond the parked vehicle stopped her from saying anything at all, and suddenly, his reason for asking about her shoe size made a whole lot of sense. The arena complex couldn't be mistaken against the backdrop of the dark sky with its towering height and domed roof.

She turned to him with a big smile. "We're going skating?"

Lucas shrugged, his gaze darting from her to the building as he tried to explain, "I know it's not something crazy. Maybe we didn't need the blindfold, huh?"

He had no clue ...

"I haven't been skating since I was like thirteen," Delaney said, her memories rushing back to a different time in her life.

"That long?"

"It's a bit of a story," she admitted.

"You don't need to tell me if you don't want to."

That was the thing, though.

She *did* want to tell him. His gentle kindness radiated, and he seemed like exactly the type to be a strong shoulder to cry on over her lost girlhood dreams that had been replaced by a cold reality. It just didn't seem like the right time to tell him.

"We can skate, that's what we're here for, sweets." Lucas dazzled her with a lopsided grin. "I've got brand new, freshly sharpened skates in the back. I booked the whole rink out for the next two hours. It's just you and me."

Strange, she thought.

Just him and her sounded perfect, actually.

*

"This is *definitely* not the right outfit for skating," Delaney said as she did the final lacing on her new, sleek figure skates. Lucas winked, unashamed, at her from where he already stood on the ice with his arms resting one on top of the other on the sidewall of the rink. She pretended not to notice, even if her body broke out in goosebumps to say she'd seen his suggestive gesture perfectly well, and admired the skates that did great things for her bare calves and legs. "I've never had a pair in black before. They weren't standard in competition back then. You lose points for that."

"You did figure skating?"

Ah, *shit*.

She hadn't meant to go there.

The man listened better than she assumed—most men only heard what they wanted.

"I did," Delaney eventually said, opting to stand on the skates so she could get a feel for the tightness around her ankles. Good support was a must in skates someone might be jumping or spinning in. Nothing could ruin a skate faster than a broken ankle on ice.

"How do they fit?" he asked.

"Perfect," she beamed.

Lucas, clearly pleased with the answer, offered her a hand from over the wall even though she didn't need it to keep herself steady as she walked along the rubber coated floor under the benches to where the door opened to the ice rink. Nonetheless, she liked her hand tucked inside his, and those first few seconds after her skates hit the ice required a bit of adjustment from Delaney.

Mostly, getting used to the sensation of gliding across crisp, clean ice on thin blades again.

Remembering.

It took her a minute.

Just a bit to get the hang of shifting her weight from skate to skate to propel over the ice and maintain her balance without barely lifting a blade. Lucas patiently waited, his shiny, new hockey skates keeping him upright and alongside her as they headed for the red center in the middle of the ice.

Still hand in hand.

"Like riding a bike," she muttered to herself.

Once a person learned, they never forgot how to do it. No matter how much time passed. Skating proved no different.

Lucas chuckled. "Yeah, pretty much."

"Do you skate a lot?"

"Used to. I did hockey all through school, and played for a charity team once a year up until I turned thirty and didn't really have time anymore," he said.

He shrugged at her questioning stare, adding, "Life gets in the way of a lot of things I used to do just because I liked to, you know what I mean?"

She did.

Adulting sucked sometimes.

A few feet from center ice, Delaney dropped Lucas' hand to kick away from him with enough room to widen her skates as she spun to glide backwards.

"Aha," Lucas exclaimed, full of praise and clapping.

Delaney held up one finger, quieting him, before her backwards skate turned into a triple twirl on the spot. She could have tried for more spins before coming to a full stop, but lack of practice meant she forgot the most important rule about spinning.

Keep your eyes on one spot.

She came out of the spins with a bit of a dizzy wobble, and a breathless laugh that had her bent over at the middle. Not an intentional bow, but it worked to end her show.

She would not do that again.

Wouldn't *dare*.

The last thing she wanted to do was fall flat on her face on the ice, and give another kind of show should her dress ride up too high on her ass.

Delaney's toothy smile matched Lucas' as he skated a wide circle backward around her. She faced the large scoreboard on the far wall of the arena hanging beneath a massive Canadian flag stretching from one side of the rink to the other.

"See, you still got it," he told her.

"I really shouldn't do that after drinking wine," she replied.

Lucas only chuckled. "You barely even blinked."

She eyed him from the side, shaking her head a little.

Maybe it was the smell of the rink and the chill of the ice that did it, or it could have been the gorgeous man who never took his gaze off of her, but her willingness to share came back in the form of a tightness in her chest. The words practically rushed right out the second she opened her lips.

"My grandmother put me into figure skating when I started kindergarten," Delaney said, her words never once breaking Lucas' clean circle he continued to make around her. "I guess, to teach me how to skate, mostly, but I took right to it."

"What did you say earlier—thirteen you stopped?"

Delaney exhaled a breath she could see in front of her face. It ached coming out of her lungs. "Lucky me, I was an early bloomer."

The pucker of his brow said he didn't understand. Funny ... she hadn't either, back then.

"My parents pulled me out of it, refused to pay fees or replace my equipment and things. I always needed new costumes ..." Delaney trailed off, knowing none of those things really made sense to clear up the reason why she had quit as a young teen. "It wasn't really about the money. My father was more concerned with how short my costumes were and how people could see the shape of my body when I skated."

Lucas shredded ice as he instantly came to a stop. "What?"

She shrugged one shoulder, but her attempt to laugh off the seriousness in her delivery was nothing less than weak. "Oh, yeah. I listened to him rant for weeks every time we sat down at the dinner table." Not *just* then. All the time, really. "The second skating got brought up somehow, he started. My mother—she sat there and let him do it. It was his house, anyway, or so she always said whenever one of us had something to say about the way he did things. She didn't care. I tried to argue for a while. I wasn't doing anything wrong. I didn't skate and sin."

"What does sin have anything to do with it?"

"Well, when I kept coming up with what I thought were smart arguments to keep skating, being a thirteen-year-old starting to grow into her own brain that didn't automatically believe everything they told me, he just took me to church. Instead of him shouting at me about how I was going to become a whore because of figure skating, the pastor spent four hours counseling me about my sinful and wanton behavior, and how it seduces boys and men when I pranced around in short, shiny skirts and tights."

Lucas blinked, standing strong like a pillar, close to the middle of the ice.

Delaney suddenly wished she hadn't allowed herself to go to that place—that horrible place where God and her faith had been twisted and manipulated by the people around her for their selfish desires and needs. Very rarely had they considered *her*. Anything about her, really.

"Shit, Delaney—"

She held up a finger at the pitying tone Lucas took one, and wanted to stop that in its tracks. "I learned something when they did that to me—when they took skating from me. They taught me something important about my family."

"What did it teach you?" Lucas gestured at nothing in particular, muttering, "I can't imagine that would teach a teenage girl anything good—to what, hide her body even in sport because *she's* responsible for the thoughts of the opposite sex?"

Delaney nodded. "No, I was already used to being told things like that. If you were alive and had a vagina, you'd hear that nonsense coming out of church every sermon." From the time she could walk and talk, really. As soon as she understood that she was the girl, and by default, always the reason in a bad or inappropriate situation. Especially when it came to men. "They taught me if I had to question them, or the things they told me, they were probably wrong."

A small smirk pulled at the edge of Lucas' lips. "Oh?"

She pointed at her head. "Like I said, I started to think with my own brain instead of the way they told me how. Every question I had for God didn't seem to be answered in the Bible, and I wasn't exactly encouraged to think outside of our safe little box. The voice

I heard in my head when I was alone didn't sound like the one they wanted me to listen to when I started asking the questions I thought were important. It sounded real—more like *me*."

For her parents, that fucked up everything, and it changed all their lives forever. She refused to apologize for that.

"Jesus, okay," Delaney said suddenly, needing to get them off this conversation and back to the happy place the two of them had found moments ago. She kicked off on the ice, starting a wider circle around Lucas than he had previously done to her. He, on the other hand, began a slow skate backwards. "Are we skating, or what?"

Lucas flashed a cheeky grin. "Want to race?"

Did he really have to ask?

She couldn't say no to a challenge.

Delaney spun fast, and headed for the far side of the rink with a holler, "First one to that side and then the back wall wins!"

"*Brat!*" She heard him shout.

Hey.

He had way longer legs.

She deserved a head start.

To be fair, Delaney really had to work for that win. Cold air whipped past her pumping legs even as she came to a dangerous stop at the back boards before jetting toward the other side of the rink. Lucas was not far behind.

She barely got herself stopped at the other side and turned around before the man rushed her. All of him. Every towering foot of him that loomed over her as he shredded ice again to come to a stop mere inches in front of her at the back boards. She felt the prickles of ice shavings dance up her bare legs, but she couldn't even make herself look away from Lucas as he inched closer until her back pressed against the boards and his hands caged her in on either side.

He grinned big.

Even when she peered up at him and whispered, "*I win.*"

Delaney earned herself that bruising, breathless kiss she'd wanted in the car. He didn't ask for it, but he didn't have to this time around. Her tongue tangled with his—so demanding, taking more even when she gasped for air around their trembling kiss—as their bodies melted together against the boards. She enjoyed the sensation of being pinned under him a little too much for her own good, but she couldn't bear to push him away.

So, she didn't.

"I'd break my rules for you," she told him, shivering even though she wasn't all that cold anymore once Lucas had pulled back from the kiss. "I *would.*"

If her cousin wasn't at the apartment waiting …

If he just kissed her like that again …

She would break *every* rule.

He made her think it might be worth it.

Lucas wet the seam of his lips with the tip of his tongue as he tried to catch his own breath. The way he stared at her—hard and long, unmoving—said he wanted her to do exactly that. Break every and any rule.

His mouth said something different.

"Don't," he told her, shaking his head and pushing away from the wall to skate backwards. "Don't ever lower the bar for me. Set it even higher."

Goddamn him for saying that, too.

It made her like him even more.

"Best two out of three for the race, then?" she asked. "If you want a chance to save your pride, I mean."

Lucas laughed loudly. "You bet your pretty ass. It's so on."

13.

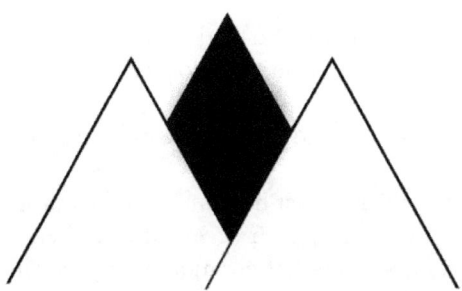

"Delaney?"

Bexley's muffled voice filtered from deep within the darkened apartment when Delaney finally got the door open after she wiggled the key the right way in the lock to loosen the final tumbler on the deadbolt.

"Is that you?" her cousin followed up.

"Its me," Delaney called back. "You're still up?"

A chuckle echoed behind Delaney. A dark laugh that definitely did not belong to Bexley.

"It's not that late," Lucas said. "Almost eleven."

Fair enough.

Maybe she had been secretly hoping her cousin would be out— enjoying the town herself, like Bexley usually spent her evenings— or sleeping. Although, it wasn't like Delaney needed another reason to break one of her rules.

"No, just getting out of the shower. Give me five minutes to get dressed," Bexley said, her voice a little louder for a second before Delaney heard the distinct click of the bathroom door closing.

With a handful of minutes to spare, Delaney turned in the opened doorway of the apartment to face the grinning man standing just outside in the hallway. Both his hands pressed flat to the doorjamb so he could lean down closer to Delaney.

"You really didn't have to walk me all the way to my door," she said. "Inside the front would have been fine, too."

Lucas shook his head like that wasn't even an option. "No way. I watch too much true crime to let you do that."

Delaney lifted an eyebrow high in silent question.

He shrugged, adding lower, "Hey, you don't know the kind of

porn buddy upstairs binges for twenty hours a day, you know what I mean? I'm just saying."

Yikes.

She didn't want to know the kind of true crime rabbit hole he had found if those were the kind of concerns he kept in the back of his mind.

"And maybe I wanted to do this one more time but out of the cold," he said.

Before she could ask what he wanted to do, Lucas showed her. He caught her lips with his own when she tilted her head upwards, but the softness in the kiss left her mouth tingling with the ghost of him even after he'd pulled away.

"Get some sleep," he told her, pushing back from the door to stand to his full height.

Delaney didn't move from the doorway. "Are we gonna do this again?"

Lucas didn't hesitate for a second. "Absolutely. The first chance we can."

"I could let you know what my next couple of weeks look like?"

"Please do."

Delaney's smile bloomed. "I'll do that. For what it's worth, *I* don't mind the drive to Saint John, either. And I love to watch the ships in the harbor."

"Good to know," he murmured.

For a moment, Lucas waffled on the spot as his gaze traveled to the end of the hallway where the exit door to the stairwell waited to take him back downstairs to the main entry floor. He shifted from one shoe to the other, and even shoved his hands into his pockets.

She thought she knew what he wanted.

Maybe.

Because she wanted it, too.

"One more for good measure?"

Lucas' gaze swung back on her, but it blazed. "And sweet dreams?"

That sounded perfect to her.

"Please," she whispered.

He met her in the doorway again, and his arms snaked around her waist to cage her close. Where the lit of the hallway and the shadows of her apartment met. His first kiss landed on the apple of her right cheek before he quickly dropped another on the other side. Delaney's fingers curled into the open lapels of his blazer in an effort to keep them both there in that moment, when his soft lips pressed against her forehead with hushed words.

"More than one—just because," he told her.

Well, she wanted the extra.

He *definitely* deserved it.

Her head fell back so she could catch the last kiss where she wanted it the most. Not that she needed to test her already-fragile self control where Lucas was concerned, but she couldn't stop from losing herself in that lingering kiss.

For a second, anyway.

They both knew it couldn't last forever.

The other person in the equation reminded the two of that fact when Bexley made her entrance from the bathroom. The short hallway connected to the bathroom and bedrooms walked straight out into the middle of the apartment where Bexley had a good view of the two still standing close together in the doorway.

"Oh!"

Delaney grinned, and patted Lucas' heavily rising chest with both hands as he backed away. "Call me tomorrow?"

"You bet," he murmured.

"Have a good night!" Bexley called.

Lucas waved two fingers in return for a goodbye, but saved a wink for Delaney before she had to watch his back retreat down the hall. Her hormones did all the internal screaming for her demanding that he stay—screw the fact the apartment had thin walls and her morals were beginning to get even thinner in the process.

The click of the metal fire exit door at the end of the hall closed the chapter on the night for Delaney, but she remained leaning in the doorway for a beat or two longer. Not because she expected the man to turn around—Lucas didn't seem like the type to push boundaries—but because she wanted to enjoy the culmination of their evening together.

A hell of a night.

Considering they didn't end up in bed together.

"Well?" Bexley asked after Delaney had shut the door and retreated into the apartment to remove her coat and boots.

She hung her bag up, stuffed full with her mittens, hat, and scarf, on the same wall hook as her jacket. "Well, what?"

"How did it go?"

Delaney hid her smile by pretending to rummage through the pocket of her jacket for nothing in particular. "Um ..."

"Delaney, *come on*. I've been dying here all night."

Her laugh filled the apartment like the lights flooding them overhead when Bexley hit the switch in the living room.

"It was great," she told her cousin.

Bexley smiled knowingly. "Yeah?"

Delaney shrugged. "He's a good guy."

More than.

"And I had a lot of fun," she added.

Which was what mattered.

Lucas, in the span of a few hours, proved to be many interesting things all wrapped in a very attractive package. Delaney honestly hadn't expected to end the evening ready to make plans for the next one, as soon as possible, but she wouldn't complain that it turned out this way, either.

"I'll probably see him again," Delaney said, turning to face her cousin with a grin.

"Oh, just probably huh?"

"Well, everything is just a maybe until it isn't, right?"

The world wasn't as scary when Delaney saw things that way.

Bexley only sighed.

"I think I'm gonna take a bath," Delaney said, heading that way.

"You really had a good night, huh?"

"How can you tell?"

Bexley's laugh tinkled through the apartment. "Because you haven't stopped smiling."

Well, then ...

"I guess that speaks for itself, doesn't it?" Delaney asked before slipping into the hallway.

*

Beautiful dreams, sweets.

The goodnight text lit up Delaney's phone seconds after she slipped into bed. She wondered if he, too, had just found his way back to his own bed, and still had her on his mind. Who didn't crave to be wanted?

"*You, too*," she messaged Lucas back.

It wasn't good enough. She had to make herself put the phone down to keep from hitting the call button just to hear his voice.

Delaney didn't know what to do with those feelings.

That bubbling anticipation.

It started the second he greeted her at the front door of the apartment building and hadn't dissipated throughout the evening. If anything, it just got stronger. And there Delaney was, left buzzing with all her nervous energy and excitement, but alone in bed.

She couldn't stand it.

Hell, she barely understood it.

Delaney picked up her phone again, but this time, she bypassed Lucas' contact in her list for one not too far below.

Gracen.

The cell number Gracen would answer, no matter the time or day, rang four times before Delaney started to think her best friend might be asleep. Her suspicions were confirmed when a gravely, familiar male voice picked up the call.

"You know it's almost twelve, Delaney, right?" Malachi asked, not even bothering with a proper hello.

She didn't blame him.

It *was* late.

"A little after twelve, I think," she returned. "Is Gracen—"

"Sleeping. It's been a long week. The morning sickness really kicked in hard. She hit the bed before nine."

A first time for everything.

"Okay, well tell her—"

"Who's that?" came a sleepy voice in the background.

Malachi sighed while the rustle of movement echoed over the phone. "Go to bed, babe."

"Who called?" Gracen asked. "Is that my phone?"

"I can call back in the morn—"

Delaney didn't even finish her sentence before the speakers crackled in her ear as the phone was handed over. Or, guessing by the muttered *hey, be nice* by Malachi, Gracen had simply taken the phone from him without asking.

"Delaney?" Gracen questioned, her voice less wobbly with sleep.

"How did you know it was me?"

"Nobody else calls me this late."

Fair point, she thought.

"What about the manor?" Delaney asked.

"It wouldn't be for anything good," Gracen mumbled.

Yeah, true.

Delaney hadn't considered that.

"Okay, so it's me," she said quickly.

Gracen laughed. "It is *really* late."

"I know, but I can't sleep."

"Why not?"

Genuine concern coated Gracen's question.

Delaney might have beat herself up internally over the time, and the fact that she could have waited until the morning. "Listen, I'll call tomorrow morning after you have some sleep. It's not that important."

"Everything is important. Just in different ways. We talked earlier, things were good, right?"

"Things are great," Delaney admitted.

Better than they were, anyway.

"Great," her friend echoed.

She heard the confusion there, too.

Just spit it out, Delaney.

"So I did something tonight—I mean, I went out with somebody," she told Gracen.

Silent seconds ticked by. One after another.

Delaney stopped counting once she hit ten.

"Gracen?"

"Yeah, I'm here," her friend muttered in a groan like she was lifting out of bed. "Like, you went out with a guy?"

"A guy?" she heard in the background.

Malachi again.

"Lucas," Delaney clarified, even if his name didn't offer much information.

"Lucas," Gracen repeated.

"Who the fuck is Lucas?" Malachi asked loudly. "What is happening?"

Gracen didn't clue him in.

Delaney finally moved on to the crux of her call. "It was kind of amazing, and I needed to tell somebody. You're the only person I really want to tell."

At once, Gracen seemed to understand.

After all, what were best friends for?

"Okay," her friend said, all thoughts of sleep gone as she had more important things to focus on now, "so tell me everything."

14.

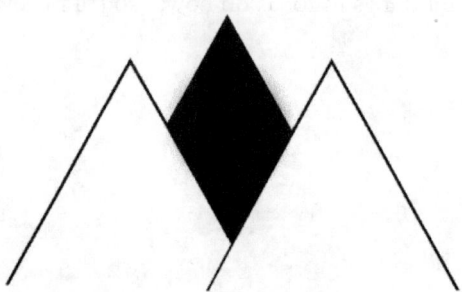

Lucas rolled into the brewery's employee parking lot with a grin on his face on Monday morning. A change from his usual mood lately. A *welcomed* change, really. He was even willing to overlook the fact that his good nature didn't stem from the fact he was heading into work, but rather, the last string of text messages on his phone.

It had nothing to do with beer.

Or work.

Delaney owned his smile entirely.

Lucas pulled the Bronco into the parking spot designated for him without a concern in his mind about the day that lay ahead of him. He barely passed the plaque with his name and COO title engraved on gleaming bronze a glance as he put the car in park, already thinking about something else that he had to get back to.

Delaney's last text, that was.

He couldn't risk texting and driving—more for the safety purpose than the ticket he could surely afford. She'd left him on a bit of a cliff-hanger from her last message when he had just stepped out of his apartment to start the day, and it deserved an appropriate response.

She deserved his attention, rather.

Lucas climbed out of the SUV with his phone in one hand that he worked to unlock while he slid his tan leather commuter bag over his shoulder with the other. He was already scrolling back down to the end of a conversation that had bled over from the late hours of the night before when he slammed his car door shut, not even concerned about locking it with the keys he'd tossed into his bag.

Likely lost at the bottom, and he couldn't be bothered to dig into the bag to find out when he had left the apartment fifteen minutes later than usual. Not to mention, when he came up behind the city bus on the east end that had seemed to have a penchant for refusing to move over into the designated bus lane.

Oh, well.

He'd send Nola, his secretary and assistant who tried to keep his days on track for the most part, on a coffee and donut run for the morning meeting, anyway. Every employee in the offices upstairs, from accounting to the design department, were far happier and much more willing to sit through the more boring parts of their standard mid-month regrouping when sugar and caffeine were involved in the process.

Nola could lock the Bronco for him on her way. Hell, sometimes she took the Bronco to get the food, if the roads were particularly icy; his vehicle certainly handled the weather conditions better than her Buick.

Lucas had better things on his mind.

Delaney, of course.

His grin widened again as he reread their attempts to come to an agreement about another date and time they could get together. In between tangents where she—or even he—had offhandedly mentioned something that took the two down a rabbit hole of conversation in the form of text messages.

He typically spent his night with a glass of spiced rum and the Telegraph Journal opened to the most recent news stories featuring their province, but not over the past couple of nights. Instead, he spent them distracted by a black-haired beauty an entire city away who snuck him phone calls in the evening when her cousin wasn't close to listen in and snoop.

Lucas blamed Delaney for his distraction.

Wholeheartedly.

Not that he had any complaints.

He typed out a response to Delaney's last message as he strolled the recently salted walkway around the side of the brewery to the front entrance. Sending it through as the automatic doors slid open to welcome him into the smell of wood from the paneled walls of the reception gallery and the distinct aroma of hops in the air, he faintly heard the woman behind the front desk say her usual good morning to the boss.

115

A faint *"Beautiful day, Mr. Dalton."*

Maybe he waved?

Lucas didn't even realize his own distraction until he glanced up to find neither of the two elevators leading to the upstairs offices were open for him. Because he hadn't actually pushed the button.

Not really bothered by his sudden absentmindedness, Lucas chuckled it off, and pushed the red button between both panels. The one on the right opened instantly, and he stepped inside at the same time Delaney's response came through.

He punched the appropriate button to head upstairs, and then went back to Delaney's most recent message.

"What do you mean?" she had asked.

His question?

Are you adverse to flying?

Their attempts to come to a day and time when he would be in her city when she was also on her days off from the salon that kept a rather strange schedule didn't seem likely. He had all the time in the world to do whatever he wanted when it came to his time in Saint John. Less if he had to work it around her days off in Freddy. As it stood, a random couple of hours on a midweek day before he'd probably be jetting out again didn't seem like enough.

Delaney agreed.

He had a second option but had held off on mentioning it.

If she would agree …

Lucas didn't think explaining his twenty-four-hour access to a helicopter—that made the two-hour drive between cities a single hour sprint through the sky that was far more interesting—over the form of text messages gave the right impression. He wasn't exactly trying to impress Delaney, the helicopter was simply there to be used, and the last thing he intended was to brag about it either. After all, it wasn't technically his.

The helicopter should only be used for company excursions, and typically was—however, his grandfather and father had both been known to book the flying machine off the record of the business. As long as the helicopter was back on the pad when it needed to be, the money didn't come out of the company's accounts, and the pilot got paid, nobody cared.

Another benefit to a non-publicly owned company like theirs. There weren't any investors breathing down the backs of their necks in regards to the way money got spent or even how business matters were handled at the end of the day.

Instead, it was all a family affair.

Private, entirely confidential, and easier on the taxes at the end of the year. On the flip side of that same coin, he had become intimately familiar with the cons of being a shareholder in a privately owned company as well.

Mostly, being in business with his father.

Either way, what good was his privilege if Lucas didn't sometimes use it, right?

That's what he told himself, anyway.

On his way up in the elevator, Lucas sent Delaney another message: *Could you fit me in for a call today?*

An inside joke, really.

Despite admitting the schedule of the salon was a little strange compared to the norm, she proclaimed to love it. She worked half the days of the month and got the other half off when it was all worked out. Not to mention, she practically made her own schedule with her clients, and walk-ins like him were few and far between when her time slots booked up rather quickly.

"Is lunch too late?" she asked back seconds later.

The elevator slowed to a stop before the doors slid open to reveal the upstairs lobby for the office employees. The space bustled with quiet activity as his secretary chatted on the phone behind her desk in front of the large company logo with backlit lights that made it look like it was hovering in front of the wall. The parcel carrier, the same one who always brought their packages and mail upstairs, unloaded his cart with the help of another woman who kept things on track upstairs.

He didn't expect to find the office as low energy as it was when he stepped beyond the elevator door. Usually, on Mondays, someone had a story to retell from their weekend exploits that kept the upstairs laughing until well into the afternoon.

Today, he even found the doorways to the offices closed as he headed for the long hallway that led to his own. On the way by, Nola called at his back, "Uh, Lucas, there's—"

"Give me five minutes, okay?" he interrupted.

Delaney remained at the forefront of his mind while he typed back a confirmation that lunch would be fine to call. In fact, he'd make sure his own was entirely open for whenever her call came through to his cell.

"Sure, but ..." Nola trailed off when her phone rang again, and over his shoulder, he watched her wary stare drift down the calls she already had on hold that blinked at the top of the receiver.

"Five minutes," he repeated, already too far down the hall for the woman to see him from her own desk.

Lucas had just shoved the phone into his back pocket when he pushed open the door to his private office.

And there sat his father.

Scowling behind Lucas' desk.

"Ah, son," his father said with a snide smile forming on his face that was like looking into an aging mirror for Lucas. Right down to the cleft on his chin. Jacob had the same. Their dimples came from their mother. It was the only thing that set the brother's apart from their father, and he tried to focus on that feature of his face rather than the rest. It was hard to see the reflection people proclaimed to be good-looking staring at him in the mirror when he more often saw the similarities to his father as a focus.

Probably something he should take to his therapist.

"Nice of you to finally show up in the office this morning. You're what, twenty minutes late?"

"Ronald," Lucas deadpanned.

No hello.

Not even: *why are you here?*

Lucas bypassed all that bullshit and went straight to the important matter at hand. The fact that his father was sitting in his office, *at his desk.* Who gave a fuck if he showed up an hour late? That didn't change the fact that Ronald only sat where he did to get a rise out of Lucas, and he wouldn't go for the bait.

They'd played that game before.

It never ended well.

Suddenly, the somber mood in the office and the not-so-cheerful greeting of the young woman at the reception desk downstairs made a lot more sense. Not one person in the bottling and brewery factory could muster a genuine smile when Ronald Dalton walked through the front doors.

Actually, he didn't even use the front.

A parking spot beside Lucas' that had been designated to Ronald's CEO/CFO position remained unused, but five feet closer to the entrance than his son's. Which was all the man wanted at the end of the day. It didn't matter that he worked most of the year on the other side of the country. He simply enjoyed making Lucas know who had the most control, and that his seventy-five percent share of the company would always be greater than his son's twenty-five.

In every way he possibly could.

Not that it mattered. Ronald didn't use his parking spot. Instead, he parked in one at the side of the building near an exit door that he had personally hired a locksmith to install with a private lock that only he could use to access the stairwell. The lock was put in almost immediately after Lucas' grandfather died. Ronald stopped pretending that he cared about the company or its employees at all after that—right up until the point he hauled ass to the west. The man couldn't even be bothered to enter through the front like every other employee to have his face seen and say hello.

In some cases, that wasn't a bad thing.

Except the man could at least pretend to respect the people beneath them in the company hierarchy. The employees worked hard. Harder than Ronald *ever* did, and they deserved recognition for that, at the very least. Not that his father could muster the energy to do so.

No one really expected it from the man anymore, either. No one expected *anything* from Ronald Dalton unless it would be something unpleasant.

"I called," his father said.

Lucas blinked. "You mean, at four-thirty in the morning?"

Who the fuck was even up at that hour?

Not a sane man.

No, he had not bothered to dignify that early morning, missed call with a response because Lucas had been clear about his boundaries. Ronald didn't care if he crossed them, of course, but Lucas no longer fed into his father's nonsense on his end.

A choice he could make and control.

That's what counted.

"I messaged over the weekend, too," Ronald added, giving his eldest son a pointed stare.

Ah, right.

The meeting his father wanted.

"You didn't think to give me a couple of days to get back to you? I do other things besides work, Dad."

Not that he had any intention to share what those things were

with his father. If anything, the man wouldn't care. At worst, well
… anything was possible. Ronald didn't keep his displeasure with
Lucas, and his acts against his son, strictly within business hours.
His personal life was not off limits, if Ronald thought he could get
away with it.

He didn't have to search very hard for reasons to keep a safe
and healthy distance between the two of them. Ronald made that
shit easy.

"Are we letting the whole office hear your complaints about my
phone calls?" Ronald asked, gesturing at the open door behind
Lucas.

His cheek twitched with the effort it took for Lucas to keep his
mouth clamped shut, so he didn't ask Ronald whose fault that was
between them.

"It wouldn't even be the fifth time they heard it," Lucas replied
dully, his molars aching from the pressure he released from his jaws
to speak.

And sadly, not untrue.

He did close the door because the office employees deserved
the same dignity and respect that Lucas liked, including keeping
family matters at home whenever possible, but Ronald liked to
make that hard.

His father said nothing as Lucas milled around the office,
dropping his commuter bag onto the corner bucket chair with the
scalloped back in front of his desk. The closest he came to Ronald,
who crossed his left ankle over his right knee and reclined in Lucas'
chair to watch his son handle his usual morning business in the
office, was when he hung his jacket and scarf on the wooden coat
rack next to the desk.

Right beside Ronald's hanging fur-lined parka.

Did he plan to stay?

Lucas couldn't help but notice the stack of Post-It notes left for
him by Nola. Reminders for the day or different calls that had been
requested of him for one reason or another.

Ronald noticed his stare, muttering, "You should really get her a
better mode of communication than scribbles on rainbow paper.
It's a little juvenile, isn't it?"

Oh, God save him.

Lucas tried the breathing technique his new therapist had
suggested. Although he'd only managed one appointment with the

man since starting, during that hour-long session, he'd pointed out the obvious areas in his life that needed immediate attention.

Including his patience.

Or lack thereof when it came to his father.

A grounding method had been suggested by his therapist to allow him at least ten seconds of mindfulness before he cut out at Ronald with whatever response was on the tip of his tongue.

One breath in—count to five.

Let it out, and count again.

Simple, right?

If only.

Lucas came out of the technique still wanting to bash his father's brains across the desk. The amount of hostility his father brought forth in him actually scared him sometimes. He was ashamed of himself that this was the position where he seemed stuck up against Ronald.

"You're never happy anyway," Lucas said, "so even if she did everything exactly as you wanted her to—and she would try her hardest, because she's a perfectionist but struggles with ADHD that she's got diagnosed on record which is on her health insurance forms you undoubtedly looked at."

The drawer where Nola's file could be found was slightly ajar to the rest of the five in the cabinet. Just how fast had Ronald moved from one side of the office to the other in and effort to hide what he had been doing when Lucas came down the hall?

Yeah, he looked for everything.

Didn't miss a click.

Not when it came to good, old Dad.

"Which I know you know," he told his father, shrugging one shoulder as he rounded the front of the desk where he stood with his arms crossed over his chest. He nodded at the fifteen rows of filing cabinets against the back wall of the industrial styled office. "Let's not pretend that you don't dig through personnel files like it's not past time reading for you, Ronald. It's interesting to see that not much has changed no matter how long you stay on the other side of Canada, eh?"

His father's dark, bushy brow jumped higher. "Excuse me?"

Lucas wasn't done. See, his father had gone ahead and so easily made a rude remark about a woman he knew nothing about at the end of the day. A forgettable moment in Ronald's day chalked full of negativity and toxicity, maybe. On Lucas' end of the spectrum, however, he gave a shit about the young woman who was the eldest daughter of a guy he used to work out with, and couldn't let the casual disrespect of people Ronald cared nothing about pass.

"Not that it would matter to you," Lucas said, keeping a stone-straight face as he delivered his next words to his father to make sure *everything* was clear, "but that young lady uses her pile of notes as a way to dump out her most important thoughts during the day so she doesn't lose them. I noticed one day, and—"

"Lucas—"

"Shut up, Ronald," Lucas interjected at a decibel below raising his voice.

His father's jaws snapped instantly shut.

"I let Nola make me a pile of notes as well," he continued like the two of them hadn't missed a beat. "And since they're not meant for you to begin with, I haven't the first clue why you felt the need to comment on them. Other than purposefully looking for a way to make a jab at a twenty-two-year-old secretary who really likes her job."

Lucas smiled, then, but sadly.

Ronald had barely even blinked.

No, he sat there and stewed.

Fumed, really.

A knock behind Lucas on the office door dropped his blood pressure instantly. He knew who it was without turning around.

"Come in, Nola," he called.

She pushed open the door with a creak. "Are we still doing the meeting at ten-thirty, or—"

"Move it up fifteen?" Lucas asked. "Please."

"Sure, and um ... are we doing the usual?"

Right.

Who knew how long this shit with his father would last?

Lucas decided to give everybody a reason to smile and give a bit of grace today. "We'll do the donuts and coffee for lunch. And pizza, for the plant. Yeah? Could we find somebody who could get that done in a couple of hours?"

"*Someone* will," she assured.

There were a whole city of restaurants capable of making pizza.

"Thank you," Lucas said over his shoulder, smiling at the wary-looking Nola who hadn't completely come inside the office.

Her gaze snapped back to him with a puckered brow. "Otherwise?"

Her way of asking—as she always did throughout his day—if he was okay.

"Otherwise, nothing," Lucas confirmed with a shrug of one shoulder.

Nola nodded before retreating. The door closed, leaving Lucas alone with the cold reality of his father still sitting in his office.

"I'll head that meeting today," Ronald said, dragging Lucas' gaze back to him instantly where he shook a finger in the door's direction. His smile, cunning but cruel, turned on his son. "I don't think you'll mind, right? Otherwise, I'll head the table in my chair while you talk from the side. Hmm?"

Ronald even raised his brow high like that was a real question.

Seventy-five to twenty-five.

It wasn't real.

He just wanted to point out the discrepancy; that he *could*. Most importantly, that he always would. As if Lucas could forget.

Without another word, Ronald stood from Lucas' chair and walked around the desk with a careful eye on the wall and contents of the room. He left his blazer jacket still hanging over the chair where Lucas should sit.

Where his jacket should *go*.

"I noticed you redecorated," his father muttered, his muscular back bulging against his silk dress shirt from the grip at which he held his hands behind his back. It had tension written all over it.

Ronald needed to make a point, now. His pride wouldn't forgive him if he didn't because in some way, he must have felt like Lucas got the better of him that morning. It always happened, and unfortunately for Lucas, he long ago figured out that regardless of whether he engaged his father or not … the end result remained the same.

"I took a few things off the wall," Lucas said. "I had them sent over—"

"Mmm, it's in the garage," Ronald interrupted as he came up to one glass shelf that hadn't changed in the office. The one where Mitchel Dalton's urn sat next to a picture frame of his last company approved photo, and a plaque with relevant details. One other condition, and request by default, of his late grandfather's final Will and Testament.

"Should have taken that and tossed it in the trash like I'll do for the rest of it," his father uttered.

No, they weren't doing this again.

Lucas had far better things to get to, and not enough emotional energy to expend at his father's sick expense.

"If you're done, I have work to do," Lucas said, opting to get right to the point. "I can move the meeting up if you'd like to get right to that and head out. Isn't that why your head office in the city is downtown? I thought the rattling of the bottles give you migraines?"

Any excuse.

Ronald used it to make everyone's life hell.

His father turned on him with a shrug, but the gleam in his eye told Lucas he had tread close to dangerous waters. "I'm thinking of making the transfer back, actually. Even put out some feelers about filling my position out west."

Lucas balked. "What?"

Was that his heart in his stomach?

Or his stomach in his chest?

"You know," Ronald said, moving past Lucas in the office as he headed for the door, "when I couldn't get a hold of you this morning, I called Jacob."

Lucas froze while those organs inside his body rearranged themselves once more. This time, he couldn't make his mouth work.

At the door that he yanked open unceremoniously, Ronald faced his son with an unfeeling gaze. "At least, he answered."

"It's easier when you just leave him alone, you know?"

Ronald chuckled dryly. "Right, I suppose. I thought maybe you'd whined to him about having to see me throughout the winter, and he'd say that's why you were ignoring my calls."

No.

Really, he just had things to do.

Of course, Ronald had to go and bring Jacob into it. A young man who already felt unwanted by the people who were supposed to love him, had far more than enough proof to know he was right, but also hoped it might someday change. An early morning call from one's father just to abuse and bother him because his older brother wasn't available wouldn't help Jacob toward that change.

Not that Ronald gave a single damn.

Another fragile soul to toy with.

He *knew* just how fragile Jacob's was, too.

"I'll see you in the meeting," Ronald said, taking his leave without another word.

Lucas had his phone pulled out of his back pocket before the door even swung closed. He'd thought it odd that morning when Jacob didn't call or text like he typically did, but sometimes that happened on Mondays when they both ran late. Especially if his brother's work at the gym, or animal rescue where he spent the rest of his free time, ran particularly late on the previous Sunday evening.

Jacob stuck to a schedule.

It helped to keep him on track, and his nose clean.

In more ways than one …

"Answer the phone, bro," Lucas muttered down into the screen of his phone as he waited for the call to connect on the screen.

It didn't.

Five rings took it through to voicemail.

Lucas tried again.

Same thing.

"Fuck," he muttered, already trying again. *"Come on, Jacob."*

The concern growing in his chest wasn't for nothing, because once upon a time, Lucas had done this very thing with his little brother. Called and got no answer. *Knew* something was wrong because of the pit of pain that formed deep in his chest. He tried not to let his mind go to that place. Jacob had spent years proving to Lucas that they would never return to that awful day again.

Yet, there he stood.

In that exact office.

Doing the same damn thing.

Why wouldn't his brother pick up the phone?

15.

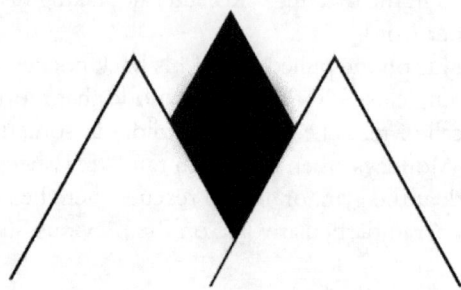

Delaney blinked awake to a darkened bedroom. The second she came to awareness, her gaze cut to the window where a crack in the pulled shades would tell her what she already knew without picking up her phone on the nightstand to confirm.

For no particular reason—except maybe the universe had decided it would be fun to fuck with Delaney—she had woken up every morning that week an hour before her alarm. She blamed a certain someone for her brain's inability to shut off at night but considering it had been almost three days since she spoke to Lucas last, she refused to give him more of her time. Even if it was just thoughts passing her mind by.

Besides, she didn't have a lot of time to waste.

Not the type to be able to fall back asleep, even if she could get a solid hour more before her alarm started beeping, Delaney snagged the phone from the bedside table off the cordless charge. The five o'clock time made her scowl into the glow of the phone's home screen before it deepened when noted the empty notification box at the bottom for her messages. Nothing new to see there, either.

Don't do that, Delaney. The guy would have called you if he really wanted to or gave a shit—how many messages have you left since Monday?

Nope.

She wouldn't do that with herself, either.

Lucas owed her nothing. They had one date. It didn't have to be more even if it had felt like it would be right up until everything seemed to change last minute.

Oh, well.

Delaney spent the first two days of the week playing that foolish game with herself and her feelings all because a man didn't want to pay her any attention. Or really, that's how it boiled down to her. And she didn't like that.

Couldn't *stand* it.

Or herself, for that matter.

Delaney made herself get out of bed to start the morning of her third shift of a four-day week. She put her focus into getting up and around, on the day ahead booked up with cuts, blowouts, and colors, and didn't look back. She muddled about the apartment, taking a quick, hot shower before getting dressed in white skinny jeans and an oversized black sweater that would prove hard to keep clean throughout the day. After, she moved to food, frying a couple of eggs to eat with buttered, jam-smothered toast. Not that she needed the caffeine, but the cup of coffee she made to go with her breakfast couldn't hurt her overall mood for the day, so she tried to savor that, too.

It was all about the little things.

The sun climbed over the cloudless sky as Delaney washed the handful of dishes she'd made in the sink at the same time her cousin finally started moving around in her room. The two didn't speak when Bexley came out for a glass of water before heading to the bathroom, but that wasn't unusual. Neither were morning people.

The shower started seconds later.

Delaney rifled through her purse on the table, making sure everything from her wallet and keys to the mints she liked to suck on throughout the day were all in order. Not that it made much of a difference because everything went to hell as soon as she tossed the slouchy bag over her shoulder. Still, it gave her something to do.

To focus on.

Instead of the quiet phone that she swore felt like it had eyes where it sat on the table. Or that could have just been her inner bitch begging to pick it up and make one last phone call. One that would get *all* of her feelings out of her chest.

It wouldn't hurt, then.

Distracted by her angry daydreaming, the loud knock on the apartment door made Delaney jerk in surprise. The apartment manager, who lived in the only ground floor apartment of the thirty-one unit building, would never intrude on the tenants so early unless an emergency had come up, but everything seemed quiet. On the other hand, if Bexley had a friend coming over, one of the girls she attended nursing classes with, then she absolutely would have told Delaney as much.

No one should be knocking on their door at a little past six in the morning. The second set of knocks banged louder than the first, and couldn't be mistaken that it was, in fact, their door. Delaney blamed her confusion on who it could be, and the time, for the reason why she immediately yanked the door open instead of checking the peephole first.

A stupid move.

She lived in the city long enough to know better.

Nonetheless, it wasn't something—or someone—bad waiting on the other side of the apartment door.

Mostly.

"Lucas?" Delaney asked, his name coming out of her mouth like a question because she couldn't make sense of his image standing there.

No matter how hard she tried.

He wore the same jacket from his last visit, but the red scarf looped loosely around his neck was new. More interesting was the way his gaze avoided hers to survey the framing around the open doorway while his hand raked over his mouth and down the new scuff on his jaw.

He'd been clean shaved last week.

And every time she saw him before.

Like his hair, his face never looked unkempt. As if the slightest bit of facial hair or more length to his style gave off the impression that he might be lazy.

"I, uh …" He trailed off, his hand dropping to his side as he forced his gaze upwards to meet Delaney's hurt, wary stare looking back at him. "I'm sorry—this is a stupid fucking time to knock on somebody's door, isn't it?"

She blinked, but a nervous bubble of laughter burst out of her chest. Somehow. Even though she tried to stop it. "Yeah, it kind of is."

Lucas offered a small smile.

It *wasn't* true, and it didn't reach his eyes.

Hell, it fell as soon as it started.

"What's wrong?" Delaney asked.

She saw it in the dark sadness behind his eyes; not to mention, the dark circles underneath and how it seemed to take him effort to even lift his eyelids. When was the last time this man slept? The invisible heaviness weighing his strong shoulders forward radiated around him in the empty hallway.

He raked a hand through the short crop of his hair, and a visible tremble raced across his fingers before he hid the shaking by shoving both fists into his pockets.

"I called," she said when he remained silent, her words gaining his pained stare again. "You didn't call back."

"Ah, yeah," he breathed, a choppy, exhausted laugh falling flat between them. "Sorry about that. My phone, it uh … fell into some water. Nola's been trying to keep up on my voicemail. And I hadn't exactly mentioned you to her, so she may have passed over a message you left. She just got the new phone for me this morning before I headed out. I haven't even bothered to turn it on properly yet."

"Nola?"

He closed his eyes, and his brow pinched. "Sorry, that's my, ah …" A sigh rattled out of Lucas before he muttered, "She's my secretary and assistant."

The way he struggled for his words confirmed Delaney's suspicions that he had not been sleeping, and something *was* very wrong.

"Lucas, can I call someone for—"

"No," he interjected fast.

"Then, why are you here?"

"Maybe I shouldn't be?" he asked back. "I honestly wasn't even planning to leave the airport when we stopped to fuel, but …"

He left the sentence hanging, unfinished.

She couldn't figure the puzzle out.

"I'm paying the taxi by the minute, anyway," Lucas added. "He won't care how long I stand in here, right?"

Delaney, unsure of the stormy waters she had waded into by opening the apartment door, couldn't come up with something appropriate to say. He took her silence as a different kind of answer.

"I'm sorry," he said for what felt like the millionth time. His left foot moved back a step, and he turned to the side, adding, "I should go. I thought … I had a stupid idea, but really, I'm just tired, and I know you're working today. Last shift, you said?"

She didn't know what to deal with first.

That he planned to *leave*.

His incorrect assumption about her schedule.

"What idea?" she settled on asking.

Lucas hesitated in the hallway, but he didn't turn to face her completely when he said, "I never really got an answer about your aversion, or not, to flying."

"I've never been on a plane, actually."

An almost desperate chuckle escaped Lucas, then.

"Shit, I bet a helicopter is way out of the question, huh?"

What?

"Are you sure you're okay?" she asked, not able to make sense of his rambles.

"No," he said simply, his gaze shooting upward to zone in on the hallway ceiling. "No, I'm not."

"Okay, so I *should* call someone for you."

And she would, as soon as she got a person, or number, out of him. Worst case, she could take him to a hospital ER, if things turned tricky.

Delaney didn't want to get ahead of herself, though.

"You weren't coming back to Freddy until the end of the month, right?" Delaney asked.

That was one of the reasons the two of them had so much trouble trying to come up with a day and time that would work to get together again. Her schedule didn't help things in that regard, either.

"Plans changed," Lucas said under his breath, looking back at her with those haunted eyes and his heavy shoulders. "Everything changed."

"Could—"

"Delaney, is everything okay?" came the question from her cousin, deeper inside the apartment.

Delaney didn't turn around to acknowledge Bexley. In fact, she hadn't even heard her cousin leave the bathroom or turn off the shower. The man in the hallway took every ounce of her attention and held on for dear life.

Something was wrong.

She wouldn't let him go.

"Everything is fine," Delaney said over her shoulder, forcing herself to meet Bexley's stare where she lingered near the kitchen. "Give me a minute?"

Her cousin wrapped the fluffy housecoat tighter around her sprite-like frame. "Yeah, sure."

It took Bexley more than a handful of seconds to actually make her exit from view. Back in the hallway, Lucas' expression turned pained as he squeezed the bridge of his nose with still shaking fingers.

"Let me know how I can help you right now," Delaney said.

Lucas exhaled harshly. "I was trying to do that when I came here, help myself, I mean, but now I'm wondering if I didn't think it through."

He laughed a hollow sound.

It hurt Delaney's heart.

"You didn't actually tell me why you showed up here," she pointed out. "Starting there might help."

It certainly couldn't hurt.

"Would you do something crazy?"

His question had her brow dipping low. "*Crazy?*"

"Foolish, maybe," he muttered. "That might be the better word."

"Foolish," she echoed.

"I'm taking a few days, just a handful, away," Lucas explained.

Although, not well.

"Where?" Delaney asked.

"I own a hurting camp—a little place." He shook his head, but something wistful flashed across his features all the same. "We spent weekends there with our grandfather."

"We?"

"My brother and I," he clarified, but otherwise, offered nothing more about his brother.

"Oh. Nearby?"

It was possible.

The entire Saint John River traveled for what seemed like forever along and through small rural communities with no end in sight. Surrounded by kilometers upon kilometers of raw land and farmers' fields that rolled up and down for days along the peninsula. There were lots of spots outside of Fredericton where someone could keep a hunting camp deep in the woods without the barest hint of civilization.

Lucas shook his head. "Further upriver. Birch Ridge. You probably never heard of it."

"I have. I do know it, actually," Delaney replied. "My friend, Gracen, likes to hike. Maggie's Falls is a great trek and a good pay off, so it's one of her favorite spots."

And only an hour and half drive from Delaney's hometown. She didn't mention that, or how close the location was to her friend's home on The Flats.

Lucas nodded absentmindedly, but his hard swallow was audible to her ears. "Yeah, so, that's where I'm headed. It'll be the longest I've been in the air in the helicopter, but—"

"You're flying there?"

"Yeah. As long as he's got enough clearance and flat land, Millard can drop the chopper."

All of the sudden, Delaney understood one part of the puzzle that she had been missing in this strange conversation between them.

"That's why you asked me if I would fly? You wanted to ask me to go there with you?"

Lucas' gaze swept over her once more—studying the clothes she'd put on to spend her work day, and even the high pony keeping her natural waves out of her face. "I did say it was foolish. I told you that."

Right.

She had work.

They didn't really know one another.

Not *well*.

Would they even have a way out of the hunting camp once the helicopter was gone? She didn't assume it, and the pilot, would stay.

"Well, I planned to fly you to Saint John for the weekend," he muttered like an afterthought. "That's why I asked the first time."

Huh.

Except ...

"Something changed," she filled in.

Lucas nodded once.

"Will you tell me what it was?" Delaney asked.

"I will."

"But—"

"Delaney, are you gonna drop me off this morning?" Bexley

asked, making a reappearance in the kitchen once more. "It looks kind of cold outside."

Fuck.

Her cousin could walk to uni—that's how close campus was to their apartment. Her intrusion felt more like a check on the situation between Delaney and Lucas rather than an actual question about a ride in the Jeep.

Lucas, never acting like Bexley's presence concerned him, told Delaney, "I will tell you. I'm just trying to make sense of it myself, right now. I gotta keep it together long enough for me to do that where nobody else can see. That's all."

His words said a lot.

His eyes said more.

There, he begged for somebody.

For *something.*

He looked empty and lost; a part of her, deep in her gut, recognized that bleeding heart he tried to hide on his sleeve and the wild stare ready to bolt. That was a dark place to be, stuck inside the hell of your own mind. Yes, she knew that look and the place he found himself. Because more often than not, those same demons looked back in her reflection every single day.

It was hard to run from pain that came from within.

That never stopped a human heart from trying, though.

"Delaney?" Bexley asked again, saying her name more forcefully the second time around.

She still didn't answer.

Beyond the door, still watching her, Lucas asked, "Would you do something crazy—will you go with me?"

His soul screamed silently in that empty hallway.

Hers heard and answered back.

"What should I pack in a bag?" she asked.

16.

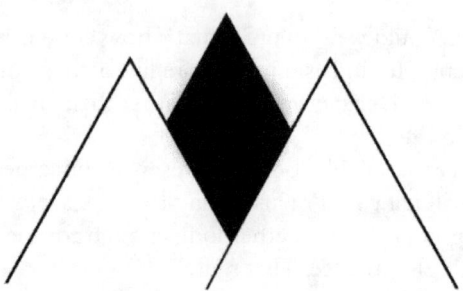

"You're not seriously considering this, Delaney. You don't even know that man—you've gone on a single date with him! He could be dangerous."

Bexley's last warnings to Delaney as she'd packed the warmer items of clothing Lucas had suggested she bring still rang in the back of her mind as the chopper held steady high above the Saint John River. Her cousin's words didn't linger because she thought Bexley made a fair point—her cousin knew Lucas even less than Delaney did, so who was she to suggest a man who showed up on their doorstep looking broken had any ill intentions?

No, it was the last thing Bexley said.

Her parting words.

"I'm calling Gracen."

Yet another person in Delaney's life who didn't need to worry about the choices she made, but Bexley tossed the comment out like a threat. As if telling Gracen of Delaney's unexpected—and perhaps, slightly foolish—plans would stop her at all.

It didn't.

Here they were.

High in the sky.

Despite the cab of the helicopter being heated, the pilot, who introduced himself as only Millard, unpacked two heavy quilts with thick fleece lining for his passengers to use. Just behind the man who kept the helicopter safely traveling upriver, occasionally pointing out the many dams and small rural communities on the way through the headset comms each person wore, Delaney and Lucas sat strapped into seats with only a foot of space between them.

He saw her shiver once and doubled up his own quilt before

adding it on top of the heavy weight of hers. Her argument for him to keep it, or even share, fell on deaf ears of the man who pretended like he couldn't hear her over the chopper's noise and the downward pressure making their voices an echo in the comms.

He could hear her, though.

She knew it.

Delaney had expected a bumpier ride, but other than the initial lift off that sent her stomach jumping into her throat, the first hour and a half had gone by smoothly. The view, and Lucas' warm hand holding hers under the quilt resting against her jean-clad thigh, certainly gave her something else to focus on other than the scariness of a new experience.

Really, it wasn't that scary at all.

Just ... *different.*

Delaney started to recognize the shape of the forested mountains on the horizon, and the large bridge connecting one side of a familiar town to the other, before the man heading the chopper did. Her fingers tightened around Lucas' when the chopper started to climb higher. Something it had done before during the flight.

He'd felt her squeeze; his gaze turned on her.

"You see that first range, the small one there," Millard noted from the front as he lifted a hand to point out the lower mountain in question compared to the ones further behind. "That's—"

"Montgomery Mountain," Delaney said, her voice a crackle to her own ears in the comms.

Millard glanced back with a grin. "That it is, Miss Reed."

She was more focused on the town they currently approached from up above. Not once had Delaney been able to make it this close to home without falling into some kind of panic-induced fit. She still felt the tension, of course, tightening her shoulders and vibrating through her body as her gaze instinctively searched the ground for the hole in the landscape of a town where she'd put so much of herself, her life, and love ...

In the seat next to hers, she heard Lucas mutter, "Hey."

Through the comms.

She kept looking down from the windows, searching for that blank spot in the canvas of her previous life. It took her far too long to finally pinpoint why she continued overlooking the place where their salon had once stood.

It had been turned into a parking lot, it seemed. For the lawyer's office next door, apparently. The high snowbanks pushed against the far end of the lot and the handful of cars parked in various spots made it difficult to picture what the salon must have looked like from the sky back before it burnt to the ground.

Maybe it was the new perspective, being so high, but she found it easier to swallow the many changes—and familiar sights—of her beloved valley town. Cars crossed the bridge connecting the main streets as they always did. The thick sheet of ice blanketing the river had tracks from one side to the other where everything from skidoos to people used to make the trek.

Still tiny.

Sleepy.

Only a little had changed.

"Delaney?" Lucas asked. "Are you okay?"

He shouldn't be asking her that. Not when his eyes were still a pool of sadness and pain that he had yet to explain. Yet, his stare leveled on her where they sat side by side in the back of the chopper, and she could only shrug.

"This is my hometown," she explained.

Not loudly.

The soft curve of his smile told her that he had heard what she said, nonetheless. His hand flexed around hers, a silent confirmation that he had taken in the information, before his profile swung the other way so he could take another look at the quiet town down below.

The place that made her.

And hurt her along the way, too.

"Another thirty minutes, maybe?" Millard asked at the front. "How are you doing back there, boss?"

At the question, Lucas grunted some form of a reply, and waved a hand. Millard, satisfied, looked ahead at the horizon and the rolling hills of mountainous tree-topped terrain they still had to cross.

"Hell of a trip," the pilot noted in the comms. "A beautiful day for this, huh?"

It really was.

Delaney had never fully realized or appreciated the vastness and raw beauty of her home province quite like she did in that moment as the chopper cut through the sky. There was nothing quite like it.

*

Even though Lucas had said the pilot could land the chopper just about anywhere as long as he had flat ground, she didn't actually understand that he meant it. Quite literally. Millard used a field of juvenile fur trees that seemed to stretch on for miles with a patch cleared that connected a snowy trail to the main road to drop the helicopter down.

By far, the freakiest part of the whole flight.

She had been way too distracted by the landing chopper and praying that the snow-covered ground below looked as flat as it seemed, to pay attention to the surrounding area. She thought she knew Birch Ridge quite well. A rural trek deep in the peninsula covered in thick, dense forest with few inhabitants and quite a ways from any main towns. At some point in the Ridge, the telephone poles even stopped lining the roads and the government plows didn't clear the snow or even sand.

Were they that far out?

She couldn't tell.

In the summer, or any warmer months, the place could be a haven of nature away from the normality people found in their communities. Rolling fields for as far as the eye could see allowed ATVs to go full tilt for kilometers on end.

She only saw white.

Snow-covered trees and glistening, icy fields for days.

Blustering billows from the chopper's spinning blades didn't help.

Millard kept the machine running, proclaiming the engine would run better hot as he directed the passengers in the back to remove their headsets. A clue it was time for Delaney to shed the quilt, unbuckle from the five-point harness keeping her safely in her seat, and help with the couple of bags loaded into the back.

"You called ahead to get things sorted, eh?" Millard asked, flicking switches at the front while Lucas unbuckled himself.

"I left a message," Lucas replied. "The Smith boys keep the gas changed out so it doesn't go sour throughout the year. If they didn't get up here by now, they will. I'm not concerned. All we need is a fire tonight."

"Ah, well—I thought I saw a tuft or two of smoke coming

from the gully," Millard said. "Maybe one of the boys did get down to the camp, huh?"

"Let's hope."

"The Smith boys?" Delaney asked.

Lucas clapped a hand over her quilt-covered thigh. "Friends in the area. They keep an eye on the cabin, check the well so nothing freezes up, and makes sure no one's stopped in to make a mess when someone isn't around."

Huh.

"And the gas is for what, exactly?"

"The old truck," Lucas replied. "And the generators, too."

Of course.

She had her answer about just how far out in the country they were at that statement. If someone needed generators, there wouldn't be power lines.

"There *is* running water and indoor plumbing, right?" Delaney questioned.

He did mention a well, but ...

"Sure. Once I get the gen-set up and running," Lucas returned, chuckling. Delaney just unlatched the harness at her chest when Lucas stepped past her to open the side door, saying, "Bundle up, sweets. We've got a little walk from here."

What?

He had told her to wear a warm pair of boots. Her wide-eyed expression caused him to laugh. The sound lit up the cabin of the chopper despite the noise, and for a brief second, his features, too. She welcomed the sight considering their entire flight had been spent with him in a somber silence that prickled at the sore spots on her heart.

"Not far," Lucas assured. "I promise."

"How far is not far?"

"Depends on how well you can wade snow."

Delaney blinked, laughing at the absurdity in his statement. "Are you serious?"

He shrugged. "The hard work is at the camp, anyway."

She had no clue what he meant.

Delaney didn't dare ask, either. Any regrets or concerns she had about this trip were too little, too late. The cold blast of air that brought wind and spiraling snowflakes into the cab of the chopper when Lucas pushed open the door told her as much.

"Quick is best," he called over his shoulder. "Keeps the blood moving."

Right.

She could tell.

The only thing Delaney cared about now?

Getting *warm.*

*

There was nothing quite like minus-twenty degree cold to make a person re-evaluate every life decision that brought them to a singular moment in time. Despite thick mittens, a fleece-lined parka with the hood pulled up, and a fifteen-minute trek that took the two out of the tree field and down the road, Delaney's fingers still felt numb at the tips by the time they reached the private drive for the hunting cabin. The driveway only stood out against the backdrop of dense trees because it was the only hole in them along the road.

Someone *had* cleared the snow.

Or rather, the tracks of a snowmobile led them down a trail of packed snow under the cover of tree branches that criss-crossed over their heads like a snowy canopy. No wonder she hadn't been able to find the cabin from the sky.

Could it even be located from above?

"Here, give me that," Lucas said, snagging the overnight duffle Delaney had packed for herself and adding it to his own shoulder load of two bags. He nodded ahead at the snow-crusted path and the trail that didn't look like it widened or opened to anything in the twenty feet or so ahead that she could see. Besides the cracking and flutters of a frozen forest, only their shoes made noise crunching along as they walked. "Go on—get warm."

"I'm good," she assured.

A lie he could surely tell.

Her words came out on a puff of breath that made a cloud between their two faces. Her fingertips might have been numb from the cold, but the rest of her shook like a leaf in the wind. Some Canadians liked to say that cold was just a state of mind during winter in Canada as the more brutal temperatures settled in, but in that case, so was hypothermia.

Nobody came back from that.

Lucas gave her a look. "*Go*. We both don't need to be fucking icicles out here before we even get to the cabin. I'll be two minutes behind, max. It's not that far. There's a little hill, you'll see it around the bottom bend. The cabin's just beyond it. Somebody's been down here today. I bet one of the boys made a fire that's probably still got some hot coals."

That word never brought out happy or content feelings and reactions from Delaney, but in that moment, all she heard was warmth. The promise of it, mostly. Just the idea of heat seeped into her veins to thaw out the chill that had settled deep into her body during the walk down from the road.

She couldn't refuse.

Not considering the circumstances.

"All right," she muttered. "Don't freeze without me?"

Lucas rumbled with one of his husky laughs, but his dark gaze had yet to lose the tired sadness shining from within. The emotions, pained and heavy, still radiated from him like a cloud he couldn't escape, and her closeness meant she couldn't help but feel it, too.

"Sweets, don't worry about me. I'm fine."

Which one of us is lying now, she thought, but better yet, *how did he do it so easily?*

Delaney saved that question for later and pinned it in the back of her mind. For when her teeth didn't chatter on every word, of course.

*

Considering the location, Delaney wasn't sure what to expect of the hunting cabin, but the quaint cottage, positioned side by side with a similarly sized shed that had large double doors, took her by surprise. Pleasantly.

She passed the electricity wires connected between the shed and cottage a look, taking a safe guess where she could locate the generators and truck Lucas mentioned, before she took the three wooden steps leading up to the brown wooden front door. She found it unlocked when she tried the door and could almost feel the heat seeping through the thick wood. She gave the covered veranda—that seemed to wrap around the entire building—painted the same brown as the door, one more look before heading inside.

Someone had started a fire.

She shut out the cold as soon as her boots hit the hardwood floor of the cottage. What was to find and see inside the small cabin welcomed Delaney the moment she stepped inside. A kitchen with limited counter space from a single island that doubled as a table if the stools along the side were any indication. Natural stained, oak cupboards made up a pantry framing the stove and oven with only one burner on top and a tiny bar fridge off to the side sat open, and off, in the side corner. The sink basin, larger than even the stove, took up all the space beneath the window overlooking the front property that currently appeared to be a winter wonderland of beauty.

From the safety of the warmth inside, obviously.

The power and amazement of winter could actually be appreciated when one could hear their thoughts between constant shivers and mind-numbing cold.

An open-concept layout welcomed guests to the largest section of rooms with the kitchen first. Beyond that, and the ticking wood chief currently pumping out all the heat sat in the very middle between the rooms, blocked up on a circle of red bricks with a black pipe jutting up from the stove and through the ceiling to the roof outside where the smoke left the chimney in tendrils.

A stairwell, with a smooth, stained railing led up to a loft that couldn't be properly viewed from downstairs, but that she could make out the legs of what appeared to be twin beds. Just beyond the stairs and using the back end of the stairwell as an enclave entry for the sitting room, sat an old couch that looked comfortable and two worn recliner chairs facing a rear bay window that peered into the quiet, cold forest.

The wood paneled walls greeted Delaney with picture frames filled with images of a young boy, and a man she knew on sight. The similar features in their smiling faces reflected one another and didn't escape her notice, but also remained the same in the age progression in the many photographs filling the walls as she moved from one side of the cottage to the other.

One, in particular, had the younger boy holding a large trout while a gentleman behind him, who she didn't recognize but shared the same smile and cleft chin, stood behind him in shorts and a polo. He'd smiled for the shot with a hand on the boy's shoulder.

A younger Lucas kneeled in the background of the photo,

clutching to fishing rods and smiling like he hadn't expected the picture.

A lot of the photographs had a similar theme—woods, nature, and the great outdoors. Not to mention, the *people* within the photos remained the same, with only a few different guests between the many framed shots, mostly candids, that appeared to span years.

Lucas' family?

The age gap between Lucas and the boy in the photos made her question who he could be, if only because her mind didn't go straight to a sibling at first. That *was* possible, though. Was the younger boy his br—

"See, not so bad inside," Lucas muttered as he lumbered into the cottage, bringing the cold air with him. He slammed the front door shut, scuffed his snow-dusted boots off on the entry rug of faded, woven colors, and dropped their bags just beyond the danger of any melting ice they bought in with their travels. His gaze found her across the cozy cottage where she stood haloed in the afternoon light spilling in the rear window. "I guess the Smith boys got my call after all."

"Good thing, huh?"

Lucas let out a hard breath, nodding as his stare drifted around the place he had tried to call a hunting cabin. "In my head, it's always bigger. Like when I was a kid."

Delaney smiled, hearing the memories he held back. "I could see how you could really be just a kid, way out here."

He cleared his throat, and his wistful grin wobbled for a split second. Not lingering on whatever pain he'd felt, Lucas pulled the gloves from his hands and nodded toward the kitchen. "Did you check the stove?"

"Why would I?"

"*You* wouldn't." Lucas winked. "The Smith boys, their mom— well, she always sends something to get us through the first night before we can drive into Arthurette for whatever we need."

"I've never actually been inside that store," Delaney said as Lucas made a beeline for the stove.

A good twenty-minute drive out of the deep, quiet Birch Ridge sat a small county of a couple hundred residents that called Arthurette home. Located between a desolate stretch of raw, rural New Brunswick that connected The Flats where her friend called home, and the nearby town of Plaster Rock, it had exactly one general store that doubled as a gas station.

For people making the long trek from one side of the mountains to the other, and needed to stop for gas, of course. Or a pack of smokes.

"You haven't missed much," he said, grabbing hold of the oven's handle. "We may need to take the truck into town."

She had yet to even see the truck.

Her disinterest in the chilly outdoors kept her from asking important questions about the vehicle—like if it was even licensed or legal to drive. Way the hell out in no man's land, maybe nobody fucking cared.

At the moment, she didn't.

"Aha," Lucas proclaimed, stepping aside to show Delaney what waited inside.

Two, white plastic shopping bags sat on the oven racks, with one filled to the top with containers meant for food storage. Lucas grabbed both, but only one clinked interestingly.

"Liquor?" she asked.

"And food," he told her, pointedly.

Like that was what mattered.

"What does she put in there for you?" Delaney questioned, making a slow trek across the cottage floor.

"Whatever Mack's got on the shelf, usually," he muttered, hefting the bags onto the island.

He pulled out a pint of scotch first.

"Mack?"

"Mack Smith," Lucas said, gesturing broadly at the front of the cottage that faced the hill leading them into the gully. "He owns that half of the Ridge, practically. That lot of fir trees we landed in keeps him going in the winter."

Ah.

"Christmas trees," she said.

"They do sleigh rides and all sorts of things. They make a whole season out of it, anyway," Lucas said, distracted by the second bottle he'd pulled from the bag.

It wasn't liquor.

The amber gold, a sweet favorite for every Canadian's breakfast table, filled the tall glass bottle with a corked and wax-sealed top.

"Maple syrup?" Delaney asked, reaching for the bottle to look at the homemade label on the front.

The *best* kind.

Deadpan, and suddenly frosty, Lucas handed over the bottle without a word before yanking his gloves back out from his parka's pockets. "I've got some things to do on the outside. You'll want light, running water, and a working fridge by tonight, I imagine."

"You okay?"

His back, ramrod straight as it faced her where he stood at the front door, hunched a little. At her question "Yeah, I've just got things to do to get the camp up and going. It won't take me long."

He disappeared into the cold in the next breath. Only the slam of the door and the icy wind that swept across the cottage broke the silence and kept her company once he was gone and only his snowy footprints remained on the rug.

On the one-liter glass bottle filled with maple syrup, a note had been taped to the middle of the label.

For Jacob, it read in neat handwriting. Under that, the person had added, *Hope that'll do him for the year, friend.*

17.

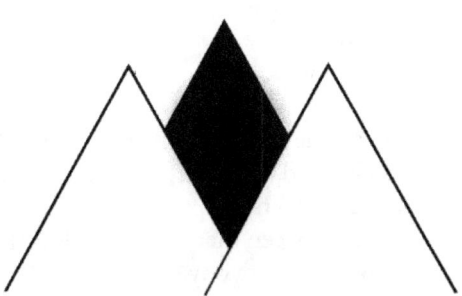

I won't be long.

A lie, and he knew it, the second the words left Lucas' lips. Maybe it wasn't as devastating of a lie as his assurance that he was, in fact, fine, but it just piled his dishonesty higher on the mountain that had become his most recent days.

Pretty soon, that mountain would crumble. Or Lucas might find himself breaking under the massive weight.

Not if he could help it, though. Lucas would hold himself together, by ripped seams, if need be, until he absolutely couldn't anymore.

Life had not taught him how to manage, or keep on, otherwise. He didn't have a choice.

The rural cabin did require quite a bit of set up work upon arrival, so heading outside to get a start on those duties gave him something to do. Getting power running and clean water coming up from the well dug beneath the cellar were easier tasks in the summer when cold and snow wasn't a factor.

One didn't have to concern themselves with clearing the driveway leading out of the gully of snow outside of the winter months. A requirement, really, because the old truck with all season tires that he used to travel in and out of Birch Ridge when needed couldn't get up the hill without a clear path. Which was often why Lucas didn't find himself this deep in New Brunswick's countryside during the harsher times of the year.

More work.

For the moment, he didn't mind it.

Even if his hands ached and shivers kept him jittery as he flipped on the switches for the generators before pulling their start cords to get the gas engines running after filling both with the gas left by one of the Smith boys. He barely considered the cold; his focus stayed on the work of getting the cottage usable and safe to leave, if needed, instead.

He couldn't let his mind wander.

Lucas couldn't go *there* yet.

The two generators, one hooked up to the main lights and the out-building's electricity, and the other, wired directly to the kitchen appliances and submersible pump down in the well, used a good thirty liters of gas between them a day to keep the place livable. By modern standards, anyway.

Given the constant consumption of gas, trips out of Birch Ridge had to be regular. Every other day, or so, during a stay. Hence, the need for a vehicle.

Or, in the unlikely case of an emergency.

Things happened.

His grandfather, who had left the property to Lucas after his death because the Dalton brothers had enjoyed it for years alongside him, had made sure both his grandsons were equipped and capable of maintaining and living in the cabin. Including an education on running and maintaining the generator system, and closing the cottage down, essentially, at the end of any given season.

Dropping the empty gas jug in front of the garage doors he'd pulled close to help with the chill while he readied the generators, Lucas waited as the bare lightbulbs overhead came on one by one. A good sign that at least one of the generators, and wiring, hadn't suffered in the last two years that it had been left to the wayside.

Life got in the way.

Lucas didn't have time.

Jacob … well, he wouldn't have come without his brother.

Sure, the Smith family a few kilometers down the road kept an eye on the place and exchanged out the gas to keep it fresh and usable if the Dalton brothers showed up unexpectedly, but a house was not a home without a heartbeat. A long stretch of time with no movement inside could certainly leave the cabin in disrepair after a while.

He was happy to see things working.

Even if it was bittersweet.

After uncovering the old Chevy truck under the worn painting cloth and adding what remained of the gas from the second jug that had been left in the corner of the building for Lucas to find, he grabbed one of two shovels hanging from a large nail sticking out of the wall. The smaller scoop, easier to push through heavy snow, was his preference.

When clearing snow was required.

Not a job he particularly liked.

Cold hands and feet were a better option than a broken heart and mind, though. So, he kept that knowledge at the forefront of his thoughts as he headed out of the garage and back into the cold to begin the long, hard, and tiring work of clearing the massive driveway.

He didn't care that it would take him hours.

That already, his fingertips and toes were numb.

Lucas would rather shovel snow until his limbs turned black and fell off from frostbite than listen to thoughts in his head, or the memories playing on constant repeat there.

He just needed time.

Anything except—

"Can I do something inside?" came the soft question from his left as he stalked across the drive. Lucas came to a halt, his boots crunching against the snow, and turned to find Delaney where she had come to stand on the front veranda. Her unzipped parka made him think she had come outside as soon as she noticed him leaving the garage. "The lights are working, and I found the linen closet in the bathroom where all the quilts and stuff are packed in totes, so I pulled them out and got some stuff out ... I wondered if there was anything else, that's all."

Right.

Good to know things worked inside, too.

That saved Lucas an extra five minutes.

"It'll take the hot water tank in the cellar a bit of time to fill and warm up," he said, "but otherwise, you could run the water in the bathroom taps for a bit. It cleans out the pipe and gets any shakiness from the ground out of the water as everything settles. Unless you don't mind a bit of dirt at the bottom of your drinking glass."

Delaney's nose, pinked from the cold, scrunched up sweetly. "No, thanks. I'll run the water, then?"

"That'll help."

"How long?"

"Maybe a half hour. You can check, and see what a glass of water looks like, but it should be good," he explained.

History told him a half an hour would do the job to clear any sediments sitting in the well water that the pipe might bring up. Once the water ran clear, nothing tasted better than mountain water pumped from a water vein a hundred feet in the ground.

"Okay, sure," Delaney said with a nod. "I can do that."

Figuring the conversation had come to a natural end with that, Lucas started his trek toward the bend in the driveway that would lead to the hill going up to the road. The fact that he didn't hear the front door of the cottage close behind him should have been a clue.

"What are you doing?"

Lucas came to a stop again and glanced over his shoulder with the shovel held out where she could plainly see. "Clearing snow. Unless you *don't* want to make a trip to town for gas tomorrow. I've got lots of wood piled behind the garage to keep the furnace going, but only so much gas."

And practically no food.

They had to go, really.

Delaney's head bobbed up and down as she hugged her jacket closed and shivered on the step. "Do you want me to help? I can."

On another day, maybe he would have taken her up on that offer. No doubt, she had experience clearing snow or dealing with the weather of their country. Nobody's hands were too soft to shovel snow when a storm rolled through.

"I got it," he said.

"If you're sure ..."

He continued heading for the long work ahead, saying only, "I need to do *something*."

Lucas couldn't just stand there and *think*.

That would kill him.

*

Lucas didn't time himself once he started shoveling at the top of the hill, but if he had to make a safe guess, it took him close to three hours to reach the bottom of the drive again. He couldn't be totally sure, but the movement in the sun told him a significant bit of time had passed, and the growl of his empty stomach suggested it was about to revolt after missing breakfast and lunch.

Hell, did he even eat yesterday?

Lucas couldn't remember.

He'd been struggling with other things.

"They said if the family is insisting on writing the piece for Jacob," his secretary's last message had said on his phone before he boarded the chopper in Freddy with Delaney. *"The Telegraph's editor can give you until Wednesday night at the latest for it to still make the run on Friday, Lucas. Otherwise, they'll run a standard notice."*

Christ.

He still had things to do.

Lucas tried not to think about it.

Even if he was running out of time.

Goddammit.

Hadn't he done so well, too?

His arms ached and protested with the last ten or so shovelfuls of snow that he had left to clear away from the front of the cottage, but he worked through it.

His back hurt like nothing else, as well, but at least the pain gave him something to keep his mind on instead of trying to process the unimaginable pain building there. Even if that same pain had started to bleed into the rest of his nervous system because he could no longer pretend like it didn't exist.

It was real.

Worst of all?

He couldn't change a thing.

No one got to rewrite the past.

In his boots and thick ski gloves, the cold had eventually seeped through the fabric to leave his appendages numb and tingly with every shift and movement of his body. The nice thing about physical labor in the winter was that it kept the body warm as long as the person continued moving.

So, he did.

Until he felt every step rattling his spine, and each breath he pulled into his lungs worked to cool his internal temperature down so that he didn't sweat himself into a fever by the time he did finish the job.

Maybe it was the quiet stillness of the land around him, or the sprinkle of snowflakes dancing down from the sky as he finished shoveling, but he put his guard down. Not a lot. Just enough that the wall, keeping him shielded from the painful new reality he faced, crumbled.

The torrent of memories rushed in.

A happy kid.

His little brother.

The man Jacob could have been—the one his older brother knew he had desperately wanted to be. He'd tried ... nobody could ever say that Jacob didn't at least *try*.

"*Fuck,*" Lucas uttered, the harsh cuss following his hard stab of the shovel into the snowbank where it stuck straight up without his help.

Good.

It could stay there, too.

Lucas rubbed his gloved hand against his forehead, willing the thoughts in his mind away, so that he could cling onto the comfortable, safe pretenses in his mind that allowed him to keep it together. He didn't need to haul any wood from behind the garage when a tinderbox sat on the porch full, and God above knew his back could use the break for the night, but he made the long trek around the back through the snow, anyway.

For something to do.

He *had* to keep moving.

Or else—

"She sent turkey, potatoes, and some other veggies—cupcakes, too," Delaney called from the crack she had opened in the front door as Lucas hauled an armload of wood from the back of the garage. "I warmed it up. Come eat."

Was she still watching him from inside?

Could she feel how he was dying inside?

Lucas didn't get the chance to ask before Delaney closed the front door, making it clear that she hadn't warmed the food to suggest he eat. That's what she expected him to do. He couldn't imagine sitting down to eat when all he really wanted to do was scream.

Because he hurt.

Life never promised to be fair.

Did it have to be cruel, too?

A crater had formed where his heart should be inside his chest. Cracked open, bleeding, and deep, every breath made him more and more aware of the pain.

Was it finally time?

Lucas stood, frozen, only a few steps away from the cottage with an armful of wood and alone, as he stared at the door and tried to answer that question.

Is it time, Lucas?

The doctor had asked him that question, too. Late Monday evening in a dimly lit hospital room while his brother lay prone in a bed with a tube down his throat and machine keeping his organs working. Nothing worked because Lucas had been too late, and Jacob was already turning blue around the lips by the time his brother pulled him up off the bathroom floor.

The needle that did the job had splintered to pieces under Lucas' shoes as he tried to keep from slipping in the water falling from an overflowing tub. Never letting go of his little brother while he had desperately dialed 9-1-1.

"*I think it is time,*" the doctor had said in the end, making Lucas finally listen. Nobody seemed to care that he didn't want to.

Was it time?

Was it, *really?*

In the end, it didn't matter.

Lucas didn't get a say.

Jacob took the choice away.

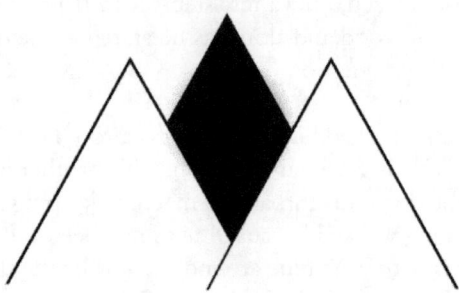

18

The cabin welcomed Lucas inside to the quiet heat that instantly wrapped around his broad shoulders like a hug as he shed his outdoor clothes. "Jesus, it's cold. My fingers are icicles."

The tips of his fingers throbbed with sharp pain as the warmth started to seep into his frozen skin.

Delaney, flipping through an old magazine next to a plate of warmed up leftovers, didn't glance up from the glossy pages resting on the kitchen island. She sat cross-legged, quite a sight in painted-on white skinny jeans that accentuated her hips and legs in the best ways, on one of four stools rounding the makeshift table and countertop that helped save space.

"Two hours in twenty-below weather will do that to you."

"It's definitely closer to thirty," Lucas returned. "Only two?"

She peeked over at him, then, and the corner of her lips lifted into a half smile. "Yeah, a little more. Did it feel longer?"

Lucas had been positive it was, actually.

What did it matter, now?

Delaney nodded across the cabin toward the sitting room. "I put your plate on the coffee table."

"I could eat out here with you," he said, toeing off the boots that, in his opinion, would not work for up to below forty-degree weather. They barely survived the temperature outside. At least, he was smart enough to put on a thicker pair of thermal socks that morning.

Lucas used *some* forethought.

Where it counted.

"But do you *want* to?" Delaney asked. "That was the question I asked myself, and I think we both know the answer. You look like you want to be alone."

Lucas tried not to take her comment to heart, but that was easier said than done. They hadn't even been at the cabin for a day, and already, he gave her the impression that she wasn't wanted. The furthest thing from the truth.

Lucas moved closer to the wood stove in the middle of the floor, keeping his back to Delaney as he mulled over his thoughts and warmed his hands over the iron top where a kettle sat full of simmering water. "Would you eat in there with me?"

"Of course."

The stool scraped against the floor the instant those words left Delaney's lips. She passed him by at the stove with her plate of food balanced in her hand on top of the magazine. He snagged her wrist in his grasp a second before it was too late.

"I asked you to come here with me because I didn't want to be alone, actually," he told her.

Delaney nodded. "I didn't think I upset you earlier, but—"

"You didn't."

"Okay, good to know."

"I'm sorry if you felt that way," Lucas said, wanting to explain his sometimes loner-like nature. It wasn't always a choice when it felt like a requirement for his mental health, more often than not. "It may come as a surprise to you, as we haven't known each other long, and you don't have an inside look at my personal life, but I live a very solitary one. I have a handful of people I consider friends, but whom I don't spend a great deal of time with because my days are entirely wrapped up in work. I care about people deeply, more than I should, I'm told—but it's hard to see that in between putting on the suit and tie for work and the scant handful of hours I have at night before I close my eyes. I can only give so much; that doesn't change the fact that I also need to take time just for me."

He released her wrist as Delaney asked, "You can't be all alone, all the time, right? Don't you have some family ... your brother, maybe?"

Her gaze darted to the wall closest to them, and the many photographs in a collection of different picture frames he, Jacob, and even their grandfather, at times, had picked up at yard sales in the area over the many summers. It seemed she must have caught onto the likeness between the siblings in the photos and made a safe assumption about the relation between Lucas and Jacob.

The dull ache in his heart didn't let up.

It even hurt to think of his brother's name.

How long would that last?

"You didn't mention your parents, either," she noted softly.

No, he hadn't.

Not now.

Not on their first date.

Never—that would be Lucas' ultimate preference. He never wanted to talk about Ronald and Penelope Dalton if he could help it. The nuances and complexities of his strained—fractured, really—bonds with the people who created him made them feel unimportant to what he was doing here. At least, where Delaney was concerned.

She didn't need to be affected by the toxicity of people who would likely care nothing for her existence, other than how it related to him.

"We're not close," he settled on saying.

"Oh," she whispered. "Sorry. I'm not really close to my parents, either. Although, to be fair, I desperately wanted to be. I wanted them to love me and tried to do what I could to make that happen, but it never worked out for us in the end. My mother and father's love came with conditions I couldn't meet, and so, they made it clear in a lot of hurtful ways that they would have nothing to do with me."

Lucas chuckled from the irony of the fact that she, too, had a difficult relationship with her parents while he nervously scratched a spot over his eyebrow. "An interesting pair we make, eh?"

"As long as it's not a sad pair," Delaney joked with a grin.

Ah, shit.

Well …

"Give it a minute," he muttered.

That melted her happiness away in an instant. "I'm sorry?"

Not yet, Lucas.

Shouldn't they eat, at least?

"Let's sit down and get some grub before it goes cold, huh?" he asked, gesturing toward the sitting area.

The press of his hand against the small of Delaney's back kept her from asking questions as he guided them into the small room that also connected to the cabin's tiny bathroom off to the side.

The cabinets meant for storing bedding, and the stackable washer and dryer, took up most of the space in the bathroom while a toilet facing a pedestal sink and a standing shower in the corner made up the main facilities. In order to use the washer and dryer, however, one had to redirect the power supply from the appliances in the kitchen to the bathroom through the wiring in the cellar panel by flicking a switch.

There wasn't a lot to see.

The place wasn't fancy.

It did the job, though, and for the moment, the cabin out in the middle of buttfuck nowhere served the purpose Lucas needed. To be away from the city where he couldn't take the time to privately process and accept what had happened to Jacob because there, his life was so intrinsically woven into work and his dysfunctional family.

Here, he didn't have that.

Just memories of his brother.

The peace of nature.

And a woman with a kind smile, Lucas thought to himself as he took a seat on one of two recliners.

Delaney sat across from him on the couch and pointed at the plate next to his on the coffee table with two chocolate frosted cupcakes. "I hope you plan on sharing dessert with me, by the way."

"Shelly did send two," he noted of Mack Smith's wife.

His joke, and tone, fell flat.

Delaney didn't miss it. "Whatever it is, I hear it in your voice."

"I know," he murmured. "I do, too."

Worse yet, he had to feel it.

All that grief, it compounded, grew like weeds full of thorns in his chest from his heart, and now seemed as if it would swallow him whole.

A never-ending, inescapable prison.

He did his best to stuff the sorrow down, reaching for the plate and utensils Delaney had placed on a napkin for him to use. "Let's eat, yeah? I'm starved."

He welcomed her responding silence, and the comfortable quiet that followed as the two dug into the reheated food the neighbor had been kind enough to send. It wasn't lost on him that, other than his secretary who also handled his assistant duties, had been the only person in his life that knew the truth of what happened Monday morning.

He didn't tell his pilot.

Or the neighbors who probably suspected Jacob had come along with Lucas for the trip as he usually did.

Not even his family doctor when he requested an official written order for time off work to handle an emergency family matter. Even if that note hadn't been technically needed, sending it into the brewery would make it clear to at least one person that Lucas was unavailable and unreachable for an undetermined amount of time.

Ronald, that was.

No excuses.

Unfortunately, soon, everyone *would* know. Once the newspaper ran Jacob's obituary, whether Lucas wrote it himself or not, on Friday—everyone across the province would see the news.

Jacob Dalton, youngest son of the Dalton brewery dynasty, was dead at twenty-five.

Lucas could already see the headline; his father's complaints about family matters and privacy, and other shit that didn't matter, were distant echoes in the back of his head. Hell, he didn't even know if someone let Penelope know her youngest child was dead or not. Someone eventually would.

Frankly, at this point, Lucas didn't care.

His parents hadn't come to the hospital when calls were made. *He* was the one who remained steadfast at Jacob's bedside, angry and confused as he poured through weeks and then months of his brother's public social media profiles in an effort to explain the clear signs he must have missed.

People didn't just *fall* right back into addiction.

Lucas had tried to prove that to himself by staring for hours into the glowing screen of his phone while he combed Jacob's timelines of posted photos made up of animals he handled at the rescue, gym shots, and candid ones with friends at college.

Nothing had stood out.

Or so Lucas thought, then.

"He'd started to wear a lot of sunglasses, and long sleeve shirts when he worked out," Lucas said, his shitty attempt to bring Delaney into the conversation that was his thoughts.

"Hmm?" she asked around a bite.

"My brother—Jacob," he clarified. "He's ten years younger than me."

Was, he corrected internally.

Lucas let out a breath that shook on the way out, and placed his half-eaten plate back on the coffee table so he could just get through his moment. "We had a big gap in age, so I always felt like I had to look after him. It couldn't be just brother to brother. I had to be more because he didn't have anybody else being that male figure in his life. I guess that took up a lot of my teenage years and even becoming a young man … I ended up being my brother's second father. Basically."

Delaney, still chewing, glanced at the wall of pictures like she wanted to put the face to the name again that he spoke of. Lucas didn't have to look around to remember or know Jacob's face. He'd die with his brother's memory permanently scarred into the back of his brain, now.

"Having me didn't really change what he knew he didn't have, though," Lucas added after a pause. "It didn't change how the lack of attention and basic needs a parent should provide to their child wasn't really offered to Jacob by our mother or father. Oh, he had what he needed in a physical way, sure."

Until he didn't, and Lucas had needed to fill in where Jacob's life lacked there, as well, but that was a conversation for a different day.

"Maybe you'd understand," Lucas said to Delaney, "seeing as how you felt love from your parents was a conditional thing."

Her mouth free of food, Delaney asked, "What do you mean?"

"If you weren't meeting the conditions, I suspect you didn't have their love, right?"

"In a way. Or, the love they offered was really just abuse that they said was needed to correct or fix what was wrong with me."

Lucas nodded, but the idea made him angry. A lot like Jacob had once felt as a kid whose parents couldn't be bothered to even eat with him at the dinner table, but had no problem making sure his private tuition for school was paid so they wouldn't have to see his face five days out of the week.

"Well, my brother never had any love at all," Lucas said, shrugging. "It took me a while to figure out that was why he had so many insecurities as a young man. Why he felt like he wasn't good enough or had to work harder than everybody else. He was overlooked and worthless to his own parents, and that made him think that's just how love was. And for a long time, he believed that. So he found the only kind of love he really knew in a lot of bad places with not-so-great people."

Lucas glanced down to where his hands wrung together forcefully enough that three of his knuckles crackled. "Who didn't always do the best of things. He told me once it started with Xanax bars at parties because he couldn't stand alcohol—our mother is an alcoholic."

He shrugged, chuffing under his breath before adding, "No matter what I did, I couldn't make him see that just because a doctor wrote the prescription didn't make it okay."

Of course, Jacob's struggles were an easy excuse for their parents—separated by then—to throw under the bus as the reason for their distance from their youngest son later on. As if the first half of Jacob's life had never existed in the first place which certainly led him down his chosen path, in one way or another.

Lucas didn't have to search hard for the reasons why he couldn't even stand the sight of his parents. He had a whole goddamn list.

"Hurt people aren't really great at making good choices," Delaney said, drawing Lucas' attention back to her instead of abusing his hands. "It's kind of like a survival thing, after a while. You know what I mean? It's ingrained in you."

"Sure, and he worked hard to change that in himself," Lucas replied, massaging the pulse of pressure starting behind his forehead. "After he ran out of money from what our grandfather had left him and instead of snorting prescriptions from his doctor, he'd moved onto shit he could buy on the streets where he found something he loved even more, I guess. Needles."

Delaney's brow lifted high. "I'm sorry."

Yeah, that felt like an appropriate response.

A lot of people used it.

It hadn't been *his* pain, back then, though. Jacob hadn't been chasing his next high because he was trying to numb Lucas' pain or to fill the empty hole left in his brother's heart from their parents' emotional neglect.

That was all Jacob's.

"I guess that was rock bottom for Jacob—maybe, at the time, he knew how far he'd gone because he came to me and asked for help," Lucas muttered.

Which he did.

Without question.

At only twenty-one years old, Lucas could see how that situation would have been a cold and lonely place for his brother to find himself in. No wonder Jacob had accepted help so easily back then. His only other option had been working for his next fix.

"I got him into a rehab in British Columbia for a few months," Lucas continued, determined to get through this conversation because he believed it would help to put it all out on the table. Even if it meant he might be at fault for how things ended with Jacob if only because he loved his little brother too much. "He relapsed thirteen days out, overdosed a week after that, and then never touched the shit again when he came out of the hospital."

"That must have been scary."

Lucas wet his lips, laughing a sad note. "Fucking terrible. It was terrible. But he got a sponsor and worked the Narcotics Anonymous program after that, and he found the gym, so I got him into school again because it seemed like he found a real passion in that too … things have been good. I really—*really*—thought things were good."

The biggest lie of all.

Clearly.

Delaney, who had stayed mostly quiet during the duration of his jumbled story that jumped back and forth, seemed to piece something important together that he had yet to fully explain. "You said he started wearing sunglasses and long sleeves, or something?"

God.

Why did his chest have to hurt so much?

Couldn't he just breathe?

Lucas leaned back in the chair to stare up at the ceiling. "In every picture he posted for the last two months, actually. I tried to check his place when the paramedics were trying the Narcan on him, but I was just panicking because I couldn't stand there and watch them, so I couldn't even do that properly. I don't know how long he was using again, or *why*."

The real question he wanted answered.

Among so many others.

Lucas had questions.

It killed him to think he might never know the truth.

"I didn't call back on Monday because my phone did fall in water," Lucas told Delaney, sighing as his head fell forward and their eyes locked together. "He'd been running a bath ... he liked those in the mornings, but he nodded off on the toilet and the water overflowed to the floor. That's how I found him."

"Lucas—"

No, he had to get it out.

Every last bit of it.

"The ER doctor amused me, at least. Bad word choice, maybe," he told himself, cringing. "Anyway, he hadn't been breathing before I got there in the morning, and nothing they did changed that fact until they put him on a ventilator. They gave me a few hours until the scans and tests came back, but ... well," Lucas finished lamely, shrugging.

All of the sudden, the woman across the way didn't seem to know what to say. Her wide hazel gaze, wet with unshed tears, watched him, unashamed.

"I spent Tuesday making what arrangements I could for his cremation—there's a small service to celebrate his life next week," Lucas explained, the numbness seeping back into his fingers and toes even though he wasn't cold anymore. "And I sat there after in my place feeling like the silence kept screaming at me, and I couldn't do it. I couldn't stay."

It took one pill to kill somebody.

The next hit *could* be the last. To an addict, it wasn't until it was, but then would always be too late.

Jacob was proof of that.

It took Lucas until that moment to realize his pain and grief was the unintentional consequence of his brother's decision. One he would live with forever.

"I'm so sorry," Delaney whispered from the couch, the tears freely falling down her cheeks.

"Yeah, me, too," Lucas uttered, standing from the chair, and grabbing his unfinished plate. The food didn't hold much appeal. "To rub salt in the wound, I have a few hours left to write my brother's obituary if I want the paper to run something that wasn't written by some fuck in a cubicle."

"It would still be appropriate and respectful," Delaney tried to assure.

Lucas scoffed on his way to the kitchen where he dropped the plate unceremoniously to the island before moving to the cupboards to find a glass for water. "But it wouldn't be *meaningful.*"

That held more weight to Lucas.

The end of Jacob's life couldn't be for nothing.

Lucas wouldn't allow that to happen.

"I need this to do something … *mean* something," he attempted to explain.

"I could help you write it?" Delaney asked from the sitting room.

At the sink, Lucas ran himself a glass of water while her selfless request tugged at his sore heartstrings. "Would you?"

Her voice was a lot closer the second time. "I'm here, and I have nothing else to do. Nothing else I want to do," Delaney clarified at his back. "And thank you."

Sipping from the water, Lucas turned to face her as his back leaned against the sink. She placed her plate next to his on the island.

He eyed her. "Why are you thanking me?"

"For asking me to come here. I don't need you to say it to know this place is special. And besides that, it takes a lot of courage to admit you don't want to—or *can't*—be alone, Lucas, never mind telling it to a stranger."

He tried to smile.

It felt miserable like him.

"You're not so strange," he offered back.

The best attempt at humor he could do.

Delaney leaned against the side of the island. "Yeah, *well*. I'm not sure how exactly you're going to send the obituary out if we do get something written that you like," she said, making a face. "I can't get a single bar of service on my phone here."

Ah, that little troublesome detail.

A minor inconvenience of Birch Ridge.

No service.

Lucas waved it off. "There's a booster upstairs. Your phone has to stay on it, but it works."

"Oh. There's also twin beds up there."

"Mmhmm. I prefer the couch."

Delaney nodded. "I wondered …"

"What?"

"If we could just shove the two beds together?"

Lucas welcomed the directional change of their conversation, if only for the moment. "To keep warm, I imagine?"

Delaney grinned.

The sight sped up his heart rate.

"That's a bonus, too," she agreed.

"I can shove 'em together, no worries there."

Her expression turned somber. "I wish I knew what to say about your brother. I'm sorry doesn't seem like enough, does it?"

No, it wasn't.

It barely scratched the very tender surface.

Lucas sighed. "I guess, it's the best we've got, huh?"

19.

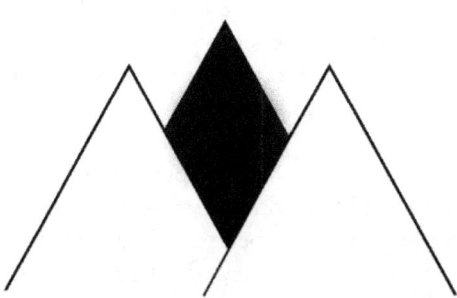

There was something to be said about a person waking up in an unfamiliar place without a sense of fear. Delaney blinked awake to consciousness with warmth wrapping her tight, focused more along her front, and a heavy weight resting across her body. She didn't start awake by the fact that she couldn't move, or that the gentle rumble of a snore coming from somewhere above meant she wasn't alone in the bed, either.

And she knew instantly ...

They hadn't moved once in the night.

Delaney did her best to stretch under the heaviness of Lucas' arm wrapped around her back to keep her tucked close to his bare chest under the quilt, but it only served to jostle the sleeping man enough that he pulled her tighter. His snoring, a sound she hadn't heard throughout the night, cut in and out for a choppy couple of seconds until he settled into sleep once more, satisfied with his shifting.

Delaney peeked up to find Lucas' lax profile sunk into a pillow. Her arms, tucked up in around her head, had acted as something to rest on because she hadn't wanted to move. Not after the big bear of a man had slipped under the quilt with her the evening before and found her shivering in the bed.

It wasn't from any chill.

Even if he had taken it that way ...

His arms and the quilt had become the cozy cave wrapping around Delaney, keeping her warm and shut out from the new surroundings and the faint smell of firewood burning in the cabin. Why would she want to move?

His chest, dusted all the way down a toned belly with dark hair, lifted and fell rhythmically with steady breaths and snores. Delaney, the type to curl into a ball with her knees pulled high, had somehow gotten her lower limbs entangled with his during the night. The cotton fleece of his sleep pants were soft, but heavy, around her legs as she tried to unweave the two of them enough to get the sleep out of her lower half.

It didn't work.

He kept her caged in like his own personal teddy bear, but Delaney kind of liked it. It didn't escape her thoughts that Lucas, the same man who shared the bed so intimately with her while she wore nothing more than an oversized T-shirt and boy shorts to sleep, held her like he might for a lover.

Yet, he'd not even asked her for a goodnight kiss.

She'd been the one who pulled him closer to her under the quilt to shorten that gap between them, needing to feel the plush softness of his lips pressed to hers. If only for a few seconds. Oh, she'd certainly wanted to kiss him, but she had also desperately wished that kiss would wipe his sad frown away.

It had.

For a moment.

Delaney understood his deeply rooted pain, though, so she didn't hold his quietness against him when all he had seemed to want and need was to hold her tight. She let him do that, too.

She did manage to wriggle one arm out from beneath the quilt. Only to instantly find chilly air waiting to kiss her skin the minute she was free from the warmth their close bodies provided. A chill raced through Delaney.

"Oh," she breathed, quickly jerking her arm back into the safe, cozy confines of the quilt and Lucas.

That time, she did wake him up.

His snores stopped.

She peered up to watch his brown eyes blink away the dreams—good ones, she hoped; he deserved those. Lucas let out one hard breath before his chest tightened and so did his arm around her.

Delaney laughed as he crushed her into his warmth once more. The sound caught his attention, and that dark stare of his found her safe in his arms with only the top of her head peeking out from beneath the blanket over top of them. Recognition bloomed in his features, and all at once, he seemed to understand that he had kept her tangled with him all night. Not that he did anything about it.

Their legs remained interlocked.

His arm didn't loosen.

Her perfect cave stayed intact.

"Good morning," he grunted out.

Not *unhappily*.

That, at least, gave Delaney some joy.

She didn't think he *shouldn't* be sad—especially about his brother—but a part of her couldn't help but try to put a smile on his handsome face or light happiness in his eyes all the same. Anything at all to take his mind away from that dark, lonely place. If just for a moment …

"Morning," she whispered back, grinning. "It feels a little cold?"

Lucas' brow lifted, and his head rolled back on the pillow while he stretched the arm high that he'd slept with it tucked under his head on the pillow. "Fuck, let's hope the fire's not all the way out, huh?"

Oh, yeah.

There was *that*.

"Don't tell me you can't build a fire," she joked.

Without warning, the hand that Lucas had been stroking up and down Delaney's spine jumped to her side where he tickled her mercilessly under the quilt until she squealed for peace. The second she said stop, he did, replacing his palm flat over her sleep shirt at her spine.

"*Mean*," she gasped, "that's so mean!"

"Can too," he muttered, using his thumb and forefinger to rub his eyes until he blinked down at her again. "I can build a fire, thank you."

Oh, he took that personally.

Delaney snickered. "Got it, big man."

"*Mmmhmm*," he rumbled in a deep, sleepy hum that did wonderful things to Delaney's body. "And don't you forget it, either."

How could she possibly forget?

She figured out exactly why he preferred the larger couch downstairs when the size of him practically swallowed both of them in the combined twin beds. If he wrapped around her, she didn't think she *would* need a blanket in bed with him. And there was the not-so-little matter of the thick ridge bulging in his sleep pants that she had felt pressed against her belly from the time she had opened her eyes that morning.

Even if she *was* trying to ignore it; his very large, and prominent, erection made that hard. No pun intended.

Lucas came to the same understanding of his predicament from his close quarters with Delaney at the same time—by chance, he'd stretched, and the movement drove their bodies firmly together. Her wiggle, and shift against him, brushed her hand along his drawstring pants, and erection.

"Jesus," Lucas breathed, his eyes flying wide as he instantly tried to put distance between the two in bed. Not that he went far before almost toppling off the side of the bed. He caught himself—barely—but the sudden movement tore the quilt off enough that there was no mistaking the cold in the cabin.

"Sorry," he muttered.

"Give me the blanket, you're gonna freeze me out," she demanded.

His morning wood was the least of her concerns.

And the easiest thing to deal with, being honest.

Lucas reduced himself to embarrassed chuckles as the two resituated in the bed, protected from the cold and comfy tucked together under the quilt. In the same position as before; Delaney demanded that, even reaching to pull Lucas' arm back around her.

"*Warm cave*," she mumbled into his chest, tucking herself there like a kitten in a ball while her legs slipped in between his as they had been before. "Not moving."

His laughter rumbled like thunder.

"I can't believe I was awake for at least two entire minutes before I figured out I had a hard-on," he grumbled from outside the quilt.

Delaney grinned wickedly. Maybe she liked the disbelief and awkwardness coloring his voice, if only because he missed a bigger part of the picture that she saw just fine.

"Or sex isn't the first thing on your mind in the morning—even if that part of you thinks differently," Delaney returned quietly.

Not so low that he couldn't hear it.

Lucas inhaled deep, and let out an equally slow, trepid exhale. "And as you say that very thing to me, I feel every word coming out of your lips brushing against my chest, and I can't say you're right at the moment. My dick's still hard, I know it *now*, and—"

That was okay, too.

Delaney showed him why without saying it by tipping her head up to watch his face while her hands went *down*. Not under the stretchy waistband of his sleep pants, though. Her fingers curled around the band first, and she asked the man who suddenly couldn't look away from her, "Can I make you feel good?"

Lucas swallowed hard, saying only, "We both know you will, please fucking do."

His lips captured her smile when she tried to reach up for a kiss, but couldn't quite reach. He did the hard work for her in that regard. Delaney did the rest by getting her hands inside his sleep pants, and shivered when she found the silken flesh that wrapped his hard erection hot and sensitive to her touch. Both her hands circled his shaft, one on top of the other, but she still had at least three inches of him to stroke, eliciting the sweetest hiss from Lucas that whooshed along Delaney's forehead.

"Kiss me again," she said, pouting.

She stroked him tight with both hands, from root to tip, and demanded, "Kiss me and show me how you want to come, Lucas."

"Fuck, *woman*."

Why did that sound like a warning?

Why did she *like* it?

Delaney pushed him a little harder, lust swimming in her veins and pooling low between her thighs where she felt a pulse in her clit with every beat of her heart. "You can even use me—*would you do it?*"

She'd let him.

She'd do anything for him, right then.

His gaze blew with, and the darkest pools of desire landed on her in the bed a second before his mouth slammed down on hers. He devoured her with firm sweeps of his lips coaxing hers apart until their tongues tangled. She tried to keep the tight strokes going along his shaft, but he made that hard for a brief second when he pushed Delaney to her back and climbed on top of her. The change in positions came so abruptly that Delaney felt swallowed by Lucas when he suddenly loomed over her in the bed.

But in the *best* way.

The quilt fell down around their bodies as he fit between her widened thighs. His hips pumped his cock into her tight grip while his weight pressed Delaney into the bed as he leaned in for another kiss that left her breathless, and her lips tingling. His hands, so much larger and rougher than hers, slid under her shirt, bunching the fabric higher until he had her small breasts firm in his grasp as he worked for his pleasure.

That got Delaney off.

She didn't like to be treated as glass.

Every rock of his body into hers drove her a little crazy, and a bit closer, to the heaven of her own, but it wasn't quite enough to get her all the way there. She didn't mind, more enraptured with the way his lips trembled along her jaw with husky words that coaxed her into a pleased desire that she was doing it for him.

"Oh, my good girl," he told her, "fuck, Delaney, let me do it just like that, huh?"

Could he feel how shameful wet she already was beneath the thin cotton of her boy shorts as she fruitlessly tried to find some relief rubbing into him? She could feel every thread of the damp fabric tugging and pressing with the shifts of her hips. It just wasn't enough.

Yet.

She kissed the underside of his chin. "Come. Won't you come, Lucas?"

"*Christ.*"

His left hand found purchase on one of the posts of the combined twin headboards as the thrusts of his hips came faster and harder. She felt the pulse in his cock, how it started at the base and moved up, before warm semen spilled over Delaney's fingers and dripped down to her stomach.

A sticky mess she didn't mind.

His relief came with a low groan of her name.

So pleased.

It shone in his eyes that stared down, awed and blissed, at her.

Delaney's teeth abused her bottom lip as she tried to subdue the satisfaction she managed to feel from his orgasm. She didn't have to get off to feel those same ripples of pleasure. Serving him fed the same purpose.

It didn't have to always be a give and take.

Oh, but when it *was* …

"*Sweets,*" he murmured, a praise she felt touch her all over.

"Better?" she asked him.

"Mmm, so good."

He wasn't flaccid in her hands. Still engorged and tender with every gentle sweep of her fingertips, in fact.

Lucas couldn't be aware because she wouldn't share it, but it brought Delaney some relief to know, at least for that morning, she took his mind away from his pain. She hoped he wouldn't blame her for wanting to keep him in that protected bubble with her for a little while longer. His eyes were so much brighter when the sadness wasn't holding his mind entirely hostage.

"When's *your* turn?" Lucas asked.

Delaney squinted through her blooming smile, and the shiver from the cold air in the cabin kissing her exposed breasts; her nipples peaked from the chill. "Get a fire going first."

The request sent Lucas pulling away from Delaney instantly, but not before he dropped a quick peck to the tip of her button nose. "On it now."

He left her laughing, and happy, in the bed after covering Delaney with the quilt. To her satisfaction. Not a fingertip or toe outside of the heavy fabric that smelled like Lucas and wrapped her in the same cozy warmth.

Delaney allowed only the peek of her face to be free from the cocoon of the blanket as she watched Lucas' back retreat down the stairs, away from the upper landing. Overwhelmed by the trickle of need still teasing her nerves, Delaney rolled to her back in the bed and eyed the massive glass gun rack that framed the wall behind the beds. Full of rifles and a couple of nice looking hunting bows with displayed quivers, it gave her something else to focus on instead of the urge to get herself off.

She could do it quietly.

In less than thirty seconds, actually.

However, patience served Delaney well. It brought good things.

Delaney heard Lucas' movements change from one side of the cabin to the other downstairs before a door slammed. The bathroom. Twenty seconds later, the toilet flushed, and a minute after, he exited the bathroom with a call back up to her.

"You want coffee, sweetheart?"

"It wouldn't be stale, right?"

Lucas laughed. "No, that shit stays good for years."

"Mmm, yes please."

Water ran in the kitchen before the sound of the cast iron kettle clinked onto the wood stove in the middle of the cabin.

"Good news," Lucas' voice traveled from downstairs, "there's coals, but we came close to just ashes."

The rustle of fabric and the stomp of boots told Delaney he had gotten his parka and footwear on a second before the front door opened and slammed shut in the same breath. Not two minutes later, the light of the lamp on the bedside table that had sat between the two twin beds when they were previously separated flickered on where it now sat in the corner of the loft.

The generators got turned off at night.

It saved gas.

Lucas entered the cabin with news that it wasn't as cold as yesterday, by far, and that would do well for the old Chevy in the garage that didn't like running in below minus twenty temps. Or so he explained. She tried to listen.

Did her best, really.

Delaney just wanted his mouth and hands to be doing other things, now.

"I'll let it run for a bit before we head out. Get the engine nice and warm," he explained as she listened to him feed logs into the wood stove.

Every minute that passed with him working down below made Delaney curl tighter and tighter into herself as she waited for him to return to her.

Where she wanted him the very most.

The need vibrated through her sinew. Maybe that spoke to the length of time she had allowed herself to go without sex, or any physical intimacy with a partner, but she'd not met a man in recent years who woke her up like Lucas did.

She could taste it, even.

He made her feel alive.

That was the key for Delaney.

What she needed most to really want a man.

"Where's my coffee?" she jokingly asked as Lucas climbed the stairs to the loft.

He winked, moving to the bed where he could get a good grip on the edge of the quilt she had hidden herself inside like a burrito, and she could see what he had in his other hand. A washcloth from the bathroom. "You'll get that as soon as the kettle squeals. Let me in—I want to clean you."

Well ...

"Fine," Delaney mumbled, but not very happily.

She helped him to unfurl the quilt, but little did he know that she had used the sleep shirt to wipe away the stickiness he left behind on her hands and stomach. She pulled the shirt off once she was sitting up in the bed, and tossed it to the pile of dirty undergarments the two had left in the corner the night before.

Try to keep it to a load or less, it helps the old washer.

Those were his words.

Fine by her.

Lucas didn't hide his appreciative gaze drifting over her naked upper half as he carefully cleaned her hands with the warm washcloth before she laid back against the pile of two fluffy pillows to give him better access to her stomach.

The shift of her legs, sliding together, drew his stare lower. There was no hiding the slit of wetness peeking out from her panties at the apex of her thighs.

"You left me in a bit of a spot," she explained, opening her legs to give him a flash before she closed them again.

That was as much of an apology as Delaney would ever make for her pleasure, or her want for it. She stopped letting herself feel shame about being a sexual being a long time ago; her body was *hers*. And she could do what she wanted with it.

Lucas smirked. "Should I help with that?"

"You do it, or I will," Delaney returned.

Just to make things clear.

The facecloth met the same fate in the corner pile, and his knee hit the bed as that large hand of his fit perfectly between her legs. Even over top of her panties, he found the right spot to rub to make Delaney's thighs loosen and open wide for him. His fingers scissored and tightened up and down along the hood of her clit above her wet panties. Already, her body wanted to sing for him, and it showed in the fervent grind of her hips into his hand.

"Oh, God, yeah," she whined. "Just like that."

He kept those fingers moving against her, but she watched with wide eyes as he brought his other hand up to lick the tips of his fingers. That hand then went under her boy shorts while he hooked the others to the crotch of her underwear and pulled them aside.

"Look at that pussy—let's make her cream, sweets," Lucas told her, the sexiest grin pulling at his lips.

"Is it my turn?" she asked.

It was crazy how she ached to feel him inside, his substantial size would stretch her open so good, but knowing they would have to wait. His fingers, slick with spit and the arousal he found pooling between her pussy's folds, rubbed faster and firmer around her swollen clit.

"Your turn now," he agreed.

20.

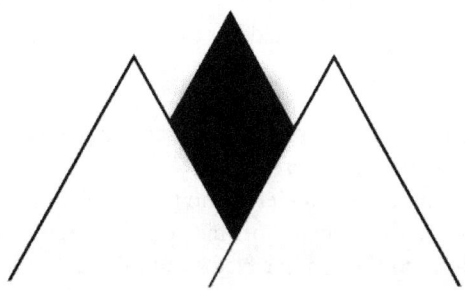

"What are you doing standing there and shivering?" Lucas asked Delaney. Before she could come up with a quick response for her reason as to why she waited outside the rural gas station while he filled the extra gas cans on the back of the old Chevy, he nodded toward the store, telling her, "Go find something sweet for us to have tonight—and whatever else you like, huh?"

Delaney considered arguing the point or just standing her ground and waiting to enter the store with Lucas once he finished, but the wind had picked up since she first left the truck. The lack of trees surrounding the store, instead hugged by expansive farmer's fields for as far as the eye could see, offered no protection from the cold blast of wind whipping through the quiet community of Arthurette.

If not for the wind, the cold might be bearable.

Except, no.

Her skin just *stung*.

"Yeah, all right," Delaney muttered, tightening the hood of her parka closer around her face before asking, "Anything else I should look for—do they even have food?"

"Usually," he agreed. "Potatoes, and things. Get whatever you want, okay? I'm paying."

That wasn't an important detail to Delaney, but she didn't let Lucas know as much. With another encouraging nod from him, she headed for the single door at the front of the store that acted as the entrance. Chilly air blasted her from up above as she stepped beyond the threshold into a tiny enclave where people could wipe off their boots on the rubber mat, use the payphone in the corner, or survey any one of the many flyers and notices posted on the walls.

Delaney wasted just enough time in the entrance to wipe off her boots and look over the photo of someone's missing cat with a date at the bottom that matched her graduation year.

A long time ago.

Damn.

"Hope you found your cat," she muttered, pushing through the second door to enter the store.

The man behind the register at the front welcomed Delaney with a wide smile that showed off his gold canine tooth, and a wave, friendly even though her face wouldn't be one he recognized as a regular in the area.

"Hey there, how ya doing?" he asked.

"Trying not to freeze," she returned.

He chuckled but nodded in understanding. Although, standing there in his T-shirt and denim jeans, she didn't think he *could* appreciate the cold outside the heated store at the moment.

"Aren't we all. Liquor's that way," he said, pointing to the small corner of the store sectioned off by sliding doors with the familiar NB Liquor sign hanging above. The man went back to watching the news broadcast going over the previous week's highlights on the small flatscreen television positioned overhead from his register, adding, "Give me a shout if you need something else."

"Potatoes?" Delaney asked.

Only because she figured if there were bags of potatoes to be bought in the store, whatever edible food the place sold would also be in the same spot. Or very close by. Not that the store was particularly large at first glance, but the four aisles that stretched a good fifty feet back from the front looked like it displayed everything from bags of dog food to paper towel in the very back.

She wasn't interested in those things.

"Go 'round the side there," he told her, pointing at the farthest aisle from the front cash.

"Thanks."

He waved two fingers over his shoulder, already more interested in the television again, as Delaney headed for the aisle in question. She hadn't noticed any shopping carts, or even a basket to use, upon entrance. Her arms would have to do the heavy lifting.

So to speak.

She did find ten-pound bags of potatoes piled on the bottom

shelf at the front of the far aisle. Setting a bag to the side, where it could safely lean against the corner of the shelf, she headed further down the section where rows of various bread, bagels, and other grain options waited. Sandwiches or toast made a few meal options possible, so she grabbed two loaves of white bread and a bag of carrots, along with a pack of cinnamon and raisin bagels.

Plus, a package of cinnamon buns with a best before date that allowed a couple of days grace before the sugary treat would go stale.

Not the worst thing.

In the next aisle, she found cans of soup, bags of sugar, and even jars of peanut butter and jam. Before long, Delaney had gathered enough items that she had to take an armload to the front where she piled it all on the cash with a sheepish smile.

"I'm not done yet," she admitted.

The man looked over the items, and chuckled. "No worries, missy. I'm paid by the hour, not the sale."

Well, they weren't exactly busy, right?

Not at the moment, anyway.

"If you're looking for some frozen stuff, there's a big chest freezer in the back," he offered.

Huh.

"Good to know," Delaney said, spinning away from the cash to go on yet another search.

It didn't take long for her to find the freezer in question. Six feet long and deep enough that she wouldn't be able to reach all the way to the bottom if needed—she could tell just by standing alongside it—Delaney opened the freezer to find a gold mine.

Frozen pizzas.

Mozzarella sticks and mad caps.

Ice-cream, boneless chicken breasts, and even packs of bologna waited for her eager hands to paw through and decide what would be best to take back to the cabin. A delicate balance for her to consider given the small fridge that had an even smaller section for frozen goods.

Could just stick it all out in the snow, she thought.

Not seriously, of course.

That was a good way to feed wild animals.

Little else.

According to Lucas, the chopper wouldn't be back in Birch

Ridge until Sunday morning. They had at least three days of meals to get through, and while they would make another trip to the store for gas before they had to leave, Delaney liked to plan.

She wouldn't apologize for that.

Besides, Lucas did say *anything*.

Or rather, whatever she wanted.

Delaney kept that in mind as she pulled out a frozen pepperoni pizza, a package of bacon, and a one-pound bag of ground beef. On her way back to the front of the store, she nabbed a box of King Cole tea—it reminded her of Gracen, and she preferred it to coffee if given the option—and a bottle of instant coffee.

Apparently, there had only been enough for one cup that morning. For what it was worth, she made Lucas share it with her. Even if he had insisted on giving it all to her.

She made one more trip to the row of coolers along the side wall, facing rows upon rows of various chips and other bagged snacks with too much salt and sugar. At the cooler by the back, she found milk, butter, eggs, and even prepackaged subs and other easily heatable meals. She skipped over the instant options for the basic needs.

Things she could do something with.

The milk, butter, and eggs, of course.

In her search through the store, she also noticed the various cleaning and other house supplies offered for sale. Even feminine hygiene products and a small section of hanging items for party supplies. At a much higher price than she knew it could be bought in one of the nearby towns—that couldn't be overlooked, either. She hadn't given much thought to the price stickers on the pile of items she took to the front, but no doubt, those too were overpriced.

Not surprising given the location of the store.

Buttfuck Nowhere, Canada.

Basically.

If someone needed what was on the shelf and couldn't make it to town, then so be it. Pay the price on the sticker or suck it up and figure it out.

Those were the choices in rural Canada.

Even gas got knocked up a few cents per liter outside of town limits. The sad fact of the matter came down to people having no other option but to pay much more to live in their small communities outside of the busier, more populated counties surrounding them. Nothing came free. No, their tax dollars paid for that side of things.

Back at the front of the store, Delaney dropped her last armload of items on the counter just as Lucas made his way inside with a shiver a muttered *brr*.

"Did you get something to drink, sweets?" he asked.

Delaney gestured at the food. "Priorities."

His laugh matched the man behind the counter as the two shared a nod and a polite hello.

"Beer's that way," the guy manning the cash said.

Lucas headed in the direction of the liquor storage with a wave over his shoulder. From the high-piled boxes of beer and a wall of bottles blocking the windows, she couldn't see what he went for, but Delaney had an idea. He proved her theory right when he exited the cold storage with a twelve-pack of beer held up for her to see.

The familiar Dalton logo, foiled and prominent on the box, glinted under the overhead lights. No question, his brand all the way.

"It's all about the loyalty," she said, doing her best impression of him as he placed the box of beer down to the counter.

"That it is," Lucas returned, but his gaze stayed fixed on the man bagging and tagging items on the cash register. "You added the gas?"

"I got the gas," the guy confirmed. "Anything else?"

Lucas hummed over the pile of items Delaney had chosen and drummed his fingers along the edge of the counter before he pushed away. "Let me do a check."

"What do you need?" she joked as he headed down the first aisle.

"Snacks!"

"Snacks?"

"Well, I can't only eat *you*."

A surprised, but amused, chuff came from the man who didn't miss a beat, piled the food into bags as Lucas disappeared around the aisle. Delaney, ignoring the sudden heat burning up her cheeks, pretended like *nobody* had heard his comment.

Their total had already crawled over two hundred dollars by the time Lucas came back with three different bags of chips—a variety

of flavors—and a dill pickle dip he must have found in the rear
coolers. Lastly, he lifted a pack of toilet paper high for the guy
behind the cash to see before he placed it to the floor.

"Better to have too much than not enough," Lucas explained at
Delaney's questioning stare in regard to the toilet paper.

True enough.

His gaze locked with hers. "Did you want something other than
the beer? Red wine or—"

"You wouldn't share your scotch with me?" Delaney
interjected, only teasing.

Lucas grinned. "Are you a scotch kind of girl?"

"Get me a little drunk, and I can turn into a try anything kind of
girl, really."

"Tell me more."

Delaney winked. "I just might."

Physical intimacy changed a lot about the way two people
interacted—it didn't even have to be full on sex for that to be the
case, either. Delaney had first learned that important life lesson as a
teenager when she found herself in the unfortunate circumstance
with a boy who she let get under her skirt.

With only his hands, of course.

Nonetheless, that boy had wrongly assumed that the moments
the two of them shared meant more than it actually did and
behaved toward her accordingly. Until it got to be too much, and
Delaney had to let him know exactly that, too. In the end, she came
out of that experience careful about who and how she shared
herself—but especially her body.

It changed things.

It changed *people*.

Delaney would be a liar if that suggestive, knowing glint in
Lucas' eye didn't call to something twisting viscerally inside her gut.
In a *good* way.

For a moment, the two of them had seemed to forget that they
weren't back in the cottage deep in the quiet stillness of Birch
Ridge. The man, who had finally finished tallying their total on the
cash register, cleared his throat as a way to bring the two back to
earth.

"Should I add a pack of these into the mix for good measure?"
the man asked, producing a moderate-sized box of condoms from
beneath the cash.

It made sense to keep items like that—probably a high theft item—where they couldn't be easily seen or found.

Delaney could *not* meet the man's eyes, no matter how hard she tried. Instead, she tossed the question to Lucas without saying a word, but by shifting her entire body toward him as if to ask, "Yes, should we?"

Lucas stepped forward to pay, giving the pack of condoms the man held a shake of his head to refuse the offer, and pulled his wallet from the back pocket of his dark-wash jeans with a cocky grin. "Let's get this show on the road, eh?"

Delaney *wished* she could get the redness out of her cheeks, but no such luck. Her blush held strong through the time it took Lucas to pull out his debit card and stick it into the machine.

Behind the cash, once he got the paid confirmation on the debit machine, the man only replied, "Happy to do business, sir."

All in all, their items fit between four bags with Delaney taking the one with more fragile items and the lightweight pack of toilet paper on the floor, and Lucas handling the other three bags and the box of beer between his two available hands.

He gestured, with dangling bags, for Delaney to head out of the store first, and so she led the way. Shoving the door open by turning her back to get the job done hands free, she found Lucas had stopped a couple of steps away at a rack he must have missed on the way in.

He stared, quietly subdued, at the sight of the newspaper rack for the Telegraph Journal and the other community papers. Tomorrow, the Telegraph, in particular, should be running the obituary Lucas had written for his brother.

In the end, he hadn't needed very much of her help penning out the words on an old legal pad of paper with a pencil he'd sharpened using a kitchen knife. She didn't ask to read it because he hadn't offered, but she sat quietly beside him as he typed it out on his phone in the loft upstairs until he was satisfied with his work. Then, he asked her to read it before he plugged in the booster for the phones to send the obituary out.

Other than a passing moment before they left when she asked about a particular photo of an older Jacob—clearly adult age—and Lucas that she'd noticed on the sitting room wall, he hadn't willingly brought his brother into their conversation. Delaney didn't want to push him. Lucas should be allowed to grieve, even if that was silently, however he needed to.

No exceptions.

She'd simply agreed to be here while he did it.

That was all he asked of her.

His lengthy pause at the newspaper rack continued long enough for Lucas to ask over his shoulder, "You get the new edition for the Telegraph every day it runs?"

"By noon, at the latest. If the weather's bad," the man tacked on like that counted for something.

"Good to know," Lucas murmured.

At that, he nodded once more to Delaney who continued holding the first interior door for Lucas to pass. He held the second for her.

*

Set on top of a small hill off the main road, the store had a good view of the logging trucks blowing past on their way to the sawmill upriver. Delaney helped Lucas to load their bags, and other items, into the back of the truck where he'd parked it alongside the hill after filling up with gas.

"At least nothing's gonna melt sitting on the back," Delaney muttered, still bitter about the cold and not afraid to complain.

Lucas didn't seem to mind.

Much.

"It's not that bad today, come on. There's snowshoes in the cellar, by the way. We could get out on the trails—take a walk."

That didn't sound too bad, actually.

"Can we do something else today?" she asked.

Lucas leaned against the side of the truck and arched a brow. "Like what?"

"The main road is bare." Which really meant that a driver had a better view of the asphalt covered in black ice. Lucas had managed the truck well, so far. What was thirty more kilometers? "How would you feel about taking the truck on a little drive?"

His lips split with a smile. "How little?"

"The Flats?"

She didn't explain why she wanted to go to the quaint farming community just outside of the valley on the other side of Montgomery Mountain, but if he asked, then she would tell him on the drive. Delaney couldn't justify being this close to her best friend's home, and not making some kind of effort to visit Gracen.

Her *pregnant*, soon-to-be married best friend.

Didn't they have things to catch up on?

Delaney couldn't pass the opportunity up. Especially if she didn't have to show her face in town where her family still lived and attended their long-time church, practicing their faith to the same smothering letter that had once sent her running away. Lucas being a part of her process of returning home, in a way, just happened to be a bonus.

Besides, the food would stay cold on the back of the truck, and hadn't Lucas earned something—a drive and the chance to meet new, friendly people—to keep his mind off the sadness in his heart?

She thought so.

"That's twenty minutes or more from here," he said. "What's there for you, family or something?"

Close.

"The only family I care to know," she returned.

The best family was the one a person chose, after all.

No hesitation, Lucas nodded at that. "All right, sweets, then let's go."

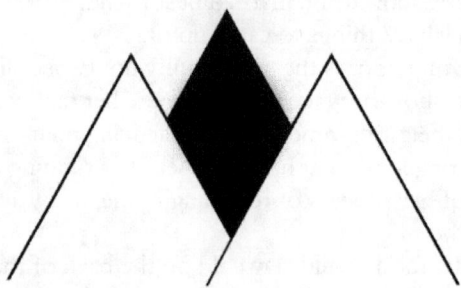

21

"Did you think we *wouldn't* need the condoms?" Delaney asked.

The question that had been plaguing her mind from the moment the Arthurette store faded into the background in the passenger mirror.

Next to her in the truck, Lucas cleared his throat. "Sorry, you just ... came right out with that question now?"

Perhaps it wasn't the right time.

But *still* ...

"It's the next driveway—with the wooden bin and white painted numbers," she informed. "But back to the condoms."

Lucas chuckled. "Right, back to *that*."

"Well, you told him to put it back. I'm still trying to figure out why."

"I'm not going to assume we're sleeping together until you say we are, sweetheart," Lucas said, matter of factly.

"Were your fingers being inside of me this morning not enough of a clue?" Delaney returned.

The pleased, dirty smirk he leveled on her as they approached her friend's driveway did the best, and worst, things to Delaney's insides.

Goddamn this man.

"Well?" she squeaked in question. "I just wondered ..."

"We can stop in again on the way back. The store stays open until nine Monday through to Sunday."

Huh.

Delaney turned to stare out the passenger window instead of at Lucas as the truck slowed on the quiet road. "Good to know."

"*Yep.* Is this the pregnant one?" Lucas asked, navigating the rumbling Chevy into the narrow mouth of a familiar driveway. At the crest of the gully situated along fields the farmer's used for wheat, corn, or cows depending on the year.

Gracen sent pictures to Delaney of the cows that greeted her one morning—her second on the property.

Delaney laughed, not knowing how else to respond to Lucas' question at first.

"What?" he asked. "Jesus, they must get a lot of wind, huh?"

Nestled deep in the gully behind a wall of tall birch trees sat her best friend's two-storey farmhouse directly across from a tall gray barn. Sitting between both was the garage her friend's fiancé had converted into a wood shop while Gracen had a small salon built onto the house shortly after the fire that devastated their beloved Haus.

"First," Delaney said, "don't call her the pregnant one."

She couldn't see that flying over well with Gracen. A woman was more than whether she currently carried a child in her womb, right?

Lucas rolled his eyes and scoffed behind the wheel. "I would *not.*"

"Well, you just—"

"I only asked because I meant to follow it up with whether or not it would be appropriate for me to congratulate her," he filled in, matter of fact.

Enough that Delaney's jaws snapped to keep from saying another thing to chastise him. She should have known better. Lucas proved often, and consistently, that he considered the people around him in ways others might overlook. Not being able to relate to someone else didn't seem like an excuse he used not to be kind.

"She isn't far along, right? That photo I saw—what are those called?"

"Sonograms?"

Lucas made a noise under his breath as the truck slowly rolled down the winding drive with snowbanks piled high on either side. "Whew, would not have thought that was the word."

She laughed. "Are babies out of your realm?"

Delaney couldn't imagine Lucas saying yes to that question, honestly. He seemed like exactly the type to make a good, devoted father. If he cared deeply about people he might as well consider strangers, what kind of love would he show to a child that belonged to him?

Then again, being a good man didn't necessarily mean that man also wanted children.

He considered that question before answering. "Experience-wise, yes. That's a bit out there for me."

Fair enough.

But everybody could learn.

Delaney tried to do the math in her head, but couldn't come up with a firm, exact week number for her friend's pregnancy. Although, she was sure Gracen would know the second Delaney got the chance to clarify and ask. "If she's past her first trimester, it's barely. And no, Gracen doesn't complain about the wind. I guess it kind of rolls off the crest of the gully, and the trees keep the house from getting the brunt."

"Huh," Lucas said under his breath.

Not that he differentiated the non-response to anything in particular.

Delaney grinned over at him. "Are you nervous?"

"What, why?"

His head swung her way, and those soul-deep eyes of his slammed into hers.

"I don't know," she said, suddenly more interested in pretending to pick at the French tips on her manicure. "I mean, I might be nervous if you asked me to randomly meet your parents, or something."

Not two seconds after those words left her lips, Lucas pulled the Chevy into park behind Malachi's truck parked next to Gracen's new Four-Runner.

A recent purchase.

She wanted something bigger when the baby came, apparently.

"I assure you stopping in for coffee, or whatever, with your long-time friend is not comparable to meeting my parents, on any given day of the week," Lucas tacked on at the end.

As if for good measure.

Delaney's brow furrowed. "I know you're not close, but do you think that given the current circumstances, things might change in the future?"

She chose every word carefully.

Lucas wasn't as kind. "No. If you're at all curious what a meeting with my parents would look like, it'd probably include my father finding something trivial about you to insult as a way to poke at me, and my mother would somehow play the perpetual victim, so she can feel better about all the shitty things she's done. The casualty in every story which I can safely say would make everyone else the villain."

Delaney blinked, unsure of how to respond.

Lucas shrugged, adding, "That is, if you could even get the two of them in the same room together. The divorce seemed to draw a firm line there. I think they've been face to face maybe twice. You know, once the ink dried."

She *tried* to form words.

Even something sarcastic.

A joke, maybe.

Nope.

Delaney settled on a lame, "They sound … lovely."

"Yeah, some people just suck the good right out of you, I guess." Lucas laughed darkly. "Let me say, next week should be very interesting."

"Why?"

Oh.

The second the question slipped from Delaney's lips, she realized the glaring answer that she missed. She doubted, especially if they were the type of people who cared about appearances, that his parents would miss their youngest son's celebration of life. Even if their oldest son had been the only one who made sure that memorial would even happen.

"Jacob's memorial," she filled in before Lucas did.

He smiled sadly as he turned the engine off and removed the keys from the ignition, but rolled his shoulders indifferently before reaching for the latch on the driver's side door to shove it open. "Well, I'll deal with that when I get there, huh?"

Delaney didn't answer, but Lucas hadn't bothered to wait for a response before slipping out of the truck, and closing the door behind himself. She couldn't help but notice that he went with that *when-or-if-it-happens* outlook a lot. He put things off if they weren't an immediate cause of concern. Who was she to judge the way he chose to deal with his issues?

Including his parents.

Who the hell was she to talk there at all?

So, Delaney didn't.

Climbing out of the truck as well, she leaned over the bed of the truck on the passenger side to watch Lucas reposition the bags of groceries further away from the gas cans he'd secured to the far corner with rope. He worked in a sober silence. Even if he wasn't nervous, as he'd claimed earlier, she couldn't discount how he might be feeling otherwise.

"Are you okay?" she asked. "I can understand why, or if, you would rather not do this today."

"Sweets," Lucas grunted, shifting the pack of toilet paper with the bags, "we're already here, and if I didn't want to be, we wouldn't have come. Let's go inside. My balls are freezing off."

"Nice," Delaney muttered as she rounded the front of the truck to meet him at the grill.

She found her way tucked under his arm, close to his side, the second she was within his reach. Lucas dropped a firm kiss that lingered on the top of Delaney's head as they crossed the snow-packed drive to head up the stairs leading to the wrap-around porch and the front door of the farmhouse.

"Sometimes, you gotta say it how it is," Lucas told her when she reached out to knock on the glass.

As it were, someone already waited, distorted by the frosted privacy glass designed with etched flowers and vines up the long panes, just behind the door. In fact, he opened the door just as Delaney told Lucas, "Gracen *will* like that part about you."

"Gracen will like what, now?"

When it came to his woman, Malachi Anders never missed a click.

Delaney learned that lesson very soon after meeting the man, and thankfully, it was a quality she appreciated about him. She never had to worry about her best friend finding herself heartbroken and alone like she once did because there wasn't a soul on this earth who loved Gracen the way Malachi did.

"Nothing," Delaney teased, grinning.

Malachi smiled wide. "Hey, you. Long time, no see."

"It's not been *that* long."

"Long enough," Malachi returned.

She couldn't really argue.

Then, his gaze shifted to the man standing just behind Delaney on the porch, quiet and still but an indisputable presence all the same. Lucas loomed tall at her back, his shadow spilling over her and onto Malachi. She could tell by her position that he had a few inches of height on the man who answered the door.

"And you are …?" Malachi questioned, trailing off but keeping his tone friendly.

"Lucas Dalton," came her companion's smooth reply. He leaned around her side to stick out a hand for Malachi to take and shake, which her friend's fiancé did. "Nice to meet you. I almost felt like I could see this place before we got here. Delaney described it—"

"Delaney?"

The shouted call—clearly questioned—came from deep within the house.

Instantly, Malachi's stare cut back to Delaney.

A knowing gleam found her there.

"Yeah, babe," he called back over his shoulder.

The patter of footsteps from somewhere inside came like a herd of elephants getting closer to the front door.

"*Delaney!*"

Gracen's background shrieking continued while Malachi only shook his head and opened the front door wider with a gesture inside.

"Come on it, get out of the cold—coffee, tea?"

"Coffee," Lucas muttered, stepping in behind Delaney in the entry enclave, "would be perfect."

Malachi smirked her way. "If I make you tea, she's going to want you to have a splash of rum in it because she can't. Your call."

Delaney's brow lifted high at the news. "Eh, I'll try it."

Anything was worth a shot once.

Right?

Once inside, Delaney understood the reason for the loud patter overhead when Gracen jogged down the stairs with loud footsteps. Never once had her ranting stopped, although, it only became clear when her feet finally touched the bottom level.

"I've called you ten *times*! Your damn voicemail is full! I was worried *sick*, Delaney!"

"Babe, there's somebody else—"

Gracen didn't hear Malachi's warning at all, zooming into the entry with arms open to barrel rush Delaney into a hug the second her friend's eyes landed on her. Delaney barely had time to brace for the impact, or even appreciate how cute her friend looked in a baggy crochet sweater and winter-themed leggings, and every bit of air rushed out of her chest when Gracen tightened her arms around her like bars and squeezed impossibly tight.

"Bexley called—*so* worried," Gracen muttered into Delaney's neck. "That was crazy! *What the hell were you thinking running off with some random guy like that?*"

"Well," she tried to say.

Gracen let her go, but not far. Her hands stayed fixed on Delaney's shoulders as she separated them apart just enough for the two to stare at one another. She couldn't help the guilt that gnawed on her heart at the genuine concern in Gracen's blue eyes.

"Well, *what?*" Gracen asked.

Then, she seemed to realize she had another visitor.

Lucas, still lingering close to the front door, waved two fingers high when Delaney followed Gracen's gaze over her shoulder.

"Oh," her friend said awkwardly. "Um, hello."

To his benefit, Lucas grinned. "Hi. I'm the random guy."

*

Gracen managed to make it fifteen entire minutes before she pulled Delaney out of the homey, primitively decorated kitchen with a promise of showing her the work she and Malachi had done to what would be the baby's room. Delaney thought it might be a little early to do those sorts of things—setting up the nursery—but it wasn't her pregnancy or baby, so she trailed alongside her friend in silence up to the second floor.

With their arms hooked together, Gracen made sure the two of them stayed locked tight together so Delaney couldn't return to the man she'd left behind in the kitchen.

"Malachi better—"

"Better what?" Gracen interrupted.

Dammit.

"You know what," Delaney tried to warn.

Her friend only cackled.

It helped Delaney—in a way she didn't really understand—to see Gracen smiling and happy. The scant amount of times the two women had been able to enjoy one another's company since Delaney's move to the city were far and few between. She didn't always trust that Gracen's photos, pretty with filters, and always featuring a smile, were true.

Honestly, it wasn't about Gracen.

Delaney just missed her best friend.

"This is good," Delaney noted before taking another sip of the orange pekoe tea flavored with enough rum that one could smell it in the steam rising from the mug. "Better than I thought it would be, anyway."

"Tell me about it." Gracen shot Delaney, and the mug at her lips, a look that screamed jealousy. "You have no idea how much I miss it every night. Here I was, just trying to do something that made me think of Mimi, and what'd I get?"

"A habit?"

Gracen laughed hard again. "Well, it's not that bad, but I miss it. A lot more than I thought I would, I guess."

Delaney untangled their arms so that she could wrap hers around Gracen's side for a one-armed hug. Plus, a little pat to her friend's not-so-round midsection. If someone didn't know about the pregnancy, they definitely wouldn't be able to tell upon first glance. Gracen had yet to start showing.

"But you're getting something amazing out of it," Delaney said. "So, is it worth it?"

"Mostly. This puking shit is for the birds, though."

That sounded like something Gracen's grandmother would say for sure.

"How is Mimi?" Delaney asked.

"Good ..." Gracen let out a sigh and shrugged as the two came to stand in front of a closed door that belonged to one of the two smaller bedrooms upstairs. "Well, the Alzheimer's is more apparent, but she's still there more often than she isn't."

"They call it the long goodbye for a reason."

"Yeah, it's hard, but ..." Gracen trailed off with a shrug.

Delaney peered back down the short hallway where a waist-high gate had been installed at the top of the stairs but remained open for people to pass freely. Another one had been put in at the bottom. She knew for a fact that Gracen wasn't that far ahead of the baby game when it came to getting things ready, and her friend and Malachi didn't have animals that would need gates to keep them from going up or down the stairs.

And that gate would do nothing for Mister Kitty—Gracen's

beloved pet cat, a gift from Malachi. The tuxedo cat could climb the walls when he felt like it, and sometimes did. No gate would keep him out.

"What was that for—that *hmm*?" Gracen asked.

"Did I see chalk marks on the wall going up the stairs?"

Gracen rolled her eyes. "Malachi had to measure it for the chair lift."

It seemed her friend had other news to share.

Gracen offered the missing piece of the puzzle without Delaney prompting. "It took a while for me to get to the point where I thought I could actually do it, but I *can*. And more importantly, we want to. We're capable and have the financial means to hire a daily nurse to come in to help with things. We're in the process of installing extra security to make sure she's safe. These are the last years of Mimi's life, and I want her to enjoy them as much as she can. I want my grandmother to be home with me."

"It kind of sounds like you're about to have a really big year," Delaney pointed out.

A baby. The wedding in the spring. Now, her grandmother would also be moving from the assisted living facility to the farmhouse on The Flats.

"Big changes," she added quietly.

Gracen didn't look bothered.

Ready, if anything.

Her friend nodded. "I know. It'll all work out."

"You always were better at seeing the bright side of things than me," Delaney admitted.

Gracen scoffed at that. "Never heard a worse lie."

Maybe.

Or perhaps time just changed things.

Delaney included.

"Are you showing me this nursery, or what?" she asked.

Gracen squinted one eye closed as she reached for the doorknob, muttering, "*Well ...*"

"What?"

Delaney learned exactly what when Gracen flung open the door to an empty bedroom with bare white walls, and gleaming hardwood floors. Well, mostly empty.

A few boxes—the largest being a crib in the corner and a glider with a matching ottoman—sat in the corner, unopened and ready to be assembled.

"You told me you had things fin—"

"Get in the room," Gracen said without warning, practically shoving Delaney inside. The second they were both in what would eventually be the baby's nursery, her friend shut the door behind them and then turned on Delaney with narrowed eyes. "Seriously, what were you thinking? Since when do you take off with random guys you don't know, Delaney?"

Jesus.

They were back to that again?

"Lucas is—"

"He seems nice," Gracen interjected.

"Stop talking over me," Delaney said. A bad habit the two of them shared. It wasn't just Gracen. She did it to her friend, too. "He *is* nice. The sweetest guy I've ever met, to be honest."

The statement had Gracen arching one eyebrow higher than the other. "Oh?"

"*Yeah*, and you didn't need to drag me all the way upstairs out of his earshot and sight just to get that information out of me, Gracen."

If there was a facial expression for *no regrets*, Gracen plastered it on.

"I did call," Gracen pointed out. "Several times."

"We flew out to Birch Ridge."

"Ah," her friend said, knowing the spot immediately. "No service."

"Mmhmm."

"Wait—*flew?*"

Ah, yeah.

That.

Delaney shrugged. "It's not a big deal, don't make it one, okay?"

"What isn't?"

"You know the second largest brewery in the province?"

"Not off hand, no," Gracen replied.

Delaney blew out a frustrated breath. *Fine.* She could spell it out for Gracen, then. "The Daltons, you know? They're kind of like the Irvings of New Brunswick when it comes to beer. Except you know, beer and not *gas*."

A prominent family.

A well-known name.

Gracen blinked a few times. "*The* Daltons?"

"Well, he's Lucas—"

"Dalton."

"You're doing it again, talking over me," Delaney pointed out.

Gracen only laughed. "Wow, okay. Now I get why you didn't want me to make a big deal out of it. And the flying thing ...?"

"A company helicopter."

A low whistle cut from Gracen's lips. "*Damn*. I can see why you'd say yes—"

Now it was her turn to interrupt.

"No, and who Lucas' family is has *nothing* to do with why I came here with him. Okay?"

Gracen nodded. "Okay, fair enough."

"I know it's not like me to just up and go like that without a word, or *planning*," Delaney stressed, the most important point of all.

"Yeah, how did you manage that, anyway?"

That side of things was simple.

"He needed somebody," Delaney answered, shrugging.

"And you want that somebody to be you?"

"I never said it like that."

Gracen didn't miss a beat, stating back, "You don't have to say it to still want it, Delaney."

Those were dangerous suggestions. Mostly because Delaney found it surprisingly easy to get lost in the tumble and rumble of her thoughts. The ones that whispered how perfect and amazing Lucas seemed. How great he had been to and for her so far. At every chance he was given, the man took it and made the most out of it when it came to Delaney. What woman—a sane one—wouldn't look at that man and think *forever material?*

He fit the bill on every level.

That sort of thing could be scary.

She was allowed time—and to be fair, she hadn't exactly had a lot of time with Lucas, yet—to make sure that it wasn't just attraction and the surface feelings making her see him that way. Hadn't he been the one to say she should put the bar higher for him?

Okay, so it was.

She wanted to see what he would do with it.

"He's kind of great," Delaney settled on saying.

The most she would give.

For now, at least.

"Great enough to be your date at my wedding in May?"

"Now you're asking the hard questions," Delaney returned.

Gracen smirked as she passed Delaney by to open the bedroom door once more to expose the hallway outside. Mister Kitty had made his way upstairs to lay directly in front of the closed door, and Delaney swore his expression looked offended at the fact it had been shut on him.

"Really? That's tough for you?" Gracen asked. "I thought the hard questions would start somewhere around me asking if you'd slept with him yet."

Nope, that was the easiest answer.

"Working on it," Delaney said on her way out of the bedroom. "Now, let's go visit all my purses and things that I haven't seen in forever."

Gracen shook her head, following behind Delaney. "I'm gonna start charging you rent ... or storage fees."

She would not.

Mister Kitty didn't move out of the way for them, either.

22.

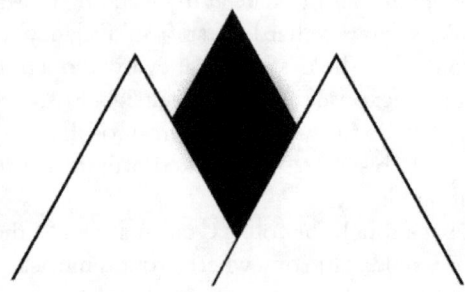

"Is that an '82?" Malachi asked.

Lucas chuckled from his seat at the table. The man had spied the truck from the window over the sink five minutes ago and hadn't looked back. "Close. Three."

Malachi whistled. "Damn. It's in nice shape, man."

"Yeah, Mitchel kept it up. I didn't have the same sentimental feelings about it that he did, but I couldn't sell it after everything was said and done."

"Mitchel?"

"My grandfather," Lucas clarified, smiling apologetically when Malachi glanced his way. "The camp in the Ridge was his—the old truck came with it when it switched over to me. Of course, it's got to a point when something breaks on it, they've gotta go four acres deep into a junkyard to find a part on another one to fix it."

"I bet," Malachi replied absentmindedly, his focus back on the Chevy that could be considered an antique at this point. "Why'd he keep it for so long?"

"Said he got laid in the truck once upon a time, and never got over that one. Never specified whether it was the same truck or not, fair warning."

Malachi chuckled. "Good to know."

The last fifteen years of Mitchel's marriage with his wife before she passed had been fraught with her sickness—cancer truly was a bitch—but Lucas barely even remembered his grandmother now. In fact, he had clearer memories of when his grandfather bought the old truck. His grandmother was dead before his early childhood memories really started. Not known for his romantic nature, or even friendliness on a good day, it really said something that there had been a woman in Lucas' grandfather's past that lived rent-free in the back of Mitchel's mind.

"Anyway, he loved the damn thing because of it. Kept up on the body work and only drove it when he came to the camp."

Malachi grinned wickedly. "Shit, eh? *Really?*"

Lucas shrugged. "That's what he told me."

And anybody else who asked, too.

Some stories couldn't be told enough, apparently.

"So, hey, if you ever wanna sell it," the man hedged.

Lucas laughed. "Seriously?"

Malachi shrugged, and turned away from the sink and window with the half emptied glass of water sloshing from the fast spin. "Yeah, no joke. Gracen would only want to kill me for a little while—she'll like taking it out in the fields in the summer, though. It'll work itself out."

The guy had it all planned out, clearly.

Lucas glanced down at the creamy coffee in the mug between his cupped hands on the barn-style table. "I should get rid of the damn thing and store something newer at the camp with a better set of tires. I don't usually come upriver in the winter."

"Put a number on it," Malachi returned, coming to sit at the head of the table with a lazy posture that spoke of his comfort in the spot. "Let's see if it meets the one I've got in my head."

"Right now?"

"No time like the present," the man said, smirking back.

Shit, all right.

He wasn't playing around.

Lucas liked that. "Twenty, and you take it as is."

Malachi tipped his head to the side like he was considering the offer. Even his left eye squinted a bit as if he might be doing math inside his head and needed the extra focus. His concentration gave Lucas the time to survey the interlocking wood panels that made up the walls, and the many framed photos, some seemingly spanning years, decorating the space.

Cozy with history.

It reminded him of the Smiths' place. The home of a family.

"And if I found you something decent to replace the truck— with a set of studded winter tires in case you do come back to the area at this time of year?" Malachi counter offered.

Like he had already said, Lucas didn't have emotional

attachment to the truck. And if he came out square in a deal with something better at the camp to drive than the old Chevy that ate gas like crazy?

Fine by him.

"You could take it," Lucas said. "Nothing older than fifteen years. Ten's even better."

"Perfect," Malachi returned, clapping.

He stuck a hand down the table for Lucas to take for a shake, and the two settled the agreement with that, and nothing more.

A word was all a man had, after all. Lucas didn't mind finding out if Malachi was a man of his, too.

Malachi rested back into the captain chair with his hands folded at the back of his head, a wide smile saying he was pleased at how the interaction turned out. His stare focused back on Lucas, and for a split second, his smile slipped.

"*Dalton*," Malachi muttered.

Lucas arched a brow, refusing to fill in silent details. People tended to assume things about those they believed were wealthy or powerful in some way. He refused to be a stereotype; and especially not another statistic that his parents shoved out into the world.

He wasn't *just* a Dalton, and frankly, his financial portfolio said nothing about him as a real person.

That wasn't the man Lucas wanted people around him to know.

"Lucas Dalton," Malachi mumbled against his hand that he rubbed across his mouth. "I've heard that before."

"Probably."

Malachi drummed his fingers against the side of his jaw as he pondered the familiar name. "Mitchel, you said?"

Lucas sighed. "Yeah."

"Not the *beer* baron Mitchel Dalton," he pressed.

There it was.

"Yeah," Lucas echoed.

At the confirmation, Malachi's brow lifted noticeably higher in surprise. "Shit, we're just sitting here talking about trading a pair of beaters like you can't head to the nearest dealership and buy two of anything to have for a couple of play toys to use on the weekend, man."

"If I spent money like that," Lucas returned, "would I have a lot of it?"

"Fair enough."

Lucas lived a modest life.

He didn't care for frivolity.

For the most part.

Malachi shrugged, adding, "But I bet there's a good chance you could comfortably live off whatever interest comes out of that old money, too."

That *old money* wasn't worth the sacrifice Lucas had paid in the form of broken, estranged relationships with his parents, and the privilege of a renowned family name and business sitting on top of a crumbling mountain of pain and heartache.

It cost him to be a Dalton.

Too much.

He didn't expect Malachi to understand, though.

"I'd rather work," Lucas eventually offered. "It gives me something to do."

"I suppose you can't drink too much beer while you're working, huh?" Malachi asked, reverting back to his previous good nature and smile.

Lucas chuckled. "You know, sometimes, that might make things easier at the plant. If I could, of course."

Or at least, it would make working with his father a hell of a lot easier. Something he struggled the most with that would surely get worse for Lucas over the coming months. If his companion's next words were any indication, Malachi had heard the big news for the Dalton family business, too.

"Didn't I just read in the paper how your father announced he's returning to Saint John and expects to have the transition done by spring?"

Lucas smiled tightly. "He dropped that bomb on me at about the same time everyone else learned it, too."

Malachi didn't miss the tension. "Shit, I found a nerve?"

"No," Lucas returned, forcing a charm on his face and the indifferent wave of his hand away from the coffee mug. "Just stuff I'm trying to keep my mind away from, you could say."

"Ah," came the understanding reply.

Yeah.

It wasn't Malachi's fault.

Surely, because Ronald wasn't a complete monster, the man hadn't meant for his announcement about returning to the Maritimes that he made to the brewery on Monday morning, to coincide with his youngest son's overdose. Either way, both things had slammed into Lucas like separate tons of bricks falling from the sky one after another.

He barely had time to get back up.

Hell, he couldn't find a reason *not* to leave the city after all that. Lucas didn't want to revisit any of it now.

"Delaney said you guys had a wood shop set up between the barn and garage?" Lucas asked, hoping the two of them could resituate the conversation to a better place.

Malachi didn't seem to mind. He nodded. "We make furniture with some epoxy work like river tables and sets on commission if someone wants something specific."

"How'd that happen for you?"

The other man laughed, but the sound came off wistful like his far away stare. "My skills with wood were limited to construction, at best, when I first met Gracen. I got into the finer details and then we kind of stumbled into a middle ground we both liked, and she and I learned along the way together. Honestly, she spends more time in the shop with me—especially if she's playing with epoxy—than working in her salon, but I like that, too. The days are better when she's with me."

The brewery's corporate meeting room had a long river table with the company's colors accenting the inner lights that made the middle glow between two thick slabs of cherry oak. That was delicate work. He appreciated the style.

"I'd love to see something if you've got anything in the works," Lucas said, genuinely interested.

"We're doing a wall piece with rock maple that's just about done," Malachi offered with a shrug, standing from the table.

Lucas followed the same path. "Let's see it."

*

Lucas held the truck in park while Gracen still leaned into the passenger's side window where she hugged Delaney for dear life. The man standing a few feet behind her offered Lucas an apologetic widening of his arms as if to silently say *what can you do?*

Apparently, it had been a while since the two women spent time together, and as he learned over the passing morning as the day neared noon, Gracen and Delaney's friendship went *way* back. The high school days and years of living together had long been in the rearview mirror for the two, but the many photographs of them together that he noticed throughout the farmhouse said it was a friendship that would undoubtedly last.

Christ.

They practically grew up together.

"Okay, okay," Gracen said, finally releasing a laughing Delaney and stepping back from the truck. Her gloved hands remained wrapped around the door frame, not yet ready to let go. "If you don't make it back down this way before you head back to Freddy—"

"I'll call as soon as I'm home," Delaney reassured.

"I guess I'll call Bexley?"

At that comment, Delaney only rolled her eyes. "I can't believe she actually called you."

"Give her a break. You didn't explain much."

"I didn't give her much to tell," Lucas clarified.

He didn't mind taking the heat.

It *had* been his fault.

Delaney only shook her head his way, but otherwise, she didn't broach the reason why the two of them found themselves in this particular part of New Brunswick. If he were being honest, Lucas had done his very best so far not to think about Jacob and the lonely, painful reality waiting for him back home.

He'd get there.

Not yet, though.

Gracen's stare affixed to him behind the wheel, and she offered a kind smile that he returned. "It *was* nice to meet you, Lucas."

"And you," he returned. "You'll see me again. I definitely want one of those wall pieces of my own for the cabin. Malachi sketched out something for you. He said you do all the color work, apparently."

She peeked over her shoulder at the grinning man waiting there. Malachi winked back, and the gesture sent her head spinning back to Lucas.

"I guess so, huh?" Gracen asked. "Drive safe, guys. It's supposed to drop a foot of snow tonight."

"They've got lots of time before that starts," Malachi assured in the background.

Delaney waved, whispering *love you* to Gracen as she rolled up the window. The woman in the driveway mouthed the words back as Lucas shifted the Chevy into park, and pressed a light foot onto the gas.

He reminded himself to thank Malachi again for doing a quick sweep with sand over the driveway so the long, winding road up wouldn't be a problem. Before they had even reached the crest, Delaney unbuckled her seatbelt and scooted over to the middle of the bench seat next to him behind the wheel. His hand found her warm, jean-clad inner thigh while she buckled herself in once more, and her head found the side of his arm.

"Who's cooking when we get back?" he asked. "Me or you?"

"Well, *I*," she stressed, "wanted to make a soup."

Lucas perked at the news, considering the different ingredients she had picked up at the store. A large can of tomato juice had been the only thing that could act as a base, in his head, and he could already taste it. "I'm game for that. Anything else?"

He felt her grin against his arm before she kissed the same spot overtop of his parka. "Don't forget to stop at the store."

Right.

There was that, too.

23.

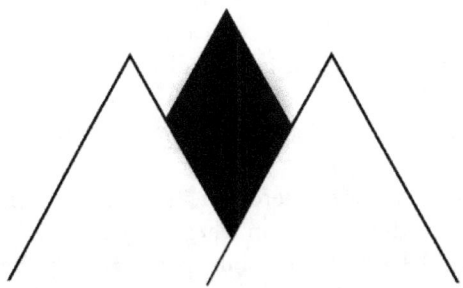

The fire back at the cabin had sizzled down to nothing but a bed of coals by the time Lucas and Delaney walked through the front door with arms loaded up with bags. After the two got the bags in order on the floor where she directed them to be put, he restocked the old wood chief and moved the kettle to the middle where it could boil while his quiet companion unloaded bags, and searched the small pantry of cupboards for the items she needed.

Lucas shed his coat and scarf at the hooks by the door where Delaney had already hung hers.

"Onion powder will have to do," she muttered under her breath, pulling the ingredient in question out of the cupboard.

The old spice, yet another thing the cabin had a lot of because it didn't go bad in a handful of months, joined the pile Delaney had already collected on the island. Fully engrossed in her task and not the least bit interested in the way Lucas had come to sit at the far side of the island to watch her work, he reveled in the homely silence of the small cabin other than the muted shuffle of Delaney's current task.

Her brow furrowed as she turned around, her attention down on the sealed glass jar full of rice in her hand. "Rice wouldn't go bad, right?"

"Probably not," Lucas agreed.

Delaney peeked up at him. "Is it against the rules to put potatoes *and* rice in a soup together?"

"It's your soup, sweetheart."

"Yeah, so?"

"*You* make all the rules," Lucas clarified.

Her lips split with the sweetest grin. "Yeah, I guess so. Okay."

With that, she spun back around.

Back at her work, it didn't take Delaney long to have a saucepan of boiling water on the stove defrosting the pound of hamburger they'd picked up earlier. On the only other burner, she had started another pot of water that she added spices to as the water came to a slow boil. At the island, she put Lucas to task with a bowl of potatoes to peel once she had moved onto her own bowl of carrots.

"I haven't been home—here, but *there*," she muttered with a tilt of her head toward the direction where they had traveled to visit her friend. "In the area, I guess, but specifically The Valley, in two years," Delaney said without warning that their work peeling vegetables would turn into a conversation.

Lucas didn't mind.

He let her talk.

"Oh?"

"Yeah," she said on a big exhale. "Coming back with you, when I didn't really plan to, makes it easier to be here. I'd made it into this big thing in my head about not being able to come home because I let it scare me. As if a town, or something, was a real thing that could hurt me just by *being*. Mostly, I just miss it here. Empty back roads and trees for days. Walking down the street and seeing people I recognize who actually wave at me. I miss those things."

Amongst others, he imagined.

Lucas kept those thoughts to himself, though.

"But even if the place doesn't hurt me, things happened here that did," Delaney said. "A lot."

Lucas, too practiced with a knife to let his gaze slip away from the blade in his hand while he peeled off the white potato skin, stopped so he could look at the woman who stared across at him. "Malachi told me something interesting when he took me out to the shop to show me around."

"Did he?"

An easy shrug feel from Lucas' broad shoulders. "I might have mentioned the area would be a decent place to settle down—asked if there was anything I should know."

"And what did he say?"

"Stay out of the mountain," Lucas said, the first and most important thing Malachi had verbalized about the tiny slice of the province along the Acadian Peninsula. "Montgomery Mountain, of course. Is that even its real name?"

"No, but if you so much as take a tree that's fallen into the ditch off that mountain—"

"They'll burn your house down," Lucas interjected, smiling tightly. Really, who did that type of shit? "Yeah, he said that, too. Just like that. I wasn't ready for it, let me say. I take it that's happened before? Is it not an empty threat?"

"Among other things," Delaney replied dryly. "All I ever got told about the mountain is certain people don't like to be bothered, and they don't have a problem letting you know. Otherwise, there are people in town who swear up and down the Montgomery family would do anything for you if you needed and asked. I've never needed something, and never had to ask, so."

That's what counted, Lucas supposed.

Lucas went back to peeling the potato as he said, "And the other thing he mentioned, well, apparently there's a church around that doesn't like to be bothered, either. He called it a cult, actually—is there a watch list for that sort of thing?"

"Probably. And they're probably on it, too." Delaney sighed, but the rhythmic grate of her utensil along the carrot shaft picked up again. "Let me guess, you wondered if the church he mentioned might be related to the overly religious parents I told you about?"

"I considered that could be possible," Lucas hedged, letting her take the bait if she wanted.

"Did he tell you that he grew up in it, too?" she asked quietly. "The church, I mean?"

Hurt colored her tone.

Accusation, too.

Lucas, not expecting those things from Delaney, couldn't quell the helpless feeling compounding in his chest when the woman across the island jumped down from the stool and headed for the stove. She worked in silence to chunk up the hamburger before draining the extra grease and water off into a bowl she placed off to the side of the counter. He managed to get through the few large potatoes she wanted him to peel and cube by the time she had added the ground beef and the can of tomato soup to the large boiling pot for the soup.

"To be fair, he didn't tell me anything about you, or whatever, if any, connection you have to the church," Lucas told Delaney as she rounded the island to take the colander full of raw, cubed potatoes he'd readied.

She took the colander, but a heat remained in her hazel eyes. "Promise?"

"Do those mean something to you?"

"Maybe, coming from you."

So be it, he thought.

"I promise," Lucas said.

Delaney's gaze shifted away from him, but it took her an extra second to nod like she believed him. "Okay. Do you want to ask me?"

That wasn't such an easy answer, and Lucas could tell by the irritation she already showed at the topic of conversation. If bringing the subject of her former church, and family ties, worked her up ... he didn't think *she* wanted to talk about it.

Maybe they shouldn't.

Except for one thing ...

"I care, you know?" he asked, shrugging one shoulder under the gray T-shirt he'd pulled on that morning. "About who you are and what's made you, *you*. The good and bad things. Why they make you smile or cry. If you expect me to apologize for wanting to know everything I can about you, I'm sorry, Delaney. I can't do that. I won't."

Her posture softened a bit.

So did her eyes.

She hugged the colander of potatoes closer to her chest. "*Well*, when you put it like that ..."

Lucas chuckled. "Honesty is the best policy, they said."

Or someone did.

Once upon a time.

"Yeah, but they never learned that the truth hurts, too," Delaney muttered under her breath.

Wasn't that, in itself, a sad truth?

One he knew all too well.

"I'll finish the carrots up while you wash those," he said, nodding to the potatoes she held as he reached for the bowl of veggies she had left unfinished.

For a second, Delaney remained standing close enough to Lucas' stool that he could reach over and pull her into his lap if he wanted.

And he did.

So badly.

The urge was nothing but selfishness, he knew. A way to distract the both of them from a tough conversation that probably needed to be had between them. He stuffed the desire down as Delaney headed for the sink on the other side of the island to wash the potatoes.

Far from his reach.

Shame, he thought.

As he promised, Lucas worked on peeling what remained of the three carrots left in Delaney's bowl before he went ahead and sliced them into a neat pile on the one cutting board she had also been using. She wandered back to him to grab the board full of carrot slices before taking them to the sink to wash as well.

The vegetables plopped into the steaming soup that he could already smell. Despite only having a few spices to add and a can of tomato juice, she produced a soup base for the meat and veggies that had his mouth watering.

His stomach growled, too.

They really should have eaten earlier.

Oh, well.

Delaney remained at the stove, occasionally lifting the lid on the pot to stir the soup before sniffing the steam rising up as if that could give her an accurate read of the taste. He doubted it, but didn't blame her for the effort.

"It smells great," he said.

"Thanks," she murmured over her shoulder.

But back to what *really* mattered …

Lucas left the comfort of the stool behind to make his way to where Delaney worked at the shove. Coming up behind her, she peeked back at him with a small smile as he sunk his fingers into the loose waves of her black hair falling to her mid-back. The soft tilt of her head every time he raked his fingers through her hair said she liked it, so he kept it up while he talked.

"I'm sorry, I didn't mean to bring up a sore subject," he said.

She shook her head. "It's okay."

"Well—"

"It is," she assured. "Well, it isn't okay. It *is* a sore subject, but neither of those things are the problem. It just takes me off guard whenever I have to talk about the church or my family. I left both a long time ago. At the same time, actually, because I didn't have a choice. I was told to live the way they said was the only acceptable way, or don't be around them at all. And when that's all you've ever known—church practically every day of the week, a patriarchal house, believing everyone on the outside is bad … the *lies*, it's scary when you start to think it might be better to get away. And making that choice forced me to grow up overnight. In a world that I had been told would hurt me in one way or another. Yeah, a little scary."

"Was it, though? Better?"

"I mean, I didn't have to hear my father call me a slut every day," Delaney said, like it was a qualifier to what came next. "Then again, he left a message on my publicly listed cell phone number every month for the first couple of years telling me I was a disgrace to God because I went to the trade school in Grand Falls to study hairdressing, and then opened my first salon with Gracen, *so*."

Lucas flinched. "That sounds terrible."

"Does it? I got used to it after a while. For a bit, people from the church used to yell at me in the grocery store, too. Those were fun days."

He couldn't wrap his mind around that.

"What, why?"

"One of the biggest rules for the women of the congregation is to keep their hair uncut and natural," Delaney said, shrugging one shoulder as she opened the pot to stir it once more. "I was probably a walking, talking fuck you to every single one of them. Not only did I leave the church, I was actively practicing outside of the limits of their faith. If anything, it just gave them a reason to be more horrible than they already were after I left."

His fingers froze at the tips of her wavy hair.

He stared down at the length.

One he considered long, really.

"How long was your hair?"

"At one point, to the floor," she said. "In grade nine, I could actually step on it. I hated it. It gave me migraines, we weren't allowed to wear it down. No woman can unless it's to bed or they're alone with their husband. It's supposed to be a woman's crown, they say. So, why can't she show it off? Why is she even hiding it?"

Lucas didn't have those answered, but he didn't think she

expected him to come up with one, either. The chance was, the fact that Delaney had started to ask questions like that at all was a big part of the reason she hadn't remained in the church with her family.

"After a few years, it got to the point where they didn't even look at me if they saw me on the street or something," Delaney muttered.

He heard the hurt there, too.

It even made him ache.

Lucas was intimately familiar with how hard it could be to desperately want and need the love and affection from people who should, above all others in the world, provide it. Only to find they just couldn't do it.

"Gracen and I owned a second salon—we sold the first," she explained, peeking back at him with a sad smile. "And bought the next one. A big courthouse we converted into a huge salon that we put everything into for years. We lived right across the river. That was our life every day. The salon. Each other."

Delaney sighed, adding, "Until it wasn't."

She hated how saying that sounded so cliché, but it was true, too.

"What happened?" he asked, sensing she left something unsaid.

"My older cousin, and my brother, Levi, set fire to the salon after Gracen and I helped my cousin—Bexley, you met her—leave the church once she graduated high school, and they couldn't legally stop her. They were also charged in connection with another fire that happened around the same time. A pizza place next door to our apartment but according to what I heard sitting in the trial, that was unrelated to me or Gracen. Mostly."

His hands clamped tight around her tense shoulders. "*Jesus*, Delaney."

"Yeah, so the Montgomery family isn't the only bunch around here that likes to burn things down if you step out of line, I guess. Although, nothing's ever burnt in my lifetime that wasn't by the hand of my own family, that I know of, so—let that tell you what you want it to. Not sure if Malachi told you that part."

"No, he did not."

"*Huh*. Funny, it's the first thing I think about every morning. As soon as I open my eyes, it's like I'm staring across the river watching the black smoke pumping out of the back of what was supposed to be my whole life," she muttered heavily. "I think about it too much, maybe. It was suggested I leave town during the trial—they held that in Woodstock—just in case."

"I'm sorry, that must have been rough."

"No, it was easy to run," she admitted, shrugging. "I tried really hard to be a person outside of that church and my family, my own person … and in one day they turned me into someone everyone in my hometown recognizes and knows because of what they did to me."

She shook her head, angrier when she tacked on, "I can *hear* it, you know? *Oh, there's Delaney Reed. They say her family burnt down her salon because she went against their church.* I can't stand it."

"*Delaney.*"

He tried her name, an octave lower than his usual tone, as a way to coax her away from the soup she continued to methodically check and stir after turning it down to a medium simmer. When that didn't work, Lucas opted to try something different.

Braiding her hair.

If it worked once to calm her nerves, and she liked it, then he could use playing with her hair to his benefit. Besides, whatever sugary-sweet spray she'd dusted it in that morning from an aerosol can—proclaiming it to be dry shampoo when he squinted at the powder she had to brush out—had made his hands smell like her, and he couldn't get it out of his head.

Like how his hands and fingers had smelled like the softest, hottest parts of her, all wet and needy because of him. *That* memory brought the tart taste of her sweetness to the forefront of his mind, and Lucas was just fucking with himself, now.

She made him addicted, and barely had to try at all. In fact, not one of the many reckless hook-ups of his early twenties left him semi-hard all morning the way rubbing a nut out on and in Delaney's hands had that morning.

Intimacy was one thing.

Real connection was another.

The woman currently stirring the soup a good head lower than his own, hit both of those on the mark for Lucas. A human connection he'd never experienced in his life before this moment. On the outside, Delaney was the perfect picture of a baby bird, if there was any comparison. Weak and needing protection. To someone else, they might see him as the protector, but he didn't.

Her petite size and sometimes quiet nature meant nothing for the strength all five-foot-*maybe*-one of her radiated. A stubborn confidence that probably should have been beaten or taught out of her—considering the people she came from—stained her aura in bright colors.

Can't beat 'em, join 'em.

Lucas separated Delaney's hair into three thick chunks that he began to rope back and forth into a braid. The way she went still at what he assumed would be familiar motions for her made him smile down at his slow work.

"It's been a while since I did this," he admitted, a quarter of the way down her hair.

Delaney laughed a lovely sound. "Who taught you to braid— any sisters?"

"No sisters. Jacob was the only one after me. Cub Scouts taught me, amongst many things, how to braid rope, tie a knot, start a fire … *boy* things, my father said. Although, I did braid my mother's hair once."

Delaney's head tipped to the side. "Really?"

It was a tender memory for Lucas, one he didn't want to delve into because it could only bring pain, but she had been kind enough to share hers with him.

"The plant out west opened around the time my little brother was born," Lucas started, trying to keep his voice level and the emotion out of it. "So, my father, Ronald, spent the first two years of Jacob's life across the country, and Penelope, my mother, barely got out of bed for the first six months. She had a nanny for Jacob, but I was a ten-year-old kid who could see that my mother was sad, and so I tried to help her sometimes."

As foolish as that had been. It wasn't good for a young mind to be exposed to bouts of drunken stupor and the emotional load adult issues put on the shoulders of a child.

Lucas understood that, now.

He was the personification of parentification.

A companion to a toxic parent who found joy in the misery of others, and was barely tolerated by the other adult in his life—the man who fathered him—on top of being a caregiver for his brother for almost all of his life. Jacob didn't get much better from their parents, of course, except Lucas refused to feel burdened by the role that was forced upon him when it came to his only sibling.

Family had meant something to him.

Even if it didn't to the people who made it.

Lucas willed himself out of those spiraling thoughts by muttering, "It was also the only attention I could get from her— the five minutes I'd get to bring her something to drink, or when she'd be just drunk enough to let me sit and watch soap operas with her in bed after school ... and yeah, once I braided her hair."

"*God*," she breathed under her breath, exasperated in tone, but he couldn't be sure.

"What?" Lucas asked, amused but wary at the same time, as the braid came to an end with the last couple of inches of her hair.

Delaney put the cover back on the soup pot and turned around to look up at him. "You're standing here trying to comfort me— ah, don't," she said when he opened his mouth to deny that had been his purpose for leaving his seat at the island. "You're comforting me like there isn't a reason why we're standing here in the first damn place. Like you're not grieving. It doesn't have to be about me, okay? And you don't need to bleed your pain out to make me feel better about mine, either."

He pursed his lips with a shake of his head. "You're grieving, too. Something different than mine, yes, but that doesn't change what the grief is. People grieve different things for different reasons, and those same people grieve differently. So what if I'm grieving?" he asked honestly. "You are, too. Both things can be true."

Perspective wasn't always easy.

Lucas decided to give Delaney some since she was so worried about him. "The fact you're here is the only reason I haven't been on some crisis hotline or draining my bank account for my four-hundred-dollar-an-hour therapist. You give me something to focus on, and that's okay with me. I'm aware that I hold things together really well. On the surface, yes. If you haven't figured it out yet, I didn't have much of a choice growing up but to do things, and get them done right the first time around."

Delaney swallowed hard, her brow pinching in pain. "*See*, like that. You say things like that and it just makes me want to hold you."

He chuckled.

That was not at all what he expected her to say. Funny. To him, he thought they kind of wanted to do the same things. Just for each other. To comfort and care.

"You can do that," he told her. "Hold me together. I don't have to be breaking apart while you do it, though."

Her chest deflated with a hard breath. "Okay, so that'll just be me doing that between us sometimes, then?"

Lucas smirked.

"What?" Delaney asked.

"You said *us*, like it's a thing. That makes it real, right? I mean ..." His eyebrows jumped high. "You said it."

That time, it was her turn to smile.

"You know, I almost broke another rule for you today, Lucas Dalton, but you surprised me again," Delaney murmured, pointing her index finger against the center of his chest. Could she feel the way his heart thundered there—did she have the first clue it was because of *her*?

"Did I?"

She nodded, but her stare dropped a bit as she whispered, "You would have been the first man I ever slept with that I didn't make label what we were before I got into bed with him."

Yep.

Would have.

Except he wasn't here to make her break rules, and he only heard one thing in all she said that mattered to him.

"So, like I said," Lucas told her, "the *us* thing—it's real. You said it first. I just agreed."

Her sneaky grin that she tried to hide as she spun around to face the stove again didn't escape his notice, and this time, he fit against her back where he could tuck his face into her neck. He kissed the soft, warm skin that pebbled under his lips and grabbed two fistfuls of her oversized sweater to keep them close, molding their bodies together, as she took the cover off the top of the pot.

"*Delaney,*" he whispered along the column of her neck.

"Hmm?"

Her question came with a shiver.

He fisted the fabric of her sweater tighter, telling her, "Definitely an *us*."

"And now *you* said it," she agreed. "So, I guess we're doing that, huh?"

"Guess so, sweets."

So there it was.

At that declaration, he pressed a kiss to the top of her head.

"I'm putting a can of diced tomatoes in this," she told him. "It'll need to simmer for at least twenty-five minutes if you want it to taste *really* good."

There was something about her tone.

Suggestive, maybe.

"Mmhmm, and?" he asked.

"For the rest of the day, all we're going to do is eat good food, fuck, *maybe* drink … and we're not going to talk about your shitty parents, or *mine*, or about anything else that doesn't make us both feel really, really good. Deal?"

Jesus Christ.

He would hate every aching second it took her to open that damn can of tomatoes, pour it into the pot, and stir it around.

So be it.

All in all, it seemed like a worthy trade to him.

"Deal," he returned.

24.

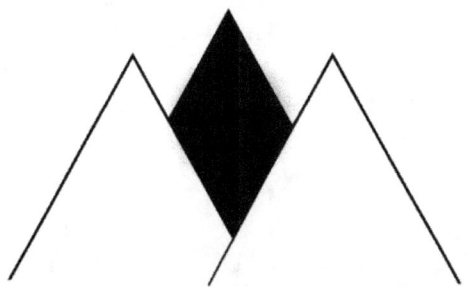

"H-hello?" came a sleepy, familiar voice when the call clicked through.

"How are you already asleep?" Delaney asked Gracen. "It's barely even nine."

"I'm *pregnant*," Gracen grumbled on the other end of the call, unapologetic. "Don't judge my sleep patterns, okay?"

Delaney snickered under her breath. "You got it, babe. Ask Malachi who's winning for me?"

She seriously doubted *he* was crawling into bed with Gracen before ten on a hockey night, and despite the flat screen in their big master bedroom, he wouldn't keep her up while he watched, either. Besides, Gracen *hated* hockey.

Gracen's muffled yell on the other end of the call made Delaney think her friend had covered the speaker. It crackled for a second before Gracen came back on the line with a surprising answer.

"The Bruins."

"*Really?*"

How many years had that been, now?

"Are they the penguin one?" Gracen asked.

Delaney only laughed. "You don't care."

"Not really," Gracen agreed, happily, humming sleepily at the same time. Delaney could almost imagine her friend snuggling deeper into the fluffy duvet and pillows that made up Gracen's big bed. "The better question," her friend said, "is why *you* are calling me at nine, huh? Didn't you tell me you were working on something earlier?"

Gracen couldn't see the way Delaney's cheeks pinked at the blatant question, but she still dropped her head like her friend could. She focused on the bright white tips of her manicure in the darkness of the cottage's loft, her fingers curled around the back of the booster that she had to keep her phone on while she talked, or it would lose the connection. Thank God for the speakerphone. Naked under the quilt she kept tossed over her shoulders as she sat on the edge of the combined twin beds, only her toes grazed the cold hardwood floor.

"I was," Delaney said.

"Mmm?"

"*Did*," she corrected.

A second of silence followed Delaney's admittance that she had, in fact, slept with Lucas before Gracen's squeal broke the damn sound barrier. All Delaney could do to keep from spilling the flood of very personal details racing through her mind was bite down on the inside of her grinning cheek.

"Do I get *any* details?" Gracen asked.

The two shared a lot together over the years.

Some things didn't need to *be* said, though.

"Ugh, you know how I am about *sex*."

Gracen laughed Delaney's excuse off.

Delaney preferred to tuck those memories of her first, only-a-little-fumbling time with Lucas locked away like a private letter she could revisit with her mind. Still fresh enough that she could enjoy the way his fingers had pinched so good grabbing her ass as they fucked, half-dressed downstairs using a stool for her knees and the kitchen island.

Her nipples still hardened at the way the cold countertop pressed against her skin in her haste to not even get her sweater off entirely before he shoved her down and filled her up. Like teenagers with shaking hands and not enough time lest they be caught, it *was* fumbling and fast and entirely fucking perfect.

She'd just wanted to feel him, to finally know he'd be as good as she thought stretching her open and fucking her hard from behind.

And it was.

He was.

Darkness fell early over New Brunswick in the winter. The dinner table barely got cleared from supper dishes, and it would already be dark. That same blanket of dark coldness carried the province through to the morning hours. A worker on a twelve-hour shift could miss the sun entirely in a single workday.

She'd still had a few spoonfuls of the beef-tomato soup left in her bowl, when he leaned across the island to take a kiss from her lips that started it all demanding politely that she pull down her pants for him. He'd let her taste the way her arousal turned tart after she orgasmed when he dropped a kiss to her trembling lips after spreading her wide on the stool and finding his dessert between her thighs, too.

The man had a mouth on him that he clearly liked to use, but it had been his tongue to start the unraveling of Delaney.

Delaney had never experienced being simultaneously turned on and almost ashamed—and truly *liking* it—at the vivid, explicit way Lucas could describe the way she tasted and smelled; or how he loved it and the things he wanted to do to her.

"*You're honey in the summertime*," he'd panted into a passionate kiss, and smeared wet with her around his lips. She hadn't been able to get his pants shoved down fast enough, but she'd tried while he kept her locked under him. "*A sin you learn to love.*"

He couldn't have known how right he was in saying that to her. Even the shame of tasting herself on his mouth after she had come turned her on. Years of being taught to be ashamed and afraid of what made her body feel good had turned Delaney into a secretive teenager who had hid all of her healthy, or otherwise, sexual exploration. The battle of her shame and pleasure became one she had always been careful not to play into lest it leave her more scarred than it already had.

Lucas Dalton, a gentleman for every moment she had shared up until she spread her legs wide for him, tempted her closer to the truth where both shame and pleasure lived. *Safely.*

She'd never trusted someone to let her revel in both without judgement until those moments with him. It had emboldened her to say as much, too.

"I want to be fucked like your slut."

"Just not called it," he'd returned, making a heat flush from her head to her toes when he'd added, "*Yet.*"

Oh, God.

He'd been so, *so* right.

Their first time had been a rushed few minutes where he gave her exactly what she'd asked for. Sore thighs and knees included. But he had made her stay still and let him touch and adore every inch of her that he wanted after he'd carried her upstairs. There, he kept her warm under the quilt with him for what she thought were hours, only leaving the bed to give her a break occasionally.

Usually, to steep another tea with a drop of rum from the mini bottles of Bacardi he'd picked up at the store as a surprise.

Never one to stop herself from pointing out Delaney's awkward stretches of silence when she got pulled into her own head, Gracen cleared her throat as if to announce she was going to ask a question. "I guess, I'm still trying to figure out why you called me?"

"Probably, huh? I swear I'm not crazy."

Gracen laughed. "You never were—your late-night phones calls are, by far, some of our best ever conversations."

She wasn't lying.

Maybe this would be another one of those?

Delaney wouldn't know if she didn't try.

"Did I ever tell you that I cried the next morning after the night I lost my virginity in high school?" Delaney asked.

She knew Gracen's answer.

No.

Never once did she share the memory of her shame after choosing to sleep with a boy she'd been dating for almost an entire year—that she believed she loved, at the time—shortly after her seventeenth birthday. There were some things she hadn't even been able to tell her best friend.

Things that, *tonight*, she had shared in hushed murmurs wrapped in the arms of a man that might as well be a stranger who felt like home, as if telling him would somehow release the ache and shame it left behind from holding it all in for so long.

It did help.

It was the sharing part that surprised her more than anything; and how his presence as he did nothing but twirl the only thing she wore between them—her cross necklace—between his fingertips as she talked and even more secrets spilled out.

Things she still wouldn't tell Gracen.

Things she didn't even like to tell herself.

"I still thought I was gonna go to hell," Delaney whispered. "That I'd ruined a part of myself."

Back then, though, the belief had felt real. As real as anything else that Delaney could touch with her own hands, hear from her ears, or see with the eyeballs in her head. There were certain things from her faith that held her back longer than others. That had been one of them.

"I would have told you that was crazy back then," Gracen admitted, sounding genuinely apologetic, "but now that we're older and I know what I do, I just want to say sorry."

"I know. It's okay."

"It's *not*," her friend returned strongly. "It's not, and it's okay for you to say that now. That the things they taught and forced up on you made you believe you weren't worthy or bad or … any of it, Delaney. Do you think it would even make a difference—if they did know?"

"They think they're right," Delaney said, "and that's all that matters to people like that, Gracen."

"Yeah," came the mumbled, unhappy reply.

It was what it was.

Even if it wasn't what it could be.

"Even though we *are* adults and smarter—or should be—now," Delaney said, finally getting around to the point of her call, "would you still tell me if something was crazy whether it hurt my feelings or not?"

Gracen thought about the question for a second. "Depends."

"On what?"

"If you're happy," her friend returned instantly.

Ah.

Delaney should have known.

Perhaps her best friend had caught onto the point of her call after all.

"I could wrap myself around him and stay in that place forever," Delaney said, the words coming out on a breath of air that she worried Gracen might not hear.

She did.

Perfectly fine, too.

"Just because it's happening fast, or feels intense and too good to be true, or doesn't even make a lot of sense, doesn't mean it's not real, Delaney. Sometimes, that's how this is supposed to be."

"Yeah, okay," she muttered, trying to hide the thick rush of emotions lodging in her throat or the wetness welling in her eyes.

"And you don't have to say it right now—it's okay to let it all be scary good for a while—for it to still be true inside of you, either," Gracen added softer.

"You won't say what *it* is?" Delaney tried to joke.

Gracen's seriousness never faltered. "When you do, sure."

*

Delaney had just said her goodbyes to Gracen—with a promise to call again if she needed anything—as Lucas returned inside the cabin downstairs. The *brrrraapp* outside as a skidoo put distance under its skis leading away from the cottage, Lucas' voice traveled upstairs.

"You want another tea, sweets?"

"I want you," she returned.

"*Well*," came his husky reply.

Lucas, having shed his parka and boots, climbed the stairs to the loft as the skidoo's engine grew fainter in the background.

"What did your visitor want?"

"Ah, that was just Kenzi," Lucas said, coming to stand at he top of the loft.

Delaney had dropped the quilt to a pile around her naked body where she still sat on the edge of the bed. Lucas grinned at the sight.

"He's fifteen, and *not* ready to see a woman like you naked on a bed," Lucas praised.

She winked. "You put on pants. I could have, too."

"Nah, he didn't plan to stay. Just pass along a message."

That had her curious.

"Oh?"

Lucas crossed the space from the stairs to the edge of the bed where she could reach out and touch him. The fact that the urge made her fingertips practically itch told Delaney she should just do it, and feed into the new monster growing, happily fed because of Lucas, inside her chest.

Her fingers curled around the waistband of the cotton drawstring pants he'd pulled on to go outside after leaving her behind, naked in bed.

Lucas watched her from above as she slowly stroked the hard planes of his toned stomach, dusted with soft, dark hair, below the waistline of his pants. There was no hiding the way his erection began to thicken under the thin pants.

"Mmhmm," he said in a nod. "Seems someone figured out I brought a guest along on this trip—probably the guy at the store talking too much. You know how it is."

Around here?

Yeah.

A new face got talked about.

To anyone who cared to listen.

"What about it?" she asked.

"The Smiths thought you might like a sleigh ride and trip to the maple camp tomorrow, if you're feeling up to it," he tacked on at the end like an afterthought.

Delaney smiled. "Shouldn't it be if *you* feel up to it?"

He only shrugged.

"What about snowshoeing?" she asked.

"Oh, don't worry. We'll probably need those, too."

Of course.

She should have known.

"I could go on a sleigh ride," she said. "And what's this about a *maple* camp?"

"You'll see," he returned, the huskiness returning full force to his tone as her hands finally pulled his pants down so she could get his big cock in her hands. "I thought we agreed you were going to jump in the shower before I shut down the generators for the night."

Delaney abused her bottom lip with her teeth before asking, "And if I want to taste you like you did for me first?"

It was a fool's question.

It wouldn't end with her sucking his dick.

She wanted his thickness making her feel too full again. Maybe she'd ride him this time, reverse cowgirl style, just to make sure he left a few bruises behind on her ass from working her body hard against his own so that she could feel it on the sleigh ride tomorrow.

Any of it.

Delaney would take it.

Lucas smacked his tongue off the roof of his mouth as he piled Delaney's loose, fuck-mussed hair into a messy bun on the top of her head. Never once did he break their stare, even as her grinning lips found the underside of his shaft to graze.

He still smelled like them.

And latex.

But the *sex.*

It drove her nuts.

In the most wicked of ways.

That she'd made him wet to his balls. How he hadn't even had time to properly clean her off before they were interrupted by the unexpected visitor on a skidoo. She licked him from root to tip, moving her fingers along the way until her mount encompassed the head of his cock where she sucked hard.

"Holy hell, girl, you're gonna kill me tonight," Lucas breathed from up above, his broad chest heaving, "but let's see what you can do with that pretty little mouth."

25.

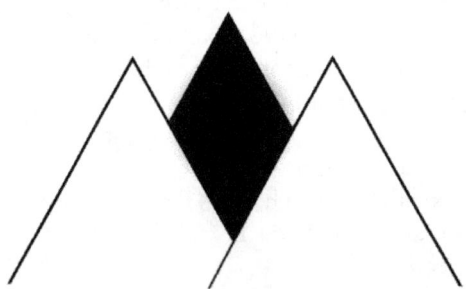

"I've never seen horses that big," Delaney said beside Lucas in the sleigh.

Her comment didn't go unheard by the woman in the seat directly across from theirs with her back facing her husband who minded the reins connected to the twin Clydesdales. Their black hides glimmered on the clear, crisp winter day from a fresh brushing while their braided manes and tails looked soft enough to touch.

Just not while they were working.

Mack Smith made that clear to Delaney when she stepped outside the cabin earlier to greet the horses, although she refused to leave Lucas' side. Even making him walk alongside her as she had rounded the horses to say hello and to check out their gear and the fancy leather tassels that clicked and rattled with every clip-clop of their hooves.

Not that he'd complained.

Theresa—Teddy, to her husband only—grinned big at the compliment. "They're gentle giants, really. More scared of the occasional mouse that scurries across their pens than anything else."

"Their hooves would squish a mouse into *nothing*," Delaney returned. "It'd take one step."

The other woman only laughed. "They're too concerned with getting away from the mouse, actually."

Interestingly enough, the horses didn't seem to be bothered at all by the occasional scream of the skidoos rounding back and zooming past the sleigh on the well-groomed forest trail. As if the animals were well accustomed to the antics of the teenaged Smith boys and their sleds, the horses didn't so much as bat a tail hair in the direction of the two testing their limits with their father.

"I'm telling you!" Mack shouted at the oldest, Dylan, who cut out in front of the horses a little too close for comfort on the trail. "Goddamn it, Teddy—you gotta talk to those two again," he tossed over his shoulder at his wife.

To her benefit, she only nodded indulgently.

Like that solved the issue.

Lucas chuckled. "Let's be honest, he lets 'em do it, too, right?"

Theresa winked. "You know it."

As he suspected.

One thing Lucas had learned about the Smith family over the years that he had made friends with them from their homestead down the way from his family's cottage was that their boys could do no wrong. Mack might like to whoop and holler about, or at, his sons every once and a while, but that was as far as his discipline went, most days.

To be fair, the boys were good kids.

Sure, a little wild than most.

Loud like all boys, too.

They were also capable in the woods, independent, hard-working alongside their mother and father on their family's farm and business, and not once had either teenager come face to face with Lucas without taking their caps off their head to shake his hand when they said hello. Respect counted for a lot where he came from.

For them, too.

Who cared if they made a bit of ruckus?

Wasn't that what made them fun?

Mack and Theresa raised a good pair of boys that would turn into decent young men soon enough. They might as well enjoy the two as they were now—it wouldn't last forever.

"They'll only be young once," Lucas added.

Mack, still heading the sleigh, laughed with a boom that carried up the trail. "True, friend. That is very true."

Lucas, having been to the maple farm owned by the Smiths a couple of times before, knew the first leg of the journey felt like the longest and wasn't the most interesting. A long trek through a maintained woods trail to the back part of Birch Ridge where there was nothing to see but land and trees for days. On the way, however, one only had the horses and trail to enjoy.

Delaney shivered next to him on the seat, and he pulled her tighter into his side beneath the pair of quilts the Smiths had brought along for them to use.

"Put your hands in my parka, if you need to," he told her. "We've got a ways to go yet."

Her eyes sparkled up at him. "Just how far, exactly?"

Theresa answered that question. "Another half hour on the trail, at least."

At the news, Delaney snuggled in even closer, and beneath the quilt, her mittens worked their way under his parka after getting it unzipped to find the warmth at his chest. Lucas laughed.

"Good news," Theresa added, "is Mack sent the boys up this morning to get a fire going in the warming shack where we boil the syrup. It'll be perfect when we get there."

"Perfect," Delaney told him, "just a half an hour more in the cold to go."

He chuckled. "You'll survive."

"Barely," she teased right back.

Conversation dwindled in the sleigh as the horses took them deeper into the trail. The canopy of tree branches over their heads let off a constant stream of falling snowflakes from the wind rustling overhead. If he could have taken a picture of that moment to keep forever, Lucas would have added it to the many decorating the walls of his cabin.

Instead, he imprinted it to memory.

And the way Delaney smiled with her head propped against his side.

Distracting himself with tucking the stray strands of her hair behind her ears and fixing her toque once he was satisfied, Lucas didn't pay much mind to the quiet conversation happening between the couple at the front of the sleigh.

Until he heard a name.

"*Jacob.*"

He missed how his brother's name had come up.

Or *why*.

The shift of his attention at the name being used wasn't missed by the woman sitting across from him. Theresa shot a sad smile his way.

"We're sorry to hear about Jacob," she explained, her hands

fidgeting under the quilt she used to cover up and stay warm during the ride. "We weren't sure if we should mention it, or ..." Mack shot a glance over his shoulder, adding, "They mentioned it on the radio this morning. I heard it in passing."

Ah.

Given the obituary for his brother should have run in the Telegraph Journal that morning, it wasn't a surprise that the news of Jacob's untimely death had also found other media outlets. There were so few Daltons left in New Brunswick. Especially with a connection to the infamous brewery that made the family so powerful.

The death *was* news.

Under the quilt, Delaney's hands found Lucas' and held on tight. A silent support that he hadn't known he needed for the conversation.

"I wouldn't have sent the syrup had I known," Theresa added.

"I'm gonna save it for the cabin, if that's okay," Lucas returned.

Her sending it hadn't caused any harm.

Maybe it was a little bittersweet, though.

She only nodded.

"Guess you were looking for some time away from it all?" Mack asked from the head of the sleigh.

"And time to breathe," Lucas replied.

Delaney had helped with that.

A lot.

Mack's head bobbed understandingly. "Too young—that's a damn shame, Lucas."

Tell me about it, he thought.

"I know," was all he said instead.

A quiet moment passed before the *bbrraappp* of the skidoos in the distance broke the silence first.

Lucas asked Theresa, "I assume they said nothing other than a notice of his passing?"

"Basically."

Mack cleared his throat, but never turned away from facing the horses as he asked, "Was he still struggling, friend? The last time I talked to him, all he talked about was keeping his nose clean, you know?"

Lucas heard what the man didn't ask.

Sometimes, the things people didn't say were more important

than what they did, and knowledge was power, after all.

Delaney squeezed Lucas' fingers, woven with her own. Her kind smile helped him to verbalize the truth about Jacob that he'd been keeping inside as a way of protecting his brother. Even if he didn't need that from Lucas anymore.

"Yeah," Lucas responded to Mack, "he still struggled up until the end. I guess I hadn't noticed it the way I used to when Jacob found trouble."

Or perhaps, his brother had gotten better at hiding it.

Either way …

"There's no struggle for him now," Lucas said quietly.

He said it for himself.

And the others in the sleigh who were listening, too. If they needed to hear it like he did, so be it.

Everyone seemed to understand.

Lucas doubted returning to Saint John in a couple of days where he would be expected to return to work amidst the service that would also be held for his brother—surrounded by people who knew Jacob, including those that didn't deserve to, in his opinion, like his parents—would be easy. Certainly not like delivering the news of his brother's passing to long-time friends who were intimately aware of the demons that had haunted Jacob for a good portion of his life.

He didn't look forward to his inevitable return to the city, and what would be his new normal with Jacob gone, and he wouldn't pretend to.

He only cared to enjoy the moment because those were the seconds that counted most to Lucas right now. His brother's life might not have played out the way it could have or should have, but Lucas wouldn't allow his to end as a consequence of Jacob's choices.

They only had one life to live, after all. He desperately wanted to fill his with happiness and all the things that made living on this earth worth it.

Jacob would want that for Lucas, too.

*

The maple camp—a shack, really—sat on the highest crest of the land overlooking the rest of the ridge. Surrounded by towering maple trees with blue lines running between each and taps dripping cold syrup into steel buckets hanging from every thick trunk, the stillness of the forest seemed to welcome the noise that accompanied the Smiths, their guests, and the large, galloping horses.

By the time Lucas had exited the sleigh and offered a hand to help Delaney down, Mack had begun tying off the horses to the railing of the warming shack while the man's wife packed up their blankets and headed for the rickety steps leading to the cozy indoors. The boys, one handling firewood to bring inside and the other heading off for a harvest to bring back, went straight to work without prompting from their parents.

Everybody had a job to do.

Except for him and Delaney, apparently.

"Let's get warm, sweets," he urged, coaxing her toward the shack.

Delaney didn't need a lot of encouragement to go. "Did I hear someone say something about hot chocolate?"

"I even keep rum to spike it if you're feeling up to it," Mack said at their backs.

"That'll definitely make you feel warm in the chest," Lucas told her on their way inside.

Sure enough, the shack—a twenty-foot by twenty-foot camp with a big wood stove and handmade shelves and stools lining the four walls—greeted them with warmth and the smell of fire pumping out of the wood chief in the very middle. It didn't take Delaney long to shed her coat and mittens, but she kept her toque on her head as she hung her garments from a free hook on the wall next to the front door.

For the moment, Lucas kept his winter clothing on.

Mack might need help outside with something, not that the man would ever ask a guest he brought along to do any hard work. He wasn't the type.

In fact, Lucas found himself wandering the small shack with Delaney, overlooking the many items and trinkets that hung from the rafters overhead and sat atop dusty shelves. All the while, the Smiths moved around them, coming in and out of the shack, without a word of expectation for them to help while they hauled in snow to melt in a pot on the wood stove and Kenzie, the youngest boy, hauled in an armful of wood for his mother to stock the fire.

"We'll make some fresh syrup, and roll some out on the snow to eat for a treat—how's that sound?" Theresa asked the two as she tossed another log into the front of the wood stove.

"I've never done that before," Delaney admitted. "What's it do—freeze the syrup instantly?"

"Makes it tacky," Mack explained as he finally entered the cabin with a shuffle of his boots at the door to clean them off of any remaining snow. "We'll clean off a couple of sticks, roll it along the syrup as it chills in the snow, and make popsicles."

"It's good," Lucas assured her.

He remembered the sweet treat from when he was a kid, actually.

This would be his first time enjoying it at the maple camp with the Smiths, however. He liked how it felt appropriate that he would be able to share the experience with Delaney, as well.

"After we get it all made, of course," Theresa added for her husband. "That's the funniest part."

"Not the liquor-spiked hot cocoa?" Delaney asked.

The other woman didn't blink. "Oh, no. That's the fun part, too. Give me a few minutes."

Delaney grinned Lucas' way, and he had all he could do to keep from pulling her in close for a kiss that he was sure would make the others in the shack a bit uncomfortable. Besides, if the last twenty-four hours had taught him nothing, he learned one important thing.

Lucas had little to no self control when it came to Delaney.

One touch wasn't enough.

A taste wouldn't satisfy him.

He *couldn't* stop at a kiss.

Nor would she let him.

"Oh, is that—"

"Uno," Lucas said, coming up behind Delaney as she spied an item on a shelf next to the only table in the whole shack. A circular table, with matching chairs made of oak, that had clearly seen better days if the scratches on top were any indication. "Jacob taught me how to play that—I lost every time."

Now, Solitaire, on the other hand …

That was a card game Lucas preferred, and it had nothing to do with the fact he could play it alone. *Mostly.*

Delaney grinned back at him. "Wanna lose to me, too?"

Well, why not?

He reached over her shoulder to grab the tall stack of old cards from the shelf, replying, "I guess I could let you whip me for a round or two."

Delaney beamed. "I really like this place—and there's not even power or plumbing."

"There's an outhouse around the back, though," Mack said where he had come to stand next to his wife at the stove. "If you don't mind freezing your ass."

The sprite of a woman at his side barely blinked a lash.

"Good to know," Delaney said. Then, to Lucas, she whispered low so only he could hear, "I'm holding my pee until the end of time, if I have to."

They all had to make choices.

She was certainly entitled to hers.

*

"She's a *real* pretty one, Luke," Mack told Lucas after Delaney had disappeared into the cabin. The ride back as the day had crawled closer to dinnertime had been as uneventful as the ride up to the maple cabin, but at least the temperatures leveled out a bit, and he still found it enjoyable. With the sweetness of Delaney close at his side, how could he not?

That made things better, anyhow.

The horses, anxious to get on their way home, stomped against the ground while Mack continued his conversation with Lucas in the driveway.

"Yeah, I like her," Lucas replied, grinning to his old friend. "You never know, I might bring her back around in the spring. Get her out on a wheeler for a rip—she won't have a choice but to take a leak in the woods, then, huh?"

Mack's shoulders rolled with laughter. "Not sure she's entirely cut out for the woods, but hey, neither were you for a while."

That made him chuckle.

The man told no lies.

"Somebody had to toughen up these hands, eh?" Lucas asked.

"We got you there after a while even if it took a bit of work," Mack confirmed. "Theresa said you're both welcome to come down for supper tomorrow, if you'd like. You're leaving Sunday morning, right?"

"That's the plan. I can't say yes or no to tomorrow, though. I'm trying to take this shit one day at a time, you know?"

He didn't know what tomorrow looked like.

Or how he'd feel.

Mack nodded as if he understood, and reached down to clap Lucas on the shoulder. "You're going to get through this, Luke. Right now it's a big ball in your chest pushing on every nerve you have, but it'll get smaller after a while. It won't press on the sore spots as much. It just takes time."

Right.

One step after another.

This day, and then tomorrow.

Grief was like that. Never-ending, but at the same time, a person could find ways to forget it was there for a while. He'd done that so far this week, but Lucas knew he was running from things that couldn't be changed, too. The inevitable would still be waiting for him at the end when he came back home.

No matter how good he felt now.

"Thanks, Mack," Lucas muttered, willing his rising emotions down.

"I'd say to send my condolences to your mother and father, but they probably wouldn't care to hear from me, huh?"

"It matters to me," he told the man.

More than Mack would ever know.

Heading the sleigh and horses, Mack straightened his shoulders and flicked the reins just enough to get the horses stirred up again. "Well, I better get on down the road, eh? Can't let those boys be on their own for too long lest they get some bright fuckin' idea."

Lucas laughed loud. "They're *good* boys, Mack. I bet he even stocked the fire when he was here just because."

Because his dad taught him to. Mack's sons didn't have to be asked or told to know what was right or proper. They offered respect and courtesy to their neighbors as an engrained trait carried over from their mother and father.

"Let them be a little wild," Lucas added. "It's what helps them grow the most, man. We were that age once, too."

Mack tossed a nod his way. "I suppose—Kenzie said Dylan dropped off your gas and the paper you wanted from the store.

Said thanks for the extra fifty bucks."

The hundred-dollar bill he handed over to the Smith boys to make a trip to the store for gas and a newspaper had been money well spent, in Lucas' opinion. No matter what the boys chose to do with the extra.

"Good on 'em," Lucas said. "I hope they spent the rest already, too."

"My guess, they filled up on junk and if they take off up to the camp, I won't see them for the rest of the weekend. What do you wanna bet they've been in my liquor cabinet, too?"

"They would never."

"Right," the other man scoffed. "I caught Dylan behind the house smoking a cigarette last week. The *shit*."

As he said that, Mack patted for the pack of cancer sticks he kept close in the top pocket of every coat—or shirt, in the warmer months—that he wore.

"Just doing what he sees," Lucas returned.

Mack opened the pack, and stuck a cigarette in his mouth before he muttered a lame, "*Yeah*, well ..."

He lit the smoke and inhaled one long drag.

Lucas only shook his head.

It had been a great day, despite the cold. His old friends helped to take his mind away from the harder things for a short while, and at the same time, reminded him why he liked being at the camp in the first place.

"Give my love, and thanks, to your wife."

The man winked back. "I'll thank Teddy for you tonight."

Lucas waved his friend off with a laugh as Mack snapped the reins with a low *yep* sending the horses jolting forward. "Keep it clean, man!"

The wind carried Mack's reply back.

"You know it, buddy."

Lucas did his cursory check of the outside of the cabin and the generators, running smoothly but ready for a top-up on gas, before he headed inside to find Delaney. He shed his winter clothing— including the ski pants the Smiths had brought along for him to borrow from Mack's collection—as Delaney filled the kettle at the sink.

Already undressed.

Well ...

He would get her out of the baggy, gray sweats and hoodie soon enough.

"We've got two nights left in this place before I have to return to hell," Lucas said, still standing on the entry mat.

Delaney's smile melted away at his frank attitude. "When you're just enjoying the day, it kind of feels like it will never end, doesn't it?"

To say the least ...

"Would you come back here with me?" he asked. "When it's warm, and we could really get out and do some—"

"Would you go to Gracen's wedding with me in the spring?" she interjected, grinning big and showing perfect, white teeth. "I'm the maid of honor, and I need a date. Since we're apparently making plans, I'd like that date to be you."

Did she now?

"When's the wedding?"

"May."

Another two and a half months, or so. He could make that work.

Lucas didn't even have to think about it for long. "I'll take half the damn month off ... I could keep you out here in the woods for that long, right?"

Delaney swung away from the sink and headed for the stove to boil water, laughing like he was joking, but they both knew he was not. "I'd be willing to let you try, anyway."

Well, then.

He noticed then how she had pulled items from the fridge and cooking pots out of the cupboards to begin making them something to eat to get them through the evening.

He liked how she looked there.

So domesticated.

Happy with him.

Here, she felt like his.

Like he had really found her.

Lucas just didn't know how to say that outside of his head. Something he had to work on, maybe. He started doing that by crossing the cabin's floor until Delaney was close enough that he could wrap her in his arms, which he did. When her head tilted back and those pretty pink lips of hers pursed for him to give her a kiss, he gave her exactly what she wanted.

She still tasted like the maple syrup candy she'd been sucking on like a lollipop the whole trip home. Her eyes stayed wide and on him the longer their lips stayed firmly pressed together, searching for something in him like he did for her.

Did she find it?

Whatever *it* was?

He sure thought he did.

"I know I said it already," he whispered against the softness of her mouth, "but thank you for coming here with me."

Delaney dropped down from her tiptoes, and then popped right back up again to press another quick kiss to his mouth, making Lucas's grin stretch wide. "We both know you don't need to keep thanking me for that. I want to be here with you."

But he would.

As long as she let him.

26.

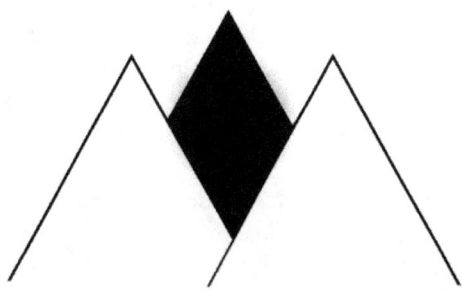

Delaney awoke to an empty bed but the robotic, feminine voice echoing from downstairs had her sitting up to catch the tail-end of what sounded like a voicemail box.

"Press one to listen to your message—"

Beeeeep.

Delaney blinked at the punch of a button that seemed to go on for seconds. A familiar chime sounded right after, one she recognized from when she tried to call out to Gracen, as the call dropped.

"Fucking *Christ*," Lucas swore severely.

Only to try to dial through to his voicemail again right after. Still trying to figure out the time, considering the darkness keeping the loft shrouded in darkness, Delaney tiptoed carefully off the bed, leaving the warmth and softness of the fresh-smelling quilt behind.

She made it halfway down the stairs before realizing Lucas must have gone outside to turn the generators back on from the glow of the lights spilling into the kitchen from the living space. Of course—he wouldn't have been able to use the booster to call out on his phone—even to his voicemail—if it wasn't plugged into the wall.

Her bare feet hit the warmer floors downstairs at the same time his call went through to his voicemail. She came around the den's wall created by the stairs to find a frustrated Lucas hunched over his phone and an opened newspaper on the table. Pinching the bridge of his nose as he scowled down at his phone giving options for his voicemail, he pressed one before the instructions had even finished.

This time, the call didn't drop.

"Lucas, it's Nola—I know you've seen the obit by now. Or if not, I guess I'm getting ahead of it," came the rushed words from a young woman. "Geoff from the Telegraph said Jacob's father requested the edits, and he apologized, but felt comfortable running the changes. I'm working on getting the date and time out for the memorial. So please don't worry about that. Okay, so if we chat before you get back to the city, great. If not—"

Beep-beep.

The second beeping chime sounded an octave lower than the first. The sad dullness of the final beep let the quiet room know the call had dropped again.

This time, he didn't redial, only sighed hard.

Delaney finally let him know she was just a few feet away under the staircase enclave. "What time is it?"

"A little after eleven," Lucas muttered, not acting the least bit surprised that she stood there.

She would have guessed even later.

Their busy, final full day at the cottage left her tired, and willing to crawl into bed earlier than normal.

"Weren't you the one who told me I didn't need to mop the bathroom floor because *we* could sleep?" Delaney asked.

Lucas dropped the hand hiding his irritated expression to clap on top of his denim-clad knee. "I couldn't, and you looked so peaceful that I didn't want to wake you with my restlessness. I made coffee ..." He trailed off, reaching out to flip the edge of the newspaper hanging dangerously off the coffee table in front of the couch. "Finally opened that goddamned newspaper."

He had left it right where the Smith boy put it on the kitchen island for over a day. They spent their last day and night at the little cottage prepping it to close down. Which mostly consisted of cleaning everything, packing away what wasn't perishable or needed, and doing a small load of wash for the towels, sheets, and quilt they had used. The chopper would land in the small field where it had dropped them off just before noon, if all went according to plan.

She hadn't quite accepted that their time in Birch Ridge was coming to an end, nor that her bed tomorrow night would welcome her home.

Would it really, though?

With just her alone?

Delaney, in a T-shirt she'd stolen from Lucas that smelled like the leather and musk cologne he dabbed on his throat and wrists every morning, found the spot next to him on the couch. Tucking her legs under her bum, she snuggled in only to feel the tension tightening the ropes of muscles that made up his biceps loosen up at her proximity.

"My father had the obituary I wrote for Jacob changed last minute," Lucas explained, making sense of that voicemail she had overheard moments earlier. He learned forward, rocking them on the couch, in his task to grab the paper and bring it closer for her to see. "Here, you want to read it?"

He didn't give her an actual choice.

The thick newspaper fell apart, pages falling to the floor as he brought the only one he cared about back to the couch, spreading it wide over Delaney's lap. In the many columns of death notices, she found Jacob Dalton's easily because after spending a handful of days at the cabin, she became accustomed to seeing his smiling face staring back at her from the many framed photographs on the walls.

The photo of Jacob chosen to be printed in the paper along with his obituary, if she had to guess, looked to be in the last five or so years. Older than a boy. Barely even a man. He kneeled between two large Mastiff dogs with a wide smile that said there was no place he'd rather be.

Beneath the photo were words that vaguely matched the obituary Lucas had spent a great deal of time writing before insisting Delaney read it over. As if she could find some mistake to point out like he hadn't been the one to agonize over the placement of a goddamn semicolon.

Really, she had thought Lucas just needed someone to read it, and to know every word he put on the paper was true.

Except, a lot didn't match, either.

Instead of the opening he wrote that told the reader that a heartbroken Dalton family was devastated to announce the passing of their youngest son after a brief stay at the Regional Hospital, the obituary simply announced the place and death with no mention of Jacob's relatives at all. His living, and deceased, family were listed in the next sentence, as Lucas had originally written the small piece, but it lost the personal touch without the family's note at the beginning. To rub salt into the wound that Lucas must have been feeling, at the end of the obituary, the request he had made for donations to FAR Canada—Families for Addiction Recovery—and the date and time of the public memorial for Jacob had been cut out as well.

A private memorial is to be held for immediate family, it read instead.

"Lucas," Delaney started, not quite knowing where to start or how to apologize for the careless cruelty of the edited obituary.

"It's all about appearances," Lucas muttered, tossing the newspaper back to the coffee table without any sort of grace or patience. Delaney didn't flinch at his show of frustration because she was more concerned how his tone twisted with pain. "That's all my father gives a damn about—that nobody, or as many people as he can control, will know. Not his son, no. Jacob wasn't an addict or a junkie, or useless and worthless. Not unless he needed something from Ronald, then he was all of those fucking things."

"Lucas."

She placed a hand to his forearm, squeezing to remind him that she was there.

"They didn't have to do *anything*," Lucas snapped, his hands and arms flying wide at nothing in particular. "Not one damn thing. I spent those last hours with Jacob making sure they wouldn't have to do anything but show up next week, and this is what they fucking do?"

"Did your mother—"

"Who'd know," Lucas interjected viciously. "If she did anything, it probably included turning her phone off, because everything else would be too much for her."

"Hey," Delaney tried again, tugging on the sleeve of his sweater. It didn't work.

Lucas booted the edge of the coffee table with the heel of his foot, sending it crashing across the living space, and into the reclining chairs. Pages of the newspaper scattered in no particular pattern to the middle of the floor.

Delaney froze at the aggression.

His anger *radiated*.

Had it been anyone else who acted out physically around her, then Delaney would have made it her first priority to get out of their way and presence immediately. A raising under the fast foot of a looming man who hadn't been scared to boot his kids in the rear end if they didn't move fast enough for his liking left her with a few, reactive scars.

So to speak.

Loud and angry usually set her anxiety spinning sky-high, but in that moment, she only saw the situation from Lucas' perspective. She stayed rooted to her seat, unmovable and not a bit scared.

Grieving, he left his city.

Where he couldn't be reached; a place that clearly brought him good memories and felt safe; and because of that, someone close enough for it to hurt on a deeper scale had used his distance and unavailability against him to get what they wanted where his brother's death was concerned.

He should be mad.

So, she said and did nothing.

Delaney let Lucas stew in that anger beside her, vibrating and glaring at his cell phone, still attached to the booster, unplugged where it had landed by the wall. The scowl hadn't eased from his features, but his chest started to rattle with every breath he took.

Each one came a little faster.

In all the time they spent there, he hadn't cried. At first, she expected him to—most people expressed their grief in that normal, healthy way. It hadn't taken Delaney long to realize Lucas held control of his emotions above all other things in his life—the one place he had the most power—even if doing so was to his own detriment. As if that was the last rope he would grab onto trying to save himself from drowning. She'd wondered if his inability to express his emotions, or the willingness to stuff it down as much as he could inside himself, stemmed from not having an environment where showing them was safe or acceptable.

Or perhaps, that question answered itself.

Having that understanding made the first sounds of his sobs as he scrubbed shaking hands over his face all the more painful for her to hear. Delaney didn't think about what he might want or need from her before she wrapped her arms around his heaving chest, and held on tight. Her head rested against his ribcage where every beat of his head echoed into her head, and the noisy breaths he couldn't steady vibrated them both.

He kept crying.

She just held on.

"They don't *care*," he muttered thickly.

She couldn't say any different, so she didn't. It wouldn't make anything better for him.

Delaney hugged him harder.

"I already had to go home and deal with Jacob being dead, but now I have to go back to this shit, too," he added with a gesture at the mess on the floor. "And they really don't care. It's just another game of public relations to these fucking people. Smile on the outside. Die on the inside."

As proverbial as those papers were scattered below them, the actions behind the reason for their place on the floor were knives that could leave irreparable scars. In that moment, she tried to be his Band-Aid so it didn't hurt as much while his pain bled out.

"They don't care about Jacob, or me ... about anything but themselves," he mumbled sadly, his palms catching the words and his tears.

His pained words, that he so clearly struggled to say, made her ache. She was aware of her helplessness. That she couldn't make this better or easier for him, and all she had to give to ease his anger and grief was herself.

So, she kept holding him.

After all, he didn't shove her away.

*

"One last tea for the road?"

Delaney smiled and took the cup of steaming tea—no rum, that she could smell—from Lucas' outstretched hands keeping the mug level lest it spill. She was forced to resituate on the couch to drink the tea, but making room served a better purpose.

Lucas slipped under the quilt they had pulled from the back from the couch with her. Despite waking up to her smile as he had every morning at the cottage, he had still been hesitant in taking his good morning kiss. Shame had kept him from meeting her eyes.

The shame of what, she couldn't say.

Crying?

The outburst, even?

He'd tried to apologize for the night before while she peered up at him from the pillow of her folded arms on his stomach, but she didn't let him get far. Delaney had chosen to let Lucas know with a lingering kiss and a touch of their foreheads that shame wouldn't be useful between the two of them, and his regret was for nothing.

No one should apologize for being human.

"Maybe we should have slept on the couch the whole time," she muttered around the rim of the mug.

Lucas chuckled. "Yeah, I guess so, huh?"

Outside, daylight had already crawled above the trees. It took a quick check of the phone Lucas had left on the floor to tell them that they had very little time to enjoy the rest of their time in Birch Ridge. Sleeping on the couch hadn't been the best for Delaney's back, but she hadn't complained the night before while snuggled on top of Lucas. Even if he made for a very *hard* pillow.

She couldn't say he cried himself to sleep, because that wouldn't be true, but he let it out what needed to be released, anyway. It had to help.

He didn't wake up angry.

That was a start.

Throwing an arm around Delaney's shoulders, he pulled her in closer on the couch while she sipped from the mug, and his lips found her temple for a soft, sweet kiss.

"If you think your boss is going to give you any trouble for taking off without much notice, get her to call me," Lucas said. "I'm definitely on her good side."

She laughed. "What would you do, bribe her to keep me on the payroll? Technically, I'm not even on the payroll. Hell, I pay her a chair rental."

Lucas didn't blink a lash. "Maybe, if that's what it took."

She smacked him lightly over the quilt. "You can't do that."

"Can't and shouldn't are two different things, sweets."

"I wouldn't *want* you to do that," she said. "How's that?"

Lucas frowned up at the ceiling. "Fine, you win."

She rolled her eyes. "It's not a race or something."

"Says you," he mumbled playfully under his breath.

Yeah, said *her*.

Delaney knew there wasn't a single chance on earth Lucas would overstep a boundary she made clear because that just wasn't in his nature, so she let him have his joke. It changed nothing that she had told him, though.

The minutes ticked by the longer the two of them remained on the couch while the old wood chief pumped out a constant stream of heat to keep them cozy and snuggled together. Snowflakes blowing off the roof danced in front of the bay windows, giving the two a show to watch instead of the mess still on the floor.

"I hate that I won't be able to see you tomorrow," she admitted, the words slipping out under her breath although she desperately wanted him to hear them.

Lucas sighed noisily.

"Or the next day," he agreed. "Or the ones after that."

Delaney pouted. "Rub it in good, huh?"

He tipped his head her way, ruffling her hair with his fingers at the crown of her head until she peered up at him with a meaner expression.

"*There she is,*" he whispered.

Had he thought he lost her?

Delaney had news for him.

"I'm not going anywhere."

Even if after today, she was a phone call away.

Lucas nodded, his throat bobbing with a hard swallow. "Yeah, I know, Delaney. I might need that—*you*, I mean. I might need you."

She wanted to ask a lot of things.

The whens, hows, and all the *whys*.

None of them mattered, though, because she'd still be there. If he called, or should he show up looking heartbroken on her doorstep again.

She'd be right here.

They cuddled closer on the couch, and while he waited for her to finish her tea, Lucas held onto her like she had done for him the night before.

"How am I supposed to get through the next week?" he asked.

Rhetorically, maybe.

Lucas continued, saying, "I can't imagine showing up to work Monday morning, where my father *will* be waiting, and just going on as if he did nothing. But that's what he'll expect, and frankly, it's what the people we employ deserve."

She couldn't begin to understand how it must affect Lucas to be forced to work alongside someone who seemed to enjoy his son's suffering. Never mind being the face of a company, that as he had explained it to her during their stay, would be going through a transitional period with the CEO—his father—returning to homebase.

"Nobody's gonna expect you to go back and be ... perfect," Delaney said.

"No, but I'll still try. Because the fact our family can't stand to be in the same room together shouldn't affect the day-to-day lives of the people who work for us, and especially not their jobs. It just ... *fuck*," he uttered, jaws tight.

It killed him inside.

She heard—and felt—what he couldn't vocalize.

"I still don't know how to do it, though. How to pretend like I'm okay. It shouldn't be hard. I've done it for most of my goddamn life."

He shouldn't have to.

That was the thing ...

Delaney knew very little she could say would change the difficult upcoming days he faced back in the city. "You take it all one minute at a time, and you don't have to make excuses if you need to get away from certain people or things—unless they're offering to help you, don't let them hurt you. You're allowed to say when enough is enough, Lucas."

Nobody would do it for him.

He nodded against the top of her head, but otherwise, said nothing.

Sometimes, silence was the better answer, anyway.

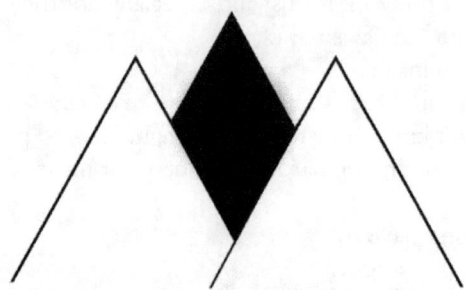

27

"I just saw the changes on your schedule," Nola said the second Lucas picked up her call. "Do you want me to run you over some breakfast or coffee before I head into the brewery?"

He smiled. Her concern came from good intentions. The icy roads he could see from the seventh floor of his high-rise apartment at the top end of the east side provided Lucas with a reasonable excuse to keep Nola from dropping by.

"You just worry about getting to work on time," he replied. "I'm good."

"You know," Nola went on, never missing a beat, "I had a whole stack of notes for you today. I even used the company colors. I might have been looking forward to you returning more than I should have."

Lucas chuckled. "Oh?"

"Well, *Mr. Dalton*," Nola muttered, stressing the *mister* like Ronald did in his condescending way, "couldn't walk past my desk last week without making a comment about them, so I tried to keep it all out of sight, but …"

Damn.

Lucas should have been in the office by the time she arrived. Ronald's comments wouldn't sting, or be nearly as loud, with Lucas in the building to keep his attitude under control. He tried not to feel too badly about taking a couple of extra days before returning to work.

Nola's next words helped him in that regard. "Anyway, I know you probably have a lot of personal calls and things to catch up on …"

"Too much," he filled in.

An understatement, really.

Every voicemail belonging to Lucas, work and personal, had been filled with messages from people, some he hadn't spoken to in years. Friends from his high school days. People connected to Jacob, either through his recovery programs, college, the gym, or his time with the animal rescue, filled his phone and email with text messages.

How did they even get his number and email?

Lucas stopped asking that question after the first thirty he clicked through—reading the words of people who Jacob had touched, in one way or another, became a way for Lucas to find hope in his current darkness. His brother *couldn't* be forgotten. It wasn't even a matter of whether he would be forgotten—that wasn't possible. The people who loved Jacob, struggles and mistakes included, found a way to show Lucas as much.

He intended to get back to each person, in one way or another. Some by reaching out for a conversation, because he'd admitted to himself that his responsibility-filled life took him away from his brother more than it should have lately, and some of Jacob's friends had extended the invitation to chat or even meet. Others, he simply wanted to thank for taking the time to think of him, and for reaching out, after learning about Jacob's passing.

He'd get through it all.

Eventually, anyway.

Lucas needed the time to get through the mountain that had built up during his time away. He came home to a mailbox full of personal letters sending love and condolences. In the city, the news of his brother's untimely passing had managed to get around before it came out in the papers, but Lucas had left it all behind.

Or rather, he put it on pause.

"So, I guess I'll let you go," Nola said. "Call me if you need anything, but everything at work is fine. Before you ask, because I know you will."

Lucas laughed. "I would not."

No doubt, the brewery had continued running at top speed from the moment he chose not to walk through the front doors. It might be a busy time of year with the accounting department closing year-end books and the plans for the new year being put into action, but it wouldn't all go to shit because he didn't show up for a few days.

Ronald would make certain of that.

Of course, Lucas' absence would be just another weapon for his father to use in one way or another, but Ronald had already pulled the proverbial trigger first by announcing his return to the province on the same day Jacob overdosed.

There came a point when Lucas couldn't be polite.

They'd hit that point now.

"But you should know, Lucas ..." his assistant hedged on the other end of the call.

He could only imagine.

The way Nola eased their conversation into whatever she had to tell him and waited until the end of the call to fit it in, already had stress crawling over his shoulders to tie them into invisible knots. He tried to focus on the far view of the east end leading down to the horse track cloaked in a sheet of crisp, white snow instead of the irritation caused by a mention of his father.

Don't apologize for doing what you have to.

You say when enough is enough, Lucas.

If they're not helping, then they're hurting you.

The words might not be exactly as Delaney had told them to Lucas, but he repeated the sentiments silently to himself all the same. Apparently, he needed the reminder. He couldn't take care of anyone else if he didn't prioritize himself first.

"What?" he eventually asked.

Might as well get it over.

Rip it right off like a Band-Aid.

"He's redecorated the big office," Nola said. "*Already.*"

Surprise.

Ronald had his own priorities.

Lucas sighed into the hand he scrubbed across the facial hair on his chin and jaw that he'd trimmed into a goatee after his early morning shower. "And *my* things?"

"They're boxed and in the storage room beside Kimmie's office. I guess it's not going to be a storage room if you're in there now?"

Ah, their head of accounting. At least, he'd have a worthy neighbor. Nobody worked harder than Kimmie. The silver lining kept him from focusing on the blank, windowless space that was better suited for old boxes of paperwork piled high than a desk where he would be expected to work.

He didn't say that out loud.

"Perfect," Lucas returned.

"It's not really, is it?" Nola asked.

"No, but I won't let my father know as much, either," he said, ending the call with a quiet goodbye after.

He couldn't afford to let Ronald think he had any control over him, really. Negative, or otherwise. Look where giving that kind of power to his father had gotten him so far.

Not very fucking much.

Time to make hard choices, Luke.

That time, it wasn't Delaney's voice in his head. She never used that nickname, or any other; but he came to understand that he preferred her breathy or sweet calls of name, anyway. No, that was his own brain telling him what he already knew.

Ronald had gone too far this time.

On the other hand, the fallout, and what it all meant, had just begun for Lucas. He forced himself to look on the bright side of the unfortunate situation before him: at least the ball was finally in his court. He just had to figure out what, exactly, to do with it.

*

"Sweetheart," Lucas said, the relief in his voice clear as he picked up Delaney's early morning call, "hey."

"You sound happy—to hear from me?" she asked, as if that should be a surprise.

"Why not?"

Her muffled laughter trailed off on the other end of the phone, but the background noise from the call came with the shuffle of feet and a click of a door closing. That spread of silence allowed him the chance to resituate his phone.

Lucas set the phone to the edge of his desk in the spare bedroom of his apartment that he used for an at-home office. On speakerphone, he could continue typing out the email he'd drafted during the extra twenty minutes he had before he had to run for brunch. A meeting he didn't particularly want to keep, but couldn't refuse at the moment, either.

"I don't know, seems sus," Delaney muttered, coming back on the line.

Her heavy sigh, full of tension, floated over the phone followed by a tiny groan.

"You okay?" he asked.

"Are you one of those guys that needs to pretend like your girlfriend doesn't bleed once a month or takes a shit, or something?"

Her frankness took Lucas by surprise—so much so that he missed a letter or two in the alphabet for his next word and needed to hit the backspace button repeatedly to start over again. All the while, he blinked at his screen.

"You are ..."

Lucas searched for the right word.

"Fucking amazing," Delaney mumbled on the other end while water tinkled in the background.

She then let out her own sigh of relief.

She had the best way of snapping him back to reality. "Yeah, you are."

Delaney giggled. "Honestly, I meant this bath. My period started this morning, and I have been waiting for Bexley to leave for classes so I could make this bath so hot I needed the door wide open," Delaney informed.

Lucas cringed—in sympathy, of course.

"Sorry about the period," he settled on saying.

It seemed appropriate.

Delaney snickered. "Please, no apologies needed. It means I'm not pregnant—not possible anyway—and I have better orgasms when I masturbate over the next week. It's a win-win for me. The first day is the worst, really."

Just like that, his fingers froze where they hovered over the keyboard of his laptop. As if the image his mind conjured up instantly at the mere mention of her masturbating was the only thing it cared to focus on. Not even blinking made the image behind his eyeballs go away.

Damn.

What an image it was.

"Yeah, fucking amazing," he managed to murmur.

She made the sweetest noises under her breath as water sloshed in the background before she finally seemed to settle into the bathtub he couldn't quite picture. His mind had no problem filling in the blanks with his own ideas, even grasping onto the belief that she would look like heaven in a clawfoot tub surrounded by hot water and silky bubbles.

"And don't think I forgot about you sounding happy to hear me," Delaney said, giving Lucas something to latch onto instead of his dirty thoughts.

He chuckled.

"Honestly, I was just happy I looked at my phone before I screened the call," Lucas said. "I've rejected—" he picked up the phone to check the exact number on the notification ribbon of missed calls from one particular number "—eighteen calls from my father in the last hour."

He made a dismissive noise, adding, "Could have been you."

"Yikes," she returned quietly.

Regardless of the reason, he was happy to see a call from her show up on his phone that morning. Even if he had kissed her goodbye less than twenty-four hours earlier before handing her off to a cab he'd arranged ahead to take her home from the airstrip just outside of Fredericton.

"Wait—eighteen?" she asked, tone pitching high.

"Yep."

"Aren't you guys in the same building today? I thought you would be at work already. Can't I hear you typing?"

Ah.

"I'm currently drafting a letter I plan to send out before I leave here shortly—in the company newsletter. It'll explain my extended absence, considering recent events, and a reminder that my privileges to take time off for family emergencies or mental health matters are just as important and valued as their right to do so. My father will hate that part the most," he tacked on the end to make sure the point hit home.

This time, it was Delaney who needed more time to form a response.

"Oh," she finally said. "Will it help, do you think?"

"Help what?"

"How bitter you feel toward him," Delaney filled in.

The answer seemed easy.

It really wasn't.

"Yes and no," Lucas decided to say, "and neither of those, or my father, are more important than the fact you called me this morning. Can we get back to *that?*"

She chuffed on the other end of the phone.

He smirked to himself, returning to typing the last sentence of his letter to the company's employees.

"My cousin is kind of mad at me," Delaney said, filling the silence with something that he found interesting. And a little sad.

"Because of last week?"

"And you."

Ouch.

That hurt a bit.

"It comes from good intentions, doesn't it?" he asked. "Because she worries about you, clearly."

"Yeah, but she's not very good at showing it. Or in this case, how she *says* it."

The way she tiptoed around the topic made Lucas think she didn't want to talk too much about it. He wouldn't push.

"*But,*" Delaney continued before Lucas could say anything at all, "she's gone for the day, so I get a few hours of peace, anyway, and I don't have to work until Wednesday this week. Well," she corrected, letting the word trail off.

"What?" he asked.

"Linda asked me to lunch tomorrow afternoon—to check in, she said."

Delaney didn't sound like she believed that.

"It was my fault," she added after a moment, "I called yesterday to let her know I got back in town, so."

"I see. I hope I haven't put you in a situation with your job—"

He should have known better than to say anything.

Delaney wasn't having it.

"I'm an adult who makes my own choices. If I lose my job because I took off and lied about having a family emergency, so be it. Losing a position isn't going to change the fact I still have a valuable skill I can put to work literally anywhere," Delaney said.

Shit.

He was glad she had all this figured out.

Lucas couldn't say the same even if he was working on it.

"So, what's your morning look like if you're not going to work, huh?" Delaney asked.

"My question first," Lucas said, doing one last scan through the email before pressing send to push it through to every employee on the mailing list. "Deal?"

"Hey, now, the last time we made one of those, I got bruises up the front of my thighs from getting bent over a counter," she replied, laughing.

"Exactly. This can only go in a good direction, right?"

She might have squeaked under her breath.

He kind of loved it.

"Okay, what?" she breathed.

"Since we're asking personal questions on this lovely morning," he muttered, pushing away from the desk to head out of the office, "and *you* brought it up first, what exactly, are you planning to do in that bathtub when you hang up with me shortly?"

Delaney scoffed at the question.

High with embarrassment.

Thick from desire.

He heard both clearly.

"Come on, Delaney," he urged, already passing through the hall connecting directly into the master suite across from his office. His bed, still unmade, didn't even look inviting. Like the rest of the place, it all felt like an extension of a life he had made to fit a person he could no longer be.

He didn't have to think about those things when he put his attention back on the woman waiting, breathing a bit heavier, on the phone.

"Tell me," he coaxed, grinning.

"You are *so* terrible," she uttered.

"Do you use toys, or just those fingers? What am I licking clean next time, baby?"

"Oh, my *God.*"

"Which one?"

"Either will do," she managed to say.

"And today?"

"Toys."

"Toys," he echoed, husky in the back of his throat because he could already feel his dick growing hard under his slacks.

Maybe he shouldn't have wasted time getting dressed just yet.

"Two, actually."

"*Two.*"

He was starting to sound like a parrot.

"Mmhmm," Delaney hummed. "A waterproof wand I put right on my clit and—"

"Oh, let me guess," he jumped in before she could ruin the

surprise.

Her breathless giggle did wicked things to his body.

Lucas would work on fixing that problem shortly.

"What?" Delaney asked. "What else do you think I use?"

"Probably some thick vibe you use to fuck your tight, little hole just enough that you can feel the way you pulse around it—I remember what you liked."

A heat—needier than ever—colored up her words. "God, why are you so right, too?"

He only laughed.

She liked what she liked.

"Are you using either right now?" he asked, honestly curious.

And already popping open the button on his slacks.

"I swear on *everything* that I did not plan to call you at work for phone sex today," Delaney put in.

As if that had ever even mattered.

"Sweets," he told her, "that is not what I asked."

She sighed, defeated.

In the best possible way.

"It's not nearly as big as you," she admitted. "Blame my period for this, okay? It makes me unfairly horny."

She already had her whiney whimper coming out to play, too. Fuck him for having other things to get to that morning because he'd spend the rest of the day listening to Delaney get herself off if that's what she wanted to do.

Yes, please, he thought.

"Is unfairly the right word?" he asked. "Because from my position, I'm not complaining."

He turned and kicked his bedroom door closed with one foot while his hand worked to free his erection from the confines of his briefs, unashamed about his open fly and hastily pulled down pants.

"Good," she mumbled shakily. "Are you gonna play, too?"

"Until I have to go. Don't worry, it's no one important. They can wait thirty minutes for me to show up instead of it going the other way around."

Delaney didn't ask *who* Lucas would be meeting.

For that, he was grateful.

There was nothing like talk of his mother—or the therapist he'd booked for a second appointment to see after his planned brunch with her—to make his dick soft.

That's not what Lucas was trying to do here.

"Oh, my ... *Oh*," Delaney exclaimed in a squeal he knew well.

Lucas pumped his cock with a snug grip, picking up the pace. "That's one, Delaney. Edge yourself out at least once or twice. I want to catch up."

28.

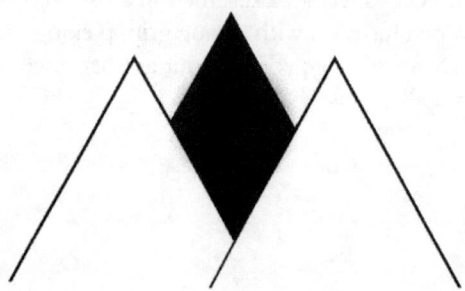

Lucas had not been prepared to have brunch with his mother while another companion sat across the table, but he hid his surprise—and annoyance—with the smiling man who greeted him by standing and offering his hand to shake.

Maybe he shouldn't have been shocked by Penelope's husband joining them. He had been the one to reach out and make the request for the breakfast between Lucas and his mother in the first place.

"Hanson," he replied, shaking the hand of his mother's new husband.

Well, was he new?

The two had been married for a couple of years.

"I'd apologize for being late for this," Lucas went on, "but it's been a rough week. I'm doing what I can."

"Terrible about Jacob, isn't it?" Hanson—Hanny to his friends; Lucas did not pretend to be one of those—asked, offering a sympathetic smile as he took his hand away and returned to his seat next to Penelope.

A *drinking* Penelope.

It wasn't even noon.

"I take it the healing spa in Florida didn't really stick then," he noted when his mother lifted her screwdriver for a sip.

One of many rehabs where his mother had found solace over the years, and preferred to go back to whenever she wanted to dry up for a bit. Hell, she'd traveled all over Canada and the United States attending one program or another. Only the best of the best would do. None of them seemed to help with her chronic alcoholism that had tainted the memories of his childhood. Once he got into his adult years, Lucas had put distance—and what he thought were healthy boundaries—between him and his mother. As much as he could, anyway. He wouldn't show up to be the ride home from the drunk tank on her worst nights—or the person who cleaned up her vomit after a particularly bad binge.

She didn't know her limits, and he couldn't set them. She only saw her son's space as a betrayal. Certainly not what it really was—him protecting himself.

"You don't have to be so judgemental," Penelope finally responded once her glass clinked down to the shiny tabletop between them. "It's *a* drink and seeing you today … It made me nervous."

No, it didn't.

No shock that she used him as the scapegoat for her drinking, though, and those alcohol glassed eyes said it wasn't just *one* drink, either. There began the tip of the iceberg that made up the dangerous waters that were his mother.

"Making an observation that you're drinking before noon is judgemental?" Lucas asked. "Is that what you tell the doctors every time they remind you that you only have one liver for life, Mom?"

Okay, that one was a lot more direct.

Lucas still wouldn't apologize for it.

Penelope, who hadn't even asked him for a proper greeting when he joined the table which usually included a kiss to her wax-like cheek, focused on stirring the speared cherry tomato around the rim of her drink. Lucas desperately searched for the small part of the boy left over from his childhood who always found *some* sympathy for his mother, but there she sat, at sixty-seven years of her clinging onto a long-gone youth with her heavy makeup and face frozen full of Botox.

Liquor on every breath.

Still, he tried to find the excuse or justification to get him through that brunch—barely an hour, if he ate fast. Just like he would have years ago, finding reasons for yet another bad week, one of her tantrums, or the long stretches of silence and neglect in between.

He didn't have that ability anymore.

Every time she walked away from him, or hurt her sons, especially in recent years … well, it taught Lucas how to live without her.

That he wanted to at all, really.

Hanson, to his benefit, cleared his throat next to his wife, drawing attention to himself for a moment. The clean lines of his suit and slicked back hair, somewhat helping to hide the balding patch on the top of his head, was a far cry from the frizzy, messy pile of his mother's dyed red curls, but at least he kept her dressed up nice.

To be honest, Lucas noticed over time that his mother preferred men—especially after the separation, and later, the divorce from Ronald—who liked a project. So to speak. Men who gravitated to broken women they thought could be fixed. By their hand, of course.

Clearly, that was not working out for Hanson, the retired realtor mogul with his penthouse in Florida, and Penelope, who'd called her son drunk to brag about the size of her engagement ring and how she'd thrown the one from his father into the bay.

Sentimental, *who*?

Nobody here.

The husband of the current decade—if he lasted that long, who could say? —tried to defuse what he saw as a brewing situation between Lucas and Penelope by saying, "Okay, okay—aren't we all here to have something to eat and talk about Jacob on this beautiful morning?"

Lucas didn't flinch. "It's minus twenty outside, nothing is very beautiful today."

Except a woman two hours away, out of his reach.

He didn't add that part out loud.

The fact his earlier phone call with Delaney had left him relaxed and blissed was the only reason he decided to even show up at this excuse for a brunch. Dopamine could be a fucked up thing. That, and because Hanson had taken the time to personally reach out to Lucas over the last week—when he couldn't be reached—to make the request for his mother. Not that he'd included *his* involvement in the brunch—a tidbit Lucas was sore about.

Two years of spotty contact with his mother—mostly by his choice because Penelope had a way of making things worse than they already were—made him feel like he at least owed her this today. Couldn't he put on a suit, show up at a restaurant he wouldn't otherwise eat at because of the cost-to-food ratio alone, and grit his teeth through an hour of her non-apologies and victimhood?

Her youngest son had died.

Lucas imagined that *did* hurt.

So, here he was.

Trying.

Even if she drowned all of her grief out, like everything else in her life, with too much liquor and a handful of sleeping pills at night.

Hanson shifted in his chair, his gaze darting away from Lucas awkwardly while he slung an arm over Penelope's shoulders to coax a tepid smile out of her. "Yes, well, we don't have to make it more painful than it already is to be here, right?"

Oh, didn't they?

Jesus, Lucas hadn't even asked for this *brunch*.

Where was the goddamn food, anyway?

"Are we eating?" Lucas asked. "I'm starved."

Penelope, glass-eyed and loose in her movements in the chair covered with a silk slip that matched the rest of the private dining room, looked to her husband for a way to proceed.

"The waiter will be here shortly," Hanson explained.

Lucas rubbed at the spot of pain beginning to form beneath his temple with two fingers. "Oh, wonderful."

"We're flying to Florida tomorrow," Penelope blurted out suddenly.

He blinked at the news. "What?"

"You know how snowbirds are," Hanson added, trying to add his two cents into a conversation where Lucas didn't particularly want the man involved. "We thought we could make it through a winter back here, but it's been a hard one."

Had it?

Lucas laughed, and it came off so *bitter*.

He couldn't even hide it.

"Jacob's memorial is Wednesday," he said to a table that he was sure had no intention of listening or hearing him.

Penelope proved that by muttering, "I was told Ronald made it clear there would be no services for Jacob, so I didn't think it would be a problem."

"You didn't think it would be a—" Lucas clamped his mouth shut, and pinched the bridge of his nose to give him the focus he needed to help subside the flood of disbelief and anger. "He was your youngest *son*."

"Ronald said—"

"Ronald's a fucking idiot," Lucas interjected hotly, dropping his hand where it slapped against the table, jostling the setting.

Even his mother jumped across the way.

Hanson, to his benefit, only stared at Lucas with pity.

He hated that even more.

"There *is* a memorial on Wednesday," Lucas said, deciding to get out what was most important before he let the anger consume him entirely. Inevitable when it came to his mother—much like his father. How could the people who had created him be the same ones that caused him constant, unwavering struggle?

Year after year.

All the decades of his life so far.

At what point did Lucas get to cut the cord and say enough was enough.

Right about now, honestly.

"The memorial is on Wednesday," he repeated, "and I know every person on my contact list got the email, voice message, and a text from my secretary letting them know as much. Including the two of you, so—"

"You must have really pissed your father off last week," his mother interrupted like what he said didn't even matter. "It got to the point he called me to see if you'd been in contact. He doesn't want a memorial."

"It's not about him, *mother*," Lucas snapped back. "It's too bad for Ronald if turning my phone off and taking bereavement days burns his world down. I'm done being the idiot trying to put the flames out. Stop acting like you don't know about the memorial this week. At least have the respect to tell me to my face that you don't want to be there because there isn't a preapproved guest list, Mom."

"We'll still be flying out tomorrow," Hanson put in quietly. "Either way."

But *firmly*.

As if it wasn't up for discussion.

Lucas nodded, frustrated again but willing to hide it for the moment if they could get on with this brunch so it could be over quicker. "Fine—it'll be mostly friends and people who knew Jacob outside of his family, anyway. I'm not sure you or Penelope would fit in very well. Let's see it as a bright spot, huh?"

Penelope took a big gulp of the orange poison in her glass, and set it back down harder than necessary. She peeked over at her husband, but the scowl affixed to her slightly-overfilled lips told Lucas something nasty was on the way.

She didn't fail.

"So, we'll be missing the drug addicts he made friends with and whoever else he met playing around with mutts," she said.

Nope.

Lucas couldn't do it.

He *tried*, though.

No one could say he didn't try.

Standing from the table, annoyed that he'd checked his coat in at the front and couldn't just put it on and leave immediately, Lucas raked his shaking fingers through the short crop of his hair before turning to stare down the couple across the table.

Neither of them moved.

Hanson didn't get up this time.

Good.

"Did anyone ever tell you that when you fade your hair high," his mother started, "you look even more like your father?"

Yep.

That's why he'd always hated it. Except he wasn't anything like Ronald Dalton *at all*. The backhanded comment barely even stung.

"Who's the judgmental one now, Mom?" Lucas asked. "I guess because you can afford to stay drunk all day is the way you tell yourself that you were better than Jacob? Now I get why you couldn't stick to AA. Accountability isn't your strong suit."

Penelope gasped, her hand fluttering up to cover her chest as if his words had actually hurt. He hoped they did.

It felt wrong calling her a mom.

A mother and mom were not the same things. Any woman could birth a child grown in her womb, but what happened when that same baby found its way into her arms that couldn't care or love at all?

Well, they were looking at it.

Lucas.

Jacob.

They were the result.

His brother might have needed to find outlets for his pain and issues in the same thing that had ultimately killed him, but Lucas ... well, he wouldn't continue to let these people poison him in the same way they'd done to his brother.

They didn't get to say what he deserved or when—he made those choices.

He wasn't the one in the wrong here.

Penelope only glared at Lucas, openly hateful in the way her familiar brown eyes, heavy lidded from whatever liquor she'd consumed before the screwdriver, tried to pin him to the spot where he stood. It wouldn't work.

He was so numb to her now.

To all of it, really.

A sad fact he didn't like facing because that meant admitting he, too, played a part in their family's unraveling. It always devolved into this type of thing—every dinner or family gathering was an eye roll away from an explosive argument fueled with name calling and vitriol. Only in the face of the public or their family's business did the Daltons manage to put on a good show. Having time away from his parents while Penelope enjoyed her new marriage, and Ronald ran off to the west had lulled Lucas into a false sense of comfort. The days that melted into weeks and months between contacts or phone calls didn't help any damn thing.

They were all still toxic in the same room together.

"Don't call me again," Lucas told Hanson, not even looking at his mother as he delivered the final blow to a relationship that had been crumbling for years.

Good.

This was what they all deserved.

It was human nature to try to save a part of yourself. He recognized that in the helpless way he'd attempted to please or be available to his parents over the years as their estrangement became worse and their bonds were irreparably damaged. As if he truly believed he was the thing that could fix all of them, but really, he was the punching bag in the middle taking the most abuse.

It was what it was, yes.

For a long time, he'd tried to think how it wasn't what it could be, though, and wasn't that worth the effort? Didn't it count for anything? Now he understood everything was exactly as they'd made it out to be—it had practically nothing to do with him. So, why keep trying?

"Don't call me for anything," he added, shrugging, "not for her, not if she's dead … not for one single thing. Do you understand me?"

Hanson drew in a deep breath. "That's a little much, son."

Really?

They never even got close to *that.*

"Oh, fuck off," Lucas returned, his sardonic laugh filling the quiet space partitioning them from the rest of the dining guests.

It paid to be a Dalton.

"Stop it, someone might hear," his mother snapped, sloshing her drink when she made a messy grab for it to take a sip she still choked on. Penelope let out a phlegmy cough. "Isn't it bad enough I've already got people calling me at all hours of the day because your brother did what he did?"

"He relapsed and overdosed, Mom. Say it. I know you don't like those words because they come with responsibility," Lucas added with a shrug. "Doesn't change what it is, huh?"

"We all *know*—"

Lucas dismissed whatever Hanson planned to say with a flick of his wrist. "*Not* you."

"Lucas, don't be like—"

Something inside Lucas finally snapped.

"Go to hell, Penelope. Jacob wanted to change, and even if he failed in the end, I hope it kills you to know at least he tried to get back up once. Whatever, you're too busy hiding from being blamed for why he was the way he was, anyway, because you *can't* change."

Hanson stood fast from his chair, casting a shadow of disappointment across an unconcerned Lucas who tipped his head sideways to look up and dead stare the man.

"Lad," Hanson said, his Nova Scotian childhood coming out thick, "I'm going to need you to show some respect."

He had to be six-foot-three, *easy.* Eye-to-eye, or close enough, to Lucas. He lacked the solid two-hundred-*plus* pounds of muscle Lucas grew into before he had even hit puberty. Built barrel-chested with a back and arms meant to work, passed on to Lucas from good genetics and a hearty family bloodline that could be traced back to Denmark, Russia, and Germany. Hanson, on the other hand, was lanky enough that a good shove from Lucas could seriously hurt the man. Lucas opted to continue his lingering stare down, letting the obvious speak to Hanson so he didn't have to.

I would murder you.

Lucas didn't need to say it when his eyes did so for him.

"Coming here was a waste of my time," Lucas said, breaking the silence first.

"Stop it, we're all just a little worked up," his mother scoffed, eerily gleeful.

The fact she could enjoy this triggered Lucas all over again. His first instincts had been right. Nothing would ever stop the toxicity from bleeding freely inside their family.

"This is over," Lucas said, ignoring the man who sat down again without a word, and deservedly embarrassed. Hanson could lick his wounds another time. "And I knew it was over before I even agreed to come here today. Enjoy what's left of your life— look at me like I'm dead, too, because to you, I am. Finally, you can be childless like you always wanted and smothered in affection from a man who'll apparently love you right into a grave. Is it as beautiful as you thought it'd be?"

He let that question be the final words he planned to say to his mother. Choosing to draw his last line—more like a wall to keep her out—came with the best relief he'd ever felt in his whole life. Like a weight had just been thrown from his shoulders. His steps were lighter than he thought they'd be on his way to the front of the restaurant where he grabbed his coat and apologized for not waiting on the server, but put his card down to prepay whatever bill Penelope and Hanson racked up.

He didn't want their damn food, anyway, but that was probably the best few hundred dollars he'd ever spent on a meal in his life.

Lucas had just exited the downtown eatery and crossed the street where his Bronco sat with chunks of ice clinging to the wheel wells when a figure slipped out the doors, as well. Focused on getting into his vehicle and starting the engine to hide from the cold, he didn't notice his mother's husband until Hanson came to stand outside the driver's side window.

He glowered at the man, but didn't roll down his window. "What?"

That should be clear enough, right?

Hanson lifted an envelope where Lucas could see, prompting him to roll down the window a couple of inches to grab it. "A few pictures—your mother thought you'd like to have them. Better you than her, she said. You'll do something meaningful with them."

So *he* said.

Lucas only heard: *they don't mean anything to her.*

His brow furrowed. "Pictures of what?"

The man shrugged. "Your brother, I guess. All of you throughout the years. I only looked at a few. She went through them last night. She *does* care, Lucas. This hurt her, too, but—"

"Stop right there. The second you put *but* into the conversation, you're also saying I should forget everything else that came before it. And let's be honest here, I'm done doing that. I think it's obvious at this point," he said, determined to let that be the end of this awful conversation and morning.

He had better things to do.

An appointment with his therapist.

Jacob's apartment to start clearing out.

Anything—literally anything—except this.

"Have a safe flight," he told Hanson, rolling up the window at the same time, and turning his gaze onto the windshield and road ahead, "but don't call me for her ever again."

The other man backed away from the vehicle.

In his lap, the envelope full of pictures grew heavier while Lucas maneuvered the Bronco out of the parallel parking. He tried to pretend like the pile of images—probably ones he'd never seen before—didn't leave an invisible ache behind already.

Lucas tossed the envelope to the passenger seat once he got the Bronco on the road. It was something that would have to wait.

29.

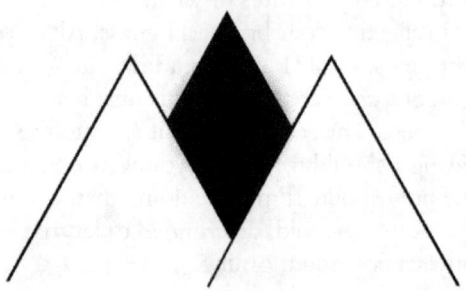

"You're not still mad at me, right?"

Delaney, trying to decide between a sweater that bared her spine with diamond shaped cut-outs or a dressy blouse, hadn't properly heard her cousin's question. "Didn't you have classes today, or …?"

The blouse felt more appropriate for lunch with her boss, but there was something about the black color of the sweater that drew Delaney in that direction. She made no apologies for the lack of vibrance in her wardrobe.

The way it made her look spoke for itself.

"I guess that answers *that*," Bexley bitched under her breath before spinning on her heel.

"Hey, *whoa*."

Delaney turned away from the mirror, realizing too late that she'd been more absorbed in her reflection than her quiet cousin who had lingered in their apartment long past the time her first classes for the day had started.

"I'm sorry, I wasn't really listening," Delaney admitted.

Bexley, who had stopped just beyond the bedroom threshold, peeked over her shoulder quickly, and gave a cursory look at the items Delaney held. "Just wear the sweater—you know you don't want to put on the blouse."

Was it that obvious?

Delaney tossed the blouse, still hanging from a metal hanger, onto the bed. "Yeah, you're right."

"And the being mad thing?" Bexley asked. "Am I right about that, too?"

"What, am I mad at *you*?" she asked.

"*Well*—"

"Are you still mad at me?" Delaney interrupted before Bexley could get another word out.

Their matching grins eased the bit of tension created by the initial overreaction. Without prompting, Bexley turned to lean against the door frame so she could watch as Delaney slipped into the back-teasing sweater after removing her push up bra.

"See, cute," Bexley said.

Delaney smiled at her reflection. "It is, huh?"

She smoothed down the front of the sweater while turning enough to enjoy the view of the back.

"Are you going to say sorry for calling me stupid—*twice?*" Delaney asked.

Bexley sighed. "It's not good enough to admit I might have a bad way of communicating my feelings when I'm worried?"

"Nope, it's not."

Because that wasn't an apology.

"Would it have been better if I had told you I thought what you did was reckless, and the fact you didn't call me for days—"

"Reckless isn't *stupid*. They're not the same words, and they don't have the same meanings. I'm sorry that we had to listen to people tell us we were stupid every time we turned around growing up," Delaney said, moving on to the wall rack next to the mirror where her variety of bags waited to be chosen. "It sucks that it's the first thing to fly out of your mouth every time you have an argument with someone, and it hurts. It's hurtful."

Bexley pursed her lips, but muttered, "I know, like I said, I don't deal with stress well, and I'm working on it."

"That's not an apol—"

"And I'm sorry," Bexley said, one octave louder than Delaney. Clearly to be heard.

There was only so much oxygen in the room, after all. Some people, like her, did it without even knowing it.

That was Delaney's fault to own. Sometimes, she made herself louder than she realized in conversations, but especially arguments, where she felt like she wasn't being heard. None of them were perfect, including her.

"Yeah, me too," she told Bexley over her shoulder.

A black handbag decorated in metal buttons caught Delaney's eye above the other selection of bags she'd collected since moving to Fredericton. Her last collection, much larger, ended up safe in the walk-in closet that Malachi had renovated for Gracen.

Delaney tossed the bag to the end of the bed, and then dropped down beside it where the boots she'd already chosen from her closet waited at her feet. "But all of these apologies change nothing," she told her cousin lingering in the doorway of her bedroom, "because I'd do it again in a second. He needed me."

Bexley nodded, the exaggerated motion rocking her body forward and back from the chest up. "*Right*, his brother died—you told me that."

She tried not to flinch at the almost careless delivery of Bexley's words. Her cousin didn't mean for it to come out as cold as it did, likely, and Delaney had to remind herself that Bexley didn't have every single detail about the situation so she could be careful to sound less heartless.

Delaney thought it wasn't for her to share.

"Do you have to say it like that?" Delaney asked.

Bexley's brow lifted higher on her forehead. "Well, I mean, you wouldn't even tell me a phone number for the guy before you left, so—"

"You need to know how his brother died, or even that he had barely finished making arrangements before he showed up at our apartment door to care about the fact that he needed someone, and he asked for that person to be me?"

There was no good way out of this conversation.

In only a few words, Delaney had backed Bexley into an impossible corner, and they both knew it. Her cousin either needed to admit defeat, and accept she had been the one in the wrong between them entirely, or ... sound like a total bitch.

There was no in between.

Bexley tried for a few seconds to come up with something, only to settle on a flustered, "I was worried about you!"

"I know you were—and I am sorry," Delaney said. "Next time—"

"Next time, she says," Bexley cut in, laughing. "Is that something I should start trying to plan for? I'll make a checklist for the next time Delaney runs off with some random man for a week away."

Well ...

Delaney shrugged. "Anything is possible."

It just wouldn't be for *any* man.

There was only one.

One above all the rest for Delaney.

Bexley rolled her eyes. "You drive me crazy—okay? There, I said it. I don't know how Gracen lived with you for like five years, or whatever."

"We had a few rows together, too."

"You remind me of Mom," Bexley muttered under her breath.

That comment froze Delaney as she reached for her boots. "What, why?"

Her aunt, the sister of Delaney's father, had been a severe woman with a wooden spoon at the ready to swat whatever kid wasn't fast enough to get out of her way. Shrill when she yelled, and pious to an extreme, a lot like Delaney's own mother, she was the last person who anyone should want to be compared to.

"You're hard to talk to," Bexley returned, turning again to make her leave, "you know, when you're not giving someone the silent treatment for days."

"That was only *Sunday!*" Delaney yelled at her cousin's retreating back. Her piss poor way of stepping back from the situation after Bexley called her stupid. Two freaking times. "Come on!"

"Same thing!"

Okay, Delaney thought, *that's enough.*

She let Bexley return to whatever she'd been doing in the apartment while Delaney finished getting ready for her lunch with Linda. The coffee shop close to the salon was a favorite spot of her boss, quiet with a cozy vibe and great coffee.

With soup and bread on the side, too.

Despite having a hundred good reasons for continuing the argument with Bexley, mostly because Delaney happened to be right, she didn't have the damn time. Besides, she was *nothing* like her aunt, or her own mother, and now she resented Bexley for saying that, too.

It was what it was.

Delaney exited her bedroom with leather ankle boots buckled tight and her handbag ready to get everything transferred from the one she had been using to the new bag. She plopped it onto the table next to the bag from the week before, unceremoniously dumping one into the other while Bexley huffed into the couch just a few feet away.

"I'm *not* like your mother," Delaney said, unable to keep it inside.

Her cousin's messy bun swayed back and forth in her view.

"Did you know giving someone the silent treatment is another form of abuse when it's used—"

"For *one* day—because you pissed me off and called me stupid! Get over it, I could have said mean things like you, but I chose not to say anything at all. Which one is better, Bex?"

Better yet, what was really going on?

This issue had gone on longer than it should have.

Delaney had questions.

"How about you just say whatever it is you want to say, and get it over with?" Delaney asked. "Get it out and be done with it."

Bexley swung around on the couch, her gaze narrowing with hurt on Delaney across the room. "I heard you talking to Gracen last night on the phone in your room, and how she mentioned you could take over her salon if you went back home because she's too busy making her little art, or *whatever.*"

Delaney's eyes widened in understanding. "We were just talking … not being serious, or anything. It didn't *mean* anything. I don't have plans to leave."

"You looked *so happy* after you came back. She told me that, too, you know. How happy you were when you visited her, and how good it seemed to do you to be back there. I couldn't even get you in the car to go home for a *Saturday*, Delaney."

Fair enough.

Situations changed, though.

"Are you jealous that I like being with my best friend," Delaney asked, "or worried that I'm going to leave you behind here, Bexley?"

The angry squish of her cousin's mouth said what Bexley wouldn't.

Or couldn't.

Both.

The answer was both.

"Are you considering it?" her cousin asked, then, quiet but still demanding. "Moving back home?"

Like she needed to know.

"What are you going to do next fall?" Delaney asked instead.

"When you're graduated and should be starting your career in nursing—are you staying here or going home? Did you consider me, or what I would do, when you thought about those choices?"

"What does that matter? That has nothing to do with what I just asked you. Also, your name is on the freaking lease. I only moved into this apartment because you wanted to get a bigger bedroom."

"Yes, it does," Delaney returned, refusing to take the bait about the lease issue. A non-issue in her mind, really. "It's the same thing."

Being adults meant they could both make their own choices. Delaney gave Bexley the respect, but she expected it for herself, too. At the end of the day, the only thing she really owed Bexley regarding their current apartment and the lease was her half of the rent for the rest of the term. Money her cousin could find in the back of the freezer inside a rolled up Ziplock bag under a pack of frozen trout that neither of them would ever eat.

That wasn't the real issue, though.

Delaney could tell by the way Bexley's shoulders hunched and she dropped her head before turning back around on the couch to sink beneath the blanket. Meanwhile, her favorite television series played on the flat screen television mounted to the wall. For a brief second, Bexley had looked like a little kid trying to hide away from the rest of the world.

Or just the things scaring her.

Delaney forgot that, other than her, Bexley didn't have very many people around her. Sure, she'd made friends at school, and her part-time job at the hospital, as well. Her older cousin, however, had been the one person who had been there to hold her hand through these last couple of years. From leaving her family and their religious sect behind to a rough first year in nursing school that damn near had Bexley bowing out.

She would have, too.

If not for those late-night study and quiz sessions with Delaney that got Bexley's final exam grades over passing so she could continue on.

Bexley needed Delaney.

Or, she thought she did.

"Hey," Delaney said, trying to coax her cousin back out from beneath the blanket.

It didn't work.

Delaney left her purses behind to round the back of the couch. Twisted like a burrito into the blanket, only the back of Bexley's head could be seen against the sham pillow. Delaney folded her arms and used them as her own pillow to rest against the back of the couch as she talked.

"The truth is, a part of me does want to go home," Delaney said.

"*Knew it*," Bexley muttered.

"And I might, because I really haven't given it the time or thought it deserves, so I can't say I've made a final decision yet."

Her younger cousin sighed loudly.

Delaney only rolled her eyes.

The silence between them pressed on.

Delaney reached down to hook a finger under the edge of the blanket so she could pull it down enough to see the way her cousin gave her the side-eye glare. "Careful, or your face will stay frozen like that."

The smartass comment, another familiar one from their childhood, had Bexley barking out a hard laugh.

"*Bitch.*"

"Tell me about it," Delaney replied, letting the blanket go and resuming her previous position.

Bexley pulled the blanket down and rolled to her back. "I don't know if I'll ever want to go back after everything ..."

Delaney nodded. "Then, maybe you shouldn't."

"Do you think I can make it here without a roomie?"

"I'm not going to leave you hanging like that. Trust me."

"If you do go, are you still gonna visit?"

Delaney grinned. "At least every other week—I can't do rural shopping again after living in the city. What do you mean?"

Bexley laughed again.

True *was* true.

"Aren't you going to be late for your lunch with Linda?" Bexley asked.

Delaney shrugged. "Yeah, but you didn't even go to classes today, so ..."

"It's not a competition. Plus, my period started. Give me a break."

"Good to know yours is starting."

Bexley's brow furrowed, disgust coloring her voice when she asked, "What, why?"

"It means mine is nearly ending."

Four day periods were common for Delaney once she started taking birth control pills to help with the worst of her cramping and heavy bleeding. What had felt like a punishment from God in her teenage years, before her mother absolutely refused to let their family doctor prescribe something she proclaimed was nothing more than man-made sin, changed to something more tolerable the second those twenty-eight days of pills came into her life. Like clockwork, she could predict the ending of her own cycle with how the beginning of her cousin's lined up to the timing of her own.

"You track that stuff too much," her cousin mumbled, rolling back over on the couch. "It's weird."

Nah, she didn't think so.

"It's not weird to know what your body is supposed to do," Delaney replied. "It means you're informed and prepared if something's not all the way right."

"I guess you'll never have to wonder if you're pregnant, huh?"

Delaney blinked at the comment. "Um …"

"I'm just saying because you'll know the second you're a day late."

Well, fair enough.

"You know what, I'm definitely late for lunch," Delaney said, opting to end the conversation there.

Babies were not on her docket.

Not today.

*

"I'm sorry, I'm late," Delaney said the second she dropped into the bistro chair across from Linda at the corner table in the coffee shop. Her apologetic smile earned her an unconcerned wave from her beaming boss. "I know, I'm late. Did you get my text?"

"I did," Linda assured, "no worries there."

Oh, good.

"I ordered two soups and sandwiches of the day. Does that work for you?"

Delaney, who had seen the tomato soup and grilled cheese option for an all-day menu item scrawled on the chalkboard sign in the front window on her way in, nodded. "That's perfect."

Food didn't have to be fancy.

Just delicious.

The two women made easy conversation, about safe topics like the road conditions and price of gas that week, as Delaney shrugged off her parka, and shed her mittens, gloves, and hat. She made a pile of items inside her large handbag, and then hung her jacket off the back of her chair. Not two minutes after she sat down, the server in her standard red and brown uniform came over with hot, fresh coffee that Delaney eagerly accepted.

Linda got a refill on her cup, too.

"The food will be right out," the young lady with a bouncing ponytail assured before heading off to a table nearby.

As soon as the server was out of earshot, Linda asked Delaney, "So, how was last week? Did you get the family emergency handled?"

The question came with a genuine smile.

Delaney instantly felt bad. "Can I be honest?"

Linda's kind expression never waved. "Of course. Why wouldn't you be?"

Some people didn't create the kind of environment where others saw the opportunity to be truthful without consequence. Delaney had become acutely aware of her ability to tell the difference from one person to the next whether that was the case.

Her boss, beautifully sweet inside her soul, only ever proved that she cared when it came to the ladies who worked for her, or the people that came through her doors.

"It wasn't technically *my* family's emergency," Delaney clarified about the spread of days off she had unexpectedly taken the week before without much notice or explanation to Linda. "It was, however, a situation that needed me to leave town for a bit, so I did. I feel bad that I made you think it was something that had happened to someone in my family when in fact—"

"Sometimes, the family we choose is all we've got, and they need help, too," Linda interjected with a sympathetic pat to Delaney's hand.

Well, if only …

"I wouldn't say Lucas Dalton is necessarily the family I've chosen," Delaney hedged carefully, "but I did feel like he needed my help for a few days."

The same drew a spark of recognition in Linda's bright eyes.

"*I knew it!*" the other woman proclaimed, smacking the table with a hearty laugh. "I knew there had to be a reason there was a Dalton leaving messages on every phone number I have listed publicly to me. I mean, I didn't want to call your cousin and ask her if you were seeing Lucas, but … I almost did."

Delaney blinked.

The tables had turned on her so fast that she was still trying to catch up with a situation she clearly didn't understand.

"I'm sorry?" Delaney asked.

Linda, still cackling to herself and proud of whatever accomplishment she managed in getting Delaney to talk about Lucas, waved the confusion off. All the while, she dug into her own tote bag hanging off the corner of her bistro chair until she found the item she wanted.

A newspaper, actually.

"Have you seen this?" Linda asked, slapping the front page down for Delaney to see.

"No, what?"

"This," her boss pressed, pointing at the second story on the front page.

Surprisingly, a picture of Lucas shaking the hand of a man who looked a lot like him, if not a couple of decades older, and grinning for the camera with a plaque and cut ribbon between them. His father, Ronald Dalton, according to the information in the text beneath the printed photo on the front page. Along with the details of the photo; a shot that had been taken a couple of years ago during the expansion of their Saint John brewery.

More concerning was the headline at the top of the story.

Troubles inside the Daltons Worries Brewery Future.

Delaney did a quick survey of the paper—noting it had been printed for release that very morning. The first line of the article didn't exactly leave her with a hopeful feeling, either.

The infamously private Dalton family faces unprecedented times with major changes on the horizon, and discontent dribbling down from the top. The article continued on to discuss the return of Ronald Dalton to the brewery in the city, before his position had even been properly filled in the west, and the mess that would certainly cause for the company as they struggled to keep things going without issues on both ends of the country.

An impossible feat, according to the writer.

The article didn't go easy on Lucas, either, proclaiming the oldest Dalton son had not returned to work since the passing of his only sibling, despite the instability facing his family's brewery. The story, with more details about the Dalton family's shaky history of public feuds between fathers and sons, going back at least two generations, and the recent troubles stemming from Jacob's passing, continued on page three, but Delaney didn't read very far into that.

How dare the public speculate about a private man that way? She understood the Dalton Brewery company held prestige and power in the province, but Lucas didn't seem like the type to want his face and personal life speculated about on a platform for anyone to see, either.

She couldn't imagine *Lucas* reading it.

Why should she?

"I had not seen that," Delaney told her boss, pushing the paper back across the table. "Did you say someone had called you and left messages?"

Linda's expressive eyebrows, which could animate her whole face, pinched together at the question. "They started two days after you left, actually. All from the same man, if I'm to trust how he introduced himself each time. Ronald Dalton."

"Lucas' father."

More sympathy stared back from her boss.

"I take it you didn't know the family was troubled when you fell into whatever situation you're in with Mr. Dalton?"

"Lucas," Delaney corrected.

Mr. Dalton sounded like something his father would demand to be called. She knew for a fact that Lucas had already cleared that nonsense up with Linda once.

"Right, Lucas," her boss repeated. "But you didn't know— about his family, or father?"

"I didn't know his father was aware that I had left town for a few days with him at all, no," Delaney agreed.

The other bit …

Lucas made it clear there were issues in his family.

She wouldn't share them, though.

Linda nodded, and stuck the newspaper into her purse before bringing her attention back to the table once more. "I was sorry to hear about his brother."

"Me, too," Delaney murmured.

Her boss glanced down at the tabletop between them. "I only answered one of his father's calls, and immediately got the feeling he was trying to fish for information. It could have been because he instantly questioned how often his son visited the salon when he came to town, but then he called you out by name—specifically, that your name matched the one on a flight record he had access to through his business."

"We did take a helicopter to the place we stayed," Delaney said. "And to come back, but—"

"How did he connect your name on a flight record to the place where you work, Delaney?"

She didn't need Linda's tone to tell her that piece of information was concerning.

"He's never even met me," she said faintly. "I don't understand why the man would be trying to *find* me, I mean … I'm nobody to him."

That was weird, right?

Linda shrugged, asking, "Would he have access to calendars or online schedules for Lucas that might have listed you? I suspect his phone and things probably sync to the company's home office system. Would there be a reason Ronald Dalton had to seek you out?"

Delaney had no clue.

"I didn't mean to cause you any trouble, Linda," she told her boss.

"Ah, you didn't," Linda replied, grinning a bit. "I might have had a little fun dodging his calls and messages, anyway. I'm not sure what he was trying to prove, but it did nothing. I'm certainly not going to fire you over all of this."

Lucky it worked out.

Delaney still felt … *off.*

Or something about the situation did.

Could it be possible Lucas *didn't* know his father had purposely tried to seek Delaney out behind his son's back?

Her gaze traveled to the elbow of the newspaper still sticking out from Linda's purse. A more prominent question came to her mind at the sight.

Would knowing his father had done so make an already bad

situation brewing in his family even worse?

"Is that why you wanted to have lunch?" she asked Linda. "To give me a heads up about the calls and whatnot?"

Linda nodded, but winked, too. "Partly, but something told me to just check in on you, too. I know you've had a rough couple of months, Delaney."

"A rough couple of years, really."

"Exactly. I can always fill your chair with somebody. That's not the problem for me. I'm more concerned about making sure my girls are happy coming into work everyday. That's what's more important to me at the end of the day, you understand?"

Yeah, she did.

"Are you still happy working for me?" Linda asked when Delaney remained quiet across the table.

"I like my job," Delaney replied, "and dropping off a resume with you was probably the best decision I made when I came to this city."

"That wasn't an answer to my question, Delaney."

Right.

"I also miss my home," she admitted, "and the life I left on pause there."

Linda, with her smile that never faltered, only said, "Just try to give me a couple of weeks notice, okay? At least."

Delaney could do that … "Absolutely." She gestured at nothing, but her gaze traveled to the newspaper sticking out of the bag while her mind and heart went out to Lucas. His privacy invaded by too-curious journalists, and the rest of the province waking up to the article about his family. "Once I get the rest of this figured out."

"Oh, yes," Linda agreed, "I wouldn't expect anything less. I didn't see any mention of the funeral or some kind of service for the Dalton boy that just passed. Are you going to need an extra day for that? I understand."

Sweet Jesus.

Delaney didn't need to take further advantage of this kind woman. Even though she knew the location and time of the memorial for friends and those that were attached to Jacob Dalton, in one way or another, she hadn't discussed showing up to it with Lucas. Other than making it clear that he suspected his father wouldn't attend, he also hadn't asked her if she might.

Linda put the idea out there, though, and now Delaney couldn't unsee it.

"It's tomorrow, actually," Delaney hedged carefully.

The first day she should return to work for a four-day stretch.

"Do you need the hours, or ... sorry," her boss said, "I shouldn't ask that. You're welcome to take the day or not, but Neeka wanted the extra shift, anyway."

Delaney didn't need the hours.

Her savings account and lack of debt made certain exceptions possible in her life. What good was all that hard work if she didn't use it?

You kind of just did, Delaney.

She ignored her inner voice.

Today, it didn't matter.

"I'll take the day," Delaney said.

It would be four hours of driving there and back between the morning and evening, but if showing up meant she helped the day pass easier for Lucas ... That was all Delaney cared about.

Linda didn't look a bit surprised, but a softness touched her eyes. "Pass along my condolences to Lucas? I started putting the puzzle together that your emergency might have been about him after I noticed the posting in the paper about his brother ... and then the calls, you know."

"Right, *Ronald.*"

Even the name tasted bad in Delaney's mouth.

The older woman rolled her eyes upward. "Right, him. Anyway, pass that along for me?"

"Yeah, sure."

"A shame the two of you intersected at such a difficult time in his life," Linda said, more to herself than Delaney. "I hope that doesn't complicate things."

Delaney still heard it perfectly fine.

Worse, she'd thought about that being the case, too.

30.

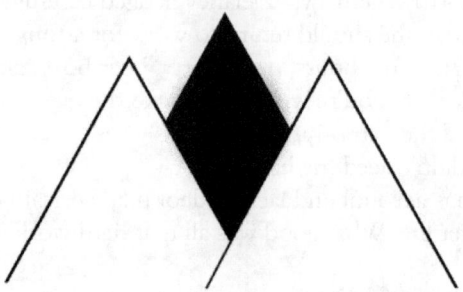

A northeaster—or nor'easter to those familiar with the intense winter storms known to pummel Atlantic Canada with cyclone-strength winds while dumping feet of snow—that had been forecasted for the later part of the week changed track slightly by Wednesday morning. It meant the Maritimes wouldn't get the worst of the storm, but the tail end that brushed along the coast could bring fifteen centimeters or more of snow and white-out driving conditions at the time Jacob's memorial rolled around by the afternoon.

Lucas had become accustomed to waking up in his Forest Hills high rise apartment to see the sheet of white covering the land. If anything, winter in Saint John looked predictable. It still took him by surprise to pull open the curtains and not even be able to see the ground below from the amount of snow blowing in the winds, however.

By then, he'd gotten the notification on his phone from the province warning about the drastic change in weather, and asking people to plan their day accordingly.

Well ...

The storm changed practically nothing.

For him, anyway.

Lucas, trying a new thing where he slowed down his morning routine so that it gave him time to focus on himself, went ahead as he would if not for the storm once the funeral home confirmed their schedule wasn't affected, either. He journaled through an easy breakfast of bacon and fried eggs on toast—a suggestion from his therapist that he didn't think would hurt to try even if he wouldn't consider himself a writer, necessarily.

Penning out his messy thoughts in his equally unreadable scrawl let him work through the jumble of emotions and the rest of the bullshit filling him up inside as the time for his brother's memorial crawled closer. Maybe if he worked through some of it beforehand, it wouldn't be so tough to get through the actual thing.

Already dressed in the suit—a black-on-black ensemble from the dress shirt underneath the tailored-to-his-frame blazer to his tie and vest—minus the jacket he wanted to keep pressed and clean until he had to put it on, Lucas watched his nonsensical ramblings change on the paper. He started as though talking to himself, hunched over the round glass-topped kitchen table the penthouse apartment had come furnished with when he bought it, but finished at the bottom of his fourth page like he was writing a message to Jacob.

It didn't have to make sense.

It *did* help.

Benson said it's not my guilt to carry, but I told him that's not gonna change how I feel when I wake up again tomorrow and you're still not here, Lucas had written, the mention of his therapist reminding him yet again why he had sat down to do this in the first place. *I didn't ask for you to be okay, Jake, just for you to be here, you know? Maybe that's why I still feel like it's my fault.*

A skipped line beneath those words, Lucas had added— *Celebration of life?* The question mark felt appropriate because that's just how he felt regarding the memorial meant to do what it said; celebrate a life. He hated the irony that came with it when the only reason they were having the celebration to begin with stemmed from a life no longer here to be lived.

He couldn't come up with a respectable way to end his thoughts coming out on the paper, so he slapped his initials at the bottom of the page and closed the leatherbound notebook with a snap as the front and back came together. The magnetic strap that connected to the front closed itself, and he left the notebook where it sat on the table as he cleared his plate. Lucas didn't want to linger on his thoughts that he'd gotten out—that defeated the purpose of allowing himself to stream them, and filter all the nonsense out, onto a page where hopefully, for a time, they could stay.

He could always come back to the unfinished bit later.

Journaling worked to get Lucas through the last hour or so before he had to leave to make the trip to Quispamsis—the thirty-minute drive just outside of the city—where the memorial would be held had likely turned into a forty-five minute or more journey with the storm.

At least, the heated, underground garage of the high rise kept the Bronco warm and ready for Lucas when he jumped into the driver's seat. He kept trying to find those silver linings everywhere to keep him on track and doing what he needed to do.

The memorial, that was.

Because a piece of Lucas internally screamed at the idea of it all being real. It would be—as soon as he entered the funeral home's gallery where his brother's urn, one he'd selected in a ready-made, easy to understand package provided for viewing online by the crematorium, would be waiting on a podium. There the truth would be surrounded by flower arrangements and picture collages made up by the animal rescue where Jacob had volunteered.

Even knowing what he would be walking into, because the funeral home director kept him informed and managed to be more respectful of Lucas' time than most other people in his life, didn't make it easier.

Nor did it make the drive *longer*.

It didn't stop the pain blooming like a bruise deep in his chest, either.

Lucas had not been prepared to arrive ten minutes earlier to find the parking lot for the white funeral home trimmed with black nearly full of vehicles. What shocked him more came in a face he recognized—Kimmie Tate, from accounting, walked arm in arm with Lucas' assistant. Nola and Kimmie waved with soft smiles as he slowed to let them pass by the front of the Bronco, where a gathering of people who made a sea of black on the front steps waited to trickle inside the double doors a few at a time.

There, people could brush off their boots, remove their winter clothing and hang everything on waiting racks, and be greeted by any family of the deceased along with the funeral director. Lucas had asked that they not wait on him.

What if he needed time?

People shouldn't have to wait to pay their respects to Jacob.

Something about the number of vehicles, and people, eased the anxiety building in Lucas' chest. If he were honest about the worst of his thoughts, the most painful ones that stemmed from all the awful shit he heard said about his brother over the years, especially from his parents, then Lucas would have to say he'd wondered if anyone would come at all. The fact that so many did confirmed what he already knew.

His parents didn't matter. Not a word they said meant anything at all to the life Jacob had lived. He wasn't the total sum of the drugs he had used, or the fact that his addiction had ultimately killed him—words their own father had spat like insults at Jacob for years. Instead, his baby brother's life had been made up of many pieces. Multi-faceted. A culmination of each person he ever met and every experience he'd ever had.

One thing—bad choices, or otherwise—didn't define him.

Jacob was so much more than just that.

By a quarter past noon, the priest who had baptized Jacob and Lucas as children would say a few things. Lucas had put out requests to certain individuals, like Jacob's old sponsor and his buddy from the gym that introduced him to the rescue, if they'd like a moment to say anything. Both had agreed.

All that left ... was *him*.

Lucas was still trying to figure that bit out.

Well, he told himself, shifting the gear into park in one of three parking spots lining the front of the large funeral home designated to immediate family—the other two were empty, of course—*you start by getting out of the fucking car, Lucas.*

So, he did.

*

"A little birdy in HR told me that thirty people called in for a sick day at the brewery today," came a quiet voice at Lucas' left.

There, he found a grinning Nola.

"I can believe it," Lucas told her, tipped his head toward the overwhelming crowd gathering in the gallery room. He ended up at the opened doorway between the entrance and gallery next to the director, despite being hesitant, because the crowd had parted for him the second he neared the front steps. Every pat on his back, muttered *sorry, we loved Jacob*, or otherwise made the ground a little easier to walk on.

He took the hug Nola offered.

A couple of steps behind her, Kimmie from accounting waved.

"Jacob always said hi whenever he stopped by the office," the brunette explained, shrugging. "I thought it was fair to come say goodbye."

Nola stepped back from Lucas with a nod of her own, and tear-filled eyes that she did her best to hide. "I'm really sorry, Lucas."

"Thanks," he managed, but his smile didn't linger long.

It couldn't.

Thankfully, nobody expected it from him today, either.

"No work talk today," Nola said, shaking a finger at him, and then Kimmie, too.

"Who said anything about work?"

"Definitely not me," Lucas said in a chuckle.

He took another hug from Nola, and a quick one from Kimmie, before the two women disappeared into the gallery to find seats before they all filled up. Lucas wouldn't have to worry about that on his side of things. A change with a seating card just for him waited at the very front where he had a view of the slightly raised stage where Jacob's silver urn sat in front of a large portrait of him taken only a few short months ago.

Grinning wide and carefree with water up to his ankles on the Bay of Fundy's shore.

From his position between the two rooms, Lucas had a good view of the makeshift alter meant to honor his brother. He wasn't sure what would happen to all the flowers, or what in the hell he would do with the portrait and collages, but each and every single thing he could take would be carefully loaded into the back of his Bronco for his safekeeping.

Another dozen guests down the line later, including a little boy—six, he'd told Lucas when asked his age—who had began fostering dogs with his mom and dad because of Jacob, and he started to feel like he needed a break.

The priest who would speak later chose that moment to slide in alongside Lucas with a heavy hand to his shoulder.

"How're you doing?" Father Burke asked.

"Take a second," the funeral director, keeping things on schedule and smooth, told Lucas.

He turned away with a nod, but didn't leave his position at the door. Instead, he opted to speak to the Catholic priest while his gaze surveyed the reflection of his brother's life made up of the gathered people and makeshift memorial of teddy bears and folded up letters making a pile under Jacob's urn.

"I'm getting through it," Lucas settled on telling the priest.

He had to look down to meet the short man's eyes, but the bespectacled priest only squinted back with a sympathetic smile.

"I worry about you, Luke," Father Burke told him. "It wasn't so bad when I saw you every other week at church—at least then I could check in on you."

Lucas opted not to discuss his decision to stop attending his family's parish in Quispamsis. He had been the last Dalton to stop attending regular services, because as he'd gotten older, his philosophical beliefs didn't necessarily align with what had been taught to him growing up. He didn't find a connection to a deity sitting in hard pews or between the pages of the pocket Bible he'd kept for years up until he left it behind on Delaney's workstation that day.

Besides, the blind faith thing never really worked out for Lucas. If there was a God, and He *did* listen, then what did it matter? God should already know what was in Lucas' heart.

The important bits.

"Thank you for doing a small sermon today," Lucas said to Father Burke. "I know Ronald probably asked you not to, but it means a lot."

"I didn't even phone him back, actually," the priest replied. "Doing this for you and Jacob meant more to me than a late-night message from your father, anyway. He really should talk to someone about his anger, though."

"Tell me about it," Lucas muttered.

At the same time, the funeral director behind Lucas greeted another guest. "Hello, thank you for coming today to celebrate Jacob's life with us. You'll find keepsakes in the gallery room."

"Thank you," came the familiar voice.

The sweetest voice Lucas had ever heard.

He spun around to find the owner of that voice dressed in a body conforming, long sleeve dress, black like everyone else, with a hemline on the skirt that fell a couple of inches below her knees. Her flat-soled knee-high boots were still wet from the snow she probably kicked off at the front door, and her black curls, swept back into a messy chignon, were only slightly frizzy from the wind and the snow still peppering her hair.

Another thing he'd done for himself that morning to make the day easier came in the form of silencing his phone—and only checking it to call the funeral home regarding whether or not the storm changed any plans.

His last message to Delaney had been the morning before. He did not expect her to show up at his brother's memorial, but the day had just become bearable from the way her presence instantly filled up the hollow space in his chest.

A snow angel had found him, it seemed.

"You came in this storm?" he asked Delaney, only slightly concerned with how she managed that in the bad weather conditions.

She shrugged, wringing her hands despite holding his gaze. "I wanted to come for you. I thought I was gonna be late."

"Nope," Lucas returned, already reaching out to pull her into the hug she deserved for being so fucking perfect, "you couldn't have better timing, sweets."

31.

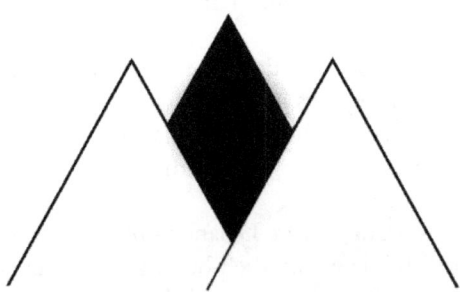

"Are you doing okay? It's been a long afternoon," Delaney said.

Lucas nodded but didn't distinguish between whether he was okay or if he also thought the afternoon had been a lot.

Apparently, he had other things on his mind.

Understandably.

"I had a moment where I got mad at Jacob this week," Lucas said. "I started cleaning out his place—my name is on the lease, and it's paid up until the end of the month, so it's something I needed to do. I figured out he'd dropped the gym just before winter, hadn't contacted his sponsor since Christmas, and it didn't take long for him to go right back to using what was cheapest. We talked about that once—how he can't possibly know what these people are cutting into their drugs, if it's even what he thinks he's buying ... *fuck*."

Lucas massaged his eye sockets with his finger and thumb, adding roughly, "I guess it didn't matter in the end? Even if back then he acted like it did. It pissed me off because what I saw was all that time when he didn't ask for help. Then I just felt like shit because fuck, he's not even here to be mad *at*, anyway."

She heard the guilt he held inside.

"Anger is a part of grief," Delaney returned to her somber companion. "That probably won't be the last time."

"I don't want to be mad at him, though."

"It'll be harder if you don't let yourself feel the things you need or want to feel, Lucas."

Wounds like those took longer to heal.

"*Mmm*," he hummed noncommittally.

Delaney didn't fault him for the distraction, considering.

In the chair one over from hers, Lucas's profile darkened with his sadness, and she wished more than anything she could be the thing that helped ease the pain. That just wasn't how this sort of thing worked.

The gallery, devoid of windows but brightly lit by long lights overhead, gave Delaney lots of items to take her attention while Lucas sat with his feelings beside her in silence.

She didn't have a reason to rush him.

"I'm going to resign."

The quiet declaration made Delaney's head snap around where she found Lucas fiddling with the photograph someone had placed on the pile of other memories beneath Jacob's urn. One of the many that Lucas picked out among the rest, and had kept tucked in his breast pocket. Lucas flicked the corner edge between two fingers as his furrowed brow and steady gaze remained on the smiling young man staring up from the photo.

One of at least hundreds Delaney had seen of Jacob over the course of the afternoon. She had believed she knew his face well from her time at the cottage in Birch Ridge, but hearing the stories and memories of those who personally knew Lucas' younger brother helped to give his life a lot of color for her. Their love for him made her feel like she had known him, too.

In a different kind of way, maybe.

"Like, quit?" Delaney asked, dumbly.

To her, it sure sounded that way.

Surely, she hadn't heard him right.

Right?

Lucas shrugged his broad shoulders covered in black silk. He'd lost his blazer long ago to the back of the chair he sat in for the duration of the memorial. "I mean, that sounds less professional, but sure."

"From the *brewery?*"

Delaney still couldn't wrap her mind around the idea.

"Honestly," Lucas said, glancing over at Delaney where the two sat side by side in red crushed velvet backed chairs, "I stayed in the family business because I didn't have a lot of other options outside of the brewery to take care of myself. My shares of ownership came later, from my grandfather's estate, and since Jacob had been left with nothing, I still couldn't leave the place to do something I wanted to, really. My hands were tied."

Responsibility could be like that.

Especially when it wasn't one's own.

"Is this because of your father?" Delaney hedged carefully.

There hadn't been a proper time over the course of the afternoon that she felt comfortable to share with Lucas how his father had attempted to contact Linda about Delaney. With the funeral home mostly cleared out of those who had gathered to celebrate Jacob's life, and only Delaney and Lucas remaining in the gallery with Jacob's urn in the chair separating the two, now seemed like as good of a time as ever.

Especially when Lucas confirmed her suspicions.

"He's not going to make things easy on me. If I go ahead and resign. He never has—but I can't do it anymore," he said.

"Would there be any reason your father might try to contact people connected to me? Like my boss, say?"

His stare narrowed at the news. "He didn't."

It wasn't even a question.

"It's not a big deal because Linda wouldn't even answer his messages back, but he found me through you. I haven't really connected those dots, I guess, but—"

"You don't have to," Lucas interjected, saying exactly what Delaney thought. The fact Ronald Dalton had somehow attempted to interfere in his son's personal life, when the man clearly had no invitation to be there, was concerning. "Who'd know, huh? Maybe he was trying to prove something about the time I took away. He hasn't brought you up to me."

Delaney nodded. "Okay."

"But we also haven't had a face-to-face meeting in … a while."

Ah.

That possibly changed things.

"The good news," Delaney said, "is that there isn't much to find. I'm not exactly infamous or prolific, so …"

Lucas chuckled. "Well, you don't have to be either of those things to mean something to me. Let's hope that's not his interest."

She almost asked why.

He continued on before she could, saying, "I'm worried that if I do what he did, stay under his thumb doing everything he demands to make life bearable, that history will just repeat itself. I don't want to wake up one day like he must have done and realize that I turned into him."

"I don't know your father, but—"

"No buts," he interjected, his jaw growing taut, and his gaze hardening. "You don't know him. Keep it to that."

Delaney reached over the urn with the intricate carvings along the top cover to place her hand on Lucas' forearm once he'd placed the photograph of Jacob next to the urn between them. "I don't know exactly what you're worried about—how you think you'll be anything like him—but I'm proud to know you, Lucas. I think a lot of people here today would say the same thing."

In fact, people had.

"And he can't change that," Delaney finished.

The only thing that should matter.

Lucas sighed heavily, and relaxed back into the chair while he eyed the makeshift altar to Jacob Dalton at the middle-front of the room. "You and my therapist are the only two people I've told that I'm considering leaving Dalton Brewery."

No wonder.

She could only imagine what would follow a choice like that for him. Would another few articles get published in the newspaper? Would he be the villain? The employees of his family's company, especially those that had shown up to support him today for his brother, would undoubtedly be affected in one way or another, too.

He'd make a ripple.

Where would the waves end?

Delaney chewed on her lower lip. "And, what'd the therapist have to say?"

He chuckled. "He pointed out I've made more than a few hasty, and possibly reckless, decisions in the last handful of weeks that all could be tied back to my, as he put it, *fragile* emotional state," he said, deadpanning every word except the one he clearly disliked. "Resigning could be another one of those, and he told me to give it a bit of time."

She tried not to grin, failing. "Big man, you don't want the world to know you cry?"

His dark stare rolled to her when his head fell to the side. "If only, right?"

He didn't need to cry to be hurt or to grieve, but she'd found him on the verge more than once over the afternoon. Eyes shining with unshed tears, he'd quickly step away with an apology to take a minute or two by himself.

His emotions, fragile or not, wasn't what he wanted her to focus on.

"Did he mean me?" she asked. "Was I a hasty decision you had made?"

Lucas cleared his throat, but muttered, "Among other things."

Huh.

Delaney didn't know how to feel about that, so she chose to sit there and stew on it. Lucas didn't let her ponder for long.

"I don't necessarily think he's right about everything," he said, "but he makes me look at things from perspectives I hadn't considered."

His hand found hers overtop his forearm, and then his fingers slid in between her own to grasp tight.

"So, maybe he had a point in a way," Lucas added, shrugging like it didn't make a big difference. "You aren't a hasty decision I made. The best one, if anything. I'm not going to let guilt or anything else change how I feel about that, or you."

Delaney smiled. "That makes two of us, then."

"But he also wasn't wrong—in the way I can't go into every decision based on how I'm feeling at any given time," Lucas muttered.

"Like the brewery?"

His free hand, not holding hers, drummed an anxious beat to the padded arm of the chair. "Yeah, like the brewery. Knowing as much doesn't really change what I want, though. That's the bit I have to figure out now."

"Which is what?"

He swallowed audibly and his hand came up to scrub under his jaw as he surveyed the collection of items and photographs that made up the overall picture of his brother's short life.

"Honestly?" he asked back.

"Even if it's crazy."

She wanted to know.

Lucas laughed, but it came off a little hollow. "Well, that's not possible."

"Tell me anyway."

"I'd take Jacob to Birch Ridge, and hide away from the rest of civilization for a while. Breathe fresh air everyday and I wouldn't keep a schedule beyond when the sun's going up or down. I don't even want to call it a break, just ..." Lucas let out a gusty breath, adding quietly, "I'm not sure I know who I am or what I want in life, and maybe I'd like to take the time to get those things sorted out. For myself."

Didn't everybody deserve that?

It hadn't escaped her notice that she wasn't something in his crazy dream. She didn't take it personally. *Much.*

"Would visits with me be included in this time away from civilization?" Delaney asked.

Lucas' brow dipped in the cutest way as he glanced over at her. "What do you mean, I thought you were going with me?"

Oh.

She wasn't included because in his mind, he already saw her there with him.

A *given.*

"Of course, you're there," he said as if he could read her mind. "In my head, I'm always trying to get back to you now. I'm thirty seconds off a phone call from you already thinking about the next time I'm gonna hear your voice. It should be crazy to me how you're the one thing I feel like I know for sure when not very long ago, we were strangers."

But it wasn't.

She heard what he didn't say.

"It's like that for you, too?"

She had crawled inside the chambers of his heart to build a home there like he had done for hers—she wasn't alone?

"It's like that for me, too," he echoed. "I don't know how to tell someone I love them, that wasn't a popular phrase around me growing up, but I do for you. I love you." Lucas looked down at the urn between them, and his expression pinched with pain for a split second before his eyes met hers again. "I'm really sorry that I found you at a bad time, and it might make things a little difficult from here on out for a while."

"I'm not sorry at all," Delaney replied. "I'll never apologize for falling in love with you."

He wasn't her burden.

This thing between them didn't have a deadline to the finish or time constraints around what they did or didn't do together. *They* got to paint the masterpiece—every inch and crevice; all the colors and shades. It didn't even have to be perfect.

They wouldn't be, after all.

"Shit, come here," Lucas muttered, tugging on Delaney's hand to pull her closer. His lips found hers for a gentle kiss that had her breath catching before he lifted their connected hand to press rapid pecks along each of her fingers when he flipped her palm over. Keeping his lips connected to her skin, he looked up at her. "And it's okay if I have to take time to get the rest sorted out?"

What would that mean?

Less contact?

No helicopter rides to the middle of nowhere?

Who cared?

"Fair is fair," she told him, "because I think I might have some things to figure out, too."

Lucas didn't ask what those particular items on her life shelf that were needing rearranging, but they also wouldn't change anything.

"I'll still be wherever, waiting," she said.

He nodded, and then kissed her again before Delaney could prepare for the way her heart had not quite recovered from the first one. That time, he ended it with their foreheads pressed together while the quiet gallery gave an illusion of privacy.

That couldn't last forever.

"Good news," came the familiar voice of the funeral director as he swept back into the room, "Kiesha's eyeglass case has been found—and Lucas, I heard back from my friend at the government garage. They're on track to finish clearing the highways within the hour. She's safe to travel back to Fredericton tonight."

Lucas put distance between himself and Delaney as soon as their guest announced his presence. To be fair, it was *his* building.

"Thank you, Kody," Lucas said.

"Are we getting everything loaded up in the Bronco?"

"Shortly," Lucas agreed.

At the confirmation, the director spun on his heel to exit the gallery and once again, leave the two alone.

"See, I told you," Delaney put in, winking. "The roads are good."

Not even her lifted Jeep meant for tough terrain had been enough to convince Lucas that he could let her leave to start the journey home. Proclaiming she had work in the morning hadn't done the job, either.

"Can't be too safe," he told her, then.

289

The same thing he told her before.

"Driving here was worse—trust me."

"Yeah, well … Forgive me for caring."

"Not necessary, Lucas. Stop apologizing for loving me … or anything. I'm not sure that's how it's supposed to work, okay?"

He squeezed her hand tight. "I'll work on it. How about that?"

"It'll do," she said, matching his smile with her own.

Effort surely counted for a lot, too.

Delaney could tell—just by the way he stared at her—that it had nothing to do with the weather, road conditions, or whether she could manage the drive. He simply didn't want her to leave. Frankly, neither did she.

There came that bad timing …

And the bits of their lives they each had to work out.

"Call me as soon as you get to your place?" he asked, dropping more kisses to her knuckles after flipping over her hand inside his own. "I'll worry, otherwise."

That just wouldn't do.

"The second I park," she assured.

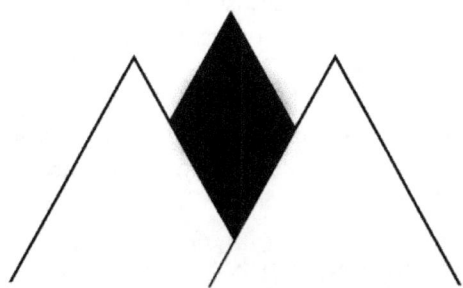

32

Returning to work on the last day of the week hadn't been in Lucas' original plans, but stepping inside the brewery on the Friday after his brother's memorial sobered him, nonetheless. He intended that to be the last time he crossed the Dalton Brewery threshold as an employee beneath his father, and that made him see things a bit differently.

Or maybe he appreciated the warm greetings from the familiar faces as he entered and made the trek upstairs more than he might have on a regular day.

This wouldn't be another one of those days.

That made everything different.

Even the elevator seemed to pick up on that change within Lucas, taking longer than usual—although, that could have been his mind playing tricks on him—to deliver him to the upstairs.

Nola, despite Lucas' friendly smile and good morning as he stopped at her desk, took note of the mood change while he dropped off her typical morning coffee and sugar-glazed donut. "Thanks—are you okay? I thought you were coming in over the weekend?"

"No, my father wanted me to come in this weekend for a meeting," Lucas explained, "and I'm in the process of making other plans."

Not that he offered those plans.

Nola peered up at him from her swivel chair that she nervously rolled from side to side. "Oh, okay. You know, he's been interviewing secretaries all week, right?"

"I didn't, actually. Let me guess, he's had you being the go-between for every interview, hasn't he?"

"Basically." She chewed her lip, and toyed with the rolling shelf on her desk that held or hid the keyboard for her desktop. "Where exactly will that person go? Because my desk is here, and the room where *your* office should be is not big enough—"

"It's storage, not an office."

And he wouldn't pretend otherwise.

Nola sighed, and her hands flitted anxiously in front of her face. "I know, but that's not the point. I'm kind of concerned about my job right now."

Honestly?

"You should be," Lucas replied.

The young woman openly frowned. "That hardly seems fair."

It wasn't.

Sadly, for Ronald, it didn't have to be fair. It was *his* company—a business where he held majority shares that remained privately owned, and as such, Ronald could do and behave as he wanted. Including when it came to his employees.

"I didn't work here back when he used to be here," Nola said lamely. "I'm not really familiar with the way he likes things or does them, I guess."

"It's not about you," Lucas said, hoping he could make that one thing clear to Nola, so she didn't take that one negative onward with her from this job. "When it comes to Ronald Dalton and the things he does to other people, it's very rarely about what you do or don't do. No matter what he says."

Nola nodded, but the way she looked down hid the embarrassment and worry skittering across her pixie-like features. "Yeah, okay."

No, it wasn't okay.

"You've got family in Halifax, right?" Lucas asked.

Nola's nervous rolling of her chair same to a sudden stop at the mention of her family. "My mom lives there—that's where her family lives."

"Yeah, we talked about it a couple of times."

"And you remembered?"

He smiled. "That you seemed happier and worked better after a week-long vacation to visit your family? Of course."

"What does my family in Halifax have anything to do with the chance I might lose my job?"

"A friend of mine," Lucas explained, being careful how he

chose his words, aware that the quiet office might have ears and eyes listening, "is coming into town in the next week or so. He's got family here, but lives and works out of Halifax. He's an artist. A bit eccentric, but—"

"What about him?"

Lucas chuckled.

Straight to the point.

That's what he'd always liked about Nola.

"He called me yesterday to apologize for not being able to travel into the city for the memorial—apparently, he's got a lot of things on his plate between his gallery here that he's still in the process of moving. He mentioned needing an assistant who would need, and preferably enjoy, the travel. He'll pay better than you get here, plus you have the bonus of the Halifax connection. I thought of you, and if you want, I can pass along your name."

Sloane Alcott hadn't specified a timeline on needing or finding an assistant to manage all the little things about the business side of his artistry, but that didn't matter. The man cared more about finding someone who came highly recommended from someone else he trusted.

Lucas, for example.

Nola fit the bill.

"What about *you*?" Nola asked. "Won't you need someone here, or—"

"I'm not sure I'm going to be here, either," Lucas said. Letting that be his final word on the matter of his employment at the brewery, he tapped the edge of Nola's desk on the way by and added, "Let me know before I'm gone today whether or not you'd like me to make that call to my friend, okay?"

"I got it, Lucas. Thanks."

The long hallway with the row of offices on one side and the view of the bottling plant down below on the other welcomed every step from Lucas with a loud slap of his leather loafers against the tile. Not surprisingly, he found every door closed, as if the rest of the upstairs employees also had a reason to shut out the word beyond their private work spaces.

Including the office at the end.

Lucas considered knocking.

Until he noticed the newly etched *R. Dalton* on the frosted glass door.

"Welcome back, Dad," Lucas greeted as he unceremoniously entered the office without warning.

All he received in response came in the form of a dull, "Did you see your new office?"

"No," Lucas replied to the question Ronald had asked without even glancing away from the glowing screen of the desktop computer. "Not needed."

"Mmhmm, well, you've certainly seen the storage room before, so."

"No, it won't be needed, Dad," Lucas said, hearing the way Ronald tried to bait him with an underhanded comment, and refusing to give in. He stepped further into the office, already scanning the walls of awards and accolades for the ones he knew would be missing—*his*. His achievements, in the brewery or outside of it, had never mattered, after all.

Lucas didn't expect that to change.

"Meaning, I won't need it at all," Lucas clarified once and for all.

That gained his father's attention.

Ronald squinted, already annoyed, around the side of the monitor. "I beg your pardon?"

Why did that question feel like a challenge?

Because it is, he thought.

Lucas refused to give Ronald an inch. A quick survey of the space prompted him to ask the man sitting comfortably behind the old, familiar desk, "It almost looks like it used to, doesn't it? Before it was mine."

Ronald scoffed. "Lucas, it was never yours."

Right.

Salt, meet wound.

Ronald rubbed it in *hard*.

"Lucky for you that I didn't make too many changes that you couldn't cover up with a painting, huh?" he asked Ronald.

The older mirror of himself, proud as could be with his arms folded over his chest, smiled coldly back at Lucas. "Does the fact that it never felt like yours say more about me, or you, son?"

More bait.

It dangled cruelly, waiting for Lucas to stoop down to his father's level of passive-aggressive insults. Bringing others around him down, by varied means, was the only way Ronald could get a person to his low playing field. He couldn't compete otherwise, and Ronald couldn't have that—he needed to be better than everyone else.

And he wanted everyone to know it, too.

Lucas no longer cared to do that.

Even if he would be right. Not even if it meant a verbal altercation might leave him feeling in control and as if he'd gotten a stroke on his side of the scoreboard against Ronald. His life wouldn't be made up of a past defined by whether or not he'd come out on top against someone else. That wasn't how Lucas wanted to treat *anyone*.

It didn't matter that the person, in the moment, happened to be Ronald. Or that Lucas hated his father, at the end of the day. Never mind the fact that he could probably sit down and write an entire list of reasons why engaging Ronald would be justified.

No, that person, who his father was, couldn't be Lucas.

He wouldn't let that happen.

Lucas put the ball back in Ronald's corner, saying, "You tell me, Dad. What do you want it to mean?"

That wasn't the response Ronald wanted.

He scowled at Lucas. "That sounds like something a fucking shrink would say. You're still seeing a therapist, then?"

"You're assuming?" Lucas asked back, amused.

"Don't act like you didn't stop inputting your daily schedule into your digital calendar for that woman to keep up on," Ronald muttered.

"Or you could say it like it is—you're pissed that you can't log into the company system and dig through my private schedule to see if there's something you can meddle in," Lucas returned.

At least, his father had the decency to shrug at the accusation. No denials or a runaround. Simply an acknowledgement of his interference. Just because he wouldn't entertain Ronald's mind games didn't mean Lucas planned to also let the man off with his more recent bullshit.

Yeah, he figured out how Ronald found Delaney's name.

The same way Jacob did so.

Once upon a time.

Maybe his hubris came at the right time for Lucas. He shouldn't have expected Ronald to give him more respect and privacy than he did for anyone else. If his father was willing, and often did, play in the employee files of others, surely he would make no qualms about opening Lucas' for a fucking password.

"I hear your mother went back to Florida," Ronald said, his attention drifting back to whatever work he had on the desktop screen. "Good riddance, eh?"

"Honestly, it's like she wasn't here at all."

Ronald barked an unsettling laugh. "God, I *wish*—the bitch."

Yes, Penelope could definitely be one of those. She earned the title in her own special way, but he couldn't say he would ever call his mother as much.

The comment made Lucas flinch.

In an instant, he could hear those abusive slurs shouting down the dark hall that had once connected his childhood bedroom to his parents' on the second floor of their old home. *Idiot. Bitch. I hate you. You're useless. Worthless.* Penelope's insults and yells in response to the horrible things her husband told her had been just as bad, of course.

Lucas had never understood why people who couldn't seem to stand to be in the same room with one another had managed to remain married for over twenty-five years.

Ronald didn't appear to notice the moment it took Lucas to recover from the flashback of surfacing trauma from his youth, thankfully. Still typing away at the keyboard, he didn't even act like someone else remained in the room at all.

Lucas' observations about the changes in the office couldn't be overlooked, or overstated, for that matter.

Sure enough, in his two-week absence from the brewery, Ronald had not wasted any time in making his return clear. In a very physical way. All the things his father had decorated and preferred for his own private office space in his rental downtown—that the man rarely used but became one of many sink holes in their accounting books for the company—had made its way to the brewery's largest office upstairs.

There wasn't a speck of Lucas in sight.

Not his collection of mystery novels that he managed to read a few pages at a time on the wall of climbing glass shelves sideways to the desk. Gone were the many knickknacks Lucas used to distract himself throughout the day from his desk while he took phone call after phone call or met with one employee after another. Every framed family photograph, including company events where the Daltons attended together, had been taken down from the walls and replaced with large oil paintings of various woodland scenes.

His father's favorite.

Returned where Mitchel had never wanted it to be.

"Never Ronald," Lucas said, loud enough for his father to hear over the click-clack of noisy keyboard keys.

Instantly, the sound stopped.

"What did you just say?"

Lucas, who had moved to the far wall where he could study his grandfather's shelf, stared at the reflection looking back. Untouched and still the same as he'd left the shelf with Mitchel's urn, framed photograph, and the gleaming brewery plaque next to both, it was the one thing in the room—the whole brewery, in fact—that Ronald couldn't change.

Ever.

"That was the running joke, right?" Lucas asked his father over his shoulder, fully aware that Ronald's hands formed fists overtop of his keyboard at the question. "It's what Grandad told anybody who ever asked—*what are you planning to do, die in that brewery, Mitchel?*"

Ronald's jaws clenched.

Lucas went right ahead with the rest of the story. Or rather, how it had always gone whenever it left his grandfather's lips. "*Whatever, but it's never going to Ronald.*"

Never Ronald became the slogan employees whispered mockingly behind Ronald's back for years at the brewery. What had been said as a joke by Mitchel actually held a lot of weight behind the private walls of their family homes over the decades. Lucas had never quite understood what changed his grandfather's mind—why that seventy-five percent ownership of the brewery transferred to Ronald after Mitchel died—but it couldn't be a coincidence that the first twenty-five percent changed hands from father to son shortly after Jacob had been born.

Lucas remembered that period in his childhood well.

For a time, while their faces were in the papers and a journalist had been penning how the family business would continue on, the Dalton men had got along. His parents had also fought less often, and life seemed happy.

Or that was the pretense, anyway.

It didn't last long.

"I took his bullshit and abuse for *years*," Ronald hissed from across the office. "Do you know how many times he called me down to the plant just to shout at me in front of everyone he could get to watch? He got a kick out of humiliating me every damn chance he could. I worked my ass off to give that man what he wanted, and that's all he ever gave me in return. *Nothing*. I got to be the fucking joke, Lucas. Well," his father said, haughty and pleased as he leaned back in his chair to widen his arms at the room, "who is laughing now?"

"You don't see the parallel, do you?" Lucas asked.

Ronald blinked at the question. "What are you talking about?"

"That it's generational. The way we hate each other—it's an ingrained trait in this family. Passed on and on. He couldn't talk about his father without getting red in the face, and there you sit, ready to jump across the desk because of how he let it bleed into you, too. I guess that just leaves me," Lucas added, turning around to face his father again, "and you. Is how you treated your sons any different?"

"I think you've got it pretty good here, actually."

"Really?"

Ronald smacked the desk with his palms, already annoyed at being questioned. "I'd say so—you practically come and go as you please. You haven't had to answer to me or anyone else in the last couple of years, and hell, you still had a parking space to roll your car into when you showed up to work this morning after fucking off for two weeks, so—"

"My brother is dead. Don't use my time off because of that as something to throw in my face. I mean, it's not exactly beneath you, Dad, but it's a sore subject."

That was Ronald's *one* warning.

Lucas dared his father to cross it.

No surprise, the asshole did.

In fact, Ronald leaped over it, saying, "Lucas, I couldn't give a damn if you mother keeled over and you just got the call before you walked into this office—and frankly, I'm glad your brother's dead. It's one less thing to concern myself with, and if you had even a lick of sense, you would see it the same way. Take it as a blessing, and move the hell on. It's not like we don't have enough to focus on here between the upcoming tax deadline and the changes to the call center home office in Fredericton. Also, you need a desk for your office. I suggest you get on that."

"I already told you, I won't need it. "

Ronald, shifting his chair back in front of his screen, hadn't even been listening. "And tell that woman out there taking all your calls to have her desk cleaned off by the end of my day. My new secretary starts tomorrow."

"I only came here to tell you I quit."

Finally, he had his father's attention.

Ronald's dark eyes nailed into Lucas from across the room. "Come again?"

"*I quit.*"

"Lucas, I'm not sure that you understand how this goes. Your grandfather left you a twenty-five percent share of ownership in this brewery. A resignation means you'll be forced to give up or sell those shares."

"To a buyer of my choosing," Lucas returned, unbothered. The kicker that would throw a wrench into every plan his father might try to work out in retaliation for the choice Lucas had every right to make for himself. "And there isn't a time limit."

"It'll be within reason, or the goddamn courts will make you."

"Is that a threat?" he asked Ronald, his grin starting to form. "They're my shares. Granddad could have given them to literally anyone else. The estate could have sold them into the open market. It could have gone to you, but that wasn't what he wanted—*he* specifically handed over a quarter of the company to me. Did he just want you to know that, in the end, you couldn't have it all? Was that it?"

"He didn't have a choice," Ronald returned hotly. The unabridged rage in Ronald's eyes trickled down to the tic in his clenched jaw. "I think we've talked more than enough tod—"

"I've actually given this some consideration, believe it or not," Lucas interjected before his father could spit out some nonsense that he didn't care to hear. Hadn't he already listened to enough of it? "I could put my shares on the market—or sell it to investors. That'll open the company, put a board in front of you that you'll have to, at the very least, entertain."

Maybe not *answer* to.

That didn't matter.

"Or I can sell it to a private partner," Lucas said, shrugging. "Make myself a nice little nest egg to stash away in investments that'll take care of me. Maybe that was it—Granddad was trying to take care of me because you sure as hell wouldn't."

"You will sell it to me," his father replied, enunciating every word as if Lucas needed that to understand.

"No, Dad, I won't. Even if I sell every single percent for a penny each, it won't be to you."

Ronald stood behind the desk—as tall and looming as Lucas, but the sight didn't have the same effect on him that it used to. As kid, he'd find a quick place to hide, and as a grown man, it'd been a learned habit to keep his father pleased and peaceful to avoid confrontation.

Those things didn't mean much to Lucas anymore.

"Then, I will see you in court," Ronald said, his nostrils flaring with every hard breath. "And you can get the hell off my property immediately, or I will contact the police to remove you since you are no longer a Dalton Brewery employee."

Lucas intended to leave.

After he did one more thing.

Patting his parka pockets, he found what he'd placed in the breast before leaving his apartment that morning. He placed the two photographs, old with worn edges and fuzzy pixelation that spoke of the years the instant, throw-away Kodak cameras had been able to catch of their family in the 80s.

Of a familiar Chevy truck.

A woman sitting on the tailgate in one, grinning at the camera with a glass of wine in hand. Lucas used a finger to slide the photo over to show the one underneath, and the baby that woman then held, although the truck in the background had disappeared.

Interestingly enough, on the back of both photographs, Mitchel Dalton's handwriting waited to tell a story in only a few words.

On the photo of Lucas' mother sitting on the tailgate of that infamous truck his grandfather had adored so much because of a woman with whom he had slept with, Mitchel had written simply: *Legs and guts, Peobe—the best parts of a woman.* He'd scrawled his initials next to the date on the back of the picture, too.

On the back of the other photograph of Penelope holding her newborn son, the youngest child, his grandfather had simply noted the birth of Jacob Dalton.

Almost nine months to the day after the date on that first picture.

"Take me to court," Lucas said, making sure he was the one to enunciate every word for his father to hear while he flipped over each photograph for Ronald. He made sure his father could see that he also knew how deep their family's secrets really went into their roots, and exactly what that could mean should Ronald make good on his threat of legal action to force Lucas' hand on the sale of the company shares. "Let's see what else we can find hiding in our family tree, Dad."

Ronald, who couldn't—or wouldn't—speak through his gnashing teeth, glared at Lucas. This wasn't like sinking down to Ronald's level of petty and bitterness at all. The truth about just how rotten their family tree really was probably went all the way down to the goddamn roots.

It started somewhere, right?

"Those came from Mom, by the way," he told his father. "I guess I can't say she never did anything for me or Jacob in the end after all, huh?"

"To what?" Ronald practically roared back.

If the employees upstairs hadn't heard anything from the office before, they sure as hell did with that.

"To what?" his father repeated, snapping every word out like a dog biting at the end of its leash. "To humiliate me, like what they did wasn't already enough—like my father didn't hang that seventy-five percent over my head for fucking years to keep it a secret? What would she share it with you for?"

That, Lucas believed, should be obvious.

"Because not everything is about you," he told Ronald, "and at least now I know the truth."

Something his father couldn't do.

Pride, ego, and image made a man like Ronald into the monster he would always be. There would be no struggle from this point forward in Lucas' life trying to find a reason why his future would not include his family. If not for his mother giving him the pieces to a puzzle in the form of old photographs, he might have still walked away from today thinking there was something *he* could have done so none of this had happened. Or worse, had he believed that staying and shouldering the remaining baggage of his family's lies could have fixed it all someday.

It wouldn't.

None of those things were true.

His father's shortcomings, every insecurity that came out in the worst ways, and even Ronald's inability to be a father … none of those things would ever be Lucas' fault, and that also meant he couldn't fix them.

Really, his mother did Lucas a favor.

A sober childhood might have been nice.

This worked, too.

The tiny possibility that Penelope did care about her children might have come in the form of old family photos she kept hidden away until the secret wouldn't hurt the living anymore—but that had only made Lucas *more* angry. Mostly at his father, and less with his mother.

Why did there have to be a reason their father hated them?

Ronald's easy discardment and constant displeasure with his youngest son—not even his real son at all—made so much more sense to Lucas now, and he despised the man more for it.

And Lucas, well …

Now he had questions.

"Was I Mitchel Dalton's illegitimate son, too?" Lucas asked.

"No, you just were the trap the bitch caught me in the first time around," Ronald snarled back, slamming his palm against the desk as his anger finally spilled over. Lucas refused to rattle at the physical aggression because it meant nothing. Bullies lost a lot of air when poked back.

"He was right, you know," Lucas said, already heading for the door but still pointing a finger at the coward behind the desk. "Your father, I mean. You are a worthless piece of shit."

Don't poke the bear, who?

Wrong move.

Ronald grabbed the closest thing he could that had any heaviness on the desk—ironically, a paperweight that had been his son's, whether he realized it or not—and threw it without a second thought. Lucas barely dodged the moving projectile that flew past the side of his face and straight through the glass door that rained around his shoes.

So much for that new etching on the outside.

"Get the *fuck* out of my brewery!" Ronald, red-faced, bellowed.

So be it.

Lucas left the photos behind.

Whatever.

He'd already scanned copies—back and front, too.
Just in case.

33.

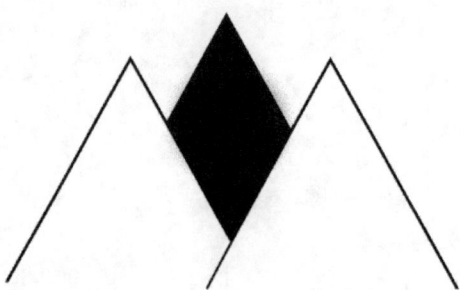

"Ta-Da!" Gracen proclaimed.

Delaney spun away from the display of jeweled and pearl-covered bridal hair pieces to find Gracen emerging from the mirrored dressing room. She laughed. "Are you going to show me a trick? *Ta-Da*," she mocked jokingly.

Gracen stuck her tongue out, and then said, "Are we or are we not talking about my dress?"

Well, maybe Delaney had made her friend wait long enough. She had already seen the empire-wasted, silk and chiffon gown in screenshots Gracen sent during their many conversations about the upcoming wedding. The rouched, shimmery bodice of the sweetheart neckline bared most of Gracen's throat and shoulders with thin straps while the layers and layers of delicate silk and chiffon making up the skirt pooled regally to the floor. More of that fragile, shimmery fabric hung loose in loops connecting from Gracen's back to her index fingers so when she lifted or widened her arms, or spun like she did for Delaney to see the dress at a different angle, the fabric billowed out like a cape.

"Do you want to put the veil on and see it all together?" Delaney asked.

"I want you to tell me what you *think*," Gracen stressed.

Delaney laughed, grinning big. "God, you look *gorgeous*. Malachi's gonna die."

Gracen did a little shimmy dance on the spot with a squeal that would surely draw the shop's manager to the back of the store where the bridal section had its own corner away from the rest of the store full of rental tuxedos and a wide variety of prom dresses. Miss Cathy's One-Stop Shop didn't get its infamous name in their little valley town for nothing.

The one and only bridal—and really, formal—shop in town unless someone wanted to travel the forty or more-minute jot upriver to the falls, or across state lines into Maine, Miss Cathy's it was.

Delaney, who had not been allowed to attend prom because it went against her family's beliefs, never got the chance to shop for her own dress once upon a time. She did lie about needing to stay after school for extra help so that she could go with Gracen to pick out hers, however.

She'd never been much of a dancer, anyway.

"I just love the way it feels and how it moves, too," Gracen said as she stepped up on the raised, circular platform a few paces away from the dressing room doors. There, she had a three-sixty view of her gown provided by the surrounding room mirrors. "This is it, right?"

Delaney smiled.

Gracen was asking *her?*

The gown had a Romanesque-slash-bohemian feel, and Delaney could already picture the way Gracen's long, soft golden waves would fall down her back under the sheerness of the long veil she'd also chosen. The gown suited her friend, picturesque and tall like Gracen loved to own. Delaney would have gravitated to the same style for Gracen had she been asked, but it seemed like her best friend had certain things figured out.

To be fair, Delaney thought she knew what her wedding dress would look like someday, too. Marriage was barely even a blip on her freaking radar at the moment.

"You tell me," Delaney said. "That's why I promised no moving all Saturday morning just so we could come into town first thing and see it."

Gracen playfully narrowed her eyes over her shoulder at Delaney. "Be nice—you're the first person to see it on me *besides* me, okay? I felt so bad, too, because Margot came home to visit her father last week, and she begged, Delaney. Begged. Come on."

Well …

"I'm playing you," Delaney returned. "You don't need me to say it, Gracen. The dress is *it.*"

Her best friend sighed happily, turning back to see her front facing reflection in the mirrors of the dressing room walls. "It is, yeah."

Then, she spun back around to Delaney. "Also, I like *this*."

Gracen's hands helped to display her favorite feature of the dress when she hugged the small roundness protruding from her lower belly. Finally starting to show in her pregnancy, she took every chance she could to admire the new swell. The empire waist of the gown certainly made the bump appear more prominent, but it also would make a hell of a picture.

Delaney had needed to blink—not used to seeing her slender friend looking so *motherly*—the day before when she first rolled into Gracen's driveway. Hadn't it just been a little over a month ago when Gracen still didn't even *look* pregnant?

Shit moved too fast.

Sometimes.

"And the extra good thing," Gracen added, allowing herself another check of the angles while she held her swell, "is that nobody can tell when I let it go."

She did exactly that.

The little bump disappeared.

Given the design of the dress, the extra eight weeks of growing that Gracen had left to do before her wedding wouldn't matter much except the prominence of her bump when she hugged it. Gracen would get to choose when she, or her bump, were the center of attention on her wedding day. As it should be.

Their laughter rang out into the store again. Sure enough, the second round of happy noise sent the only sales woman—and the owner herself, Miss Cathy—back to their corner to check on their progress. She slipped along the wall, coming up beside Delaney without making a sound until she asked, "So, are we finally taking it home today, Gracen?"

"I think so," Gracen returned with a firm nod, "It's close enough to the wedding now. I'm sure I could get Malachi to mind his business about the bag in the back of the closet until May."

"Could keep it in the closet in *my* apartment over the garage," Delaney suggested. "We both know he's not going in there now."

The office space the two used in the small one-bedroom apartment over their garage was cheap, available, and close to the place Delaney would be working considering Gracen's home-built salon had been connected to the house. It wasn't the first time Gracen had offered the apartment up for Delaney to take, but she finally said yes.

After someone else found a roommate.

Bexley's college friend took over Delaney's half of the rent in Fredericton starting the first of April. Delaney did the biggest part of her move—the majority of her things, and a few pieces of furniture—using a small U-Haul she connected up to the Jeep.

Anything else, she could bring in the back seat. Besides that, nothing she left behind had been so important than she couldn't find space for it, anyway.

Sometimes, things worked out.

Miss Cathy sighed wistfully. "I wish someone in my circle was having a May wedding this year. Spring weddings are the best."

"We're doing it on the twenty-ninth, too," Gracen added.

"*Oh*," the shopkeeper squealed with clasped hands. "That's so nice! It'll be warm enough to do it outside. And you are, right?"

"We're using the barn since it's the last year it'll be uninsulated, so …"

Miss Cathy's eyes widened. "Are you doing tulips for flowers, too?"

Gracen shared a knowing look with Delaney. "That's the plan. Do you check your email regularly?"

"Only when I'm expecting things, dear," the older woman replied, waving a hand. "Why?"

"I sent the invites out digitally last week. We made special keepsakes for the table settings instead that people can frame, or display, with our names and the date, so I tried to save on paper elsewhere. Save the planet, and everything."

Miss Cathy's eyes brightened even though her cheeks pinked. "Oh, really?"

"Mine went to junk," Delaney told the woman, shrugging. "Stupid filters. You might have to check there."

"I'm going to do that right now."

"You're invite didn't go to your junk folder," Gracen said quietly to Delaney as Miss Cathy headed back into the belly of her store.

"I was trying to help," Delaney replied, winking.

And it did.

Delaney opened her arms as if to silently ask, *So?*

Gracen only laughed, but spun around to admire her dress once more. "Almost there."

"And Mimi will be back home next week," Delaney added.

Her friend met her eyes in the reflection of the mirror. "Can't forget you—you came home, too."

Crossing her arms over her chest, Delaney leaned into the section of wall near the light switches where she wouldn't disturb anything hanging. "Yeah, I came home, too."

The unbridled joy lighting up Gracen's whole face made the anxiety Delaney felt about actually being home fade away. Or at least, numbed it a bit so it wasn't *so* unpleasant and constant. She still felt like every time she saw a familiar face, even if it was just someone waving at her on the street as they had driven through town that morning, that person thought about the awful thing that had made her leave.

Like a shoe had yet to drop.

Maybe that would get better over time?

Delaney wouldn't know if she didn't try.

*

Delaney hauled in only a few boxes to the upstairs apartment that welcomed guests into a small nook that made up a bright, white kitchen before she wished she had waited one more month to make the move back home. Not because she wasn't happy to be home—no, rather, the early spring in New Brunswick didn't look very different from late winter.

Cold.

Icy.

Blustering, blistering winds.

The heavy rain and rising temperatures they would see in the coming month would melt what remained of the snow and ice, but it wouldn't be comfortable to go outside without bundling up until early to mid-May, at least. As it did every year, over night, the little snow left would go, and the sun in the afternoon would make a person think they could wear shorts.

Until those cold evenings came in again.

Delaney tried to warm her hands up using the base heater on the entry wall as Malachi shuffled into the apartment behind her. He dropped the armload of boxes he'd carried up from the U-Haul next to the ones Delaney piled on the floor beyond the entry mat.

A shiver raced over him.

"*Jesus*, whose idea was it for you to move in the winter again?" he asked.

Delaney snickered. "Technically, we're three days into spring."

"Yeah, yeah. Some bullshit," he muttered, making his way to the baseboard heater where he squatted down next to her to warm his thin-gloved hands. "They shouldn't be allowed to call it spring if we're still slipping on ice every damn morning."

Fair enough.

"Delaney, we're putting everything marked bedroom or books in the bedroom, right?" Gracen asked as she entered the kitchen through the short hallway that connected the only bathroom and bedroom to the living room at the far side of the apartment. In her arms, she carried a box that made Malachi scowl instantly. "This one says—"

"I told you not to haul boxes, didn't I?"

Gracen glared back over the box. "Did you just interrupt me?"

"Are you carrying a box?" her fiancé returned, unbothered.

"It's full of linen! That's like … *five pounds*. Stop being ridiculous," Gracen returned, even going as far as turning away with the box when Malachi stood to take it from her. "No, I'm pregnant, not helpless. Get out of my face."

"That's mean," Malachi deadpanned.

Gracen didn't even blink. "*And?*"

"*Babe*—"

"This is why I'm spending the night with Delaney, okay?" Gracen asked, wide-eyed and as serious as could be.

"That's not why, and we both know it. You just think you can't technically do a proper sleepover if I'm in the house because *someone*—that person is you—believes I can't sleep on the couch," he countered swiftly.

"Because you can't. You're not taking this box."

Malachi, stone sober and staring down the box in Gracen's arm like it was an enemy to kill, sighed in frustration. "I can move the boxes where they need to go. Just put it down."

"I'm putting it in the bedroom," Gracen told Delaney, refusing to acknowledge Malachi at all before she turned on her heels and headed back down the hall.

"She's going to kill me," Malachi muttered through a tight smile that he turned on Delaney.

"Nah, she's just making a man out of you," Delaney replied,

shrugging.

Malachi, not the type to be prideful or get a hurt ego over a comment like that, only laughed as he rounded the table on his way to the front door. "*Right*, that's what it is. Stay up here with her and keep an eye on what she is or is not lifting—I'll get the rest of the boxes."

"Sounds fair to me."

After all, she wouldn't freeze.

Malachi had made himself scarce in the apartment by the time Gracen returned to the kitchen. This time, without a box in her arms.

"Hey," she said behind Delaney, "I found this in the box under the linen one. Should it go in your room? I can't remember you ever having a Bible after high school … didn't we donate your old ones?"

"All three," she agreed.

Delaney finished hanging up her jacket and toeing off her hiking boots before she acknowledged the pocket Bible Gracen brandished. Hanging out from between the closed, gold-trimmed pages was the cross pendant hanging from a familiar necklace.

She finally took it off.

Not to mention, she found it a better place.

"I still think the overall message has the right idea," Delaney said about the Bible.

"Just without the organized bit of the whole church thing, right?"

"Right."

The necklace worked much better as a page marker for the Bible, and oddly enough, she didn't even notice it gone from her neck. All those years it took for her to take it off had been a mental game that came to an end the second the clasp hinge broke as she dried her hair a few mornings ago.

Wasn't that how life worked sometimes?

"Lucas left that behind the first time I cut his hair—sometimes I read it, or I'll find one of the passages I used to like for one reason or another, and I go back to it again," Delaney explained. "Back when I got rid of mine, I was angry. I'm not really mad at the book, anymore, so …"

Gracen nodded, and flipped the Bible around to look over the back, making the cross flop back and forth on the cover. "Okay—

in your bedroom, then?"

"Yeah, that's fine."

"I guess we'll get good headway on unpacking and setting up this place tonight," Gracen said. "Has Bexley forgiven me yet for stealing you back from her?"

Delaney scoffed. "No one is stealing me from anyone else."

"You know, she didn't text me for like a whole week after you told her you were definitely moving."

"She still RSVP'd to the wedding, didn't she?"

Gracen snickered under her breath. "Well, that is something, huh?"

Exactly.

"She's fine—*now*," Delaney qualified at Gracen's pointed look from the other side of the small kitchen. "I get it, though. Having those couple of years to live together let me and her be *real* cousins and friends for a while. In a way she couldn't be when she was still at home, and whatever. You know what I mean?"

If anyone did, it would be Gracen.

Her friend nodded. "I get it, no worries."

"I take it the fact Malachi thinks you can't sleep in the house tonight is because you didn't tell him I'm having a guest all weekend?"

A guest who would be arriving *early* tomorrow.

Gracen grinned slyly. "He *really* likes Lucas, Delaney."

"Yeah," she agreed, "I can tell."

From the moment she showed up with her U-Haul, that was the only thing out of Malachi's mouth. He'd made a trip to the camp. He found a vehicle that Lucas needed to check out for himself that would work for the trade. Not to mention, all the things, and the headway, they had made and wanted to show him for his epoxy and wood art piece for a wall at the cabin.

Delaney's friends didn't pry too deep into her relationship with Lucas—seemingly knowing that the long distance didn't affect the fact there *was* a relationship seemed to be enough for Gracen and Malachi.

Besides, there wasn't much to ask.

Every week, something new came out in the paper about Lucas, his family, or the brewery. Delaney gave Malachi and Gracen a lot of credit about not being too nosy despite the fact both had mentioned seeing the recent troubles following Lucas. The initial suspicion about the internal upset in the family ranks proved to be true when news of his resignation from Dalton Brewery made the rounds, followed by the news he would be forced to sell his significant shares in the business.

If not for tentative, and hostile, negotiations in mediation with lawyers for both sides of the Dalton equation, and the peewee hockey team Lucas had volunteered to coach—to help out a friend—for the duration of the month of March, they might have taken a weekend together before now.

Instead, life forced them to wait.

"Not gonna lie," Delaney said, smiling over at Gracen as she moved to the sink where she could fill her electric kettle for tea, "but you might not see very much of me tomorrow after he gets here."

Gracen whistled suggestively. "I guess we should stay clear of the workshop downstairs, too?"

Delaney didn't reply other than a quiet, "*Well ...*"

That only set their laughter off again.

"Get it," Gracen murmured approvingly.

Yep.

That was the plan.

"Not sure how long I'll be able to keep Malachi away, though," her friend added. "Not once he knows Lucas is here, that's all I'm saying."

"You'll manage it," Delaney returned with a suggestive smirk. "I'm sure."

Gracen shrugged under her loose, flower-printed blouse. "Oh, probably."

For all his complaints about hating to drive long distances in the past, Lucas had none about making the trek on his last weekend of the month, that wouldn't include coaching the peewee team, to spend it with her.

After that, who knew what would happen?

His proximity to Saint John—four hours away from her now— was a necessity. *Currently*. He made that clear to her, like it mattered to him, so she dared to hold onto the promise that something good waited for them on the horizon.

What it was ... Delaney couldn't wait to find out.

But she *would*.

Lucas was more than worth it.

34.

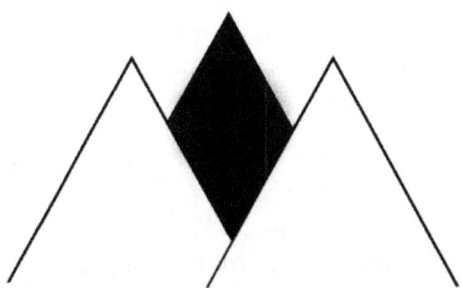

"I know you said you wouldn't take my calls this weekend," came the familiar, crackly voice of the only solicitor Lucas would ever use.

The shakiness in Lawrence's voice was the only show of his eighty-three years, over fifty spent acting as a lawyer. The Bluetooth in the Bronco made the man's rattly voice more apparent when Lucas allowed the call through. He didn't like to chat while he drove, but the trip from the bridge connecting one side of a small valley town to the other was just a short stretch away from the road leaving the town behind—into a mountain where he had already been forewarned provided no cell service.

If he had to answer the call, now would be the time.

"And yet, here you are—calling," he noted to Lawrence as his navigational directions in the background told him to turn left at the end of the bridge in fifty meters. "I'd like to hope that means good rather than bad things."

"That depends on how deep down a legal rabbit hole you're willing to go with your father, Lucas," replied the old lawyer who should have retired two decades ago.

Once my mind goes, the man would say.

"It's an expensive, *deep* hole," Lawrence added after a moment, "but I'm sure you're already aware of those things. I know you're a smart, sensible man."

If nothing else, Lucas appreciated that his solicitor maintained a certain level of respect and professionalism, no matter the circumstances. He made Lucas feel like a friend whenever he visited the man's offices in Rothesay just outside of the eastern side of the city, but sitting across from the age-weathered man who never showed up to work without his suit and tie was a good reminder about the wise.

"Of course," Lawrence went on while Lucas remained quiet on the other end of the call, "the Dalton family secrets have padded my bank account in the past, so I do understand these grudges can hang on. It's up to you, Lucas."

Right.

"So, why *did* you call?" Lucas asked, bringing them back to the most important item at hand.

"I had breakfast with Hanny—"

"Chandler Timothy?" Lucas asked, calling his father's lawyer out by name, despite the friendly nickname Lawrence used for the man that was well-known in his larger circles.

Lucas didn't feel the same way—not to use it, anyhow.

It might have something to do with the Ronald connection, and not to mention, how the lawyer had threatened to keep Lucas tied up in fifteen or more years of litigation if he sold even one percent to anyone outside of his father. Fifteen years that would drain Lucas of most of his wealth just to keep control of *who* he sold his ownership of the brewery to.

The prick.

Lucas called the bastard's bluff, anyway, and bought himself some time.

Hence, his visit to Lawrence.

"Hanny is a friend, he assured me it would be worth my while. I think it was."

"I'd love to know how," Lucas returned, "seeing as how the last month saw my face and name in the Telegraph Journal at least once a week painting me as some entitled, rich fuck trying to soak his father's company for millions. Did you see those articles?"

Lucas was *way* over Ronald's friends at the newspaper. Maybe the slander wasn't as open and brazen as Lucas spelled it out to his solicitor, but the underhanded implications hidden between every goddamn line was unbearably clear to him.

"Did you consider that's *why* Ronald got those articles printed in the paper?" Lawrence asked back.

Lucas blinked at the confusing question as he came to a rolling stop behind a Ford pick-up at the end of the bridge. "I'm sorry, what?"

Lawrence chuckled. "He knows it bothers you—do you think

anyone who has worked with you from the time you were a young man until you sat in the high offices above them really believe, or are telling anybody else, that those things in the paper are true? In case you missed the other side of the equation in those pieces, the brewery has faced more than three walk-outs by employees since your departure, as well. Ronald knows he's in hot water. Trust that."

"Well," Lucas tried to say, more interested in navigating the truck through the three-way at the end of the bridge than coming up with a decent response.

"*Well,*" the lawyer returned sarcastically, albeit with a playful note. "Come on, Lucas. Ronald is doing what Ronald does best which is poke at you. That soft heart you wear on your sleeve only gets tucked in when he's around, but that doesn't mean he's unaware it exists. If you want to go ahead with some slander or— whatever—we can rattle a cage or two for their side of things, but my suggestion is that you simply continue to hold the wall. Ronald will get bored when he realizes he isn't getting the reaction from you that he wants."

Jesus.

Just like a schoolyard bully.

"Why should I do that, exactly?"

Because there was a small possibility that Lucas might enjoy suing the newspaper and his father for their bullshit over the past month. Small, but there.

"You should do that," his lawyer replied, "because if we get started filing paperwork for anything else, the offer Hanny brought me this morning will be void. Like I said, your father is very aware of the position he's put himself in. Shame, I think the employees quite miss you, Lucas."

Yeah, well …

Lucas cleared his throat. "I can't return there if my father is a factor, so."

He knew how he sounded. The way his words put more distance between him and the man who had helped to create him, like he needed the extra space. No doubt, Lawrence picked up on it, too. This was how it would have to be from now on.

"Funny," Lawrence said, his voice echoing through the speakers into the quiet Bronco, "I once sat across a table from your father as he shouted something very similar to your grandfather."

"I'll give Ronald that one," Lucas replied just as fast, "considering his father apparently knocked up his wife—maybe that was due."

"What about you?" Lawrence asked. "Is your anger *due*?"

The reasons didn't have to be the same.

Or equal.

"What was the offer?" Lucas asked his lawyer.

Lawrence sighed heavily into the phone. "*Now* you're interested."

He chuckled. "Actually, I need you to make it quick because I'm approaching a spot upriver with no service for a stretch."

And on the other side of that mountain?

A woman waited.

His woman.

Lucas just needed to get there.

"I could call back," Lawrence suggested.

Lucas had a better question.

"Would I *want* to hear it?"

"The offer?" his lawyer asked.

"Yes."

"It's … Frankly, I'm not going to lie to you. It's a good one, Lucas. I think it's something you, more so than your father, would personally prefer. In my opinion, it's a big win for you."

Oh?

Lucas couldn't be sure. A big part of him didn't want to make deals with Ronald. It felt like letting the bastard win. At the same time, how long would a battle of wills like this last, outside or within the courts?

Fuck him for just wanting it all to end.

His last cord to cut.

"Okay," Lucas said. "Let's hear how he plans to screw me over."

"Technically, with this, *you'd* get what you wanted. He wouldn't own the shares, but they'll still remain within the company, and by-proxy, his control."

Now that made Lucas slightly curious.

What trick did Ronald think he could play?

"All right, I'm listening."

*

Getting to the farmhouse located on The Flats coming upriver wasn't quite the same as taking the main road straight from Birch Ridge. The view driving through the mountain he had once flown over with Delaney in a helicopter truly made Lucas appreciate the size and vastness of the tree-capped range. The gully road, weaving around tight turns all the way through the mountain, eventually spit Lucas and his Bronco out on the other side to a view he recognized.

Snowy fields stretched on for as far as his eye could see. It wouldn't be very long before rain and warmer weather came to take the snow away, but the familiar stretch of land made it easy for him to find the first driveway on the right, cutting from the crest of a hill, after leaving the gully road behind.

Lucas made it halfway down the long driveway when a figure emerged from the barn off to the far left of the property. His hand lifted from the steering wheel to return the wave Malachi Anders greeted him with. The man smiled wide once the Bronco got close enough for him to see who sat in the driver's seat.

Parking the Bronco where Malachi directed Lucas next to the line of vehicles in front of the two-door garage situated between the house and barn, he didn't even get the engine turned off before his companion came up along the side of the vehicle.

Lucas rolled the window down with a laugh. "Long time, no see."

Malachi grinned back. "Yeah, I guess, eh? Imagine, not one of those two told me you were coming down this way today."

"I'm here for the weekend, actually."

Slapping a hand against the top of the Bronco, Malachi scoffed. "Someone is really keeping secrets, then."

Lucas didn't know much about that, but in any case, it could only mean good things that Malachi wasn't unhappy to see him there. "That was four more hours in a vehicle than I would have liked to spend driving, let me say."

"Ah, you made it. Now I know why Gracen wanted to order enough pizza to feed a fucking army later."

"I could do pizza," Lucas said. "Beer, too?"

Malachi nodded. "Definitely beer. Are you getting out or sitting in there all day?"

Well ...

Either might work at the moment.

Lucas hated to admit that an old hockey injury from his younger days made sitting in the same position, like behind the wheel of a vehicle, particularly difficult. Stiffness and pain were the most common symptoms, but nothing a hot bath, a few beers, and a couple of Tylenol couldn't fix.

"Yeah, I'm getting out," Lucas said, sighing as he pushed the button to roll up the window before he removed the keys from the ignition.

Sure enough, stepping out of the Bronco made him aware of just how achy his mid-to-lower back had become over the long drive. His spine cracked, earning a grunt from Lucas, as he moved to the back of the vehicle where he placed a tote bag full of clothes and toiletry items. Whatever he needed to get him through the weekend, basically. Another bag, keeping his brother's urn and ashes safe, remained in the back and would stay there until Lucas could make the drive to the cabin sometime over the next couple of days.

He still felt like that's where he wanted Jacob to be.

"Do you want to take five minutes to check out the progress on your wall—" Malachi's offer quieted when a beep interrupted him. He pulled the reason for the disturbance out of the pack pocket of his jeans, his gaze drawn into whatever he found on the screen.

Something good, Lucas thought.

It had to be.

The man grinned like a cat licking cream.

"What about the wall piece?" Lucas asked.

Malachi's gaze darted upward to find Lucas waiting with his bag hanging from his hand before he pulled the back hatch closed. "Gracen is up to something—I can't tell you what, or even what I just saw, but she is." He put his phone away, stuffing it back into his pocket. "And now I have something I need to do in the house. Right now, actually."

Lucas chuckled. "That important?"

"Something like that," the man returned, smirking. "I suspect you probably want to say hello and catch up with Delaney for a bit, right?"

"That was my plan, yeah."

Malachi's head bobbed up and down. "Good, good." He waved a finger between the two of them, saying, "And we'll meet back up later—pizza and beer, eh?"

"Absolutely. I know where to find you."

"Sure do," Malachi replied, clapping Lucas on the shoulder as he walked on by, making a fast beeline for the house. Over his shoulder, he called, "The stairs for the apartment are around the east side."

Lucas waved two fingers high. "Got it, thanks."

The first time he visited the property, Lucas had not explored the apartment Malachi said had been built overtop of the garage. Apparently, Delaney's friend and her partner had been using it as office space and extra storage for their home-based businesses, between the salon and wood working, but didn't need the extra room in a pinch.

Hence, the offer for Delaney to rent it.

Which she had.

Knowing she would be a couple of hours further upriver than she had initially been when they first met made the time Lucas had been able to carve out for a weekend with her more special. Sacred, in a way, because they didn't have a lot of it.

So, he didn't want to waste *any* of it.

Lucas took the wooden steps on the far side of the garage two at a time. Salt, sprinkled liberally up the steps to keep them from getting icy, crunched under his shoes until he reached the large rubber mat on the landing at the top.

Someone else waited there for him, too.

Delaney yanked open the frosted glass door—similar to the main house, but smaller—with a happy shriek. "You lied—you told me you were in *Woodstock!*"

Lucas' responding laugh at his trick having worked became muffled into the sweet-smelling crown of Delaney's black hair when she engulfed his middle into the tightest hug of his life. Stopping at the edge of The Valley to finish his conversation with Lawrence proved useful when Delaney called right after, and he convinced her that he was farther away than was true.

To see her smile *so* big.

Just because her arms couldn't reach all the way around him didn't stop Delaney from trying, or taking the breath out of his lungs, either. Lucas laughed at her hard squeeze, and hugged her back with one arm while he used his other to keep the two steady and safe on the twenty-foot-high landing by holding onto the railing.

He kissed the top of her head in quick succession, murmuring, "God, yeah, I missed you, too."

He heard what she didn't say.

What her hug *did*.

Delaney chose that moment to tipped her head back, resting her chin on the middle of his chest while she grinned up at him, eyes sparkling. "I'm making something for lunch—and I stocked up on beer, which this goes *perfect* with. I promise. Are you hungry?"

His stomach chose that moment to make itself known.

She just laughed. "That's a yes?"

"I got right on the road this morning," he offered, "so that's a big yes."

Delaney pushed up on her tiptoes with lips pursed for a kiss that he happily provided, and the two lingered in that soft moment until she pulled away for a breath first. "Are you opposed to a very cheesy casserole?"

His favorite kind.

Especially with pasta.

Like the woman in his arms could read his mind, Delaney said, "I used spaghetti. Mushroom and tomato soup. Ground beef, and fry up a can of mushrooms. I'm sure you can figure out what happens to all the cheese."

Yes, yes he *could*.

Lucas didn't get to cook for himself as much as he liked, but that sounded like the type of meal he would make just to be able to reheat and enjoy again in the next couple of days. Leftovers made the best meals.

"For *lunch*?" he asked. "I heard someone was getting pizza tonight, too." Lucas brow lifted high, and Delaney winked at the unspoken suggestion that the two things were not coincidental. "That's a lot of good food."

"I see Malachi didn't miss you, then," Delaney noted.

"Nope, but he—"

"Got distracted with something," she interjected, a sly grin forming.

"You did something," he accused.

Delaney only laughed, spinning away and out of his arms to turn and enter the quiet, bright apartment. Four windows in the small kitchen gave a full view of the garage facing the front of the property leading up to the road, while standing in front of the sink overlooked the fields in the back and the tree-capped peninsula range on the horizon.

Lucas hung his bag on the coat rack by the door, kicking off his boots next to Delaney's on the entrance mat as well. "What did you do?"

"Well, nothing, really," she said at the stove where she'd left a tinfoil topped glass casserole dish sitting on the top. Opening the oven door, she put the casserole inside, closed it up, and then turned the light to have a view through the glass on the outside. Smiling back at him, she shrugged and explained, "I may have asked Gracen to give Malachi something to do when you got here so that I didn't have to share you with anyone else for a while. I mean, I'm glad he likes you and all, and not to mention, Gracen said he needs to make more friends, but—"

"You didn't want to share me."

"Like I said, I *may have* said something like that, yes," Delaney returned, unconcerned.

"Did you, now?"

"Yep. Not apologizing for it, either."

Good.

He wouldn't want her to.

The news made his chest ache, and his lips stretch wide with a toothy, *stupid* smile. Delaney, who had turned to fiddle with the timer on a stove that was probably new to her considering she had just moved in the day before, finally got twenty-five minutes on the clock before turning around to find Lucas had caged her in at the stove.

Not that she looked bothered.

Those wide, beautiful eyes of hers locked onto his, and she tipped her head back to catch his oncoming kiss without a word. Not quick or soft like their one at the top of the step, he found the tang of mint on her tongue when his finally coaxed her mouth open. She practically melted into him, her hands finding their way in between the half-lowered zipper of his fleece-lined spring jacket to his chest overtop of his shirt.

He suddenly forgot about the rest of the apartment he hadn't seen, and the promise of beer more than one person had mentioned after his arrival. He didn't even notice the way the kitchen smelled like good, hearty food already, but he felt the way

Delaney trembled as she drew in a shaky breath as their kiss finally broke.

Not that the two moved apart.

"Did someone go to town?" he asked.

By *someone*, he only meant her.

"I did—I got groceries and a few things," she said, still happy to gaze up at him while her index finger stroked his pec.

A trip to town would be a big step for her. She'd admitted to him that her biggest fear about returning to the area close to her hometown were all the familiar faces she might run into on any given day. Including ones who might not be happy to see her.

"And?" he asked. "How'd it go?"

"I got the food. The beer, too."

At that, Delaney reached over to open the bottom door of the white fridge for Lucas to see the case of canned beer, and a six-pack of No Boats on Sunday apple cider, sitting on the bottom shelf above the crispers. She moved to close the door, but he stopped her, taking a second look at the beer.

The familiar emblem—a moose's head—couldn't be missed.

"Since when do you drink Moosehead?" he asked.

Gracen winked. "It's about the loyalty, right?"

Jesus Christ.

This woman *was* perfect.

Everything he wanted.

Lucas closed the fridge for her, grabbed Delaney's face in his hands, and pulled her in for a hard kiss that muffled her giggles. "Love. You. So. Much."

Every word followed another kiss.

She kissed him back for the last.

Lucas swallowed Delaney into a hug, refusing to get sentimental over beer. Well, not any more than he already did. "Yeah, *fuck*— damn, I missed you."

She hummed happily against his chest, squirming in her oversized hoodie and black sweatpants the longer they stayed tucked together, arms wrapped tight.

The glittering of her eyes when she lifted her head again and the way her teeth pulled at her lower lip did wicked things to his mind—he knew that promising look of hers well.

"Well, guess what?" she asked.

Lucas smirked. "Do tell, sweets. I'm *all* ears for you."

She tapped an almond shaped fingernail, painted matte black, against his chest. "You've got twenty-five minutes to show me how much you missed me before this oven beeps."

Lucas wet his lips. "Oh, really?"

Delaney nodded, eyebrows lifting suggestively. "I mean, that's just before food … of course."

She wasn't wrong, and they did have time to make up for.

35.

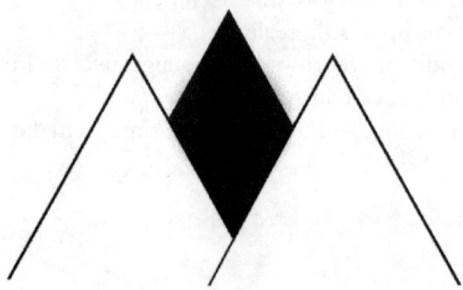

Delaney couldn't think of a better way to spend a Saturday afternoon than naked in bed with Lucas. With his arms snaked around her lower half, he used her stomach as a pillow where his lips grazed dangerously low on her bare pubic bone.

"I'm not going to pick a game if you're just going to start doing that again," Delaney threatened, semi-serious. She faked throwing the Nintendo remote but the way he kissed, and then suckled, over the same spot had her grabbing the gray and black plastic even tighter. "*God*, you're insatiable."

"Yeah," he grunted, shimmying lower on the bed to where his shoulders held open her thighs, "but that's what you get for making me come like I was getting a handjob for the first time."

He only needed a little while to recuperate.

And made *every* minute worth her while.

Of course, the timer on the oven beeped right about then, too. Maybe she could have convinced him to wait for food, but she also got to enjoy the sight of Lucas' bare rear end heading out of the bedroom, arms full of dirty dishes, so the extra wait wasn't so bad after all. Delaney then got the Nintendo up and running to play Mario while Lucas worked on clearing a second plate of food at the end of her bed.

Good thing he liked the casserole.

Eventually, after finishing the food, and coming back with an opened beer for both of them, Lucas made his way back to Delaney on the bed.

Hence, his current position.

Lucas grinned up at her, the day-old scruff on his chin scratching deliciously along her already sensitive skin. "Come on, you've tried three times to get through that level, now—"

"First of all," Delaney told him, pausing the game so she could put all of her attention on him, "I am working on banking my infinite lives."

Lucas smirked, saying only, "And now I get to make you feel alive—which one's better?"

It wasn't a real question.

The way his face lowered so his mouth could latch onto the most intimate part of her body had Delaney melting back into the pile of pillows behind her with a shiver. He had this thing that he did with his mouth and tongue. Kind of like the way he suckled on her pubic bone, but he did it around the hood of her clit while his tongue worked against the throbbing bud. The mixture of pressure and the repeated sensation while he slipped a thumb into her pussy to toy with the slick arousal he found there was enough to undo Delaney.

In mere minutes, really.

If he did it hard and fast—like earlier after she'd gotten him into her bedroom and naked on the mattress and box spring still sitting on the floor—the intensity could take her to orgasm in thirty seconds. It also left her almost too sensitive to the touch, and squealing from the way her body wanted to lift against the fast rise of pressure.

It wasn't quite the same when he did it slowly.

Like now.

Instead of her eyes squeezed shut to deal with the overwhelming rush taking her over, she had her gaze locked on his where he watched her from between her thighs. He released the suction on her clit with a soft pop but the circling of his thumb smearing her juices and toying with her clenching, greedy slit still had Delaney trembling.

"Are we going to the camp tomorrow, then?" he asked.

Delaney let out a high, air-filled laugh. "You're asking that *now?*"

Lucas rubbed his chin, wet with her, up and down her aching clit with a deliberate nod of his head. "Mmhmm."

"Fuck, Lucas, I almost—"

"Came, yeah," he interjected, winking. "I felt it—edged you out."

She whimpered as that feeling of closeness to her orgasm faded away, but the constant friction from his thumb massaging harder along her inner walls kept her body on high alert. Just not *there* like she was.

"That's one," he said, kissing her pubis, and biting the fleshy bit of skin over the hood of her clit gently. Delaney gasped, inhaling sharply when he finally let the bite go. "Do it again for me, and then when I let you come on the third one, I'm gonna bend you over and slip right in when you're nice and tight, and all hot and wet for me, huh?"

His thumb came out of her pussy just to slide the pad right up to her clit where he rubbed fast circles that made her hips jerk, and Delaney shout loud. In a good way, of course. The weight of Lucas resting into her lower half kept her pinned to the bed even as his thumb moved faster, and he recognized the telltale way her moans hitched.

And then he pulled away.

"Cabin tomorrow?" he asked again.

"Oh, my *God*," she breathed, "*yes*, yes—the cabin tomorrow."

Her fingers raked through Lucas' hair when his mouth found her clit again. Already practically at her orgasm, it didn't take long for the pressure of his sucking to take Delaney over the edge. His thumb found its way back into her cunt, catching the hot gush that came with the first wave of intense pleasure that started somewhere deep in her womb.

The sound that made its way out of her was guttural—like those first two lost orgasms came back for the third go-round to really wreck her. Her pussy was still pulsing when he withdrew his thumb and released the suction off her clit, but she barely had the chance to register the loss before Lucas had flipped her over in the bed.

His palms clapped down to her ass with loud slaps, grabbing tight to both cheeks while she tried fruitlessly to rise up to her knees.

He kept her down.

Flat to the bed, she felt Lucas straddle her on the messy, unmade bed. The weight of him rocked them on the mattress as he moved back and forth, only settling when she looked over her shoulder to find him focused. Holding his cock at the base, he rubbed it up and down the crack of her ass, letting out a slow breath.

"You sure you don't want to take a ride into town?" he asked.

Whose fault was it when they both forgot condoms?

Did it really matter *now?*

Delaney's heavy pants had yet to subside when she told him, "Let's not make it a habit, okay?"

Lucas' gaze flicked up to meet hers, and those dark eyes of his scream satisfaction as she started to push his cock between the wet folds of her pussy. On a long groan, as he took his time settling in inch by inch, he replied, "Yeah, *fuck*—okay, sweets."

He wanted this as much as she did.

Besides, she took her pills on a regular *enough* basis.

Lucas snagged Delaney's hands to hold them against her lower back while his other grabbed a fistful of her ass. The sting was so good—but so was the hard flex of his hips that seated him deep enough that all she could do was lay there and feel him.

God bless him for giving her a few seconds. Just enough time to adjust and get used to the too-full sensation of his thick nine inches. The moment she wiggled against him, though, she knew it was game over.

Lucas took that as his cue.

His fingers dug into her ass, his hand pushed hers at the wrists to hold her into the bed, and then he started the pace. A brutal rhythm that rocked the mattress into the wall under the windows with every snap of his hips. Her low whines, distorted into the bed sheets, matched the way their bodies met.

Every slap of skin pulled those noises out of her, but it was Lucas, and the way he didn't slow or tease her into coming once he was finally inside her, that really drove her crazy. She craved the way his body took over hers—in size, and strength—how he used her to chase his own orgasm made hers begin to bloom all over again.

"Hell, yes. Show me how good you take that cock for me, Delaney," he praised, voice husky and his words low.

"Don't stop, don't stop … *please, don't stop*," she chanted through choppy inhales that didn't feel like enough.

"Never. This is *my* pussy—you better make her purr for me, baby."

Delaney sobbed her way through another orgasm, the precipice cresting without warning when Lucas' hips slammed even harder into her from behind. She could feel the way her body tried to milk him; how every ripple of pleasure cascaded into steady clenching of her inner muscles wrapped around him.

That hot rush came fast between her thighs again.

Lucas' pleased chuckles said he felt it, and while his pace never faltered, the wet smacking between their bodies became louder. "*Yes*, soak me, Delaney. You fucking ruined me."

No way.

That was definitely him.

There would be no after him for Delaney—no other human, and certainly not another man, would come close to changing her the way Lucas Dalton had.

*

Delaney kept expecting a knock on the apartment door to interrupt her afternoon with Lucas—after a point, she wouldn't even have blamed Malachi for making the trip across the yard to do it, either—but it didn't come.

So, they didn't leave the bed.

Lucas seemed content to use Delaney's naked lower half as a pillow while she played Nintendo and ignored the remaining boxes she had yet to unpack in the corner of the small bedroom.

"I'm surprised how much of the apartment you got set up yesterday," he noted when Delaney got Mario onto the top of the pole at the end of the level.

She tossed the remote to the bed, her thumbs aching from a good thirty minutes of game play. "Gracen helped. Malachi hung some things."

"Can I help, too?" Lucas asked.

Delaney grinned. "I can certainly put you to work. I have a bookshelf that needs to be assembled, and a picture or two to hang."

"Good, I hate feeling useless."

Delaney frowned. "I'd never say that to you."

"No, but—"

She didn't let him get out whatever self-deprecating thing was about to leave his lips before she curled down to catch his lips in a kiss when she lifted his head to meet her eyes before their mouths touched. One sweep of her lips made his answer back. Another had them crawling closer together so he laid higher on her body, their chests rising and falling together.

"*Not* useless to me," she whispered against his lips.

Lucas let out a hard breath. "Yeah, okay."

When his head found her chest, his face nestled between the valley of her breasts, Delaney drew circles through his dark, short-cropped hair until he relaxed against her.

"I didn't want to tell you until I got here, but I had a couple of job offers come my way last week," Lucas murmured against her skin.

Delaney's breath hitched. "Oh?"

"Executive management for the sugar plant in Saint John. The money's good, as far as that goes. I wouldn't have to change much except the time I rolled into work, I guess."

"Is that up your alley? *Executive* management?"

Lucas let out a heavy breath. "Close enough."

Why didn't it sound like something he wanted to do, then?

In fact, he didn't seem interested at all.

"Huh," she muttered.

"Another one was for a rival brewery—which could be a problem if my father wanted to try and make it one, but I'm not that interested in it, anyway."

"Why not?"

"I'd have to relocate. To Ontario. By next month."

Delaney's chest deflated as she repeated dully, "Oh."

"I said no to both," Lucas told her.

"I want to hate that knowing you said no makes me happy," she whispered.

He kissed the side of her breast, making Delaney shiver. "But?"

How selfish was she, really?

Delaney had a damn good idea. "You know, my best friend once moved an unemployed, basically homeless guy into her house, and it worked out okay for her. I'm just saying … I'm sure we could figure things out."

Lucas' boisterous laugh rocked them both on the bed, but his arms only squeezed her tighter when his amusement quickly sobered. "To be fair, because I'm not sure what their situation was—your friends, I mean—but I don't think money is going to be a problem for me."

"I mean, I know you're doing okay financially, but—"

"No, because my father made an offer on my shares that I'm not going to refuse—that I can't refuse," he corrected.

Delaney's fingers froze in their circle of his scalp. "Didn't you tell me that you wouldn't sell the shares to him?"

"For a half of a million a share I will."

She blinked. "What?"

"A half of a million a share," Lucas repeated, every word skipping over her pebbling skin as he spoke. "And while the twenty-five percent would remain owned by the company ..."

"You're father," she said when he trailed off.

Lucas shrugged. "Right. However, the profit of the earnings will be split half and half between a share that's evenly distributed once a year to employees as a bonus, and the rest, to Ronald. I think he did it on purpose."

"I'm sorry?"

"The offer," Lucas explained in a sigh as he scrubbed a hand down his face. "I think he made it on purpose. Something he knew I wouldn't refuse because it's an option that helps people. Yeah, it's less than the shares are worth, by *a lot*, but the end result is what matters to me, and I'm sure he knows it, too. It's not just about him. The *company* benefits. The employees really benefit, and ... Anyway, do you know what the interest is on thirteen or fourteen million dollars in a year?"

"Not a single clue."

"Easily six figures. Can't I live on that?"

He asked it like a joke.

Most times, money wasn't very funny.

Then, he got serious.

Even though he tickled her while he did it.

"Better yet," he pressed, "could *you?*"

He met her gaze.

She stared right back.

"This isn't about your money, Lucas."

Not for her.

"That's not what I asked, and if it matters, even if I spent every damn cent of it on you, I wouldn't ask your permission to do that, either."

Well, then.

Delaney pressed her lips together to keep from smiling at his blatant arrogance, but his chuckles down below coaxed it out of her, anyway. She went back to drawing those lazy circles through his hair, eventually moving down to his shoulders and upper back where her fingertips glided over his soft skin while she tried to absorb what he just told her.

"Are you gonna do it?" she eventually asked. "Take the offer?"

"I want to," he replied, "but I also don't want to feel like somehow, he's going to win."

"Maybe it's not about somebody winning between you."

That statement had Lucas lifting his head. "I don't mean for it to sound like I want to get one up on him. Honestly, if I didn't have to see the man again, I'd be happy, but even that won't happen. At some point, I'll have to sit across a table from the bastard one last time to sign my name on a few papers. So, I'm stuck still thinking that every interaction, even through my fucking lawyer, is a way that he's trying to poke at me somehow. It's ... not good for me. I don't like what that does to me, Delaney."

He pointed at his head, adding, "In here, you know?"

She did.

All too well.

It wasn't an easy road.

A path no one wanted to willingly travel.

"I know what it's like to walk away from your parents and say that's it," Delaney replied, "because you know it has to be—otherwise, it's like they're killing the person you could be. Maybe that's where you are right now. Still trying to get away, and you haven't quite figured out what it's gonna look like when you finally are, but that's okay."

"Is it?"

Delaney shrugged against the mound of pillows at her back. "Yeah, babe. It's okay not to have the answers about what life's going to look like after this, or if it's even going to be what you want it to be. It doesn't have to be those things yet. It just has to be better than what you already have. What's better than the things waiting for you wherever he is?"

Lucas barely even thought about it before replying, "Wherever you are. That's been better for me from day one."

"Good, because here it doesn't matter. Whether you sell the shares, fight your father, or hide away from the world until you figure everything in your life that you feel like is wrong or not quite right. Here, no one is asking you to be anything or anyone but exactly who you are. It doesn't matter when you're with me because here, Lucas, you are loved either way."

That was all she had ever wanted, after all. From the time she was just a girl ... For the people around her who proclaimed to love her to actually mean it—not to put conditions on it that had to be met, in extreme ways sometimes, to get what she deserved in return.

That's not how love should work.

It would not be her kind of love.

Not ever.

"No matter what you do, I'm going to love you either way."

"That won't change?" he asked roughly.

"That will *never* change, Lucas."

36.

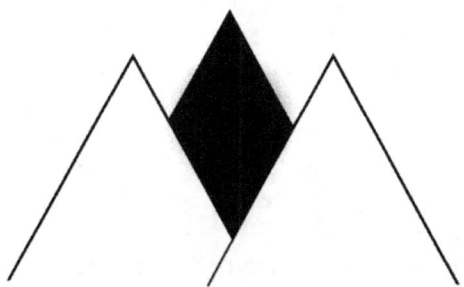

"Do you have time for one more appointment?"

Sweeping the floor in front of the large mirror that faced the one stylist chair in Gracen's attached salon, Delaney paused her end of day work to find her friend and Mimi in the open double doorway that connected the business to the rear of the house. Most of the day, Delaney kept those doors closed as she worked with clients who traveled to the home-based salon for their trims and colors. Malachi tended to be the one who came around at the end of the workday to open the doors wide for Mister Kitty to make his prowl of the place.

Otherwise, the cat meowed incessantly on the other side.

"It's *me*," Mimi declared with her weathered hands lifting high. Gracen's grandmother beamed in the wheelchair being pushed by her granddaughter.

"It's us," Gracen added in a laugh. She nodded down at her grandmother, explaining to Delaney, "Somebody's nurse headed out an hour early for an appointment, so we had time. She got it in her head that she needed a wash and set at four in the evening, so."

Delaney grinned.

Mimi always got what she wanted.

No matter how ridiculous, or seemingly impossible, Gracen bent over backwards to make her grandmother smile daily. After only a couple of weeks living at the farmhouse on The Flats, with a support nurse that came in for twelve hour shifts every day of the week, rotating days off with another home care support worker on the weekends, even Delaney could see the difference it made for the old woman's mood and mind. Sure, sometimes Mimi confused the time—like being back in the old house with familiar rooms and walls took her back to when her son and his wife were still alive; before her husband had died, too. Other days, she woke up knowing her granddaughter was over halfway along in her pregnancy and remembering the baby would be a boy.

No matter what her mind told her, or left her thinking, Mimi's good mood never faltered, and greeted everyone that came into her presence. Including Delaney.

Today seemed to be a good day for Mimi, too.

"A wash and set, then?" Delaney asked Mimi.

"Can-n I have my tea, too?"

Gracen shook her head behind Mimi, and her eyes rolled playfully. "Yes, I'll get your tea."

"A splash of rum!" the old woman added.

"And you're *so* lucky the doctor said a tablespoon wouldn't kill you," Gracen said under her breath.

Just not low enough.

"*Hey*," Mimi returned over her shoulder.

Gracen instantly bent down to press a kiss to Mimi's grinning cheek, muttering, "Love you—*yes*, I'll make your tea to drink while Delaney sets your hair. It'll be cooled down by the time your wash is done." Standing straight once more, her friend asked Delaney, "She's good in here with you for a few?"

"She's never a problem with me," Delaney assured.

Mimi's eyes twinkled. "But I could be, Lan-ney."

She couldn't help but smile at the familiar nickname Mimi had once used for Delaney as a teenager who seemed to try to spend more nights in Gracen's home than in her own.

"But you won't be, Mimi," Delaney replied, just as smart.

Gracen's snickers disappeared back into the house while Delaney headed for the wash basin in the corner of the salon where she put the broom and dustpan away first. She moved the reclining chair off to the side to make room for Mimi's wheelchair to back comfortably into the sink, and then grabbed a rolled up hand towel from the shelf over top, and a cape hanging from one hook of many on the wall.

"Are you taking your quilt off or on?" Delaney asked, rounding the back of Mimi's wheelchair.

The old woman patted the blanket made of patchwork covering her legs. "On-n."

Delaney made sure that the cape she placed around Mimi fell

far enough around the chair to keep any water from going where it shouldn't. Mimi, always happy to get pampered and attention, sat pleased and quiet while Delaney fit the towel around her neck under the cape, and moved them over to the sink basin.

"Let me get the water right for you first," Delaney told Mimi as she turned on taps with one hand, but kept Mimi from reclining fully with her other hand. "Nobody likes a shock."

"Mmhmm—a little birdy told me you have a n-new frien-nd."

"Was that birdy Gracen?"

"N-no."

"It was Gracen," Delaney returned.

Mimi, as serious as ever staring back at Delaney when her head was finally reclined into the curved neck rest of the sink basin, only replied, "I'll n-never tell."

"Are you trying to ask me about my new friend?" Delaney asked.

Mimi had yet to meet Lucas, if only because her arrival at the farmhouse came after his first visit of her initial move-in. By a couple of days, unfortunately. Having so many people on the property made it feel almost like a makeshift family, especially when the whole group, including Mimi's nurse most days, joined the large family table for dinners.

Lucas had come up.

More than once.

"She did n-not tell me much," Mimi whispered.

Delaney's grin spread wide while she used the removable spray nozzle to wet Mimi's short, white hair for the wash with warm water. "Ah, I see. Now we're getting closer to the truth. Did you consider that maybe there isn't much for Gracen to tell?"

Mimi didn't look the least bit ashamed. "*Well—*"

"What am I telling, now?"

"Apparently," Delaney returned over her shoulder to where Gracen had returned to the open double doorway, "it's what you're *not* telling her."

"Lucas," Mimi clarified. "The n-new frien-nd."

Gracen sighed but didn't suppress her tired smile as she crossed the salon floor with Mimi's teacup sitting neatly on a tea plate in her hand. "I thought we weren't being nosy? Wasn't that what you told me this morning?"

"You said that, maybe," Delaney said under her breath.

If there was anything Mimi loved the most, after her family, it was gossip. Harmless, really. She just liked knowing everything that happened around her. Especially with those she loved, and more importantly, when things were going well in the lives of those she cared about. Mimi simply wanted to feel included in those milestones and events.

Mimi's smirk down below confirmed Delaney's comment was probably true.

"Quiet, you," Gracen returned, but not very severely.

Closing her eyes when Delaney worked in a pump of shampoo that smelled like almonds into Mimi's hair, the older woman said, "So, about this Lucas ..."

"See, you've started it," Gracen said, "and now you can talk about it until her heart is content. Don't say I didn't warn you."

Delaney shrugged, winking down at Mimi who opened one eye to peek up at her from the sink basin. "What do you want to know, huh?"

Mimi's eyes squeezed shut again, but her smile remained. "All of it. A little birdy told me you love him."

Again with the little birdy bit ...

Delaney side-eyed Gracen who pretended to be busy sniffing the tea that wasn't even hers, and that she couldn't drink. "Oh, she did, did she?"

"Yep."

Well ...

"To be fair," Delaney said, "the little birdy isn't wrong."

That earned Delaney a grin from Gracen.

Mimi, on the other hand, wiggled in her wheelchair excitedly with a quiet, drawn out, "*Ohhhh.*" Then, she popped one eye open to stare at Delaney as she told her, "N-now tell me more."

*

Delaney and Gracen lingered in the doorway connecting the salon to the house while Mimi sat under the one dryer with her hair set in small curlers. She took slow, deliberate sips of her tea and flipped the pages in a magazine that Gracen had set up on a collapsible wooden table she also used for Mimi to take her meals. The dryer and curlers weren't exactly needed or even asked for, but the way Mimi lit up when Delaney suggested it, even if it meant another piece of equipment to wipe down and sterilize before her workday was over, then so be it.

Mimi's simple joy over being spoiled made it worth it.

"Thanks," Gracen said, for the third time, as she bumped her hip to Delaney's.

"Yeah, no problem."

"You don't regret it, right?"

Delaney looked over at Gracen, confused. "Regret what?"

"Moving back here so suddenly. Filling up your day with my clients instead of your own. I don't know … Come on, you know how I overthink things all the damn time."

"All the damn time!" came the loud echo from the kitchen.

Clearly, their conversation traveled.

"Shut up," Gracen called back playfully to Malachi.

"I wouldn't be here if I didn't really want to be," Delaney told her friend.

Rubbing her lips together in silent contemplation, Gracen eventually nodded like she believed Delaney. "Yeah, I guess. Hey, do you want some of Malachi's chicken stew before you head over to the apartment?"

"No, go back—why, *yeah, I guess*, like that?" Delaney asked. "You don't believe me?"

Delaney had done a lot of things she wasn't proud of over the course of her lifetime. Lying to Gracen was not one of them, nor would it ever be.

"I just—"

"I made rolls, too," came a new voice in the rear hallway of the downstairs. Malachi's figure darkened the other side in the halo of light spilling out from the dining room attached to the kitchen. "So let it never be said that I can't cook."

"Let it never be said again," Gracen added under her breath with a giggle.

"I still heard that."

"And I totally meant for you to, babe," she returned.

Delaney nodded at Malachi. "Could I just take a bowl and some rolls up to the apartment with me?"

"Sure," Malachi said, giving Gracen a look before he turned the corner back into the dining room.

Gracen, on the other hand, looked hurt. "You don't want to stay for supper tonight? It's not because I asked if you were happy, right? I didn't mean to hurt your feelings, or anything."

"You didn't. And I am happy," Delaney assured. "I don't understand why you think I'm not, though."

Her friend shrugged under her oversized, wool cardigan. "I mean, most times, you seem happy. Sometimes, though, I check on you throughout the day or notice when you get quiet, and I wonder if you are happy because you just don't look like it."

"I didn't know I had to be mindful of my expressions when I think I'm alone," Delaney said.

Only a little defensively.

Gracen didn't miss it.

She cocked an eyebrow high. "Really?"

Delaney sighed. "Sorry—that was mean."

"Yeah, you do that sometimes to protect your feelings."

Nothing could be simple, right?

"Maybe being here makes me aware of things I don't have," Delaney said, focusing on the hangnail on her thumb instead of her quiet friend. "Things that I *want*."

"Like," Gracen hedged.

"A family. A home. I'm twenty-five," Delaney said, trying to make it sound less pitiful than it did inside her head. One reason why she hated admitting the thoughts out loud. "Maybe it's because I see you settling into this nice, little domesticated life, and a part of me thinks it's time for those things to happen for me, too."

"They will."

Yeah, *when?*

Delaney didn't ask that question to Gracen.

It wasn't really for her friend to answer.

"Have you told someone else that you are looking for those things?" Gracen prodded, making it clear who she meant without actually saying his name.

"I don't want to pressure Lucas," Delaney admitted. "He's got a lot going on that he's still trying to deal with and work through. He doesn't need me on the phone crying to him because I'm in my feelings about my friend having a baby and getting married. That's a bit—"

"No, I meant," Gracen interjected, stopping Delaney's ramblings instantly, "have you told him that you want those things with him?"

"I didn't say—"

"You don't have to."

Delaney scowled up at Gracen. "I hate it when you do that. Interrupt me."

"Yeah, well, deal with it," her friend muttered. "And stop deflecting."

"I'm not. He does have a lot going on. Trying to stay out of the courts with his father; starting the foundation for his brother ..."

Delaney trailed off with a shrug.

The Jacob Dalton Foundation came as a surprise to her— something Lucas didn't mention until the paperwork had been filed, and the founding of the foundation was officially, *official.* Or, that was how he explained it to her. Meant to be a non-profit organization to help teenage boys and young men struggling with substance abuse, either in their lives or at home, through community support and programs that would give them teachable life skills along with mentors to guide them, it was still brand new.

At the beginning of something amazing.

Probably.

Lucas planned to sit in a chair for the foundation's committee, but those things still had to be worked out and set up. Other people, interested and driven in helping the same group he was, needed to be found and placed on the committee as well.

Official just meant it existed.

A lot of hard work, and time, lay ahead yet.

"I don't really know what the foundation means, yet," Delaney said after a moment.

Gracen, who leaned her back against the far side of the doorjamb opposite to Delaney, asked back, "For you guys, you mean?"

"Yeah—so, will he be staying there now? Which I get it, I'd probably do that, too, but I can't stop feeling bad that I ..." Delaney took a deep breath, trusting that judgment wouldn't come from Gracen when she admitted the truth. "I really just want him here with me."

"And you haven't said that to him."

Delaney scoffed. "No, and I don't plan to."

"Because that serves you how, exactly?"

"Well, I don't have to be the person who takes him away from doing something he feels like he has to do," Delaney said. "To start with."

"How do you know he can't do that thing and be with you?"

"Gracen—"

"Delaney, you're talking yourself in circles," her friend interjected, although with kindness.

"Okay, so maybe I'm scared he's gonna say no—that he doesn't want those things, or that he doesn't want them with me."

"I can't see that happening," Gracen muttered.

"I guess if I don't say anything, then I don't have to find out, huh?"

"And that's not realistic, so …"

There was that part about it, too.

"He told me things are better when he's with me," Delaney said, picking at her thumbnail again while she considered that afternoon in bed with Lucas three weeks earlier. "Maybe it's just hard for me not to get scared when things around me are good and happy."

"It takes a while to get beyond that," Gracen said, shrugging when Delaney glanced her way. "A year after Malachi moved in, I still thought I would wake up one day and the other shoe would drop. He couldn't be that perfect. He couldn't love me that much. Sure, he made it easier on me by proving me wrong every chance he could, but … I think being the person you are, Delaney, who had to grow up really fast, and learn to take care of yourself because you didn't have a lot of people to fall back on when you needed them the most taught you not to be so quick to depend on others. You look within to find what you want and need, or to make things happen for yourself, first before you go looking for someone else."

"And?" Delaney asked.

Gracen reached over to tug supportively on the black apron Delaney wore while she worked. "And it's okay to be afraid that you found someone who makes you want to tell them that what you really need is them. You gotta be brave enough to tell him as much, though, and trust that he's not going to leave you in a situation where you're doing it all alone."

Delaney tried to blink the wetness forming in her eyes away, but no surprise, the tears remained until one finally rolled down her cheek. "So, hey …"

"Yeah?"

"Can I eat stew here with you guys, instead?"

Gracen crossed the three feet between them to hug Delaney so hard she squeezed the breath right out of her lungs. Her friend's tiny swell, bouncing with her laughter, pushed against Delaney's side as the hug dragged on.

"You don't even have to ask, Delaney."

Right.

So what if her biological family had left Delaney a broken person, who even as an adult, struggled to find stability and emotional support sometimes? Who knew self-dependence, even to her own detriment, could be a by-product of the way she'd been shunned and abandoned as a teen? The family she had made, and still was, counted for a lot where her biological one had failed.

"I am happy here," she told Gracen. "I don't regret this."

She whispered it like a promise between them.

Gracen hugged her tighter. "I know you are, but it's okay to say you could be happier, too."

Delaney would work on that.

But in the meantime ...

"There might be another reason why these things are on my mind today," Delaney said.

Gracen's brow lifted with curiosity to the way Delaney's tone lowered enough that it wouldn't travel to anyone else downstairs. "Oh?"

Delaney chewed on her bottom lip, trying to make the words on the tip of her tongue form, but nerves kept her quiet and still. Arms folded across her chest, she allowed herself those few seconds she needed to get over it.

"A while back, Bexley made a comment to me—I'd know the second I got pregnant because I never miss my period."

"*Delaney*," came the rushed whisper from the other side of the doorway.

Delaney squeezed her eyes shut, and hunched her shoulders up closer to her ears. "Nope, don't do that—my period is *four* days late, I'd give it at least a full week before I took a test—a few days is nothing. I'm not panicking over that."

"You look a little panicked," Gracen returned.

Yeah, probably.

Delaney hunched her one shoulder upward, making it easier to feel like she was hiding part of her face when she told Gracen,

"Except you had a test upstairs that I found over lunch. Not because I was snooping, either," she added fast when Gracen's side-eye slid her way.

"I had some blood when I peed, and needed a pad or tampon," Delaney explained. "Cramps started around noon, too. But it feels just like my period. So, that's probably—"

"Did you take a test? You found them," Gracen pointed out. "I had what, one left of a box of three?"

Delaney's brow pinched, the only physical show of the way Gracen's question made her heart fall in her chest. She glanced toward Gracen, but her eyes fell to the barely noticeable bump under her friend's loose shirt and cardigan. "How many days late were you when you took yours? I never asked before—I didn't know if it was cool to ask about the whole pissing on a stick thing."

Gracen laughed, but the sound died fast. "Like five days, maybe?"

The two used the same Flo tracker app to monitor their cycles. In fact, Gracen had been the one to show Delaney how to input her periods back when they were teens. The app opened up a whole new world she hadn't known existed inside her own body— with just two or three regular periods, that app provided months of estimated data showing her future periods, days when pregnancy was more likely due to ovulation, and more. It gave her a different kind of control over her body—well, at least when it came to tracking what *should* happen.

"I bet your line wasn't hard to see and kind of spotty on your first test, right?" Delaney asked.

Whatever excitement remained in Gracen's expression died instantly. Delaney wished she had felt just as crushed but the confusion from the point she understood what was happening to when she saw the blood in her panties upstairs … she'd just not processed it yet.

"I logged the period on Flo, and the positive test," Delaney added when Gracen's apologetic expression bounced from her to Mimi still sipping tea under a dryer that had shut itself off. "It gave me a couple of articles about why it might be late—it's probably like a chemical pregnancy?"

A simple internet search had made it obvious to Delaney how common those apparently were—shockingly so, considering most women who experienced them didn't realize that's what it was and instead thought it was an irregular period.

A fertilized egg that, for whatever reason, didn't implant itself along the uterus lining.

"Not really sure why I took birth control for the last, like, eight years," Delaney stressed, "for it to fuck up the one time I didn't use condoms. That's the universe trying to fuck with me. God, maybe."

Her dark humor earned Delaney a soft grin from Gracen.

"Or you took it for all the other times it worked and helped those four days a month where you can get out of bed," Gracen said.

"Okay, fair. I feel like shit," she told her friend.

"Stew is really good for that."

Delaney laughed, and her gaze fell to the tiled floor of the salon beyond the doorway. "I definitely need some."

"Are you going to tell Lucas?"

"My period is four days late," Delaney countered. "I don't even know that's what it is, and—"

"If there's a line, and you can see a line on the pregnancy test, it's positive. That's what the instructions say," Gracen replied with a no-nonsense tone that reminded Delaney of a mother. At least, she had that down pat.

"I know what the instructions say, Gracen."

She tried to be snappy.

It kind of fell flat.

Delaney had, in fact, read the crumbled instruction booklet Gracen had left stuffed inside the open box that had been sitting in the bottom drawer of her bathroom vanity. Right where she might also keep pads and tampons. They had also been in the back of the drawer. Not a great variety, though.

To be fair, Gracen hadn't needed any in over twenty-something weeks.

"I'll probably tell him," Delaney confirmed.

"Yeah?"

"It'd be nice to know that's what it is," she added.

Gracen chewed on her lower lip for a half a minute before she said, "If you think you're having a miscarriage, that sounds Emergency Room worthy to me."

Delaney rolled her eyes toward her friend. "Stop that—just because it costs nothing to visit the ER doesn't mean I should because I'm bleeding a little heavy."

"Are the cramps worse than normal?"

"They're always bad."

Bearably so.

Women got used to that.

Gracen pursed her lips, and then checked on Mimi once more. "Let's get her out of there, we're eating supper, and take a trip to town."

"Gracen, I don't need to go—"

"They'll tell you. They'll run a blood test, tell you if the hormone is there, which it is and detectable because the home test said so, and what the levels are, and if they're too low for a viable pregnancy."

Her brow furrowed. "How do you know—"

"At seven weeks I was convinced cramping after I hiked for three hours were because I was losing the baby—no blood, or anything, but," Gracen trailed off, shrugging. "Malachi tried to make me relax, give it the night, you know?"

"You didn't?"

"Nope. That's what I pay taxes for, Delaney. I don't use the ER like a band-aid station, and I've been there all of two times in the last three years. I went down on a weekday, before nine when the diagnostics department leaves for the day. A client works in the department, so I might have had some inside knowledge on that bit, though."

Her friend checked the rose-gold watch on her wrist, and then glanced straight up at Delaney.

"It's Thursday, and we still have time," Gracen added.

That achy heart of Delaney's that she had numbed through the day by going through the motions and refusing to feel jumped to life with a beat that hurt.

"You know I love you, right?" Delaney asked.

Wordlessly, Gracen pushed away from the doorjamb to catch Delaney in a hug around her neck with both arms.

"No matter what—we're in this together," Gracen swore against the top of Delaney's head. "I told you that before, and I meant it."

No matter what, and regardless of who stuck by her throughout the years, Gracen had made that promise to Delaney when they were just seventeen. To some people, broken promises like those weren't a big deal. The fact that Gracen never broke her promise said a lot to Delaney about what it meant between the two of them.

"I know," she mumbled into Gracen's cardigan sleeves. "*Now let me go so I can breathe.*"

Sometimes, she hated being short.

Soon enough, though, Gracen released her cage-like hold.

"Come on, let's get Mimi out from under the dryer," she said.

Delaney nodded. "Right, yeah. Supper, then the ER. I still feel bad about that."

Gracen shook her head, as unbothered as ever. "*Yeah*, don't. You pay taxes, too."

A louder than she expected laugh escaped Delaney. "That's true."

Her noise had caught the attention of someone else, though.

Raising her voice so the slightly hard-of-hearing woman across the room would hear her name called, Delaney asked, "Mimi, are you ready to take your rollers out?"

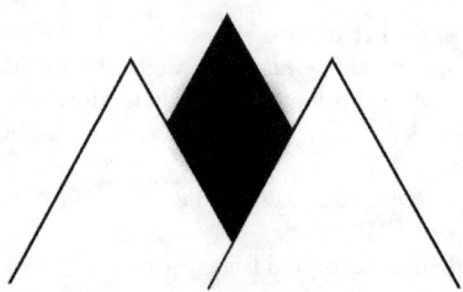

37

The entrance of the Valleyview Hospital's emergency department sat atop a hill overlooking the river splitting the town in half, and the mirrored windows along the front allowed patients in the waiting room a view as the clock ticked down time while people waited to be seen by the doctor on call.

Delaney hadn't been inside the hospital for years—at least three, for sure. As her Jeep rolled to a stop in a parking spot around the back close to the rear entrance doors, her nerves decided to make an appearance in the fast beat of her fingertips rapping against the leather of her purse.

The man behind the wheel of the Jeep didn't miss Delaney's nervous tick.

"You good?"

Malachi's quiet question drew Delaney's gaze away from the rear entry door where people entered the emergency room.

"Yeah, sure," she told him.

He arched an eyebrow higher than the other. "Nothing's ... *bad*, bad, right?"

Delaney wanted to laugh at Malachi's concern, if only to ease the tension in the vehicle, because it wasn't really needed. Except this situation wasn't really a laughing matter, and the cramps in her lower sides had picked up substantially during the ride to town.

So, she lied.

"Everything is fine."

"Yeah," he muttered, his head swinging toward the direction of the driver's door window, "Gracen said that shit, too. Yet, here we are at seven at night, sitting in the parking lot of the hospital, so. What's that tell you?"

Really, Malachi shouldn't be sitting there at all, but some circumstances couldn't be helped. He had been the one to point out that Gracen's grandmother had woken up once at night since moving into the farmhouse being confused and unsure of where she was and scared because of it. All it took was Gracen to calm Mimi down and get her back into bed, but Malachi didn't think he would be able to do the same thing should the situation happen again.

Gracen tried to argue …

Delaney had been the one to make the call. Malachi made a very good point. Hence, the deal that he would drive her to the ER, in her Jeep, just because, and he would also wait until she came back out to drive back to The Flats.

"Hey," Delaney said to her companion to gain his attention.

It worked.

Malachi looked away from the window. "What?"

"I didn't even think I needed to come here, honestly, but Gracen pressured me into it."

So, here they were.

Malachi's lips lifted at the corner into a partial smile. "Yeah, she's pretty good at doing that. Still kind of bothered that we're here, and nobody's told me why. Fuck me for caring, right?"

Poor guy.

Perhaps the truth just wasn't simple. If the reason for her bleeding and positive pregnancy test *was* a chemical pregnancy that was terminating itself, she didn't know how to begin sharing that information with someone else. She could barely process it in her own mind.

It wasn't time to share yet.

Delaney shrugged. "Don't worry about me, I'm fine. *Really.*"

Sighing, Malachi slapped the steering wheel of the Jeep. "Well, I'll be out here waiting whenever you're done. You don't need me to go inside, right?"

Oh, God.

Absolutely not.

Delaney forced on a smile. "No, that's okay."

"Great." Malachi scowled toward the rear entry door. "Hospitals give me the fucking creeps."

"Better get over that," Delaney returned, "seeing as how you've got a baby on the way."

"*Uh ...*"

The way his face blanked, and his mouth fell open at the fact point out to him had Delaney barking out a laugh. Real, true, and *hard*. It felt good. Malachi even grinned, shaking his head, in the seat next to hers.

"Get off it," he joked back.

Delaney just shrugged. "All right, better get in and register. The faster I get that over with, the quicker I can be seen."

"Text me if, for any reason, you need me to come in, okay?"

"I'm sure I'll be fine," Delaney said, pushing open the passenger door.

Behind her, Malachi stressed, "Still, Delaney. Call me if you need something. I'm not going to pretend like Gracen didn't spend a good twenty minutes arguing with me over whether or not she should come here with you. You don't want to tell me what's going on—so be it. The way my fiancée acted tells me more than enough. She wanted to be here, and you probably wanted her here with you, too. Instead, you got me. I can be inside with you in thirty seconds. Got it?"

She faced him, holding onto the edge of the Jeep door, and silently willed the deep pit in her stomach to fill with a bit of that protective love and concern she could feel radiating from Malachi. She truly did have the best kind of friends.

"Got it?" he asked again, stronger the second time.

"Yeah, I got it."

He nodded toward the hospital, and his blue eyes darkened at the sight. "Even if it does give me the fucking creeps." His gaze turned on the windshield ahead of him as he bitched under his breath. "Hate this place—they have crosses in *every* room."

Over all the doors, in fact.

As if every person who walked through the door should automatically be assumed a Christian. Never had someone else voiced that private annoyance of Delaney's until Malachi did at that moment.

"It's kind of weird, right?" she asked.

His stare cut to her, and he shrugged. "Yeah, because it's not God in there making people better. He's not changing IVs and bed pans or doling out the medication. I don't get it, I guess."

"You know what's funny?"

"Can't think of anything," Malachi joked.

Delaney rolled her eyes. "No, seriously. Think about it—people like Gracen barely look at those crosses over the doors or even think about them at all. It's like any other decoration. It doesn't mean anything to her. It doesn't stick out more than anything else. She doesn't overthink it or why it's there. It just is."

Something she saw and moved on. The sight of a cross, or the meaning behind it, didn't hurt Gracen the way it did someone like Delaney.

Delaney couldn't imagine what that was like.

Malachi's jaws tensed as his head turned away once more. "I'd like to be able to do that."

"Yeah," Delaney muttered, "me, too."

*

The rear entry to the emergency ward opened to a corridor where one could register with the receptionist waiting behind a pane of Plexiglass. Delaney stayed close to the heavy entrance door as a young mother with a sleepy toddler clinging to her arms finished checking in and waited for the person on the other side of the glass to push her son's medicare card back through the hole.

She touched the boy's forehead with her hand, and her brow furrowed at what she found. "He still feels really hot. That's bad, right? It's been since last night."

Whoever waited on the other side of the glass must have said something reassuring, as the young mother smiled and nodded, saying only, "Sure—the waiting room is just around the corner there?"

Delaney, not trying to be nosy or unintentionally invade someone's privacy, averted her gaze to the posters on the entrance wall. Everything from the birth cycle of a pregnancy to warnings about the common flu and available seasonal shots. Before long, the mother rocking the toddler in the lone hallway chair stood up with her medicare card in hand.

"Thank you," she told the person behind the glass.

Once the woman had exited the hallway to the waiting room further down, Delaney stepped forward to take the open chair. She found the small cubicle behind the glass, partially blocked by a large computer monitor facing her direction, to be empty when she first sat down. Leaning forward, she pumped a pile of sanitizer into her hand to rub into her palms before she produced the provincial medicare card with her name on it to register once the receptionist returned.

Still reading the expiration date on the card for the following year, Delaney didn't realize the chair in the cubicle had been filled until she lifted her head.

And stared directly into the face of her mother.

Well, partially.

Amanda Reed's gaze stayed locked slightly lower than Delaney's face, instead pinning to the screen in front of her as she asked simply, "Medicare card, please?"

Years of not seeing her mother face to face came to a head in that moment, and Delaney did her best to roll with the emotional punch that came along with it. Of course, she would have no idea that her mother switched jobs from her old secretarial duties for a general practitioner in town to the Valleyview Hospital. They didn't talk—how could she know?

Not much about her mother had changed.

A bit grayer, maybe, in her swept back black hair tied neatly into a bun at the nape of her neck to deal with the unmanageable length. Delaney could remember begging her mother as a preteen to be allowed to cut her feet upon feet of hair and being refused every time because the hair was a woman's crown.

Delaney's hesitance to provide the medicare card in question finally coaxed the other woman's gaze upward to find the problem. It took Amanda two blinks to recognize the person sitting on the other side of the glass.

Her only daughter.

"Delaney," Amanda said.

Once, as she left the courtroom after testifying against her brother and cousin for their part in the arson, she had caught sight of her mother sitting in the back of a black Buick. Amanda never attended court even though her husband hadn't missed a single day.

Delaney hated that she didn't know what to say. That her mind wouldn't form words. How she couldn't decide whether to address her mother by *Mom* or *Amanda*.

Life brought her to this moment.

And for *what?*

"Hi," Delaney eventually choked out.

Immediately after, she slid the medicare card through the circular hole of the pane of plexiglass that met the desk and lower wall. Amanda didn't waste time grabbing the piece of plastic, and there was nothing kind or ceremonious about the way she dropped it off to the side of her desk like she didn't want to touch it.

Amanda glanced toward the card, and her fingers worked over the keyboard. Likely inputting the number across the front. "I suppose I don't need to ask your birthdate, hmm?"

Delaney frowned.

Was that an attempt at a joke?

After she acted like the card Delaney touched and owned might *burn* her?

She tried to shake the unsettling feeling off.

"How have you been?" she asked her mother.

Amanda's lips pursed, and she swallowed hard, but her gaze never left the screen in front of her. "Oh, I'm sure you've heard about recent changes in my life. I left your father a year ago—we're not divorced, but he's moved out. Things are a lot quieter at the house."

"I didn't know that, actually."

Her mother looked over the top of the screen.

Delaney shrugged. "It's been made clear to me that I shouldn't ask about my family, the church, or anything else, really. Honestly, it's easier that way. I don't have to wonder if you give a shit about me when actions speak louder than words at the end of the day."

Flash of indignation lit up her mother's familiar eyes. "There's no need for that kind of language, Delaney. You may not be welcomed in my home or at the church, but I know I raised you better than that."

"Are you registering me in?" Delaney asked, trying to put the two of them back on task because this was going nowhere, fast. Not to mention, the stress of having to sit there and be polite to the woman who had birthed her—and who also had acted like Delaney didn't exist for the better part of the last seven to eight years—was enough to make the achy, deep cramps low in her belly worse. It bothered her that the pain wasn't any better or worse than her normal periods, but it still felt like she was losing something all the same. She tried to push those thoughts to the side, and the heavier flow settled between her legs the longer she sat there in that chair, to handle the situation in front of her first.

Her mother didn't go back to the medicare card.

Delaney's brow lifted expectantly. "Or … no?"

Amanda still didn't seem put off by the question. Unbothered, if anything. "As I understand it, some of your cousins still talk between you or Bexley, so—"

"I don't go out of my way to ask about you anymore, it never served me," Delaney interjected.

As quiet as the words were, she knew the impact they would have on her mother from that moment forward. What had long been an unspoken understanding between Delaney and her mother would now be very clear.

Sometimes, things just had to be said.

It wouldn't always feel good.

"Well," Amanda said in a sigh, her attention turning back on the screen as her fingers began to fly over the keyboard, "I had heard you were back in town. Or the area … living with the Briggs girl again?"

"In an apartment Gracen owns," Delaney replied, to be civil.

Very little else.

She didn't offer more information, and the short reply seemed to do the job of making it clear to her mother that they would not be talking about Gracen, or much else. As it was, the two had already talked too much.

For her liking, anyway.

"What's the reason for the trip to the ER today?" Amanda asked.

Holy hell.

Somehow, she had forgotten in her shock at seeing her mother that she would have to explain to her why she needed to visit the emergency department at Valleyview Hospital. The immediate lump in Delaney's throat even took away her ability to take in air for a few seconds. The internal panic was *real*.

"Uh," Delaney tried to say.

Amanda's brow lifted higher than the screen in front of her. "I need to input it for the nurse who will see you in the triage next. Are you running a fever or—"

"Bleeding," Delaney said, the word stumbling from her tongue before she could swallow it back down. Now that she got it out there, though … "I'm bleeding. I think I'm having a miscarriage. I had a positive test, but with a very faint line, and I've been bleeding for the better part of the day today."

Perhaps her mother's many years of working behind the receptionist desk for a family doctor had done something for Amanda's professionalism because hearing that news from her daughter didn't affect her as she input the information to the record for the visit through her keyboard. On the surface, anyway. Delaney could see the way Amanda's gaze shifted to her, and then widened pointedly before she asked, "Is all of your personal information up-to-date—single, person to contact is Gracen Briggs … oh, if you've moved, we should put in your new address."

Delaney's jaw ached from how hard she clenched her teeth as she repeated the new address that she had managed to memorize quickly after moving into the apartment over the garage. "And yes, Gracen still works."

"And the status, or not, of your relations—"

"None of your business," Delaney replied.

Amanda cocked an eyebrow. "I'm just asking, Delaney." Except her judgemental gaze came around the monitor to pointedly glance down toward the non-existent swell of Delaney's stomach. "Perhaps if you are single … is it not for the better? These things are often in His plans."

No way.

This isn't real, she told herself.

Someone wouldn't say that to someone else. A woman wouldn't look another woman in the eyes after she had admitted her fear of having a miscarriage just to be told it was *God's plans*.

Except there Delaney was being told exactly that by her own mother.

After all those years, not one damn thing had changed.

"Excuse me, can I help you?"

Delaney, who found herself glaring through the pane of plexiglass at the woman on the other side, didn't notice the nurse in colorful, cartoon-printed scrubs that entered the cubby from a side door. The open doorway exposed the nurses' station on the other side. Bustling with quiet activity, the waiting room sat on the other side.

"She's almost registered," Amanda said. "It'll be another—"

"I'll see her in triage now," the nurse with the kind eyes and soft smile said.

She never looked away from Delaney.

Had the woman heard what her mother said?

She hadn't noticed if the door had been cracked.

Who knew if the wall might be thin?

Amanda frowned and looked back over her shoulder at the nurse. "I don't even have her registration bracelet printed yet, Madison."

The nurse walked beyond Amanda in the office chair, picked Delaney's medicare card up to look at the information on the front, and then she slid it back through the hole for her to take. Delaney noticed the RN stamped on the name badge hanging from Madison's breast pocket of her scrub tops.

"Triage is just down the hall, it's a cubicle, you can't miss it," Madison told Delaney.

She clutched the card, standing from the chair and avoiding the confused flutter of her mother's hands over the keyboard while Delaney awkwardly moved out and around the chair.

"Thank you," she told the nurse.

Maybe that was the saddest thing about it.

In her faith of believing that *she* was right, Amanda didn't even consider that her words could hurt. Something else that wasn't new. God had been a favorite weapon of her parents for as long as Delaney could remember.

Now, the blows just left her a little bruised.

She could heal from that.

*

"Okay, Miss Reed," Madison said, "here's what we're going to do—if it's good with you, of course."

"Sure," Delaney replied, hugging her arms around her middle. "I would just like to know—"

"If it's a failing pregnancy. Yeah, unfortunately, my initial thought is it is, and it's quite common. One in four women, and even that's probably not correct because of the number of women who don't even realize a non-viable pregnancy is terminating because they mistake it for their period. Those store-bought tests are looking for the same hormone we do when we run the blood test, just in a less accurate way, and the line shouldn't show up on that test if the hormone is detectable."

Madison flipped a hand over in a wave, adding, "Apparently, it was at a detectable enough level that the test gave a weak positive. That hormone only exists in your body if there's a fertilized egg, so it is there. It's just a matter of getting a proper read of the levels, and if the doctor thinks the bleeding could be something else, like … have you had rough sex in the last twenty-four hours?"

Delaney's cheeks flushed hot pink. "No, I haven't."

Madison waved the answer off, moving right along. "Okay, well … we really need to get a proper read on the hormone level. If by chance it seems high, the doctor might ask you to come back tomorrow to run more bloodwork to see if the levels have continued to go down. Especially if the cramping and bleeding continues. I'm not sure if an ultrasound is on the table today, but we'll see what the doctor says about that, too. We'll start by getting your blood drawn, and run the bloodwork, so then we can, on paper, see if it's there. You'll know for sure, and we can start there."

She appreciated the careful, but frank and respectful, way the RN broached Delaney's current circumstances, and in a way, that gave her a little more dignity.

Delaney let out a hard breath that came with a lot of relief. "Okay, yeah. Thanks."

"It's going to take about an hour down at the lab."

She jerked a thumb over her shoulder, saying, "Should I just hang out in the waiting room until—"

"No, I'm going to ask one of the nurses to open a private room so you can wait in privacy and peace. You don't recognize me, do you?"

Delaney's brow dipped low, and she took in the nurse's distinct wide forehead and pretty blue eyes again, but she couldn't match the woman's smile to anyone in her memories. Her years of doing hair at the Haus, and the former salon she'd owned with Gracen, meant the nurse could have been a previous client.

She went with that safe bet.

"Did you used to visit the Haus?" Delaney asked.

"My younger sister—Kerry—did her practical hours for her license at the Haus, actually."

Instantly, the information gave Delaney enough information to name the face in front of her, and why it took her more than a few minutes of conversation to remember.

"You always picked her up on Fridays," Delaney said.

Madison smiled, nodding. "Yep—she talked about you guys non-stop, and it seemed like … Kerry swore that all the girls who did their hours at the Haus loved you and Gracen. Um, so maybe that's why I might have known that was your mother working the front, so when I heard her say your name, I listened in on the conversation."

She appreciated the honesty.

Delaney lifted her shoulders, muttering, "Thanks for saving me from an even more awkward conversation, I guess."

"I'll put in a complaint with the hospital's HR department, if you'd like me to. Making comments like those to patients isn't acceptable, and even if it was just a verbal reprimand, it'll be on paper, in her file, and she'll get the point the next time you have to walk through those doors."

Delaney considered it for a good, honest minute.

And then said, "No, thank you."

Madison straightened a bit in the chair across the small triage paper with Delaney's admittance paperwork spread out between them. Everything from her weight, height, and last period—that very day, unfortunately—had been tracked on the paper over the course of a few minutes.

"Are you sure? I can do it without your name being on file if you're concerned about something happening outside of the hospital because of the report," Madison offered.

Of course.

Everyone knew all too well what happened when members of the church were singled out in their small valley town. Sure, the previous pastor who had shouted hellfire and brimstone from the pulpit during her days as parishioner, and even when the Haus had been burned, no longer sat as the head of the tabernacle on the hill.

Or so she had been told …

It didn't matter.

That was the only damn thing that had changed.

"I don't want you to make that report," Delaney said, so that it would be clear where she stood, "because it's my mother, and not because she's a member of the Truth and Grace Tabernacle."

Delaney didn't have to like her mother to care about her. Amanda didn't have to know Delaney still loved her, either, because the only way she could continue to feel that way about her mother was from afar.

At a safe distance.

"You're better than me," Madison admitted, "because I couldn't say the same if it was mine."

Yeah, well …

Delaney just shrugged.

It was what it was.

"I'll get you into the room, and someone will be around shortly to draw your blood, okay?" Madison asked, standing from the chair. "Is there someone you wanted to call to wait with you, or did you just come in alone?"

Delaney followed behind Madison, exiting around the private triage corner, as the phone in her purse beeped. "I have someone outside, but I'm good to wait alone," she replied as she dug into her bag to find the phone, expecting a missed call from Gracen as she'd silenced the ringer before coming inside.

Madison gestured to another nurse behind the desk. A willowy blonde with light pink scrubs and a bright, white smile who nodded back and pointed at a private room off to the side of the nurse's station.

"Right there," Madison told Delaney. "The doctor will probably stop by to confirm what I put on your intake, but it shouldn't be long. We're not very busy today, thankfully."

She briefly looked at the room, and the number alongside it, muttering, "Sure, thanks."

Delaney had a bigger problem.

The text on her phone from Lucas, actually.

You're at the hospital?

That was all he asked.

How did he know?

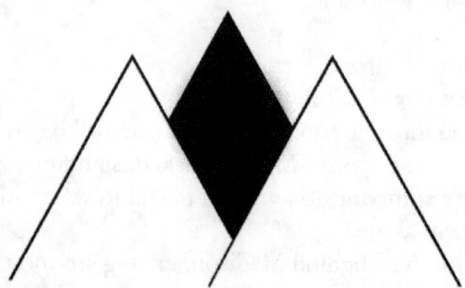

38

"Hey, what's going on?" Lucas asked the second he picked up Delaney's call. "Are you in the hospital?"

"I'm at the ER in town. It's not serious," Delaney replied.

Lucas wished that helped the painful tightening in his chest, except it still felt like someone had taken a hammer to his breastbone all the same. His soaring panic came out in the form of rushed words he rapid fired out of his mouth. "Well, what's happening? We talked this morning and you seemed fine. Are—"

"Lucas, it's okay," Delaney said quietly.

At the same time a voice called out behind him, "Lucas, we're being seated, if you're ready."

Under the alcove entrance of the downtown restaurant that served some of the best steak dishes in the city, Lucas turned to catch the eye of his lawyer up the steps nearer to the podium. He lifted a hand for Lawrence to see that he had, in fact, heard the man.

"Could you stall them for me?" he asked. "Five minutes, max."

Lawrence agreed with a nod before turning back to the woman waiting behind the podium. Lucas put his attention back on his phone call.

"I'm sorry," he told Delaney, knowing damn well he'd missed part of her explanation for being at the hospital as he made the request of Lawrence. "Tell me again why Malachi drove you to the hospital at seven at night?"

"Malachi called you."

The clipped tone from Delaney had Lucas cringing at his reflection in the entry glass facing the quiet, slushy street outside.

"Hey," Lucas said, offering the word like an olive branch meant to relax Delaney without saying as much. "Remember how I asked why you and Gracen go whispering in other rooms together, and you told me some things can't be changed?"

Delaney cleared her throat on the other end of the line, and something like paper shuffled in the background of the call. "I guess," she said blandly. "What about it? Ugh, I hate these paper sheets they put on these stupid hospital beds."

His heart squeezed painfully.

"Seriously, why are you at the damn hospital?" he asked. "Did something happen? You weren't messing around in their shop with the machines or something, ri—"

"Lucas, calm down," Delaney interjected, her voice rising over his own inside his head. "I'm already sitting here trying to figure out whether I want to cry or scream. Listening to you panic on a phone call isn't really helping that much."

Cry or scream—*what?*

"And now I'm going to have to tell my friend to put her husband in his damn place," Delaney added after a moment.

Lucas barked out a low laugh. "No, that's what I meant about the Gracen thing. Us guys have our lines, too. Mine is you. His is her. If something happened or was wrong with that woman and I knew about it, you bet your ass I would send him a text to say as much. You don't want to apologize or explain your whispering in different rooms—*well*, same."

Silence answered his unapologetic declaration.

Lucas tacked on for politeness, so he didn't sound like a total asshole, "Basically, anyway."

Delaney's sigh echoed over the phone. "I don't know whether to like that the two of you made friends, or ..."

"I was just about to have a late dinner with my father and our lawyers to sign the final paperwork on the purchase and transfer of shares—are you okay? Tell me if this is something that can't wait, Delaney."

Her silence dragged on longer.

Lucas couldn't stand it. "Did I say that wrong—is that it?"

"What could you possibly say wrong?"

"Maybe because I'm so used to somebody needing me that I keep looking for it from you, in a way. I expect you to call me and say you need me if something is wrong, but you're already over there probably figuring it out on your own, right?"

"Lucas—"

"Let me try again, okay?"

"Okay," Delaney muttered on the other end of the call. "Try again."

"I'll stop asking if you need me and start asking if you want me instead. Or that's what *you* can do, if it's hard for you to say you need me. Stop looking at it like that. Start asking yourself what you want—ask if it's me."

"I was better this morning than I am right now," Delaney admitted.

A shitty justification, in his opinion, for her lack of a phone call later when she did decide to go into town to visit the hospital. Whatever the reason.

Lucas gave Delaney a bit of grace.

"When I ask myself that question," Lucas said, "the answer is sure as hell you for me."

Delaney sniffled, but asked, "I thought you weren't doing that dinner until next week?"

"Lawrence is good at moving things along," he said of his lawyer.

Otherwise, Lawrence spoke for himself.

And his work.

"I thought if I said yes and got everything done, I could come upriver sooner than we'd discussed for a week or two," Lucas added.

"Can we start there?"

Lucas blinked at the question, but also had to move aside for a well-dressed couple that entered the restaurant. He followed the pair with his gaze as they climbed the stairs to where the host waited to take coats and greet those who entered the establishment.

"Lucas?" Delaney asked.

"Start where?"

"A week or two," Delaney clarified. "I want you for longer than that."

Lucas chuckled, the rumbling sound easing a bit of the ache in his chest. "Okay, it can be more than that. I'll figure it out. It's not like I'm going to be punching in on anybody's clock."

Not that he ever did that before, really.

Salary all the way.

"Well, there's still the foundation for—"

"The foundation is in the beginning stages and has another year or more of work ahead of me before it's functional the way I envision it in my mind," Lucas interjected. "Also, there's nothing I can't do over a telephone or video call for that at the moment, anyway."

"Are you keeping the apartment in the city?"

His brow furrowed. "Are you asking me that for a reason?"

"It's probably bigger than my little one bedroom over the garage, huh?"

"Delaney—"

"Does it sound as juvenile to you as it does to me when I want to ask you to move in?"

All at once, that pressure building inside his chest seemed to release. Finally, he seemed to grasp what she had been dancing around for the better part of their conversation.

"Is that what it is? You want me to move in?" he asked.

"You're the one who keeps saying you can work on whatever, *wherever*," Delaney returned.

Like it wasn't a big deal.

Oh, God.

It *was*.

"I thought about keeping the apartment in the city," Lucas said honestly. Because he *had* given this some thought, although he'd been waiting on Delaney to take that first step between them. He'd move accordingly, and so, now he could.

She cleared her throat. "Did you?"

"A part of me will always stay in Saint John," he said, "and what if we wanted to go for a weekend? It's there and furnished."

Delaney grew quiet on the other end of the line again. Something about that silence seemed weighted and sad to him. So heavy, he could feel it through the speakers.

"Are you gonna tell me what's going on?"

Delaney dragged in a shaky breath. "Promise you won't freak out?"

"I can sure try," he returned, "but no promises there. I won't make one I might break."

"You're so sweet it's fucking disgusting."

He grinned, but the clearing of a throat made Lucas spin around to see Lawrence had come to stand at the top of the stairs. His lawyer gestured at the watch on his wrist, making Lucas nod in silent reply.

"I *was* going to tell you—when I knew for sure," Delaney corrected, adding after, "But then someone else had to stick his nose where it didn't belong before I even had some answers of my own here."

"What?"

Lucas had no clue what she meant.

From start to finish.

"I took a pregnancy test today, Lucas," Delaney said, "and it was positive."

Stopping his heart in an instant.

She didn't give him the chance to speak, and restarted the organ in his chest, when she continued on, saying, "But I've also been bleeding all day, and not feeling great, so … Anyway, Gracen convinced me to make a trip in. Malachi drove. He doesn't know."

His mind blanked.

Just … *gone.*

Nothing really seemed important to Lucas, not even the dinner he was already late to and would need to get through lest he drag on the communication with his father and Ronald's irritating lawyer. Not a good option. The dinner, and the papers he had to sign during it, seemed so insignificant compared to the achy sadness in Delaney's voice.

That killed him.

"I'll be there before you lay your head down tonight," Lucas promised. "Are they keeping you there at the hospital, do you think?"

"You don't have to make the trip here tonight," Delaney argued. "That's a four-hour drive, Lucas."

"Are they keeping you at the hospital tonight?"

"Well …"

"What, Delaney?"

"I don't really know? Probably not, but I'm not sure. I haven't even seen the doctor yet, and honestly, I barely want to stay because my mother is doing patient intake for the ER. Really could have done without that tonight, you know?"

Lucas couldn't imagine how bad Delaney's day had gone for her thus far. He would try to make it marginally better.

"Call me when you do know. Anything at all, Delaney, do you hear me?"

"Yeah, okay. I will," she assured. "That's a long drive, Lucas. I'm serious. You don't have to come rushing here tonight. It's … if it's a pregnancy and I'm losing it, it's really early, and—"

She shouldn't have to do it alone.

She wouldn't.

"Either way, I'm coming home. I just want to know where the fuck I need to find you."

*

Lucas joined the table situated in the very middle of the large dining room—a purposeful spot that he believed the lawyers had pre-chosen before arrival to keep the Dalton men polite and cordial during dinner—with an apology for being late. The unconcerned wave of two of the three men at the table didn't seem too bad.

Ronald, on the other hand, followed Lucas with his gaze until he took his seat directly across from his father at the table. "Couldn't imagine what's more important than twelve and a half million dollars."

Lucas, more interested in the menu in front of him than the man trying to poke at his raw nerve, responded only, "Everybody has different priorities, Ronald."

He'd dropped the *dad* bit altogether.

Lucas wouldn't even call Ronald his father after today.

Chandler, the man Ronald paid a nice hourly fee to put up with his bullshit on the legal side of things, seemed to pick up on the fast-rising tension between the father and son at the table. He stepped in to divert Ronald's attention away from Lucas for a moment by pointing at something on the menu that the two began to discuss.

On his side, Lucas turned to his lawyer.

"Can we reschedule breakfast tomorrow?" Lucas asked Lawrence under his breath. "Something came up earlier that I will need to handle once we're finished here."

He didn't feel comfortable sharing the circumstances that led him to cancel the breakfast. Those details felt a little too personal and close to his heart. Maybe at a different place and table, Lucas might have felt safe to give Lawrence the insight, but …

"Your phone call?" the lawyer asked back.

Lucas nodded subtly. "I'll be heading upriver for a bit. Breakfast was all semantics, anyway, right?"

"Celebratory based on tonight, really," Lawrence replied, smirking. "It's fine. We can go over everything and what to expect with the incoming transfers into your accounts over the phone. It didn't have to be over a meal, Lucas."

"Great. My phone is always on if you call, anyway."

"Good to know he answers someone's calls," came the comment from across the table.

Even the lawyer beside Lucas heard the snideness from Ronald.

"Is there a reason I need to answer a call from you?" Lucas asked the prick across the way.

Ronald opened his mouth to respond, but promptly snapped his jaws closed when a bubbly redhead sidled up to their table with a wide smile plastered on her face. If the server could tell she came to the wrong table, the woman didn't make it known. That, or she was terribly good at her job.

Either way, Lucas planned to leave her a decent tip.

"Are we ready to get a start on the first course?" the redhead asked. Her green gaze turned on Lucas. "My name's Marley, by the way. You weren't here earlier when I introduced myself."

Lucas smiled at the server. "Nice to meet you, Marley. I'll take the special, medium-rare. Sour cream on the side, and not on my potatoes. Nothing to follow or for dessert. And no beer, thank you."

"You better drink something," Ronald interjected before the server could confirm she had understood Lucas' order. "Nobody signs paperwork without a drink to make it official—come on."

"I'll be driving tonight," Lucas said, speaking only to the server as he handed his menu over. "No drinks, thank you."

"Got it," she replied. "Anybody else ready?"

Refusing to engage his father more than he had to took conscious, consistent effort from Lucas. Especially when Ronald ordered four glasses of whiskey for the table, and a bottle of red wine that would apparently go well with the steaks. The lawyers waited until their clients had ordered before they, too, opted for the special coming out of the kitchen. Once she had all the orders noted into the tablet in her hands, Marley left with a promise to me back soon with drinks.

"No better time, then?" Chandler asked Lawrence.

Lucas' lawyer's bushy brows lifted high at the question when the man across the table lifted a legal file to place on the table between them.

"Might as well get a start on it, Hanny," Lawrence agreed.

The boring legalese that started to be tossed back and forth between the lawyers at the table was a bit much for Lucas. There was a reason he never made a bit for law school when college came up in his life a while back. He wouldn't apologize or make excuses for zoning out when Chandler opened the file and started with a glossary of terms that could be expected in the final agreement between Lucas and his father.

Instead, his mind traveled to Delaney.

Had the doctor seen her yet?

Did she know if her pregnancy had been lost?

The universe had a special way of fucking with Lucas like nothing else could or did. He should put his attention on the conversation at the table, and the question Ronald had just asked Lawrence about the thirty-day window for the money to be transferred, but all Lucas could think about was the woman he'd called home.

He even checked his phone, using the distraction of the other men at the table to his benefit, just in case Delaney had sent a text message.

But he found nothing.

The not-knowing added on top of the dinner that would be surely full of careful conversation to keep the peace with Ronald left Lucas on edge.

Just a little.

And maybe a bit distracted, too.

"We're going to have to discuss that," Ronald said gruffly, folding his arms over his chest across from Lucas. An irritated stare landed on him, bringing Lucas back to the conversation at hand.

"We're discussing what, now?" Lucas asked Lawrence.

The lawyer shifted his stare from Lucas to Ronald, but then down at the table when he filled in the blank, saying, "The Jacob Dalton Foundation. We're talking the trademarks and other things. There could be future problems with the same and its connection to—"

Lucas turned his attention on Ronald.

Zero to sixty in a blink.

Had his father done that on purpose?

It didn't even matter.

"Do you hate us that much?" Lucas asked Ronald.

He hadn't expected the frank question if the way his stony expression cracked with surprise was any indication. The other two men at the table shifted awkwardly in their seats, one clearing his throat while the other resituated the water glass away from his plate even though he had yet to drink a drop from it.

Ronald, to his benefit, didn't look away from Lucas. "How I feel about you or your brother has little to nothing to do with the brewery's registered—"

"Oh, get off it," Lucas snapped. "How did you even get wind of the foundation when nothing has even been announced? The non-profit registry only came through a few days ago, for Christ's sake."

"Easy," Lawrence muttered under his breath. "We are in public, and nobody wants to get kicked out of this establishment. Some of us eat here regularly. Keep it in mind."

Right.

Then they might not be allowed back.

Shame, Lucas thought.

He couldn't care less.

"The brewery's IP lawyer has alert systems in place should anything come up that challenges the trademarks or other registered marks of the Dalton Brewery company," Chandler explained, shrugging. "The filing, and your approval, is a matter of public record."

"I'll change the name," Lucas deadpanned, moving in the opposite direction.

It didn't matter.

The foundation didn't have to be named after Jacob to memorialize him and the difference Lucas wanted to make for young men and boys just like his brother.

Ronald moved in his seat, grunting something under his breath to the lawyer beside him. The table quieted when the redhead from earlier returned with a tray full of drinks, and the bottle of red wine. Once everyone confirmed they were happy, she left the table once more with a promise that the food shouldn't take more than an hour.

Fuck.

That long?

Lucas managed to keep his complaint to himself.

Someone else, not so much.

"There's barely three mouthfuls of whiskey in there," Ronald bitched about the glass of liquor with more ice than whiskey.

Chandler chuckled at his client's despair. "Ah, oh, well. Take the drink you wanted Lucas to have—he's not interested."

Ronald glanced back to his son who pushed the drink across the table.

"Cheers," Lucas told Ronald.

"Should have had someone drive you across town," his father said.

"I'm leaving town, so that wouldn't work, either."

Ronald's scowl deepened; his attempt to stick Lucas with another verbal barb fell short, and it showed between them.

Perhaps it was Lucas' mention of leaving town that made Lawrence comfortable enough to ask his client about his new penchant for a particular spot upriver.

In front of Ronald, unfortunately.

"Are you staying at the camp or with …"

Lawrence trailed off at the sudden turn of Lucas' head at the table.

"Apologies," Lawrence muttered fast.

The damage had already been done.

Ronald finally had enough information to put together something important in Lucas' current life. Delaney, that was.

"What's her name—Reed, right? Delaney Reed," Ronald said. "The hairdresser you started seeing just before Jacob … well, you know," his father settled on saying.

Lamely.

It felt like a punch to the chest to Lucas. He had not given his father a chance to bring up his knowledge of Delaney or her connection to Lucas. In fact, he never even brought it to Ronald's attention that he knew the man had contacted Delaney's boss in her former city of residence. A feat made easier by the fact he no longer answered calls from Ronald, and their lawyers did all the talking. As he'd hoped, it all made Ronald think Delaney wasn't anything interesting to Lucas, and therefore, not useful to his father.

Ronald put the puzzle together way too late.

Oh, well.

Unlike his father, Lucas protected the people he loved.

"I tried to check up on her, but found she'd quit her job and moved from Fredericton. I wondered why you hadn't taken one of the job offers I heard came your way. Now it makes a little more sense. Are you looking for a specific area to work? I didn't realize you—"

"She's none of your business," Lucas interjected, the edge to his tone drawing a clear line for Ronald. Or so he willed with a tight jaw and a gaze that dared his father to try.

He truly expected Ronald to prove how much of a bastard he really was in that moment. Another attempt to bait Lucas into a verbal altercation, even. Some shit never changed, right?

No.

Ronald surprised him.

His father just nodded, and reached for the glass of whiskey Lucas had pushed across earlier to take a sip. He then tipped the rim in Lucas' direction, smacking his lips before uttering, "Cheers, then."

Lucas dared to think the way his father's eyebrows and mouth drew downward came from a realization of some sadness. Did he understand the privilege to know his son's personal life had gone along with any lines of communication that wasn't through their lawyers?

Good.

Maybe the bastard did have a heart.

Lucas hoped guilt and regret tore it apart.

Pulling in a deep breath, and resituating his focus at the table to the legal agreement spread out on the table between the lawyers, Lucas asked, "Is the foundation going to be a hard line here or is there a number we can readjust to make that worth somebody's while to shut the fuck up?"

Ronald replied, "Keep the name."

"Ronald, are you sure?" Chandler stepped in quietly. "Maybe we should check with—"

"Take it out."

Lucas could feel his father's gaze burrowing a hole into the side of his head.

He refused to turn and look at the man.

"That's really it, huh?" Ronald asked Lucas, sounding almost tired.

If not bored.

"Is what it?" Lucas asked back.

"This is how you're gonna break the cycle, then? By shutting me out, pretending like I don't exist, and making a new life for yourself somewhere else?"

Lucas had said none of those things.

In fact, he never even thought about them.

Mostly.

"This is how it's gonna be," Lucas told his father, settling on that being the best out of everything else racing through his head.

Next to him, Lawrence offered a wary, awkward smile. "If we need to bring someone else in to handle the family side of things … I don't have anyone to suggest. Hanny?"

"I …"

The other lawyer came up with nothing.

Lucas rolled his eyes, and the irritation shuddered through the rest of his body with the action. He wasn't the only one, apparently.

"Oh, get off it," Ronald snapped, tossing the napkin rudely at the older man. He pointed at the papers, but Lawrence glared back, unaffected. "Let's just get back to that, huh? Stay out of the family side of things. We've gone over it a million times. The foundation was new, so take it out. We'll both sign."

Lucas then looked to his father.

"Right?" Ronald asked him, brows lifting at the question.

"Right."

It took a few more minutes for the lawyers to work their way to the end of a bunch of babble that, Ronald was right, they had gone over enough times. It all had to be official and correct—a transaction done through appropriate legal counsel. For the benefit of the company, two Dalton men would put away their private differences to handle a company matter.

Nothing more.

Twelve and a half million dollars for the exchange in ownership of Lucas' twenty-five percent share of the family brewery. The bonus of incorporating a profit ownership to employees from those shares would be great public PR for Ronald as he began looking for the people he would soon be looking to hire. His position in the west needed to be filled. Lucas couldn't say whether Ronald had found someone to take over his former position, either. The attention would also shift from private Dalton matters to what should matter more—the brewery and employees.

It benefited Ronald to get on with this situation, too. Lucas had already figured that part out himself.

Ronald signed first.

His lawyer followed.

Lucas put his name on the appropriate flagged places next. Lawrence came in last to zip through the ten pages, making a neat pile on top of the file as he finished each one. That was when Ronald leaned forward and grabbed the pile of papers, clutching tight and waving it proudly toward Lucas with a rueful smile.

His father should be happy. Ronald had everything he wanted. The Dalton Brewery was, on paper at least, a hundred percent his.

"That's it."

"That's it," Lucas echoed, no smile in sight.

That didn't bother his father.

Ronald smirked and proved Lucas shouldn't have given him any credit toward having a heart when he said, "I hope she's nothing like your mother—but don't fuck it up the way I did. Always get a prenup."

Lucas decided then that he would get his meal to go.

39.

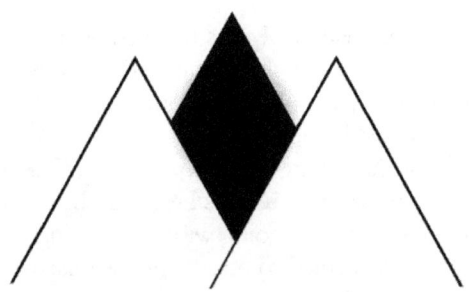

"Delaney?"

"In here," she called back.

Lucas maneuvered the darkened apartment with ease, stuffing the key Delaney had given him at his first visit into his back pocket. He checked the bedroom first in the hallway beyond the small kitchen, but quickly realized he'd chosen wrong when a soft laugh echoed behind him.

He spun around.

Delaney waved two fingers, water droplets flinging from the tips, from a bathtub filled with bubbles. Other than the entry light over the front door, only candles flickered in the bathroom to offer any light. Covered in shadows, flickers, and bubbles, her sweet smile did the best things to his heart.

Lucas hesitated in the doorway, his hands holding the jamb to help keep him from entering like he wanted to right away. "Hey."

She lifted one shoulder making bubbles and steam rise. "Hey, yourself."

She'd tied her black hair into a messy bun high on her head, and a paperback novel sat overturned on the top of the toilet seat next to the bathtub.

Lucas wished he knew what to say.

Or where to start.

Anything.

Delaney saved him by asking, "So, how was the drive?"

Lucas let out an exhausted laugh. "Long and dark."

From the start to the finish.

Pitch black highway all the way.

He rolled his shoulders, muttering, "My back hurts, but fuck it—what's it matter?"

His pain wouldn't compare to hers.

Surely.

"All in all, no complaints," Lucas finished, winking.

Delaney smiled. "I can't believe you were halfway here by the time I texted you to say I could head home."

"I told you I would be here."

Even if that meant driving fifteen over the limit and refusing to waste time on the phone because his heart had been racing too much to keep a conversation going without running off the damn road. Delaney hadn't seemed to mind. She promised to wait up, actually.

She looked up at him, then, her quivering smile hitting him in the chest like a punch.

"Good," she said, "I want you here." Her chin tipped down when she added lower, "And there was a point today sitting in the hospital when I needed you, too. So, I guess I can say that sort of thing to myself. It just takes a lot."

"I did tell you to set the bar higher," Lucas replied.

That made Delaney smile.

Only a bit, though.

"I bet you didn't bring anything with you, huh?"

"Didn't even think to pack a bag."

He didn't care, either. The extra change of clothes he kept in the back of the Bronco in a reusable bag would do for a day until he figured things out.

"How are you supposed to move in with me if you brought nothing?" she asked, only half serious.

"Let's just say you're starting with the best part."

That made her laugh the most beautiful sound in the world.

Lucas shed his spring jacket and hung it off the ball end of the rod where a towel dried on the wall. The apartment had its pros and cons. The main negative being the small size of the bathroom and kitchen, in his opinion. He barely had enough room to turn around in the space and doing so made him face all the important amenities, or the door, so hunching down next to the tub didn't exactly leave him a lot of room to move.

Delaney made it worth it by reaching for him the second he got close enough for her to touch. Those warm, wet hands of hers clung onto his forearms first before crawling higher to his shoulders before wrapping around his back. He hugged back, pulling her out of the bubbly water slightly with his squeeze, not bothered at all by her wet body leaving imprints on his button-down shirt. The fact she held tight, refusing to let go, kept Lucas in the same hunched position.

Even their breaths matched for a while.

She buried her face in his neck, mumbling, "Gracen canceled all of my appointments for tomorrow. Didn't even ask."

"Good, she should. You probably need a break."

He felt her eyelashes flutter against his skin with the roll of her eyes, but she still pressed a kiss to his neck all the same. "Don't worry—she already told me that I can't put my head down and work to get through everything."

"Well—"

"They think there was two."

Her random statement made Lucas blink more than a few times as her fingertips patted the back of his neck. Had she felt the way his surprise raced up through his spine?

"*Two?*"

Delaney's exhale came out shaky as she started to pull away. That sad smile curved her lips at the edges just enough to distract him from the strip of papers she produced from under the overturned book.

Along the edge of the tub, she spread out a roll of sonogram pictures that made Lucas' hands tremble as he picked them up. He didn't really understand the images in front of him. Every black and white and gray swirl around a circular patch of darkness wasn't exactly distinguishable.

Delaney pointed out the smaller circle off to the side of several shots. "When the blood test came back with a high hormone level, the doctor did an ultrasound. Based on my last period, and dates of conception, I would be just far enough along to see the embryo this way. If it was there," she added.

"And one was," Lucas murmured.

"That's what the doctor told me, anyway. I think I went through emotional whiplash so many times today that now I'm just numb."

Lucas' head snapped up from the sonograms to find Delaney staring blankly into the bubbles down below. "Sweets, it's been a long day for you."

She laughed weakly, looking his way with desperate eyes. "It's crazy. I went from not even thinking I wanted to be pregnant to probably being pregnant to *not* being pregnant, and then …" Her hand gestured toward the strip of sonograms he still held.

"You're supposed to have this stuff figured out before it happens," Delaney said. "Right?"

"Not everybody," he returned. "Life's different for everyone, Delaney."

Maybe that sad smile of hers had a little more fear than he'd first thought.

"Okay, well I wanted to have a lot more things in my life figured out before I had to do it with a baby on my hip," Delaney said, but even that made her frown. "I hate hearing myself say that out loud because it makes me feel bad, too."

"I can't begin to find a single reason why you need to feel bad about anything you've done, Delaney."

Her wet gaze, tears gathering on her long lashes, found his. "I don't want to feel that way at all because I need my baby to know I loved them from the start. Even if it didn't happen the way I might have planned for it to. That's not going to change if I'll be a good mom."

Lucas pressed his lips together, desperate to hold the smile back lest she take it the wrong way. "I don't think you have to worry about being a good mom. Our baby looks like a grain of rice in these damn things, and you're already worried about whether it knows you love it. Doesn't that speak for itself?"

Delaney instantly burst into tears.

Rolling down her cheeks, and all.

Not really sure what to do at that point, Lucas simply hugged Delaney against his chest while his mouth stayed pressed to the top of her forehead where he could whisper everything he wanted her to know.

"You're going to be the best mom, and no matter what, I'm not going anywhere," he assured her.

"I don't even want to *cry*," she wailed helplessly. "It's just happening a lot today."

Lucas didn't try to hold back the laughter. "I heard that happens with pregnant women, sometimes."

Her hand weakly smacked at him. "*Shut up.*"

Then, she tipped her head back.

Tears still stained her cheeks.

But she *smiled*.

Lucas dropped a kiss to her coral colored lips, and grinned back. "I love you, Delaney Reed. We're going to figure this out."

"Either way?" she asked, her voice still a little wobbly.

He tucked the flyaway strands of her hair behind her ear, nodding all the while, because he remembered very well what she had told him not very long ago.

"Either way," he echoed.

Epilogue

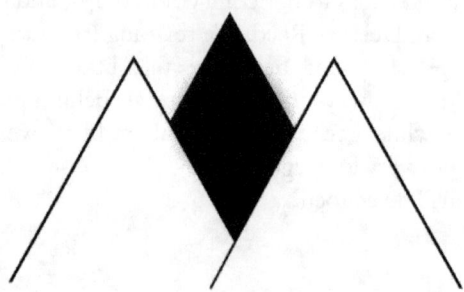

"We're definitely doing a live band when we get married next summer," Delaney said.

Lucas grinned next to her where he leaned against the barn wall. His leather loafer tapped along with the bluegrass beat coming out of the band at the far side of the barn. "I agree."

His gaze shot to the ring on Delaney's finger that twinkled under the bare bulb lights dangling across the eaves of the barn overhead. A new feature that she was still trying to get used to despite wearing the engagement ring for a little over a week.

She hadn't imagined being proposed to in the middle of a big field with the backdrop of the sky dotted with stars, but it had been perfect, all the same.

Being with Lucas?

Always.

"Come here," he murmured, catching her by the wrist with his hand to pull her into his side. He didn't even ask for his kiss, simply took it, and grinned against her mouth as his palm found its favorite spot overtop her belly.

Not that there was much to feel.

Yet.

In fact, Delaney hadn't even announced her pregnancy outside of her very small circle of close friends and the family she still spoke to. Like Bexley. Given her initial experience with the pregnancy, and the fact she had probably lost a twin, she didn't want to share the news widely until she had made it past her first trimester.

Not that it mattered.

People, especially over the course of Gracen's wedding

weekend, had more than enough things to talk about and ask Delaney other than why she kept refusing drinks with alcohol. Like the new man who was never too far from her side, and her return to the area. Those things could keep the gossip mill going for a while, surely.

Lucas nodded toward the middle of the barn where the pews and aisle from the wedding service had been removed and changed to a hardwood dance floor for the guests. Currently, the band had so many people up and dancing that the floor in the middle wasn't big enough. Gracen, in the very middle with Malachi, looked happier than Delaney had ever seen her friend before.

She should be happy.

Life had started to settle out for them both.

"Am I getting you back out there, or what?" Lucas asked.

"These shoes are killing me."

Lucas bopped her nose, earning him a half-hearted glare. "I'll go get your flats at the apartment. It'll take me five minutes and save you the rest of the night. Win-win."

"They won't look right with the dress."

At that comment, Lucas pulled Delaney close for a bruising kiss that took her breath away.

"Nobody is looking at your shoes," he promised.

Delaney grinned. "Okay, go get them for me?"

"On it, baby."

Lucas barely had time to push away from the wall before someone else joined Delaney against the barn boards. Margot, in a pink gown like Delaney's but slinkier with deeper cuts in the chest and back, teased her friend with a glass of something pink and bubbly.

"Did you try this yet?" Margot asked.

Delaney made a face. "No, I don't want to drink."

"You're missing out," Margot said in a sigh.

"Pregnant, actually."

The admission had Margot's eyes flying wide, and she coughed on the sip of spiked punch as her attention swung to Delaney.

"*What?*"

Margot was one of the last people Delaney had to tell. She didn't feel right doing it over the phone, but since their friend had returned to the province for a couple of weeks to celebrate Gracen's wedding—and be a part of it as a bridesmaid—Delaney opted to wait.

Now felt as good of a time as ever.

"Yeah," she told Margot, "I'm about nine-ish weeks."

The news earned her a tight hug from Margot and a mumbled congratulations.

"You next?" she asked her friend after Margot pulled away.

That earned Delaney a scoff.

"No way," Margot muttered around the rim of her drink. "No babies for me. Besides, you need a penis for that job. I swore off dick a long while back."

Delaney snorted. "I mean, traditionally you do, maybe."

Margot quieted next to Delaney as the band began to switch songs to a slower tune. She did well to hide the slip of sadness that fell over her expression before it disappeared, but Delaney still saw the emotion in Margot's face.

She'd also noticed how Margot arrived home for the wedding alone.

"No girlfriend?" Delaney asked, the first time she had mentioned Leya to Margot despite it being obvious her friend had returned home alone.

Margot shrugged, and her red curls bounced with the swing of her head back and forth. "Nope, it's just me. I came home alone."

"Sometimes, we need to."

That's when a person could figure out what they really wanted.

Margot pushed away from the wall but turned to walk backward so she could face Delaney as she headed toward the dance floor. "Who knows? Maybe I'll even stay."

Gracen would love that.

Delaney, too.

"Maybe you should," she replied.

Margot winked before spinning away.

It didn't take long for Lucas to get back to Delaney with a pair of sensible, black flats that absolutely did not match the pink dress she had agreed to wear—not her favorite color, but anything for Gracen—but would make the rest of the night far more comfortable.

That's what she wanted to do more than anything.

Make memories to remember.

Lucas kneeled to help Delaney out of her strappy, open-toed stilettos before holding the flats for her to step into as well.

Remaining on his one knee after she had stepped into the change of shoes, he smiled up at her.

"Looks familiar," she joked.

Lucas snorted, and then stood to catch her cheeky grin in a kiss. He hummed against her lips, swaying the two of them as their arms wrapped around one another, and the song from the band helped to urge their gentle rocking.

"Guess what?" Lucas asked her, arching a brow high and showing off his teeth.

"What?"

"I had a message from the farmer back at the apartment."

Delaney bit her lip, careful not to get too excited. "Really?"

He nodded. "Forty acres, all the way back to the wild raspberries—he'll sell it if you want it, sweets."

The slice of land next to Gracen's hadn't been publicly listed, and nobody seemed to tend the wild patch of raspberry bushes Lucas and Delaney had found on a ride deeper into the land, but the farmer who owned it had been willing to talk.

Especially to a man like Lucas Dalton.

The only man who seemed to know how to make Delaney's dreams come true. If there was a will, he found the way.

"How many acres back do you want the main house?" Lucas asked, looking *oh*, so pleased with himself.

Delaney swatted his chest lightly. "Stop it—we haven't even bought the land yet. It's not ours. You can't start building an imaginary house."

"Can't we? Who else is gonna dream our dreams, gorgeous? I was thinking back behind that first line of trees. In the field. Right where you said yes, huh?"

Good God.

He truly had thought of *everything*.

Before it even happened.

"You can't stop being perfect, can you?"

Lucas kept them swaying to the music on the spot, and his smile never once faltered. "Anything for you."

ABOUT THE AUTHOR

The author of too many novels to count, Bethany-Kris is a Canadian, lover of much, and mother to four sons, a glaring of cats, and a pack of dogs. A small town in Eastern Canada where she was born and raised is where she has always called home. With her boys under her feet, a snuggling cat, barking dogs, and a spouse calling over his shoulder, she is nearly always writing something ... when she can find the time.

Find where to follow BK and keep up to date with all her book news at www.bethanykris.com.

www.ingramcontent.com/pod-product-compliance
Lightning Source LLC
Chambersburg PA
CBHW072023020726
47501CB00006B/1927